What We Bury

Publisher's Cataloging-in-Publication Data
Names: Peterson, Alanna, author.
Title: What we bury / Alanna Peterson
Series: Call of the Crow Quartet
Description: Seattle, WA: Rootcity Press, 2022.
Identifiers: LCCN: 2022907077
ISBN: 978-1-952149-07-8 (paperback) | 978-1-952149-08-5 (ebook)
Subjects: LCSH Post-traumatic stress disorder—Fiction.
| Medicine—Research—Fiction. | Grief—Fiction.
| Family—Fiction. | Friendship—Fiction.
| Iranian Americans—Fiction. | Asian Americans—Fiction.
| Northwest, Pacific—Fiction. | Science fiction. | Adventure fiction.
BISAC YOUNG ADULT FICTION / Thrillers & Suspense
| YOUNG ADULT FICTION / Social Themes / Death, Grief, Bereavement
| YOUNG ADULT FICTION / Cooking & Food
| YOUNG ADULT FICTION / Diversity & Multicultural
| YOUNG ADULT FICTION / Social Themes / Mental Illness
Classification: LCC PS3616.E84268 W53 2022 | DDC 813.6–dc23

Book design by Unflown | Jacob Covey

Printed and bound in the United States of America
First printing 2022

Published by Rootcity Press
Seattle, WA
rootcitypress.com

What We Bury

ALANNA PETERSON

CALL OF THE CROW QUARTET
BOOK FOUR

ROOTCITY PRESS
SEATTLE

For Desmond,
who sees beauty
in the darkness

I.

Spores

Andi

BEGINNINGS OF A HEADACHE PULSED BEHIND ANDI LIN'S EYES. Even when she closed them, the trig problem still swam against that dark interior landscape, taunting her. *Just solve me*, it said. That was hard to do, though, when it felt like an enormous creature was trying to burst through her skull.

Andi closed her laptop and flopped face-down on her bed. Another stupid day cooped up in her grandparents' house in Berkeley trying to prep for her online trig final while fending off headaches. How much longer could she stand this boring routine?

At least it was a Tuesday. Mystery Box Day. That was always something to look forward to: the delivery of a mysterious package she wasn't allowed to open.

Her life was so fun.

Even though she knew staring at screens wasn't going to help her headache, she propped her phone against the wall and called Naveed.

His face appeared on her screen. "Andi! I'm out here tilling the field, so reception might be spotty—I'll head back to my cabin if the call gets dropped. Can you hear me okay?"

"Yeah, seems fine to me. Is it not a good time? I could call back later."

"No, no, I'm ready for a break. What're you up to?"

"Trying to study for my trig final, but I'm getting a headache. I swear, it's like a horror movie inside my brain. Like something's trapped in there trying to get out."

"Ah, I know the feeling." He smiled wistfully. "Nate's like that sometimes. Not the same thing, I know, but still. Does your headache-inducing-brain-prisoner have a name?"

"Hmm." In a weird way, Andi supposed she'd rather have a brain-prisoner who just caused physical pain, instead of the psychological abuse Nate inflicted on Naveed. "Maybe... I think her name is... Barb."

"Damn you, Barb! Leave Andi alone!" Naveed shook his fist. "Oh wait, I know what might help. I'm tilling with the scythe today, and it's the best ASMR. The sound of the blade cutting through the grass... it's so good. Here, hold on a sec and I'll get set up. Just close your eyes and listen."

Andi did close her eyes while he jostled his phone around, but then she opened them again. Naveed stood at the edge of a field of tall grass, his service dog Koffka resting off to the side next to Gretchen and Frida's dog, Astro. Naveed positioned the scythe with the blade near the base of the grass, then started swinging, rhythmically twisting his body from side to side. All she could hear was the rustle of falling grass and the birds chirping and the occasional contented dog-sigh.

The scene was so idyllic that she wanted to step through the screen and join him there. But it wouldn't be long until they were back together again. On Friday, her mother would drop her off at the Oakland airport and she would fly back to Seattle. She couldn't wait to step off the plane and rush to the other side of security, where Naveed would be waiting.

She wanted to stay focused on that moment. Their happy reunion. If she only thought of that, she wouldn't have to think about the reason she was returning to Seattle in the first place.

After a few minutes, Naveed set the scythe down and picked up his phone again. "Anyway, you get the idea." He wiped his forehead on his sleeve. "It's getting warm out, though. Gonna sit in the shade for a minute."

"That was nice," Andi said. "But it just makes me want to be there with you."

"Only three more days! I can't wait to show you around Zetik Farm. You'll love it here." He sat at the base of a shady tree. Koffka trotted into the frame and settled in beside him.

"I can't wait either." Andi was pretty sure Naveed remembered that she'd been to Gretchen and Frida's farm before, and the circumstances under which she'd visited—it was hard for her to even think about that place without remembering her narrow escape from Dr. Tara Snyder's research lab—but she decided to breeze over it for now. Especially because it reminded her that, in less than a week, she'd have to sit in the same courtroom as Tara Snyder during the trial.

She watched Naveed closely, his curly black hair that was veering into shaggy territory, his dark beard, the streak of mud on his shirt, Koffka's head in his lap, his fingers tangled up in the German shepherd's fur. His eyes looked a little distant, and she wondered if he was going down the same road as she was.

Andi decided to change the subject. "Did you get the email about dinner with Vanesa on Friday? You'll come with me, right?"

"I guess… actually, though, I was kind of hoping we could eat with my family that night. Kourosh said he'd cook, and Roya can't wait to see you. I'll be with Vanesa most of Saturday anyway—she's got me booked for all these *Blood Apples* promo interviews before the premiere."

"I know, but I helped organize the dinner. I should go. I want you to meet Akilah and Laurel, too. And I'm sure everyone wants to see you—it'll be a good chance to celebrate before opening night." Andi had coordinated this meeting between Vanesa and several of the organizers she'd worked with the previous spring, since they wanted to help promote the documentary film and tie it in with the work their artivist collective was doing.

"All right. But can we do Sunday dinner at our house?"

"Deal. I'll RSVP for both of us," said Andi. "I can't believe this is really happening. Our documentary—well, not *ours*, but you know what I mean—is premiering at the Seattle International Film Festival. That's huge!"

"I know. I can't wait until everyone hears your music."

"And I can't wait until everyone sees you on the big screen."

He laughed humorlessly. "Yeah. Everyone gets to watch me have a mental breakdown. Should be real fun."

Andi didn't know how to respond to that. She'd only seen the rough cut, and in her opinion Vanesa had portrayed Naveed sensitively, but she wasn't sure he would feel the same way. He'd be seeing it for the first time at the premiere on Saturday. "It's not that bad. Really," she finally said. "Don't judge it until you've seen it."

"Yeah. Solid advice. Well, guess I should get back to work."

"Are you sure?" Andi didn't want to end on that note.

"This grass isn't going to cut itself, and it's already so warm today. Better just get it done now."

"Okay. I'll try you later tonight."

"Mmm hmm. Talk to you then. Bye." He ended the call.

Andi sighed, wishing she hadn't brought up the film. Instead of stewing on it or trying to read his mind, though, she decided to invoke the pact they had made when they started going out: *no surprises, no secrets.* #ns2, she texted, using their shorthand for the pact to remind him to be open with her. Even tho I think Vanesa did a good job on the movie, I know this premiere is going to be hard. Don't worry. We'll get thru it together & you can vent all you need afterwards.

Thank you, he replied. Obviously I'm not looking forward to it but I'm so glad you'll be there with me. Oh btw i hope your headache feels better soon, tell Barb to go chill ok?

She replied with a heart emoji, then scrolled until she found her text string with Mahnaz. Shortly after Naveed had moved out, his mother had asked a favor. She had promised to give him space, but wondered if Andi wouldn't mind sending her a brief text after conversations she had with him, to tell her honestly how he was doing. Andi felt a little weird about it at first because of the whole #ns2 pact, but she totally understood why Mahnaz wanted to keep an eye on him, between his various medical problems, his suicide attempt the previous summer, his ongoing struggles with PTSD. With the trial approaching, they were both worried about him, and knowing Mahnaz was in the loop helped Andi worry a little less.

Now, Andi texted Mahnaz a "partly cloudy" emoji; they had worked out a code where his moods were translated into weather-related symbols. Mahnaz quickly responded with the cherry blossom that, between them, meant "thank you." Anyone looking at the string would probably just think they were discussing the forecast or something.

Andi was about to get back to her unsolved trig problem when the doorbell rang. Probably the Mystery Box Delivery Man. She was tempted to take her time getting downstairs—she knew from experience that Box Man would wait—but Ah-ma was asleep and she didn't want it to ring again. Her grandmother was still going through treatment for the colon cancer she'd been diagnosed with in December. Since Andi's mother had just started a new job at UC Berkeley, and Ah-gong was busy running his tea business Lu Yu, Andi had Ah-ma duty during the day.

She grabbed her keychain and headed downstairs, tightening her fingers against the small canister of pepper spray. Just in case. After being assaulted in February, she had been taking jiu-jitsu classes but wasn't yet at the point where she felt confident taking down attackers. A little chemical back-up never hurt.

She peeked through the side window and saw a young white guy standing outside holding a package. Yep, just Box Man. She relaxed her grip on the keychain and opened the door.

"Package for Betty Lin," he said.

"I'll get it to her. Thanks." Andi took the package and closed the door. She locked the deadbolt and set the box down on the kitchen table.

It was nondescript and white, empty of any company logos, with Ah-ma's name and address written by hand in neat script. There was no return address.

Every week, these packages came. Always like this, delivered not by shipping companies, but by private courier. Ah-ma had made it clear that she wanted to handle them herself, so Andi stepped away, intending to head back upstairs. But a thought flitted into her head: if she peeled the tape off carefully, she might be able to see what was inside and close it back up without Ah-ma ever knowing....

No, she told herself. *Bad idea. Ah-ma probably has a good reason for not telling me what's in the Mystery Box. Go back upstairs and forget about it.*

But that was the thing. She was stir-crazy and lonely and bored—so incredibly bored—and she wanted something to happen.

Or, more accurately: she wanted to *make* something happen.

Forget it, the sensible part of her said. *MYSTERY BOX!* the insatiably curious part yelled. *Now's your chance. OPEN THE MYSTERY BOX!!!!*

Great. Now it was all she could think about. There was no way she'd be able to concentrate on trig with Barb tearing away at her brain and *Mystery Box – Mystery Box – Mystery Box* repeating on a loop.

So, filled with an uncomfortable mixture of guilt, excitement, and dread, Andi carefully pulled the tape. It didn't come off cleanly, but if she covered it up with a fresh piece of packing tape, she figured it wouldn't be too noticeable.

She opened the flaps. Atop a pile of crumpled brown paper was a letter. Without hesitating, she unfolded it to find a photograph enclosed inside, along with a short note. *Thanks for the feedback*, the note read. *I've made a few adjustments. Keep me posted on how it goes. Also, I was cleaning out files and found this, thought you and Henry might appreciate the memento of the day it all began.*

Andi turned her attention to the photo, a snapshot of four smiling men holding up champagne glasses, as if captured mid-toast. Judging from the glossy wood behind them, it might have been taken in a fancy bar, or a hotel lobby or something. But that was not the first thing Andi noticed, because she recognized two of the men.

There, standing on the far right, was Ah-gong. A badge printed with a logo she didn't recognize dangled from a lanyard around his neck.

And right next to him was—

She had to do a quick google to make sure. Her memory had been steadily improving over the past month, but she still didn't trust herself to remember everything correctly. This was one case, though, where she hoped her instinct wasn't right.

But the image search confirmed that she was correct. The man was Alastor Yarrow. Alastor, who had headed both a supplement company and a spiritual retreat center on Lopez Island. Alastor, who had nearly killed both Cyrus and Naveed before his own wife killed him.

So why the hell was Andi's grandfather, Henry Lin, hanging out with that man? She was tempted to write it off, like maybe they had just met once and then gone their separate ways, but the note said the picture was taken "the day it all began." The day *what* began?

Andi hastily took a picture of the letter and photo with her phone, then folded the letter back up. She was just about to remove the brown paper when she heard a creak on the stairs behind her.

She threw the letter and photo back into the box and closed the flaps before turning to see Ah-ma making her slow descent down the stairs.

No use trying to re-tape the box now. Still, it was probably best to act like she had no idea what was inside until she could gauge Ah-ma's reaction. "Um, you got a package," Andi said in what she hoped was a casual tone. "I was just opening it for you."

"You didn't need to do that." Ah-ma sounded annoyed. "I'm thirsty— could you please get me something to drink?"

Andi retreated to the kitchen and pulled a glass off the shelf. She took a few deep breaths, but even so her hand shook as she filled it with water from the tap.

When she returned to the dining room table where Ah-ma was sitting, the package was nowhere in sight.

"What was in the box?" Andi asked as she set the glass down in front of Ah-ma. She wasn't sure this was the best move, but hopefully Ah-ma would take it as a hint that she hadn't seen anything.

"Nothing interesting. Just tea samples."

Had Andi not seen the letter, it would have been a plausible answer. Ah-ma did help out a lot with Lu Yu. Or at least she used to, before she got sick. But if it was just tea, why all the secrecy? Why would the letter say, *keep me posted on how it goes*?

"Tea sounds nice. Do you want to try one of the samples?" Andi said. She couldn't help herself. "I could brew some for you."

"Not right now. I think I'll go lie down. Want to watch *Fresh off the Boat* with me?"

"Sorry. I've got to get back to studying."

After helping Ah-ma get installed on the couch, Andi returned to her bedroom and closed the door. She studied the picture on her phone for a minute, staring at the other two men. She felt like she'd seen the older-looking one somewhere before, but try as she might, she couldn't place him. The younger man, who had sandy-blond hair and a neatly-trimmed goatee, seemed non-descript, the kind of person who could blend in anywhere.

She couldn't keep this to herself. She had to tell someone.

Despite *no surprises, no secrets*, she quickly dismissed the idea of sharing this with Naveed. Not yet, anyway. He had enough on his mind between the trial and documentary, and she didn't want to upset the precarious balance of his mental state.

Cyrus, though, would be able to handle seeing the photo, and wouldn't think any less of Andi because of her grandfather's apparent collusion with Alastor. Besides, Cyrus had ways of investigating stuff like this. So she texted the photo to him, adding, Hey Cy, I need your help figuring out who these guys are.

But right after she sent it, she realized with embarrassment that in her haste, she had accidentally sent it to Mahnaz, since she'd had that string open. Oops! Never mind. Sent by mistake, she quickly wrote.

Then she sent it to Cyrus for real, along with a photo of the letter and a revised message: That's my grandpa on the right. You know who's standing next to him. Do your magic. Who are the other 2 guys?

But as soon as she'd sent it, a text came in from Mahnaz. Let this go, Andi-jaan. It doesn't mean anything.

Andi paused to let those words sink in. Obviously, it meant *something*. Something that Mahnaz, for whatever reason, didn't want Andi to investigate.

Before she could decide how to respond, another text appeared on her screen. And please leave my sons out of it.

Its stern tone made hot ripples of shame rise to Andi's face—especially because it was too late now. She'd already done it, already set something in motion that she shouldn't have messed with in the first place.

Andi put down her phone and rested her head in her palms. *Well*, she thought, *today just got a whole lot less boring.*

Roya

TUESDAY, MAY 17

ROYA MIRZAPOUR LIMPED OVER TO THE CHAIN-LINK FENCE, scanning the faces of the grown-ups gathered outside the school gates. Maman wasn't there yet, but that was no surprise. She was always late for pick-up.

Roya wished she could just walk home on her own. She needed to get back to the house soon, because she had a very important mission.

Today, she was going to banish the demons.

Roya had finally gathered all the ingredients for the banishing spell, but time was running out. Tomorrow, Maman and her friend Kelly were going on a trip because the trial was starting soon and Kelly thought it would be good to take a break from all the stress. They would be backpacking at Mount Rainier—or as Maman called it now, Tahoma. She'd explained to Roya that she was trying to get into the habit of calling the mountain by its original name. Regardless of what it was called, though, she would be out in the wilderness, far away. Best to get rid of the demons before that.

Maman had been different ever since Roya's accident. It was like she was being eaten away from the inside out, drifting through life like a ghost. The only time she seemed halfway alive was when she was yelling at Roya about something.

Only one explanation made sense to Roya: invisible demons had taken control of her mother. It was like those evil spirits from the Qur'an, the shayatin, who filled your head with terrible thoughts, spreading misery and despair everywhere they went.

As wary as Roya was of doing magic on her own, especially after that night in the barn with Kass, she had no choice. She wasn't going to sit back and let the demons erase her mother. The longer she waited, the deeper the shayatin would burrow, until all of her thoughts were theirs and nothing of Maman's was left.

It would have been a lot easier if she could just ask Kass. But Maman and Baba had forbidden her to speak or write to her friend. Roya had managed to send one letter in secret, and intercepted Kass's reply before anyone else saw it. The letter said that Kass had moved in with her aunt Ilyana. She included their phone number in case Roya was ever able to call. Roya hadn't been able to figure out how to do this without being caught, since her parents had gotten rid of their land line and she'd have to ask to borrow one of their phones. There was no way they'd let her take the phone out of their sight to have a private conversation, and they never left them lying around, either. They guarded them as if they were made of pure gold encrusted with diamonds.

In the meantime, Roya had been combing through the Book of Shadows she'd rescued from Kass's old home. There were countless spells, remedies, and potions jotted inside. She copied useful-looking ones into a store-bought mini-notebook and kept her very own Book of Shadows inside the moon box Baba had made for her birthday. She set it in the center of a makeshift altar under her bed containing a few special objects that she knew were filled with magic: the agate stone Auntie Leila had given her on Lopez Island; the Hekate chalice she'd found at Orcinia;

Kass's athame, the sharp blade safely tucked into its leather sheath. She kept everything covered up with an old towel, which she figured would keep spying eyes away. Roya was the only one who could fit under there, and even though her messed-up leg made it hard to haul herself in and out, spending time with the book and the magical objects never failed to lift her mood.

Before leaving for school that morning, Roya had left an offering beneath her covered altar dedicated to Hekate, the goddess Kass worshipped. Cyrus had made some corn muffins for dinner the night before, and she drenched one in honey and left it under her bed with a small cup of cardamom tea. She wanted to welcome Hekate in, and to thank her in advance for helping with the banishing ritual that Roya would perform as soon as she got home.

One by one, all of Roya's classmates were all picked up until, as usual, she was the last one standing next to her teacher. The hot sun beat down on them. Roya leaned against the fence, sweating, trying to take weight off her bad leg without Ms. Won noticing.

Finally, Maman drove up. "See you tomorrow, Roya!" Ms. Won said. She and Maman waved at each other, and Roya was free to go.

She limped to the car and slid into the back seat. Maman turned around, and Roya gasped. Her lips were red and glossy. Her black curls were neatly arranged instead of pulled back into a messy ponytail. And she was wearing a dress Roya had never seen. "Why are you all dressed up?" Roya asked.

Maman smiled, pulling her red lips back to reveal teeth that seemed whiter than usual. "It was for a meeting," she said. "You don't have to look so shocked."

"A CFJ meeting?" Roya had a hard time believing that. Maman had Coalition for Food Justice meetings all the time, but she never dressed up. And she *definitely* never wore red lipstick to them.

"Yes. How was school?"

"Were you meeting with the mayor or something?" Roya didn't want to let it go.

"Never mind about that, Roya-jaan." She pulled away from the curb. "By the way, you have PT this afternoon. We're just going to grab a quick snack, then we need to leave."

"What? But it's usually on Thursdays! Couldn't I skip it this time? I have a ton of homework to do tonight." This was true. Ms. Won had sent home a huge packet, which would take Roya forever to finish. It was hard to concentrate on anything knowing that your mother was infested by demons.

"They had to reschedule this one. You can work on your homework in the waiting room."

"But I don't want to. It feels like I just went, and it hurts, Maman! Please don't send me to Pain and Torture."

"Don't call it that."

"That's what Naveed calls it!" Instantly, she regretted saying this. Just speaking her brother's name made her angrier.

"It's physical therapy, Roya-jaan. You need to do this to help your knee heal right. No arguments. We're going."

Roya crossed her arms. It was almost as if the shayatin were trying to prevent her from banishing them. But Roya wasn't going to let anything stop her. Even though she knew her knee would be sore after PT, making it extremely painful to get to her altar, it would be worth it in the end.

By now, Maman was already pulling up at the house. Roya hobbled straight upstairs to her room, where she was met with an even more shocking sight.

Her bedroom floor was covered in dead ants. There must be hundreds, Roya thought. Hundreds of tiny, motionless dark bodies.

She lowered herself to the ground, careful of her stiff right leg, and soon saw the reason: just under her bed, almost touching her covered altar, was one of those ant traps Maman often made using sugar and some chemical that was poison to them.

As far as Roya could tell, her altar hadn't been disturbed, which was a relief—but a sick feeling lodged at the base of her throat as she watched doomed ants cluster around the edges of the sticky substance, eating greedily, unaware of the connection between that sweet syrup and the death surrounding them.

There were a few other ants nearby, walking strangely, like they'd lost their way. Near them, one ant stood at the side of a dead friend, his antennae going crazy. Roya could practically hear his little ant-voice. *Get up! Please, please, get up!*

But the other ant remained still. The living ant circled him, tried to move him, maybe to carry away his body, make sure it would be properly buried. But he didn't get far before Roya sat up. She couldn't watch anymore.

Clumsily, she got to her feet and made her way back downstairs. She found Maman in the kitchen slicing fruit.

"Maman," Roya said.

Her mother turned. "What is it, Roya-jaan?" She sounded impatient. She was always so impatient with Roya.

"They're all dead. You poisoned them! How could you?"

Maman narrowed her eyes. "What are you talking about?"

"The ants. In my bedroom."

"Oh. They're pests, azizam. I saw a bunch of them going under your bed, so I had to make sure they don't find their way to the kitchen." She paused. "You don't have any food in your room, do you?"

The lump in Roya's throat tightened. *The honey.* Her offering had lured all those ants to her room... and to their deaths.

"Of course not!" Roya almost screamed it. "You're the one who killed them! How do you think they feel, Maman? How do you think it feels to walk through all those bodies, knowing that your friends are all dead?"

Maman's face was hard. She didn't care about the ants. She didn't get it at all. "Go put your shoes on," she said in a cold voice. "We have to leave in a few minutes."

"I'm not going."

"Yes. You. Are. Go on, or we'll be late."

"I don't care."

Maman stared at her. "Roya-jaan, what do you want me to say? I'm sorry, but sometimes you have to do things you don't want to do. Now *go put on your shoes*. Right now."

Roya knew she'd pushed far enough, and as badly as she wanted to push farther, to keep pushing and pushing, she turned around instead.

She briefly wondered if Cyrus would hear their argument and come out of his room to see what was going on, but he didn't. He might not even be home—she never knew these days. Honestly, it didn't matter if he was home or not, she never saw him either way. Well, except for Sunday dinners, the one night a week that Naveed was there too, when he would come home and brag about how perfect and wonderful everything was out at the farm.

Grudgingly, she stomped to the living room and shoved her feet into sandals. When Maman appeared, Roya stormed out to the car and shut her door without a word.

They rode to the PT clinic in silence. Roya watched Maman in the rearview mirror. Her black curls bouncing as they drove over a pothole. Her disturbingly red lips pressed together so tight. Her dark, deadened eyes.

Outside Roya's window, a group of crows took flight from a brick building as they drove past. They fluttered themselves into a cloud, which then burst apart as they flew off in different directions. Roya rehearsed the banishing ritual in her mind. She would make it happen tonight. No matter what else got in the way. The thought cheered her a little, and she returned her attention to the last group of crows, which soared alongside the car for a minute before disappearing into the trees.

Cyrus

WEDNESDAY, MAY 18

CYRUS WAS ABOUT TO SNOOZE HIS PHONE ALARM FOR THE eleventh time—or something like that anyway, he'd lost count several snoozes ago—when a text from Shea appeared. He read it and woke up instantly.

Meet me in the cafeteria at 8:15. I've got something to tell you before class.

She had sent it to the group text with Dev and Todd, so it had to be something about the business plan they'd been developing for their startup, Quirqi Media. Cyrus glanced at the clock. Shit, it was already 7:30? His commute took forever—no time to waste.

He rolled out of the bottom bunk, found his glasses on the nightstand, grabbed the first shirt he saw, threw on a hoodie and some not-too-dirty jeans, smoothed his hair, and was good to go.

Back in the day, Cyrus might have taken the time to cook himself breakfast. Now, though, it was protein bars and coffee with plenty of cream while driving to the community college where he was finishing up his junior year in an accelerated high school program.

He was fixing himself a nice tall commuter mug while making the morning social media rounds on his phone when he heard a zipper closing. Maman was in the living room, all decked out in her raincoat and hiking boots, adjusting the straps on her backpack.

Whoa, it was time for her trip to Mount Rainier already? That meant the trial would be starting next week. Cyrus had been careful to avoid even thinking about the shitshow that his family's life was about to turn into. It had been frighteningly easy not to pay attention—between working on Quirqi and keeping up with his mounting schoolwork as finals approached, not to mention recording and editing his and Dev's popular show, *Devil & Cyborg,* there had been no time for anything else.

"You heading out soon?" He hoped Maman wouldn't rope him into a long conversation, since he should've been out the door ten minutes ago. All the same, he didn't want to be a dick and ignore her.

"Yep. Kelly's picking me up in half an hour."

"Have fun, Maman." He hugged her on his way to the door.

"Kourosh-jaan." She never failed to pronounce his name the Persian way, with the trilled *r* and everything. "Asheghetam. You'll take care of things while I'm gone?"

"Of course." Not like Baba was incapable of taking care of them, but whatever.

She pulled away and looked him straight in the eye. "Spend some time with your sister. She misses you."

"I will," he said, even though he doubted he'd have time to follow through on that promise.

She gave him one of those intense *I'm reading your mind and I know you're lying* looks, and he thought she was about to call him out. But instead, she asked, "Have you talked to Andi lately?"

Um, what did that have to do with anything? Andi had texted him the other day with a disturbing photo of her grandfather standing next to none other than cult leader and would-be Cyrus-killer Alastor Yarrow. He'd replied a vague, Whoa that's crazy, I'll look into it, but had been so swamped that he hadn't yet. Plus, he hadn't exactly wanted to open the string and see that face staring at him again.

Not that he was about to bring that up with Maman now. "Not really," he said. "She's just as busy as me."

"She's coming over for dinner Sunday. Can you plan to cook that night?"

Oh, that's why she was asking. "Yeah, sure. Sorry, Maman, but I'm running late, I have to go—"

"Okay." She pulled him into one more hug, kissing both of his cheeks and his forehead, which was a little much, but he let her do it. "Stay safe while I'm gone, Kourosh-jaan."

A tickle of unease spread through his stomach. The last time she'd left, when she'd gone to a wedding in Iran, Roya had nearly gotten herself killed in a freaking barn fire, not to mention the other drama that he and Naveed had gotten embroiled in with Andi....

He looked straight into her searching brown eyes. He wanted her to know he wasn't lying about this. "I promise, Maman." He shouldered his backpack and opened the front door. "Love you."

He barely heard her response before he shut the door behind him. Quick, quick, quick, on to Dev's house, sipping coffee, eating the protein bar that tasted like sweet Styrofoam.

When Dev got into the car, he was spilling over with excitement. "Why do you think Shea wants to meet with us? You think...? Oh, I'm afraid to even say it."

"I'm afraid to even *think* it," said Cyrus. "Don't want to jinx anything."

"I thought the business plan turned out pretty great, though, don't you?"

"Yeah. It all feels so... official."

"I know! Look at us. All grown up." Dev sniffed and wiped a fake tear from his eye.

Cyrus laughed. "Okay, let's talk about something else, then. What's going on in the *D&C* world?"

Dev read him a bunch of stuff from their feed, played a few reaction videos to their latest episode, narrated comments as he composed them. Cyrus loved every second. It was rare that just the two of them were together anymore. Dev spent most of his time with Todd now. Though, to be fair, Cyrus did too—all of their waking hours were eaten up with drafting their business plan and fine-tuning *Bugpocalypse 3K*, the game app that was to be Quirqi's flagship product.

Once they arrived at school, they went straight to the cafeteria, where Shea and Todd were waiting in front of a bulletin board covered with advertisements for ride shares and dog-walking services. Dev sidled up to Todd, who embraced him a little too affectionately. Cyrus had mostly grown used to the fact that they were dating, but sometimes he still wanted to yell at them to get a room.

"There you are! Took you long enough," Shea said.

"Class starts in a few minutes," Todd said gruffly. "What's the news, Shea?"

Shea broke into a huge grin that lit up her whole face. Her freckles glowed adorably. "A potential investor wants to meet with us."

"For real?" Todd said.

"Who is it?" Cyrus asked.

"Have they already seen the business plan?" Dev chimed in.

Shea motioned for them to quiet down. "I don't know the details yet. Philip mentioned it when I was asking him some questions about database architecture." Philip Bradley was their mentor, a developer and entrepreneur who had sold his first app for an obscene amount of money. "He sent a demo of the app to a friend, whose daughter happens to be a big fan of your show… anyway, he wants us to present it to his team. Philip asked if we'd be able to pull something together by the end of the week. If all goes well… there's a chance his company would be able to grant the full amount we requested."

Whoa. This was *huge*. Their plan for scaling up had involved hiring more developers, renting office space, purchasing capital equipment, and giving each of them a generous salary. Cyrus had expected some pushback on that last part—they had each asked for a salary competitive with full-time tech workers at global companies, even though they were all just sixteen-year-olds still living at home.

Nevertheless, he really could use the money. Cyrus had watched the pile of past-due medical bills in the downstairs office grow from a few scattered envelopes into a tall stack. He didn't understand what that was about. He'd thought their settlement with Nutrexo would take care of everything; the company had agreed to pay over a million dollars in damages. But when he tried to ask his parents about it, they brushed him off, saying they had it under control.

One night last week, though, he'd overheard them having a particularly tense discussion as they made their way to bed. "We only missed one payment," Baba had said. "It has to be a mistake."

"But what if it's not? What if we can't fix it, and the foreclosure goes through?" Maman said. "This is the only place I've ever... oh, Saman, what if they take the house? What will we do?"

"Don't worry, we'll figure it out," Baba said. "It's going to be all right."

Cyrus had remained frozen long after the door to their bedroom had clicked shut. He didn't want to believe what he'd heard, didn't want to think it was even remotely possible for them to lose their home.

He wished he could have offered to help, but his *D&C* earnings had tanked now that he and Dev weren't posting regularly. He'd already spent most of his savings on a top-of-the-line new laptop, a dual-screen desktop command center, and various models of smartphones, which they'd needed for app testing. But maybe, if they got this deal in motion quickly, he would be able to bail his parents out.

"So all we have to do," Dev was saying, "Is put together a brilliant slide deck, show up and wow this guy and his team, and we might walk away with a legit business of our own?"

"Yep. Exactly," Shea said.

"So, what do we know about these people? Besides the fact that the dude's daughter is a fan?" Cyrus asked. Sure, he wanted to tailor their demo to the audience, but he was starting to wonder who, exactly, these potential investors were. He'd hoped they would be able to find an angel, some quirky tech billionaire who wanted to spread his money around, ideally one who wouldn't pressure them too much about constantly turning a profit. This sounded like something different, though, possibly involving a venture capital firm, and it was pretty much embedded in Cyrus's DNA to be suspicious of such places.

"I don't know anything but what I told you," Shea said. "We can ask Philip for more details later."

Todd checked his smartwatch. "Better get to class—let's divide and conquer at lunch. This is our chance, guys. We can't mess this up."

Naveed

NAVEED WAS DIGGING A TRENCH WHEN HIS PHONE RANG.

He only heard it because he'd left the windows open in his cabin. In the middle of the night, he'd opened them all as far as they could go, because he was desperate for fresh air. It had been one of *those* nights, the kinds that came more frequently now, where he woke up sweat-drenched and struggling to breathe, as if he'd been running from something that was stalking him, hunting him....

It was impossible to get back to sleep after that, so he'd turned on all the lights and tried to soothe his mind by carving some wood using the knife he'd bought at the market from a Muckleshoot woman a few stalls down from Zetik Farm. It was a true work of art, with its buffalo-rib handle and obsidian blade. He couldn't say the same about his current woodcarvings, which were really nothing more than sharpened sticks, but just holding the knife in his hands always made him feel a little better somehow.

As soon as the sun rose, he pulled on his boots and got to work outside. He had been digging for a long time now, but the hole still wasn't deep enough. His plan was to fit a log inside and inoculate it with turkey tail mushroom spores, then half-bury it and surround it with healing herbs. The soil was wet and heavy and he was already out of breath, but sometimes he felt like doing physical labor, the hard work of digging and moving earth, was the only thing keeping him sane.

When the phone rang, he was surprised. Andi didn't usually call this early; the last wisps of the gold-purple sunrise still lit up the sky. But his phone was playing the custom ring tone he'd set for his mother, a haunting Iranian folk song.

Koffka looked up at him questioningly, like, *You hear that, right?*

"Yeah, I've got it." Naveed leaned his shovel against the cabin and pulled off his gloves as he walked around to the door. He didn't bother taking off his muddy boots, but by the time he got to his phone it had gone quiet.

She would probably leave a voicemail—she always did—so he took the opportunity to wash his hands and take a few gulps of water. The orange prescription vials near the sink caught his eye, and he shook his morning meds dutifully into his palm, to the apparent approval of Koffka, who wagged his tail vigorously. *Didn't even have to remind you today!,* he seemed to be saying.

Even though Naveed wasn't hungry, he started throwing smoothie ingredients into the blender. Protein powder, huge scoops of peanut butter and coconut oil, hemp seeds, honey, almond milk, plus half a dozen different tinctures and plant essences that made up the traditional Iranian medicine portion of his morning regimen. He was tired of being scrawny and was trying to bulk up, but even though he drank three of these calorie-dense smoothies every day in addition to meals, he still hadn't gained any weight. He kept choking them down anyway.

His phone dinged with a voicemail notification, but he didn't bother listening to it. Instead, he called Maman back as he took his drink out to the pair of lawn chairs on the porch.

"Sobh bekheir, Maman," he told her when she picked up the phone.

"Good morning, Naveed-jaan," she answered. "How are you?"

She said that the same way everyone did, emphasizing the *are*, a constant reminder that there was something wrong with him. "I'm good. Just sitting on the porch having breakfast. Everything all right?"

"Oh! Yes, it's fine. You didn't listen to my message?"

"Not yet. Thought I'd just call you back. What's up?"

"Well... Kelly's picking me up soon, and we'll be heading down to Tahoma."

"Right, your camping trip! I forgot you were leaving today."

"I was wondering if we could stop by on our way," Maman said. "Will you be around? Or are you going to the market?"

"Frida's doing the market—I'm here today. You should come!" He tried to sound excited, even as he looked through the window at the lamentable state of his cabin. There was dog hair everywhere, mud on the floor, a teetering pile of dishes in the sink....

"You sure? You don't have too much going on?"

"Not at all! I have some spare time today. When do you think you'll get here?"

"Mmm, a couple hours? I'll text you when we're getting close."

"Perfect. Park in the front—part of the driveway got washed out in that storm a few weeks ago. I'll meet you there."

"Thank you, Naveed-jaan. See you soon, then."

As soon as he hung up, he slodged over to the main house. Naveed's cabin was way back beyond the orchards at the edge of the property where it butted up against the forest. Usually, he liked the distance. It made him feel more like he was on his own and less like he was just renting a room at someone else's house. Still, it could be a pain in the ass when it came to doing laundry or hauling things from one place to another.

He wanted to move quickly since he knew it would take a few hours to get his place cleaned up, but he was panting by the time he arrived and had to stop to catch his breath. He watched Koffka and Astro run gleefully through the fields behind him. Koffka usually took his service dog job very seriously, but Astro never failed to bring out his playful side.

Naveed climbed the stairs to the back deck and stuck his head in the kitchen, where Frida was scrambling eggs. "Morning, Frida. Could I borrow the broom? My mom's stopping by for a visit today."

"Of course! Let me go find it." With her long silver hair pulled back, Frida's angular jawline was more noticeable; she had been born male but transitioned to female a decade ago.

She disappeared to go root around in the pantry. As soon as she returned, broom in hand, Naveed power-walked back to the cabin and got to work. He cleaned the floor, wiped off the table, scrubbed the toilet. He tucked his obsidian knife into the silverware drawer and swept up the wood shavings on the floor, since he knew his mother wouldn't approve that he'd taken up woodworking again. She could only see the seemingly dangerous combination of sharp knives and clumsy hands, but he'd learned how to work around his limitations.

His bed was another problem: the quilt was covered in Koffka hair. So he hung it over the porch railing outside and whacked at it with a discarded length of bamboo until most of the hair had blown away in the wind.

When he returned inside, he noticed his inhaler was tangled in the bed linens. He fished it out and hazarded a sniff of the sheets, then pulled his head back. They smelled ripe; it wasn't the first time he'd awoken all sweaty and gross, but he hadn't washed them since he'd moved in. He made a mental note to do this before Andi came, but there was no time for it now. He'd have to make the bed, cover them with the quilt, and hope Maman wouldn't notice. The open windows made the air nice and fresh, but would she be warm enough? He should make some tea. Yes. Tea, that was a good idea.

By the time she texted him to say they'd be arriving in a few minutes, everything was tidied up and a pot of cardamom tea was steeping on the table, next to a bowl of shelled walnuts and dried tart cherries. He was proud of the quick transformation into a mother-presentable living space. It looked like the home of a normal person.

He made his way to the main house and had just put the broom on the back porch when he heard them pulling up in front. Gretchen came out from the barn to greet them too.

Maman got out of the passenger seat and gave him a big hug. Kelly greeted him from a respectful distance, which he appreciated, and he introduced her to Gretchen.

"Would you like the tour?" Gretchen asked Kelly. "I could also use a hand milking the goats, if you would like to help."

"Yes! I'd love to!" Kelly said. "Mahnaz? You want to join?"

"That's all right." Maman knew Naveed never went into the barn. It was pretty great of Gretchen and Frida to offer him this job as their live-in farm hand even though he'd told them that he wasn't able to do certain things. Milking goats was one of them.

"I was just making some tea, if you want any?" Naveed asked his mother.

"That sounds wonderful." She linked her arm in his. In general, he hated it when people touched him without warning, but it felt good to be near her. There was something about Maman that always comforted him.

They walked slowly through the orchards, Koffka trotting along at their side. Soon the cherries would be ready, and he'd be busy supervising the harvest and selling the fresh fruit at Pike Place and the Orting Farmers Market. But for now, the fruit was just a promise, not yet a reality.

Maman asked what he'd been working on, so he told her about the tilling and planting he'd done the day before, about the medicinal herb garden he was starting. Talking and walking at the same time made him short of breath, so he let her take over the conversation for a while. After they stepped inside the cabin, he went through the comforting motions of rinsing the cups, of pouring the tea, of handing her the glass mug.

"Thank you." She took a sip. "How have you been feeling lately? Nerve pain bothering you at all?"

"No. The meds are working great."

"And therapy? How's that going?"

"Fine. Haven't missed a single session."

"Good. Oh—that reminds me, did the probation office call you about your appointment on Friday?"

Shit, he'd forgotten about that. He'd have to see if he could reschedule—he was picking Andi up from the airport on Friday. "Yeah, it's on my radar."

She held her mug with both hands. "How about your lungs? You sound a little wheezy."

Dammit, he couldn't get anything by her. "I mean, they're okay. It might be allergies or something? All the pollen out here? Who knows. I'm not worried about it."

He was, though, a little. He got winded so easily now. Sometimes it felt like his lungs had shrunken, like it was impossible to draw enough breath in, and his inhaler didn't help at all. He was working a lot harder physically than he had in a long time, so maybe that was it, or maybe it was just anxiety, or a boring old pollen allergy.

"Even so, we should get it checked out. You've never been bothered by allergies before." There was a definite note of concern in her voice. "I'll make an appointment when I get back. You're due for a follow-up visit anyway."

"Okay. I'm sure it's nothing, but I guess you're right." He doubted the doctors would have any answers, and wished Maman didn't have to worry about him so much—but all the same, he was glad she was always in his corner, looking out for him.

She sipped her tea again. "I'm happy for you, Naveed-jaan. Living out here on this beautiful land, spending your days in the fresh air working with plants—it's perfect. Just don't overdo it, okay? Take it slow, and talk to Gretchen and Frida if anything gets to be too much."

"I will, Maman." This was exactly what he wanted her to believe—and what *he* wanted to believe, too. That out here, surrounded by nature in all its rejuvenating glory, he would find his way back to health and stability. But, in reality, it wasn't that easy. Yes, he loved it here; yes, he was grateful to Gretchen and Frida for giving him this chance. But he also struggled with a desperate loneliness in the quiet evenings. It always descended on him heavily, landing as a familiar feeling of tightness in his chest. *Delam baraat tang shodeh,* he always thought. The Persian phrase meant *I miss you,* though its literal translation was *my heart has become tight for you.* He missed everything so much, his home and his family and Andi and the city with all its distractions. But at least he had Koffka. That helped a lot.

Maman wasn't done, though. She added, "But… it's time for you to start thinking about the future. You can't be a farmer forever. Eventually, you'll need a good job, one that pays well, and covers your health insurance."

Frida always said this place was her health insurance, and Naveed had hoped it would be like that for him too. Soon enough, he'd have his own plant-based pharmacy of medicinal mushrooms and herbs, and he'd make his own tinctures and teas, letting the land nourish and heal him. "I guess, but I'll be covered under you and Baba—"

"Not for that much longer, though. It's important that you're working towards something. Have you thought more about reapplying to UW?"

"Not really. It's so hard for me to concentrate…."

"You have rights, Naveed-jaan. They can accommodate you."

"I know." He was starting to feel uncomfortable. It wasn't just his concentration that was a problem. He wasn't sure he'd be able to handle all the stress, either. Things always got worse inside his head when he was stressed. Not that he could confess any of these things to her. He poured himself more tea and asked, "How about you, Maman? You doing all right?"

"Fine. Just busy. Not looking forward to Monday." Opening statements of *The People v. Tara Snyder.* Naveed wasn't looking forward to it either.

She set her mug down. "Naveed-jaan… you're not going to be working the markets during the trial, are you?"

The worry in her voice surprised him. "No, Maman. They have summer interns coming—they'll handle selling at the markets. I'll just lay low down here."

"Good. That'll be best. It could get ugly."

Naveed waved a hand. "Eh, we can handle it. Been through plenty of ugliness before."

"Yes. We have."

He added, softly, "Thank you, Maman. For making sure I don't have to testify." He'd been subpoenaed as a witness, but his mother had made sure that his psychiatrist petitioned to have him removed, on the grounds that testifying could re-traumatize him. Naveed had given plenty of depositions, but still he was torn about it, because part of him wished he was strong enough to march into that courtroom and tell the world all the things Tara Snyder had done, all the ways she had ruined his body, his mind. He wished he was strong enough to look her in the eye and not be afraid.

Instead, he would be cowering out here in the middle of nowhere.

"Of course," she said. "I just want you to be safe."

"Don't worry, Maman. I've got Koffka to keep me from going off the deep end. And he's not going to let anyone mess with me, either." Koffka was the sole reason Naveed didn't mind working at the market, even though he kept half-expecting Tim Schmidt or some other crazy stalker to show up looking for him there.

Maman stared at the steam rising from her mug, but didn't say anything.

"You sure you're going to be all right?" he asked. She looked so weary.

"I'll be fine. We'll get through it. Een neez bogzarad, right?"

This, too, shall pass. He smiled at her, and she smiled back tentatively, and they sat together in his cold but sunny cabin, sipping their tea in companionable silence.

"Naveed-jaan," she said suddenly, her voice sounding strained. "There's something—"

At that moment, both of their phones lit up with a simultaneously-received text. They looked at each other, then at their screens. The text was from Kelly. Just saw the time! We're losing daylight, better get going. Can you meet us at the car?

Maman practically jumped out of her seat. "She's right. I hadn't realized how late it was getting. Thank you for the tea. Walk with me to the car?"

As they put on their boots, Naveed asked her, "What were you going to tell me?"

"Oh, nothing," Maman said. "Just that I wrote to the owner of that attari shop in Tehran, and he's looking into a few other treatments that might help."

"That's it?" Naveed asked, confused. It had seemed like she'd been leading up to something much more important.

"That's it." She squinted into the sun. "Looks like it'll be a beautiful day. I should've packed more layers. I only brought one t-shirt."

Naveed's chest suddenly felt very tight. *Delam baraat tang shodeh* circled in his head again. The phrase captured exactly how he felt. He missed her before she was even gone.

He led her through the cherry orchard back to the car. The uneven ground made him stumble, but she took his hand without saying a word, steadying him. They walked hand in hand beneath the trees together, leaving a trail of deep boot-prints in the thick mud behind them.

Andi

WEDNESDAY, MAY 18

"BE GENTLE WITH THE BROCCOLI," AH-MA SAID FROM HER CHAIR behind the kitchen counter. Andi froze, her spatula hovering just above the Chinese broccoli cooking in the pan. Apparently she'd been slapping it a little too hard.

It hadn't been the greatest day. But, Andi supposed, at least it hadn't been boring. There had been plenty of things to distract her while she waited for Cyrus to come back with news on the Mystery Box front. A term paper to finish. A piano to practice. A jiu-jitsu professor to roll with. A therapist to chat with about the confusingly intense emotions that had bubbled up after the jiu-jitsu class. Not to mention Barb, who seemed hell-bent on keeping Andi's headache pulsing all day long.

And now here she was, cooking dinner as Ah-ma talked her through the steps. The pork belly in the wok on the back burner simmered in its sweet-savory broth, four hard-boiled eggs bobbing on the surface. The kitchen was filled with the aroma of fried shallots, shiitake mushrooms, five-spice and steaming rice.

The front door opened, and a moment later Ah-gong stepped into the kitchen. "Smells good in here. How are you feeling?" he asked Ah-ma.

"Fine. Teaching Andi how to make lǔ ròu fàn."

"Hěn hǎo." He paused. "So. I have some news. Is Joyce home yet?"

"She should be back any minute," Andi said. "But you can tell us now."

Ah-gong shook his head. "Patience," he called as he walked up the stairs.

Andi turned back to the pan, annoyed. What kind of news? He hadn't even said if it was good or bad. Maybe it had something to do with the package? Probably not. That would be too easy. She grunted in exasperation. "Why does he have to keep us in suspense?"

"We'll know soon enough. Don't get caught up, just flow like water."

It was good to hear Ah-ma sounding more like her usual Zen-like self. Even so, secrets drove Andi crazy. She was tempted to go pound out something loud and intense on the piano, but she couldn't leave. Until the broth got to the exact right consistency, she was stuck here with a wok full of animal flesh.

This made her think of Brooke, who had texted a link to the menu of a vegan spot she wanted to take Andi to while she was in town. Brooke had been living in Boulder since January, but had recently moved back into her mother's house in Seattle.

Andi pulled out her phone and found Brooke's text. Oops—she hadn't replied yet. That place looks great, Andi wrote. My mouth's watering from the menu... or maybe just the pork belly I'm cooking for dinner.

Brooke replied quickly. Heheheh can't wait to seeee youuuuu

Same, Andi wrote back, adding a few hearts for good measure.

She looked up from her phone to see her mother entering the kitchen. "You're home!" Andi said, a little too enthusiastically. She stuffed her phone into her back pocket.

Her mother regarded her suspiciously. "Nice to see you, too. Everything all right?" She gave Ah-ma a half-hug.

"I'm fine," said Ah-ma.

"Ah-gong has some news," Andi said as her mother reached into the pan to steal a small clump of leaves. "But he was waiting for you, so go tell him you're here."

"Looks like dinner's almost ready. Why don't we wait until it's done before we call him."

Andi wanted to massacre that broccoli now. She stepped away from the frying pan.

When the broth was finally just right, Andi sliced the eggs in half and transferred the braised pork and Chinese broccoli to serving bowls. She brought all the food to the table as her mother called Ah-gong downstairs.

After dishing up her dinner, Andi stared at her rice bowl, stomach twisting, too nervous to eat. "So, what's your news?" she asked.

Ah-gong set down his chopsticks and looked at each of them in turn. A grin overtook his face. "It's official. I sold Lu Yu!"

"What?" Andi asked.

Her mother set down her wine glass so fast that it almost tipped over. "You sold the company? Why?"

Ah-gong reached for Ah-ma's hand. "I'm ready to retire. The offer was very generous—we'll be taken care of. All of us," he added, looking at Andi. She understood what he meant: they'd still be able to cover her college expenses, which was a relief. USC wasn't exactly cheap.

"Who did you sell it to?" Andi couldn't help but ask.

"Doesn't matter. The deal is done. I'll be finishing things up for the next month or so, preparing for the transition, but then I'll be free." He breathed a contented sigh.

Andi had never thought of Ah-gong as feeling constrained by the company. Lu Yu was his life—and now he'd sold it out of the blue to someone he didn't even want to name? Sure, he probably wanted to spend more time with Ah-ma, but still....

Her mother was congratulating him, but Andi couldn't let it go. "Who did you sell it to, Ah-gong? I want to know."

"Andi," her mother said warningly.

"No, it's all right." Ah-gong looked Andi in the eye. "I sold it to Hannigan Foods."

"*What?*" This just kept getting weirder. Hannigan Foods had once been rivals with Nutrexo, the company that had sponsored Tara Snyder's research project—but they had later bought a bunch of Nutrexo's brands, including Blazin Bitz. "Why would they want your company? Doesn't seem like they'd care about loose-leaf tea."

"I haven't made money from loose-leaf tea in years," Ah-gong said. This was news to Andi—she'd always thought this had been Lu Yu's main focus. "Not enough people buying it. People don't have the time to brew good tea anymore. They're more interested in instant tea powder, tea bags... for a while there, the supplement companies were all over our green tea extract. Not as much anymore, but Hannigan Foods wants to expand their offerings...."

"What about health insurance?" Andi's mom asked.

"I've got it covered. That was part of the deal."

The conversation moved on, but Andi stopped listening, because something had struck her. Two stray notes in her head—the Mystery Box photo and the words *green tea extract*—had come together into a chord.

"Ah-gong, did Lu Yu sell green tea extract to Metafolia?" Andi blurted.

Ah-gong stopped talking mid-sentence. Everyone's heads swiveled her way. They didn't have to say a word for Andi to know it was true. She could see it in their faces: her mother's guilty look, Ah-gong's defiant one, Ah-ma's pale, miserable-looking expression.

"You did. I can't believe you. And you never thought it was relevant to tell me this? Not even when I ended up in the ER after taking the Metafolia that *you* pushed on me? Not even when Alastor—"

Ah-ma pushed her chair back from the table. "Excuse me," she said as she rushed toward the bathroom and closed the door.

"Andi, that's enough." Her mom shot her an angry glare.

"I sell the extract to lots of companies." Ah-gong glanced with obvious concern at the bathroom door. "Metafolia was one of them. We only gave it to you because we thought it would help. And it's irrelevant now anyway. The company's gone, and—"

Andi was opening her mouth to interrupt when she heard a muffled cry and a loud *thump*. Her mother stood up so fast that her chair toppled over. She dashed toward the bathroom. Andi followed behind Ah-gong, but it was like she was trapped inside a bad dream where she could only move in slow motion.

Inside the bathroom, her mother was sitting on the floor next to Ah-ma's slumped-over body, yelling that she needed a phone. Andi took hers from her back pocket and her mother yanked it from her slow-moving hand, dialing 911, calling for an ambulance. Ah-ma lay there, motionless. The house slipper on her left foot had fallen off onto the bath mat. Andi's mom caught her eye, and even though she didn't say a word, Andi knew exactly what she was thinking. *Look how much you upset her, Andi. This is All. Your. Fault.*

Cyrus

FRIDAY, MAY 20

CYRUS SMOOTHED HIS BUTTON-DOWN SHIRT AS HE WALKED TO Shea's car. He had waited until the last minute to put it on because he knew this very important presentation would attract all the Spill-Your-Coffee-On-Your-Shirt spirits, but now it was wrinkly from being stuffed in his bag all day. Hopefully no one would notice.

"All aboard the Quirqi Train!" Todd called out his open window when he saw Cyrus coming. The guy was such a dork. Cyrus loved it.

Dev and Todd had claimed the back seat, so Cyrus rode shotgun. Shea swiveled her head towards him as she backed out of the parking space. She was wearing a summery skirt, her red hair held back with a cloth headband. She looked so hot that he had no idea how anyone could expect him to focus on their presentation.

He couldn't let it distract him, though. Shea had thrown him plenty of not-so-subtle hints that she didn't see him as anything more than a business partner and friend. Sometimes Cyrus wondered if she wasn't into him because she liked girls, or maybe she was aromantic or asexual or something, but she had never volunteered any information on the topic and he didn't know how to ask without coming off as accusatory, and anyway that was beside the point. She just didn't like him like that, and he had to get over it. She couldn't control who she was attracted to any more than he could.

"You have all the demo phones?" Shea was asking.

"Philip's bringing them. He has a copy of the slide deck too, but I've got it on a thumb drive just in case."

Dev and Todd were talking amongst themselves in the back, so Cyrus took out his phone. "Where are we going? Want me to pull the address up?"

"No. I know how to get there," Shea said quickly. "Here, why don't you go over the pitch again."

Cyrus had been practicing nonstop in his head during class, but he went through it again as they drove. He was concentrating on this so completely that he almost didn't notice they'd entered the heart of downtown, and that she was slowing down in front of a tall, black tower—one Cyrus knew only too well.

When she pulled into the parking garage beneath the building that once housed Nutrexo, he stopped mid-sentence. "What the hell? We're not—"

"We are," Shea said firmly. "The meeting's with Blanchet Capital. Twenty-first floor."

She rolled down her window and took her parking ticket. Cyrus watched the little yellow arm swing up to admit them into the bowels of the building. He thought he might puke, or cry, or both.

Dev put his hand on Cyrus's shoulder as if to reassure him, but Cyrus shook it away. "Did you know about this, Dev?"

"No. I swear."

"Look, I'm sorry," Shea said. "Philip warned me that this is the old Nutrexo building and it might be a sore spot for you. But we can't pass up this chance."

Cyrus was speechless. She made it sound like what happened here was just a little owie on his knee, something inconsequential and easily forgotten about.

He didn't have a chance to respond before Dev asked, "Isn't Blanchet the company your mom's always on about lately?"

It did sound familiar, but frankly Cyrus couldn't remember what her problem with the company was. All he was thinking about was the last time he'd been in this building. A security guard had marched Andi and him through a door somewhere around here, a back entrance with an elevator that went straight up to Richard Caring's office. At the time, he'd been certain he was about to die.

"I don't know. Maybe. Just… give me a minute, will you?" Cyrus leaned back, closed his eyes, took a few deep breaths. *No big deal,* he told himself. *It's just an ordinary building, nothing's going to happen, all you have to do is nail the presentation and then you can get the hell out of here.*

"Philip just texted. He's here," Shea said. "We'd better get inside. You ready?"

Cyrus nodded and got out of the car. He followed the rest of them numbly to the elevator bank. As it ascended, Todd regaled them with cautionary tales of catastrophic phone-related meeting interruptions, so they all powered their phones down to prevent unwelcome beeping, dinging, and buzzing. They wanted to give the impression that they had their shit together.

Philip, who was wearing a suit jacket over one of his trademark hipster t-shirts, was in the lobby speaking with the receptionist. Cyrus was slightly relieved to see that Blanchet Capital had remodeled everything. It looked like a different place inside, all sleek and modern, with a glossy white reception desk and colorful chairs with lots of hard angles that made him think of origami for some reason.

When they took the elevators up to the twenty-first floor, though, he saw the wall of plate-glass windows, the peak of Mount Rainier curving high above the horizon. He quickly recalibrated and focused on Shea's swishing skirt to distract him from the painful déjà vu.

They were led into a conference room that seemed designed for intimidation. A row of people—most of them men, all of them white—sat in regular, non-origami-shaped chairs along one side of the table. Cyrus headed over to the laptop, intending to set up his slide deck, but it was already pulled up and ready to go.

Philip was bro-hugging one of the men, who introduced himself as Kieran. He shook their hands, then gestured for them to take their seats. "Thanks for coming in. This is my team." The others nodded, apparently content to remain nameless. "Unfortunately, Ray wasn't able to join us today—he makes all the final decisions, so if this looks promising, we'll have you come back when he's in town."

"Of course. Not a problem." Philip looked at Cyrus. "Why don't we start with a demo?"

Cyrus reached into the briefcase Philip had brought and pulled out their testing phones, then distributed them to the people sitting across the table. "I could just show you on the screen, but that would be super boring," he said. To his surprise, the man sitting next to Kieran chuckled quietly. The others seemed to be perking up, too. "You'll get a better feel for the app if you try it yourself."

He walked them through the demo, noticing that everyone was instantly engaged once they began playing, even the bored-looking woman closest to the door. "So, the demo you're playing right now is set in individual mode, but we also have a cooperative mode that you can play with your friends. The object of the game is straightforward: kill the bad bugs. But you have to be careful not to smash the good ones. Kill too many of those, and it's game over."

After they'd played for a few minutes, Cyrus collected the phones. Most of them were handed over reluctantly, which made him absurdly happy. "Can we just do one more?" one of the guys asked. "I want to try out cooperative mode."

Cyrus smiled, his confidence boosted. "We'll send you a demo that you can download to your phones. But I wanted to show you how good it feels, because that's our company's overall mission: to make people happier."

Kieran was nodding encouragingly, so Cyrus went on, "Life is hard these days. People are stressed-out and unhappy. We may not be able to solve their problems, but we want to make it easier for people to get through their day, give them an outlet to blow off steam or escape from reality for a while. Not just a time-suck that turns your brain off and makes you feel more isolated, but something that leaves you in a better mood and ready to face whatever's in front of you. That's what we've always tried to do with *Devil & Cyborg,* our weekly show that now brings in over a million views per episode. That's what we're aiming to do with *Bugpocalypse 3K,* and all of the future products released by Quirqi Media."

Cyrus realized that, even though he'd been so nervous about this, he was kind of enjoying himself. He was proud of this fledgling company, of its noble mission, and he wanted it to go far. Even if it meant accepting financing from a huge firm like Blanchet.

"The game's impressive," Kieran said. "And I appreciate your vision. But my question is, why do you need the money? You've already accomplished a lot with very little capital, and you have a huge following. Why go through the trouble of forming a startup if you could continue growing organically and build more games as you have time?"

It was a good question, but they were ready for it. Shea jumped in. "Because we see a huge unmet need, and with enough resources we could build out a suite of games that are fun to play, cooperative, and pro-social. Accessibility is also a huge focus, and to be honest we all have a lot to learn about that. We want to bring in experts to consult with us. We want to beta-test multiple versions of each game with people from various disability communities so we can figure out how to build games that are widely inclusive. And while games will be our main focus initially, we'd like to branch into other types of content as well—video, webcomics, podcasts, stuff like that. To do this right, we're going to need funding."

Kieran seemed satisfied. One of the other dudes started asking about leadership structure and plans for growth and various details in their business plan, so Philip took over and fielded the nitpicky questions. Before Cyrus knew it, Kieran was thanking them and saying he'd be in touch after speaking with Mr. Whitaker. He escorted them to the elevator and sent them back to the ground floor.

As they descended, everyone beamed. "That went great," Philip said. "They were impressed. I thought your ages might be more of an issue, but they could tell that you're invested in this. That you're serious."

"Damn right we're serious. Serious about humor," Dev said with a straight face, and everyone laughed.

"We should celebrate," Philip was saying. "Happy hour appetizers are on me. Then maybe head back to the condo and break out the drones? I demand a rematch!"

"Hell yeah!" Dev said. He had just barely edged ahead of Philip to win their last race through a looping course Philip had set up in his downtown condo. Cyrus's sad little drone had quickly crashed into the wall and spent most of the race on top of the refrigerator as he tried to figure out how to get it back in the air again.

Todd started researching reviews of nearby restaurants so they could have an optimal happy-hour-appetizer experience, which reminded Cyrus that his phone was still off. He clicked the power button and waited for it to warm up.

They were walking through the lobby when it buzzed to life. He opened his messages and literally stopped in his tracks.

One of them was from Andi. She wanted to know if he'd heard from Naveed, who hadn't shown up to get her at the airport.

Well, shit. That didn't sound good. Cyrus knew how excited his brother was about seeing Andi. He wouldn't just stand her up. He texted back, Sorry just got this but hopefully u heard from N by now?

Her response came immediately. No, nothing from him all day, I'm getting worried plz lmk if you find anything out

Not good. Not good at all.

He moved on to the other new messages. They were from Baba, and had been sent minutes earlier.

Where are you? his father had written. Then, in a separate bubble, Never mind, wherever you are I need you to come right home.

Cyrus's legs didn't want to hold him up anymore. He sank into one of the origami chairs. It was surprisingly comfortable. Be there soon. Everything ok? he texted back.

Usually, when there had been some crisis or another, his parents would start with a preamble: *Don't worry, everyone's okay, but....* They would always say this before explaining, to save him those moments of dreading the worst.

Baba was composing a text, which would surely say that yes, of course it was fine, and he hadn't meant to make Cyrus worry.

But all his father wrote was, Just come home

"Is everything okay?" Shea was standing next to him. Philip was holding the front door open, and Todd and Dev had already stepped onto the plaza. Cyrus could hear the waterfall outside, thundering down the rocks into the pool below.

"I don't think it is," Cyrus said. "I think it's not. I'm sorry, Shea, but I think... I think...."

He couldn't even say it out loud. A sick feeling spread through his stomach. "I need you to take me home."

Andi

FRIDAY, MAY 20

ANDI SPRANG OUT OF HER SEAT THE MOMENT THE "FASTEN SEAT belt" light turned off. Even so, she wasn't fast enough: the aisle ahead was clogged with people taking their bags down from the overhead bins.

While she waited, rocking impatiently from one foot to the other, she opened her texts. Naveed still hadn't responded to any of her updates. She hadn't heard from him since early that morning. Sometimes he'd go radio silent if he got absorbed in some project at the farm, but she would've expected him to be checking his phone constantly for news of her arrival. Oh, well. She'd see him soon enough, on the other side of the security gates.

Her mom had sent a message while Andi was in the air. Doctors just came by. Ah-ma is still very confused and having a hard time with speech, but she's improving a bit according to their tests. Please text me when you get to your dad's.

The good news came as a relief. Ah-ma had been in the hospital since her fall several days earlier. The doctors said she'd had a mild stroke, but she should be able to make a full recovery. Part of Andi felt terrible about leaving. A slightly larger part, though, was desperate to get away. Especially after her mother told her, in no uncertain terms, that she wasn't to talk about Metafolia or ask "upsetting" questions to either Ah-gong or Ah-ma again. That didn't mean it wasn't constantly on Andi's mind, of course. She couldn't wait to tell Cyrus about the photograph, and Lu Yu's connection to Metafolia, and the fact that Hannigan Foods had bought Lu Yu out. All of this meant something, she was certain. She just had no idea what it was.

When it was finally her turn to step into the aisle, she struggled to pull her bag down from the overhead bin. A business traveler standing nearby caught it before it fell on her head, and Andi thanked them profusely. From there, it was a sprint through the B gates and out through the security exit, where Naveed—

Wasn't waiting. She slowed her pace. He said he'd be right on the other side, but he wasn't, and he wasn't browsing at the bookstore or buying tea from the nearby coffee cart. Maybe he'd gone to the wrong place? Usually, a misunderstanding like that could be solved with a quick call or text, but he still hadn't responded to any of her messages. What was going on?

She tried calling, and when he didn't answer she texted him again. She went to the bathroom, washed up slowly, wandered the shops, but he was nowhere.

Andi felt a familiar numbness that, for her, accompanied dread. But she didn't want to freak out just yet. Most likely everything was fine. His phone was probably dead, that was all. Or maybe traffic was bad. She checked the map on her phone, and it looked like there was some congestion by the airport, but nothing major. Almost thirty minutes had passed since she'd landed. He should have arrived by now.

Time was ticking, too. A few days earlier, Naveed had sheepishly admitted to Andi that he had a meeting with his probation officer on Friday afternoon that he couldn't reschedule. He'd asked if it was all right if they went to the downtown courthouse right after he picked her up. After asking if she should just get a ride from someone else—no, he'd insisted, the airport was on his way and he wanted to be the one to meet her—Andi had made plans to have coffee with Brooke during his meeting. But considering the time it would take to get downtown and find parking, they would be cutting it really close at this point.

Andi tried calling him again, but it rang through to voicemail, so she sent him another text: WHERE ARE YOU? Getting worried. Not that she expected a response at this point.

She stepped outside, wheeling her carry-on behind her, keeping an eye out for the truck he said he'd be driving. An old red pickup, one that Gretchen and Frida had let him borrow for the day. Nothing, nothing, nothing.

Andi pulled up her texts with Mahnaz. A few days earlier, she'd let Andi know that she'd be out of contact until the weekend and had sent along both Gretchen and Frida's cell numbers. Just in case you're worried and want them to check in on him, she'd said.

Andi was seriously considering it now. But before she raised the alarm, she texted Cyrus. Hey you haven't heard anything from N have you? He was supposed to pick me up but didn't show and isn't answering his phone.

No answer from him either. She watched the circling cars a little longer. Not a red pickup in sight.

Screw this. She called Brooke.

"ANDI!!!" Brooke yelled into the phone. "Are you here?"

"Yep," Andi said. "Hey, um, are you around? Can you give me a ride? Naveed was supposed to get me, but he's not here."

"That's weird," Brooke said. "But, hell yeah! I was just about to leave for downtown. I'll head for the airport instead. Yay! See you in a few!"

It didn't take Brooke long to arrive. When she pulled up, she put the car in park and got out to give Andi a huge hug.

"Welcome back!" Brooke said as she opened the trunk. The streak of fuchsia in her bleached-blonde hair looked bright in the gray afternoon, and her new sleeve tattoo peeked out from beneath the hem of her t-shirt.

Andi slid her bag in. "Thanks for getting me. Sorry—"

"Don't be sorry. I'm glad you called me. So good to see you again! Tell me all about your trip," she said as they got into the car. Andi sent a quick text to Naveed. Got a ride w Brooke instead. Plz call when you get this.

"It was pretty smooth. Except for the fact that Naveed stood me up for some mysterious reason."

"I'm sure he's fine?" Brooke probably didn't mean for it to come out as a question. "There's got to be some explanation."

"Oh, I know there is," Andi said. "I just hope it isn't something horrible."

"Amen," Brooke said.

After scanning the traffic alerts and seeing no notifications of major accidents, Andi said, "I'm going to text Gretchen and Frida. Maybe they'll have some idea where he is."

"You want to get something to eat?" Brooke asked once Andi had finished writing. "Or should we just head back to my place? I've got the house to myself since Mom's camping. We should celebrate, right? I mean, we both just graduated high school! Time to get wild!"

Yesterday had been the most anti-climactic last day of school Andi had ever had. After taking her trig final, she'd breathed a quiet sigh of relief as she clicked "Submit." That had been the extent of her celebrations so far. "Yeah, let's do that," Andi said distractedly. She didn't feel like eating. Her stomach was in knots, and would be until she knew what was up with Naveed.

"Get wild, you mean? Excellent. Wanna try something new? There's this strain of cannabis I just got, I'm totally hooked—it tastes *exactly* like banana bread. And it's mellow, it's not gonna wipe you out or anything. A good starter strain."

"I'll have to pass," Andi said. "Remember? We're having dinner with Vanesa."

"Oh. Right. Is it weird that I'm nervous for that? I don't think Naveed and I have sat around the same table since... well, it's been a long time.

And you guys are together now, which is fine, it's just... weird for me."

The two of them rarely talked about the fact that Brooke was Naveed's ex-girlfriend. In fact, Andi sometimes forgot entirely. All of that felt like a lifetime ago. "Makes sense. But Akilah and Laurel are coming, and you'll love Vanesa."

"You're right. I'm sure it'll be fun. And maybe we could even hit a show after? I think Seacastle is playing at the Tractor."

"Can we just hang out at my dad's, maybe?" Andi had tried to go to a show in Oakland one time, but being inside the packed club had stressed her out so much that she'd left before the first band even took the stage. She was still furious at Jed for ruining what had once been a source of so much happiness for her. Maybe someday she'd be able to handle concerts again, but not yet.

"Oh—sure, that works," Brooke said. "How's it been with your dad lately? Things still awkward?"

"So awkward. At least he's not seeing Patricia anymore, and apparently he's still clean. But... yeah. It'll be weird." Andi looked out the window. It was hard to think about anything but her silent, Naveed-less phone.

As if on cue, her phone buzzed. *Please be him, please be him,* she thought.

But it was a text from Frida. Andi read it aloud to Brooke. Haven't seen him all day, but heard him leave in the pickup this morning. It's an old clunker, hope he didn't run into trouble on the road.

Andi was finding it harder to ignore the ominous feeling in her gut. She wrote, Thanks. I'm sure he'll get in touch soon.

Let me know if you hear anything, came Frida's reply.

"So that explains it," Brooke said with false cheer. "He must have broken down somewhere, and can't call because he forgot his phone or maybe it's dead, and now he's, like, scrounging together bits of old wire so he can get the truck to start again."

"And when he does get it started, he'll have to go straight to his appointment. He's meeting his probation officer. Really important that he doesn't miss that."

"Yeah. So he'll call just as soon as he can."

"I hope so," Andi said. Brooke started talking about some new band she'd fallen in love with, but Andi couldn't take her eyes off her phone, waiting for the call that never came.

Naveed

NAVEED PULLED UP AT THE PHARMACY DRIVE-THROUGH WINDOW. He was annoyed at himself for putting this errand off until the last possible minute, because he had a ton of other things to get done before picking up Andi at the airport: tidying the cabin, doing a long-overdue load of laundry, taking care of his farm chores. But this morning he was down to the last two tablets of his SSRI antidepressant, Deloxin, so he finally called his prescription in to a nearby pharmacy.

"I've got a prescription to pick up?" Naveed handed the tech his debit card so that he didn't have to waste time spelling out his name.

The tech nodded and disappeared from the window. He came back a few minutes later, holding a paper bag and looking slightly abashed. "Do you have another card? This one keeps getting declined."

"Oh." He didn't. The only credit card he'd qualified for had a $500 limit, and was already maxed out. Gretchen and Frida provided him with room and board and a small monthly stipend, but he'd burned through it fast. He'd been hoping to scrape by without asking his parents for money. Still, his antidepressants usually cost less than $10 per month, so it shouldn't have been a problem. "What was the total?" he asked.

The tech consulted their screen. "It comes to $43.84."

"For one month?" What the hell—why had the price gone up so much?

"Yes—oh wait, I'm sorry, I didn't see the note on this one. Looks like Deloxin isn't in the formulary anymore, but we checked with your doctor and they said it was fine to switch you to Serovia. It's in the same category, so it should work about the same."

Serovia? Seriously? Koffka put both of his paws on Naveed's knee, his way of saying, *Dude, you need to chill. Take a deep breath. It's all going to work out.* "So, the Deloxin," Naveed said to the tech. "You just—don't carry it anymore?"

"That's right." The tech glanced at the growing line of cars behind Naveed's truck. "Do you have another card, or should I hold onto these for now?"

"Oh—yeah, could you? I don't have another card with me. I'll have to come back later."

The tech nodded. "All right. Have a good day."

Naveed pulled away from the window, then found an empty parking space. Koffka was right: he needed to chill. Already he could feel the change, his heart fluttering, prickly sweat on his forehead, his throat constricting—the beginning of a panic-spiral. Koffka whimpered and rested his head in Naveed's lap. *You don't have to go there. You're safe, you can breathe just fine, I'm here and I'm not going to let anything happen to you.*

Naveed unzipped Koffka's service dog vest and took a hit from his inhaler, more out of habit than anything. But maybe it helped this time, a little? He stroked Koffka's coarse fur. He rocked a little, back and forth, knowing that he looked insane but not caring. The motion was soothing, and he wasn't going to go back on benzos if he could help it, so this was by far the better option.

"Such bullshit," he told Koffka once he'd calmed down. "They tried me on Serovia before, at Harborview back in the fall, but it gave me serious insomnia, I couldn't sleep at all, and Nate was fucking relentless, the nerve pain too, it was all so miserable I wanted to die. No way am I switching to that right before Andi's visit. Even if I could afford it."

Better call Dr. Nguyen, Koffka suggested. Due to some insurance issue, Naveed had recently switched to a new psychiatrist and a new therapist, but he barely knew either of them and wasn't even sure how to contact their office. He'd have to check with Maman when she came back.

"Yeah, I'll figure it out," he told Koffka. "But, I mean, seriously. Can't they just read my chart? Didn't someone make a note that I had terrible side effects when I tried Serovia before? And, besides—why would they just get rid of Deloxin like that?"

He turned to his phone for answers. After a few minutes of searching, he gathered that the company who made it—Genbiotix, of course—apparently thought Deloxin wasn't profitable enough, and that discontinuing it wouldn't matter since there were plenty of other SSRI's patients could use instead.

Naveed felt like throwing his phone. It was bad enough that he had to rely on meds just to make it through each day, and now his whole carefully calibrated routine had been totally upended thanks to the decisions of Big Pharma executives who only cared about profit.

Not that he was in a position to criticize the pharmaceutical industry. He'd been dependent on their products since the day they first raised him from the dead—Genbiotix's antibiotics had been the only ones effective against MRK, the multi-drug resistant strain of *Klebsiella pneumoniae* that had almost killed him, and that had become a mostly-ignored epidemic in communities that rarely got attention in the first place: farmworkers, hospital patients, the elderly.

Naveed kept ranting about all of this to Koffka as they drove back to the farm. He rolled down the gravel road toward the cabin, inching the truck as far as he could go before the road turned into a mud-ditch that was on his ever-growing list of things to fix.

As he got out, a bird swooped right in front of his face. Startled, he froze, watching it flutter joyously through the sky. Several more followed, swooping around each other, chirping and chattering as they flew toward the trees.

Sometimes Naveed just had to shake his head. This place. Always reminding him that his troubles weren't the only thing that existed.

As he trudged out to the cabin, he spotted Gretchen and Frida's daughter in the distance bringing kitchen scraps to the chickens. Aviva lived down in Olympia, but she had been visiting for Shabbat almost every week. She paused before opening the gate, setting down the bucket and stretching her back. Her belly jutted forward, large and round, as if she'd swallowed the moon.

Naveed quickly turned away. Aviva's baby was due next month, and seeing her always reminded him of the time he'd spent with the Yakima Valley farmworkers, of their continued poverty, of the baby Marisol had almost lost thanks to MRK, thanks to him—

His phone rang. It was a number he didn't recognize. He was about to ignore it, but talking to someone, even if it was just a random telemarketer doing a survey, would be better than continuing down this train of thought. Not quite as good a distraction as a bird flying right in front of your face, but still. Any diversion was better than the alternative.

He accepted the call. He listened to the voice on the other end. And then everything changed.

Roya

FRIDAY, MAY 20

ON FRIDAY MORNING, ROYA AWOKE WITH A START. SHE SAT UP in bed, wondering what had shaken her out of a deep sleep.

The clock read 5:37 a.m. Still way too early to get up. But it was like she'd just slurped down a huge bottle of sugary caffeinated soda. Her heart was beating fast and she was wide awake.

She stretched her legs out, disturbing Pashmak, who was curled up at Roya's feet. "Sorry, Pashi," she said groggily as the cat picked her way across the blankets. "Did you hear anything? A loud noise? Is that what woke me up?"

Pashmak just yawned, then settled in on her side and started licking her paws. Roya heard nothing but the gentle lapping of Pashi's tongue. If there was someone—or some*thing*, some spirit—in here, Pashmak wouldn't be this relaxed.

Roya closed her eyes. She didn't have school today, so Baba would be dropping her off to spend the day with Khaleh Yasmin, which meant she could sleep in later than usual. She tried to fall asleep, but her mind kept traveling back to the ritual she had done the night before Maman left.

It had been... disappointing. She'd followed all the right steps. She'd cleansed herself. Cast a circle with Kass's athame. Lit a candle. (Not under her bed, of course. She'd barricaded the door to her room by pushing her desk in front of it, then set up her ritual supplies in the middle of the floor.) Inside the Hekate chalice, she'd made a little poppet out of mud and a clump of hair that she'd taken from Maman's brush, wrapped the figure in black fabric, and said the incantations written in Orcinia's Book of Shadows, word for word. She'd snuck outside before bedtime and buried it along the back pathway, where she would step over it every day when she went to feed the chickens. "Demons, begone!" she chanted as she covered the hole. It hadn't been the same as the other times she'd practiced magic, when she'd felt confident and powerful. This time she just felt silly. She worried at every step that she was doing something wrong.

The next morning, Maman came in to say goodbye before she left on her trip. She floated through the room like a ghost and sat at the edge of the bed. Roya looked up at her eyes. Still deadened and dark. Nothing had changed.

It hadn't worked. The shayatin still had their claws in her. Roya wanted to scream at them to go away, to leave her family alone. But she kept quiet. She let Maman kiss her cheek, then grumbled about wanting to go back to sleep and turned to face the wall.

Was there something here now, though? Maybe the results were delayed? Or maybe... what if she'd released the shayatin from Maman, but now they were going to latch on to her instead?

No, she reminded herself, Pashmak was calm. The cat hadn't wanted to go anywhere near Maman lately, more proof in Roya's mind that something was not right. There were no demons here now... but still....

Kass, she thought. *I need to talk to Kass. She'll know how to fix this.*

For a second, Roya imagined sneaking into Cyrus's room and stealing his phone while he slept. But then she remembered how early it was.

She couldn't call Kass at this hour.

She'd just have to wait. It seemed like her entire life was spent waiting. Roya was tired of it.

There was no way she was getting back to sleep now, so Roya got up and opened the window. The walnut tree beckoned to her. Its branches swayed in the breeze like crooked fingers. *Come outside*, it seemed to be saying.

Roya felt bad ignoring the walnut tree, because she knew it missed her, and she missed it too, missed the feeling of being up high in the branches, carried away on the sweet notes she played on her flute, but she couldn't climb it now, her knee didn't cooperate the way it used to, and the flute belonged to some other Roya who didn't exist anymore, one who'd been able to find joy in rustling leaves and music that came from her own breath.

I never made a finding song for Maman. The thought came out of nowhere, but it struck Roya hard, like a slap. She'd followed the banishing instructions exactly, but what if that was the problem? It was someone else's ritual, and she'd taken it and tried to make it hers, but it didn't quite fit right. She needed to remember her own ways of doing magic. And the flute had been her very first wand. She had used it to find her way back home, to summon crows, to save Naveed from the brink of death. True, the silver star charm—the one given to Maman by a crow long ago—had helped, but Roya had gifted that to Naveed after she used up her three wishes. The flute, though, was uniquely hers. No one else in the whole world could use it the way she did.

Pashmak was still giving herself a very intense bath, digging into the spaces between her toes with her sharp teeth, claws outstretched. "Want to come outside with me, Pashi?" Roya asked, but the cat didn't even look up. Roya pulled on a sweater and socks, grabbed her flute from the top of the bookshelf, and crept downstairs.

Outside, the sun had painted the sky pinkish. The air was cool but not cold, and as Roya stepped along the path toward the walnut tree, she thought about the poppet she'd buried. She imagined stepping on those demons, stomping them out, banishing them from Maman.

That ritual was only the first step, Roya realized. She knew from reading Orcinia's Book of Shadows that when you got rid of something, cut a cord or made a void, you had to pay attention to what you filled it back up with. If you didn't, you might unintentionally refill it with the same bad energy.

She eased herself onto the ground at the base of the walnut tree. Before raising the flute to her lips, she looked into its branches and felt that sense of calm it always brought her. It was like inhaling deeply after holding your breath for a long time.

A crow was perched on a branch just above her. She smiled, remembering Omid with his white-feathered wing. It wasn't the same crow, of course. This one was smaller than most, and she couldn't see its eyes but guessed they were blue. It was a young crow, a juvenile. Just a baby. She didn't want to startle it, so she sat in silence for a minute, thinking up a finding song for Maman. Imagining her mother's return, the dead eyes gone forever, the cold voice replaced by a caring one, the void made by the demons' flight filled with the soul that Maman had nearly lost.

Roya raised the flute to her lips and breathed out a long, low note. The crow squawked in surprise and fluttered away. She continued playing a quiet, mournful tune, thinking about Maman, until she noticed something falling slowly from above.

It was a downy gray feather. Roya watched in silence as it floated down, taking its time, lazily drifting through the air until it landed, finally, on Roya's extended leg. She stared at the feather in astonishment. It felt like a message from the baby crow: a sign that she was on the right track. She tucked it gently into her sweater pocket and continued playing her song, calling Maman home.

Naveed

FRIDAY, MAY 20

NAVEED CLUTCHED HIS PHONE, PRESSING IT AGAINST HIS EAR. Kelly was on the other end of the line, and all he could think was, *Why?*

"I'm so glad you picked up," Kelly was saying. "I tried calling your dad but can't reach him. I'm here at the ranger station because... because I woke up this morning and your mom wasn't in our tent. I don't know where she is. They're getting a search and rescue team together and... I just... I wanted you to know...."

"What? She's... I don't...." A rush of heat flooded into his head. Koffka planted himself in Naveed's path. *Don't go any further,* that meant. *You're starting to panic. Stop what you're doing and deal with this now.* Naveed sank to his knees beside Koffka and looked into his calm black eyes.

"Don't worry. We'll find her," Kelly said. "I just didn't want you to hear about it somewhere else first."

"I'll be right there." Naveed found himself saying. No way was he sitting around here when, not far away, people were combing the woods for his missing mother.

"You don't need to—" Kelly protested, but Naveed cut her off.

"I'm coming. Koffka can help—he can follow her scent."

Kelly paused, then said, "Okay. Thank you." The phone was muffled for a second, but he could hear another voice in the background. Then Kelly came back on. "Go to the Nisqually entrance. They'll direct you from there."

Naveed told her he'd be there as soon as he could, then hung up. He could barely think, his mind a swarm of questions and anxious thoughts. Why would his mother leave the tent in the morning without telling Kelly where she was going? And why hadn't she come back?

He raced to the pickup and opened the passenger door for Koffka. Astro watched from the back deck, head tilted to one side, but Naveed didn't see any trace of Aviva anymore, or Gretchen or Frida, and there was no time to look for them anyway. He backed out of the driveway and soon was on the road.

The drive passed quickly. Before he knew it, Naveed was pulling up in front of the ranger station at Longmire. He took Koffka's leash out of the glove box and attached it to his service dog vest. "You ready, boy?"

Koffka looked at him with determined eyes. *Yes.*

"Let's go find Maman," Naveed said.

Inside the ranger station, they paired him up with an experienced search and rescue volunteer named Jill, a young white woman with brown hair slicked back in a ponytail. She seemed delighted to see Koffka. "The dogs aren't here yet," she said as she led him to the trail. "So this is great! We can get a head start. Does he have any experience in SAR?"

"Uh, no," Naveed said, putting together that SAR referred to search and rescue. "But he knows my mom's scent. I'm sure that will help?"

"Yes, definitely!" Jill hesitated for a moment. "So you... will you be all right on the trails? It's a pretty strenuous hike, plus it's slippery in places since it rained last night. I could take him on ahead if you would rather be a lookout or something?" She was dancing around the question of whether he had physical limitations. Sometimes, he did, but not today. Thankfully.

"I'll be fine," said Naveed. "I'm staying with Koffka."

"Okay, great!" Her cheeriness was disorienting. It almost seemed like she was a tour guide, and they were just out here to take in some scenery.

"So where are we going?" he asked.

"We'll start at the PLS—the point last seen," she said. "A campground about 5 miles away. That's where most of the search team is right now, plus we've got a couple lookouts on the trails to keep an eye out for her. We always start with a hasty search—covering ground quickly and checking all the likely spots."

Once they were on the trail, Jill suggested they do voice checks as they walked—yelling Maman's name and listening for a response.

Naveed cupped his hands around his mouth and hollered, "Maman!" as loud as he could. If she was nearby, if she could hear him, he wanted her to know he was here.

Between voice checks, Jill asked him questions about his mother. Had she ever been backpacking before, had she been to Mount Rainier, did she have good navigation skills, when had he last seen her, what brought her here in the first place. Naveed answered curtly, with a short yes or no whenever he could. The longer they hiked, the harder it became for him to carry on a conversation. The trail was steep and treacherous. It took all his concentration to keep breathing and stay on his feet.

Soon, they came to a bridge over a rushing creek. Two people stood on one side of it. They waved as Jill approached.

"The dogs are here already?" one of them asked. "That was quick."

"Not quite yet," said Jill. "This is Mahnaz's son and his service dog."

They continued chatting, but Naveed turned away from them to look down at the rushing water. A memory struck him with so much force that he had to tighten his grip on the railing.

It had been a couple months ago on Sizdah Bedar, the thirteenth day of the Persian New Year. In keeping with tradition, they'd gone picnicking at a nearby park. Naveed had been up most of the night on the phone with Andi and was missing her more than ever, but he pretended to be having a good time because he knew his family needed this. Maman had led them over to a bridge and pulled out a bag of lentil sprouts. They had been growing in the kitchen since Nowruz, symbolically soaking up all the negativity and illness in the house. Now, it was time to discard them into a stream of running water, signaling a fresh start.

He could still see it so clearly, his mother's hands tearing apart the messy sprout-roots, releasing their green alfalfa smell, dividing them into five clumps, one for each of them, her curly black hair blowing in the wind as she kissed the top of Roya's head.

The image made Naveed grip the bridge railing hard. The water running beneath him—it was so deep. Rushing by so fast. It could so easily sweep someone away.

He was starting to feel sweaty and sick to his stomach. But there would be no panicking, he told himself sternly. The benzos were no longer here to help him, and he couldn't lose himself now.

"Are you all right?" Jill asked him.

He forced himself to let go. "Yeah. Let's keep going."

At some point, he thought he should check the time—he needed to keep an eye on the clock so he could leave in time to pick up Andi. Naveed reached into his pocket for his phone, but it wasn't there. Shit. He must have left it in the truck. "What time is it?" he asked Jill.

She checked her watch. "11:30. We're getting close—the campground's just a mile or so from here."

Okay. He still had plenty of time. Naveed looked down at Koffka, his shoulder blades rippling as he picked his way surefootedly along the trail, and allowed himself to imagine that things would work out. As soon as Koffka picked up her scent, he'd lead them to her, and they'd help her if she was injured, and everything would go back to normal.

When they finally arrived at the campground, Kelly was sitting on a log in the clearing, rubbing her temples. Out of nowhere, Naveed found himself wanting to slam into her, to pin her to the ground while shouting, *How could you let this happen?*

Kelly stood up and approached as if she wanted to hug him. He recoiled, and thankfully she took the hint and didn't come any closer. "Naveed! You're here, thank you for coming all this way, I... I'm so sorry—"

"Where is she? Did you find her?"

"No," she said. "Oh—I didn't mean—no. We haven't found anything yet."

"So what happened? When did she leave?"

"I'm not sure. It must have been early this morning—I heard her get up and unzip the tent, but I figured she was going to the bathroom or something. It was barely light outside, so I went back to sleep. When I finally got up, she wasn't there. So after I looked around and waited for a while, I left a note and headed up to the closest ranger station—"

"Wait," Naveed said. "Was there anyone else here last night? Other campers?"

"No. It was just us."

"You're sure? No one got here after dark? In the middle of the night? Or early in the morning—you didn't hear anything?" Koffka pulled on his leash, but Naveed stood his ground.

Kelly regarded him with furrowed brows. She looked exactly like Brooke when she did that. "No. I'm sure. Nobody else was here. Naveed...."

Koffka pulled harder. "I have to go." Naveed let the dog lead him onto a side trail, hoping Kelly wouldn't follow. He didn't want to talk to her anymore.

Jill, of course, wasn't far behind them. "He picked up on something?"

"I guess so," said Naveed. They threaded through the brush, veering off the trail onto a barely visible path through the woods.

Abruptly, Naveed stopped. There was something about this place, the way the sun shone on the ferns, their fronds bending in the breeze, the smell of the air here, the sound of water flowing somewhere in the distance, all of it familiar, all of it inexplicably horrifying—

Naveed felt like he had a pillow strapped to his face. He just couldn't get the air in anymore. He crouched on the ground, panting.

Koffka licked the inside of his wrist. Naveed reached into the dog's vest for his inhaler and took a few hits. It didn't help at all.

Jill was kneeling next to him. She had her radio out like she was about to call for help. He pushed it away. "I'm okay. I just need. To stop for a second. Have some water. I'll be fine."

I can't do this, he thought to Koffka as he sipped water from a bottle that Jill handed him.

You can, Koffka countered. *You can, and you are. Don't give up now. Maman needs you.*

Miraculously, after a few endless minutes, the invisible pillow eased up enough that he felt able to go on. He gave Koffka a thank-you pet behind the ears, then stood back up and continued along the path, Jill following behind.

Time passed. How much, he didn't know. He called for his mother, because that helped keep him anchored in the present, and Koffka sniffed the ground and the plants and Jill took everything silently in.

They were hiking up a steep ridge when Koffka suddenly veered off the path. Naveed looked at Jill questioningly, but she nodded. "Looks like someone's been through here. Be careful—there's a steep drop-off."

Koffka slowed down. Naveed, too, stepped more slowly. They came to the edge of a deep ravine—it must have been a hundred feet to the bottom. Naveed felt so dizzy that he reached for Koffka for support.

Something colorful by his foot caught his eye. He bent closer—it was a phone, face down. He picked it up, already recognizing the floral case, the starburst crack at the bottom of the screen from when Maman had dropped it at the park on Sizdah Bedar.

For some reason, he wasn't at all surprised. It was almost as if she'd left it for him.

He hid it, quickly, in the interior pocket of his jacket. Jill was rustling in the bushes behind him, unaware of what he'd found.

Okay, so Maman had been here. But where was she now?

Naveed stepped closer to the ravine's edge. There was something down at the bottom, something dark that didn't belong. It was hard to see what it was, but if he just walked along the ridge a bit further—

Koffka barked in warning, but Naveed didn't listen. He kept going until the shapes at the bottom of the ravine rearranged themselves into forms that made sense. One was a backpack, the same one he'd seen a million times in their garage, and more recently in the trunk of Kelly's car. Near it, a hand, its fingers limp against mossy rocks; a head, face down, a strand of black curls tugged by the wind brushing the top of her hand, which would tickle, wouldn't it, and yet she was completely still, not moving, still not moving—

He was pretty sure he was screaming, but he couldn't hear a single sound. *Maman! Maman, please get up! Please move... please show me you're okay!*

She said nothing, and she didn't turn her head. Didn't move her hand, the same hand that had ripped apart the sprouts on Sizdah Bedar, had cupped the glass mug as she sat across from him in his cabin a few days before; the same hand that had reached out to his as they walked beneath the cherry trees, always there to steady him.

He kept screaming at her, but she remained motionless. Even though he didn't want to believe it, would do anything *not* to believe it, the knowledge hit him with such force that his knees buckled and he sank to the ground. No matter how loudly he called, she couldn't hear him. She would never hear him again. He had found her, but she was already gone.

Roya

FRIDAY, MAY 20

ROYA FUMBLED WITH HER SCARF, AN ELECTRIC-BLUE ONE SHE'D found buried in the back of Maman's closet. She couldn't get it to stay on her head. It kept slipping off.

"Here, Roya-jaan." Khaleh Yasmin unwrapped the scarf and expertly repositioned it, securing it around her hair. She caught Roya's eye and smiled. "Kheyli khoshgel."

"Merci, Khaleh-jaan." Roya glanced at her reflection in the mosque's front windows. She liked how the scarf made her look. More grown up. Almost like a different person.

Khaleh Yasmin had driven her across the lake so they could go to Friday prayers together, since Roya had the day off school and Baba was leading training sessions for new engineers at his work all day. Roya had never been to this mosque before. It was Khaleh Yasmin's favorite because they had Shi'a services and gave some sermons in Persian, though the prayers were, of course, in Arabic.

Roya followed Khaleh Yasmin into the bright mosque, where they stowed their shoes in cubby-holes, rinsed their hands, faces, arms and feet with clean water, and entered the women's side.

Roya appreciated all of this: the cleansing ritual, the sacred feeling of the space inside. Khaleh Yasmin led her to a pair of prayer rugs in the back and let Roya sit on the aisle so she could stretch her right leg out instead of kneeling on it.

The service began soon afterward. Roya had no idea what the imam was saying most of the time, but that didn't matter. She liked hearing him sing the prayers, and listening to everyone's voices as they echoed phrases back, bending forward, then rising, everyone moving and speaking as one... the whole experience gave Roya a glow in her heart. It was the same feeling she got when Pashmak curled up against her legs at night, purring loudly as they both kept each other warm.

As Roya lowered her forehead towards the floor, she thought about Maman again. It occurred to her that in this setting, with the joyous energy the worshippers were raising, some powerful magic could be done.

The next time everyone sat up, she rummaged in her pocket and pulled out a small velvet pouch. The downy feather the baby crow had given her was inside, along with a trio of bay leaves that she'd been carrying around for protection. She held it in her palm as she bent forward. Instead of repeating the prayers everyone else was saying, she hummed her own incantation softly. *Please, help Maman get rid of the shayatin and find her soul again.*

When the service was over, Roya returned the pouch to her pocket and stretched both of her legs out in front of her, feeling lightened. Between the original ritual, the flute song this morning, and this prayer session, she had come up with a three-part banishing spell that was sure to work.

Khaleh Yasmin chatted with some older ladies in Persian for a few minutes while Roya leaned against her, bending and straightening her sore knee. After they said their goodbyes, they drove to a nearby Persian bakery. Roya waited in the car until Khaleh Yasmin returned with a fragrant, still-warm loaf of sangak. She draped the huge flatbread over Roya's lap like a blanket and handed her a cup of faloodeh. "It's frozen solid," she said. "You can put it on your knee for now, then eat it once it melts a little."

Roya tore off big chunks of the bread to eat as they ran into traffic on the way back, after taking off her scarf so it wouldn't get crumbs in it, then dug into the faloodeh as soon as it was soft enough, enjoying the mixture of sweet rosewater-scented sorbet and chewy vermicelli noodles.

Once they got back to Khaleh Yasmin's house, Roya spent most of the afternoon on the couch with an ice pack on her achy knee, looking at an illustrated copy of the Shahnameh and trying to decipher the words.

Baba had said he'd pick her up on his way home from work, but the usual time came and went and he didn't arrive. Half an hour later, Khaleh Yasmin's phone chimed. "Hmm," she said.

"What is it?" Roya asked.

"It's your father. He can't come pick you up—he needs me to bring you home."

"Why?"

Khaleh Yasmin shrugged. "Here, I'll gather your things."

Roya walked stiffly to the door. She wasn't sure why this change of plans was bothering her so much. It probably meant nothing, but it was still odd, because Khaleh Yasmin's house was on the way home from Baba's work. So he was already home? Had he forgotten her?

That was probably it. He'd gotten all the way home and then realized half an hour later that he hadn't bothered to pick up his own daughter.

They pulled up in front of the house just as Cyrus opened the passenger door of Shea's car. He got out and walked hurriedly toward the house, not even seeming to notice Roya.

She tried to maneuver herself out of the car. "Kourosh! Wait for me—can you help?" Her scarf, which she was now wearing around her neck, had gotten tangled up with the seat belt, making it extra hard to get out.

Cyrus turned around. Usually he was either smiling or grumpy, but right now he was neither of those things. His eyes had a haunted look. *The shayatin*, Roya thought for a second as she yanked her scarf free. But she dismissed the thought quickly. This was something different. He didn't look possessed, just... scared.

She hobbled up to him and clasped his hand. "Kourosh? What's the matter?"

"I... I don't know yet," he said. "But, Roya, I think... I think Baba has some bad news. Like, *really* bad news. The worst kind."

Roya's heart fluttered, as if it wasn't sure whether it should beat really fast or just stop altogether. "Someone died?" She swallowed, and added in a whisper, "Naveed?"

Cyrus squeezed her hand. "I don't know, but whatever it is, we've still got each other, all right?"

Roya nodded. They walked up the path towards the front door, still hand in hand, Khaleh Yasmin trailing behind them.

Cyrus opened it. "Baba? We're home."

Baba was standing with his back to them at the foot of the stairs, his hand on the banister, staring upward. Slowly he turned to face them. His work shirt was half-untucked, his hair disheveled. "Oh. Hello," he said in a tight voice. "You all got here at the same time. That's good."

The three of them remained frozen in the doorway. Roya didn't want to step inside. Something didn't feel right. It wasn't just the way Baba was acting, there was something in the air itself that made Roya want to turn around and leave.

"Come in. Close the door. Have a seat," Baba went on, which were perfectly normal words, but they seemed so wrong, like someone else was talking through his mouth.

Even though every instinct was telling Roya not to go into the house, she needed to be close to him. She crossed the threshold and threw her arms around his waist. "Baba," she said. "Baba, what happened?"

He put his arm around her. "Let's sit on the couch."

Roya didn't want to sit; her heart was still fluttery and her whole body was vibrating along with it, but she sat on one side of him, while Cyrus lowered himself down on the other.

Khaleh Yasmin closed the door softly. "Saman-jaan? What's wrong?"

"Just tell us," Cyrus said.

Baba took a deep breath. Roya leaned into his chest, not wanting to look at his face. Pashmak chose that moment to saunter into the room. Her claws ticked softly on the floorboards. Roya hoped the cat would jump onto her lap, but no luck. She curled into the armchair instead.

"Kelly called me this morning," Baba finally said. "But I was doing that training, I didn't get her message, so I didn't know...." He took a long, stuttering breath. "Your mother was missing. Kelly couldn't find her. She called me, and I didn't answer, so she called Naveed, and he brought Koffka, and they searched for her, and they... they found her this afternoon."

Okay, that wasn't so bad, right? Maman had been missing, but they'd found her.

"It rained there last night," Baba continued. "The rocks, they were so slick, and that's probably why she—why she fell."

His voice broke, and he stopped to heave out a loud sob, which was somehow a more terrifying sound than a gunshot, than an explosion, than a raging fire.

No one said anything, so Roya broke the silence. "Is she in the hospital? We should go see her—"

"No, Roya," he said. "It was... a very long fall. She didn't survive."

"What are you saying? That she's dead?" Roya looked at Khaleh Yasmin's crumpled face, at Cyrus's fogged-up glasses, at Pashmak's lazily flicking tail. "No. No, no, that's not right. She can't be dead. It's a mistake, it must be. It's someone else, the wrong person..."

"I'm sorry, azizam." Baba hugged her tightly. "It's not a mistake. I just got back... they brought her by helicopter to the hospital, and the coroner had me... identify her. I'm sorry. I'm so sorry."

Cyrus came around to Roya's side and set his glasses on the coffee table. He hugged Roya too, so that they made a giant hugging sandwich with her in the middle. Roya supposed they wanted to comfort her, but really she just felt smothered.

Khaleh Yasmin perched on the edge of the couch and wailed into her headscarf. Roya could hardly stand it—they all just believed this impossible thing? She caught Pashmak's eye and pleaded mentally for help. Pashmak jumped off the armchair and leapt onto Roya's lap. She stroked the cat's soft white fur gratefully.

Eventually Cyrus wiped his eyes and asked, "Wait, what about Naveed? Is he coming home?"

"Not sure," Baba told them. "Kelly said he was very upset when they found—when they found her. One of the search volunteers made sure he got to his car safely, but I haven't heard from him yet. He probably needs some space."

"He'll be in my prayers. You *all* will," Khaleh Yasmin said. "And Saman, if you need a hand with anything… the funeral arrangements… or anything else… I'm happy to help."

Baba started crying in that weird choking way of his, with dry sobs that sounded almost like laughs. Roya leaned into him, letting the bristly hairs of his beard scratch her forehead. She couldn't believe that Khaleh Yasmin was talking about funerals already. Maman couldn't be dead. She was coming home tomorrow, that had been the plan, she was coming home with the shayatin gone and her soul firmly back where it was supposed to be, because Roya had saved her. That's what was going to happen. It was the only future that made sense.

Andi

THE EMPTY CHAIR NEXT TO ANDI WAS VERY DISTRACTING. She'd tried to play it cool when Vanesa asked if Naveed was still planning to join them, saying he was probably caught up in something at the farm or stuck in traffic. With every minute that passed, this seemed more unlikely, but Andi was trying to hold out hope.

The dinner, though, was a welcome distraction. As soon as they'd arrived at the restaurant, Vanesa had greeted Andi with a hug and thanked her again for the perfect music she'd composed. Andi allowed herself a short happy-dance in her head. *Perfect! She thought it was perfect.* The swell of triumph temporarily replaced her worries about Naveed's absence.

As the others arrived, Andi found herself bridging the two groups. Vanesa had brought her father Fernando, along with the farmworkers Ramón and Marisol and their two kids, the chubby-cheeked baby Javier and his older sister Gabriela. At first, Andi was a little star-struck by them—they were semi-famous in her eyes, since she'd spent countless hours watching them in the documentary footage as she composed her score.

Akilah and Laurel knew Brooke but not Vanesa, so Andi introduced everyone to each other and got the conversation rolling.

Akilah and Vanesa quickly hit it off. From there, the gathering evolved into exactly what Andi had hoped for when she'd set up this dinner: a strategizing session, where they brainstormed ways to promote the film among their various networks.

Though Vanesa and Fernando did their best to translate for Ramón and Marisol, Andi wished she could talk to them directly. Laurel, who was sitting next to Gabriela, sketched some comics on a napkin, then handed Gabriela her pen so she could draw her own. At one point, though, Gabriela tugged on her mom's sleeve and pointed to Naveed's empty chair. Andi only understood two words: *Tío Nate*. The veggie fajitas Andi had shared with Brooke churned in her stomach. She sipped her watermelon agua fresca, trying to fend off the wave of sudden nausea. Her phone was still silent.

But as the dinner was winding down, Andi finally got a text. Not from Naveed, though. From Cyrus. She excused herself to the bathroom and gestured for Brooke to come with her.

"Cyrus just texted," Andi told Brooke, after making sure no one was in either of the stalls. "I'm afraid to open it."

"Do it. I'm sure everything's fine." Brooke leaned in. Andi's sweaty fingers left a damp imprint on the screen.

Hey I have some bad news, Cyrus had written. There's no easy way to say this. Brace yourself.

He was still composing the next text. *Naveed*, Andi thought. *Oh God, oh God. What happened to Naveed?*

But she wasn't at all prepared for the texts that finally appeared.

It's my mom

She died today

Andi and Brooke stared at each other in shock and horror as the texts kept coming.

I can't believe I just wrote that

And that it's true

It was a hiking accident I guess? She fell into a ravine

Kelly called Naveed to help search, he and Koffka were actually the ones who found her

We know he made it out of the park but he's not answering calls or texts and didn't go back to the farm

Plz tell me if u hear from him

Andi got so dizzy she had to rush into one of the stalls to sit down. Her brain struggled to absorb it all. She could only think in choppy half-sentences. Mahnaz. Mahnaz was. No. She couldn't. Be dead. And Naveed. Where? Had he gone?

No way could she go back to that table and pretend everything was fine. But she couldn't stomach the thought of breaking the news to everyone, either. Especially Akilah, who was close friends with Mahnaz.

"Oh my God," Brooke was saying softly. "Oh no, my phone—I turned it off when we got here. My mom's probably trying to get ahold of me."

"We'd better go," said Andi. Brooke held out a hand to help her up. When they returned to grab their coats, Akilah was laughing about something, and Laurel was twirling Gabriela around to the music on the restaurant's stereo while Marisol bounced Javier on her hip. Everyone was smiling.

Somehow, Andi and Brooke managed to say their goodbyes without dissolving into tears. They muttered excuses about how something had come up and they had to go. "See you at the premiere tomorrow!" Vanesa called behind them as they left.

"Oh my God," Brooke kept saying as they walked, hugging her arms to her chest. "Oh my God."

Andi couldn't get any more words out, but her thoughts were now moving at warp speed. Mahnaz was gone, which was horrific enough, but Naveed had been the one to find her. Andi couldn't even comprehend how *she* would deal with that level of trauma. How was he going to make it through? Assuming he was even still alive, she thought darkly, and shivered.

When they arrived at her dad's apartment building, Brooke gave Andi a tearful hug and headed straight back to her car so she could meet her mom at home.

Despite Andi's mixed feelings toward her father, she had never been more grateful to see him. She was a weeping mess by the time she got to his door, so incoherent that she had to pull up Cyrus's texts to explain. He let her sob into his shirt for what felt like ages.

Once the tears finally slowed down, her dad warmed some milk on the stove while she composed a halfway-decent reply to Cyrus: Oh my god I don't know what to say. I can't believe it. I'm so sorry, I know that's inadequate but there are just no words for this. Thinking of you. You'll be the first to know if I hear anything from N.

Then she called her own mother, which caused a crying relapse. After that she snuggled up under a blanket on the couch and turned on a reality show that was, thankfully, nothing like real life.

Her dad handed her a mug of warm milk and sat next to her. They watched for a while in silence. She couldn't stop checking her phone.

Around eleven, she told her dad she was going to bed. Andi lay down in the spare room—*her* room, her dad had been careful to call it—with her phone still clutched in her hand.

She was still so anxious about Naveed that she knew she wouldn't be able to sleep. After a brief internal debate, she contacted the Crisis Text Line. She'd chatted with them a couple times over the past few months when she'd been having an especially hard day. Sometimes she felt like her problems weren't bad enough to be classified as crises, but they never turned her away or made her feel like she was wasting their time. Their kind support always helped her put things in perspective.

This time, the counselor just echoed back how awful the situation was. Which was strangely validating. Things were objectively horrible right now. Even the professionals thought so.

Just as she was wrapping up the chat, the name she'd been waiting for finally appeared on her screen.

Andi I'm so sorry for not showing up at the airport. I'm the worst, Naveed wrote.

She responded, No you aren't. I heard about your mom. So awful, I can't believe it. Where are you?

Just been driving around can't see my family yet don't know where to go, he wrote back.

Andi typed as quickly as she could. Then PLEASE come here. Really my dad won't care if you stay the night we all want you to be safe

Four long minutes later, the reply came. ok, he wrote. Just two letters, but they literally made her sigh in relief.

She sent him the address and woke up her dad. "I can sleep on the couch—" Andi started.

"Don't be ridiculous," he said. "You need to be together. I'll stay out of your way. Just promise me you'll use—"

"*Dad*," Andi interrupted. "We're not going to... *do* anything. Jesus."

Her dad shrugged. "Grief works in mysterious ways. See you two in the morning."

When Naveed texted that he was outside, she buzzed him in and sprinted down the two flights of stairs to the lobby, too antsy to wait for the elevator. She could hear the faint jingle of the service dog tag on Koffka's harness before she rounded the corner and saw them.

Naveed's hands were caked with mud, his clothes had dirt all over them, his hair was a mess and he didn't look well at all but even so her stupid mouth was smiling because, finally, he was here. He was standing in front of her. He was alive, and they were together again.

She tried to hide her smile by pulling him in close for a kiss, but he drew back before their lips touched. She mentally kicked herself. The first rule of touching Naveed was to ask beforehand, she knew that.

"Sorry," she said as she guided him through the deserted lobby toward the bank of elevators. "It's just—I'm so glad you're here." She pushed the up arrow and the doors slid open.

"I was about to say the same thing." His voice was rough, like it kept snagging against sharp metal on the way out of his mouth.

She didn't know what to say next. Ask if he was all right? No, he obviously wasn't. "Do you… want to talk about it?" she asked, borrowing a handy phrase from the therapy/crisis text handbook.

"Nope," he said. "Not right now."

They arrived on her dad's floor. She led him inside the apartment, closing the door quietly behind her. "Okay. That's fine. Do you want something to eat? I could fix… some soup? Or cereal? Toast? Or something to drink, are you thirsty?"

Again, he shook his head. "Can we lie down? Been moving all day. But first… could I use your bathroom? I need to take a shower."

"It's okay, I don't care about the mud—"

"Please," he said. "Just, please. I really need a shower. Right now."

"Um, sure, yeah, of course," Andi said. "The bathroom's this way."

There was a damp hand towel hanging on the rack, but she had no idea where the bath towels were. "Don't lock the door," she said. "I'll bring you a fresh towel and a change of clothes."

He nodded and disappeared inside with Koffka.

Andi asked her dad for a towel and some pajamas, then fired off texts to Cyrus and Brooke to let them know Naveed was safe at her place.

She knocked on the bathroom door. "Just coming in for a second to give you your towel," she said.

Koffka was lying by the shower, and looked up at her as she entered. It was so steamy in there that she could barely see, but she hazarded a peek toward the frosted glass of the shower door. She cursed her dad for that dumb comment he'd made earlier, because now all she could think about was ripping off her clothes to join Naveed in there, feeling the hot water cascading down their wet skin, their bodies comfortingly close, pressed together in that tiny space, working out their grief in mysterious and wonderful ways….

But she couldn't tell if he was even inside. The shower looked empty. "Naveed?" she asked.

"I'm okay," he said hoarsely. "Needed to sit down. Be out in a minute."

Now she saw the black blob that was his head, floating there just above Koffka's curled-up body. She wanted nothing more than to be near him, but she restrained herself from tearing off her shirt and saying, *That's it, I'm coming in.* Instead, she went with, "I'll be right outside." She closed the door and sat in the hallway, trying to regain control of her inappropriately-timed hormonal urges.

Brooke had replied, so they kept up a good back-and-forth for a while. Andi was just about to go inside again and make sure he was still all right—it had been probably half an hour—when the water finally turned off. The bathroom door opened a few minutes later.

It was weird seeing Naveed in her dad's clothes, that old Sonic Youth shirt with holes in the sleeves and the faded plaid pajama bottoms. He extended his hand, and she took it in hers, and that small gesture made everything feel right again somehow.

He flopped on her bed. "I didn't want it to be like this," he whispered, closing his eyes.

"I know." Andi scooted next to him. "Can I—is this okay? Being this close?"

He nodded, and extended his arm around her so she could lie against his shoulder, her ear on his chest.

He shuddered a deep breath that she could hear whooshing through his lungs. Such a heavy sound. But even though she knew it was wrong, even though she knew it wasn't the same for him at all, she was filled with relief, and something else that might have been joy. Because he was here. Right here beside her. She let her hand settle in the center of his chest, and fell asleep to the gentle thud of his heart against her fingertips.

II.

Stars

Naveed

SATURDAY, MAY 21

THE WEIGHT OF ANDI'S HEAD ON NAVEED'S CHEST FELT NICE at first. It was a comfort in this room filled with unfamiliar noises: car doors slamming, people walking by outside, someone blaring music in a room nearby, the occasional siren. After growing so used to the deep quiet of night at the farm, the sounds of the city were unnerving.

Being near Andi reassured him, though. He was glad she hadn't been angry with him about leaving her waiting at the airport, and that she hadn't made a big deal about him taking such a long shower when he first arrived, though of course she hadn't seen the force with which he'd had to scrub down every inch of his body, the hot water turned up as high as it could go, because his skin was crawling and he had to get the filth off of him, and he still didn't feel he'd been thorough enough.

And now here she was, curled up beside him in a safe bed in a safe room, her head nestled atop his arm, pressing down on his shoulder and the side of his chest. Her hand right in his center. Like she was trying to ground him, to anchor him to this place.

That was exactly what he needed right now. He was terrified of losing himself.

Most of the previous day was gone. Not, like, a blur—it was just completely *gone*. One minute he'd been on the ledge, screaming for Maman, trying to will her motionless body to move. The next thing he knew, it was dark, and he was curled up hugging his knees to his chest in the pickup truck next to Koffka, staring out the window at the almost-full moon.

He'd panicked, not having a clue where he was or what had happened. The moon had reminded him. Mahnaz. *Glory of the moon,* that was what her name meant in Persian. He closed his eyes against its brightness, the gravity of what he'd lost washing over him. But it didn't help: she appeared before him, crumpled at the bottom of the ravine, her hand forever unmoving.

When he opened his eyes the fucking moon was still there, mocking him with its permanence. He tried to look away, but all he saw instead were the keys dangling from the ignition. The silver star charm winked at him from his keychain. A crow had once carried that shining star to Maman, had set it at her feet and flown away.

How could she be gone?

How could he live in a world without her?

Her phone, he remembered then. It was still tucked into the inside pocket of his jacket, warm from his body's heat. Touching it was like holding a little piece of her. Maybe it contained the key—maybe she had left it for him to explain what had happened.

But he couldn't turn it on. It was dead.

He sank back down, afraid to close his eyes. Koffka was asleep beside him; he could hear the dog's deep breathing.

After a few minutes, he worked up the courage to look at his own phone. It was right there in the cup holder. Maybe he'd left it in the truck while on the hike, maybe it was at the farm and he'd swung by the cabin to pick it up, who knew.

He turned it on to find a flood of notifications. Nearly a hundred unread texts. Three overdue reminders, including his meeting with the probation officer.

There were also a bunch of missed calls, including some new voicemails. He decided to start with those, since reading the text strings seemed overwhelming, and hearing a familiar voice might help jolt him back to himself. He selected the oldest unheard message.

"Naveed-jaan," Maman's voice said. It sounded warm, like she was smiling as she'd said his name, and for a second Naveed's anxiety went away. He must have been wrong, she wasn't dead at all, he'd panicked and assumed the worst but here was proof, she was alive, she was still alive! They must have taken her to a hospital, and she was calling to reassure him, to tell him not to worry, everything was going to be fine.

"I was just wondering if you're around today," his mother went on, and that sense of relief abruptly pulled away, like a receding wave. "Kelly and I are heading down to the mountain and thought we might stop by Zetik for a little bit if you're there. Anyway, give me a call when you get this. Asheghetam, Naveed-jaan. Ghorbanet beram."

Her voice, her voice. He would never again hear her voice saying something new. Every word she'd said was already in the past, already gone.

And, too, the words she'd chosen to end her message with. *I love you, Naveed, dear. I would die for you.* A common enough way for her to sign off, one of those dramatic Persian phrases, but still....

He had to put the phone down after that. All of this—it hurt *so bad*. After everything he'd been through, he thought he knew pain, but nothing had ever felt as intense as this. Crying might have helped, but tears refused to come. He'd already yelled away his voice, so he couldn't scream at the sky, at the mocking moon. It was like the whole universe was trying to squeeze into the shell of his body, too big to contain, his insides stretched to breaking.

He might have stayed there all night if it weren't for the film of dirt on his skin, his clothes that were still damp from sweat. It felt like tiny soil creatures were crawling all over him, and the need to escape them soon became overwhelming. He couldn't go home, couldn't face his family yet, so he texted Andi and had his phone tell him how to get to her dad's new place.

And now here he was, hemmed in by Andi on one side and Koffka on the other. He needed sleep, after that hike every muscle was stretched to the point of complete exhaustion, but whenever he closed his eyes all he saw was Maman's unmoving body on the mossy rocks.

Andi's head started to feel like it was weighing him down. Like another burden, too heavy to lift. He shifted, trying to reclaim his arm, half-hoping this would wake her up so he didn't have to remain alone inside his head. But she just moved over to her pillow, smiling in her sleep, keeping her hand on his shoulder.

She couldn't save him, couldn't take away this pain. He was stuck, exhausted body and exhausted mind with no sleep in sight, and that's just the way this night was going to be.

What happened to her? Nate roared inside his head. *Was Kelly hiding something? Maybe she was responsible? When I figure out who did this, I'm going to hunt them down, rip out their hearts the way they ripped out mine—*

No, Naveed countered, alarmed at Nate's sudden reappearance. *Go away. Seriously. I cannot deal with you right now.*

Nate kept going, so Naveed tried to focus on his surroundings to distract himself from Nate's increasingly dark tirade. He watched the red digits of the alarm clock tick slowly upward. He watched the sky brighten through the closed window blinds, and thought, *this is the first morning that my mother will not see.* He listened to the sounds of Jake getting up, showering, putting on some music, opening and closing kitchen cupboards, cooking something sizzly in a frying pan. Andi was still out cold. She must have been very tired. Must be nice to sleep when you're tired.

Koffka was up, though, asking Naveed with his eyes, *Are you okay?*

No, Naveed thought. *I am so not okay.*

Koffka knew this. He nuzzled his head closer. *It's okay to not be okay. I've got you.*

Andi opened her eyes. She turned her face toward Naveed and smiled adorably. "Hey," she said in a sleep-croaky voice. "You're here. Waking up next to you… it's like the best thing ever…." She trailed off, wincing. "Oh, no, I didn't mean… it's just… for a second I forgot."

That would be nice, too, to be able to forget for a single second that his mother was gone. But it was going around in his head the same way it had been all night. *I'm lying here next to Andi and Maman's dead. I can't sleep and Maman's dead. There's another siren, there go the red lights splashing against the walls, and Maman's dead. I feel shittier than shit and Maman's dead. She's not going to bring me tea or elderberry syrup or sit with me when I'm scared to be alone. She's dead, she's dead, she's dead, and she's never coming back.*

Jake knocked on the door. "Breakfast's ready!"

"Be there in a minute." Andi tried to snuggle back down into him again, so he sat up. Which was not easy. A soft groan escaped his mouth.

"You okay?" Andi asked.

"Fine. Just my old bones. I'm so sore after yesterday. That was a killer hike!" He found himself laughing, weirdly, who knew what the hell that was about, but he couldn't stand the concerned way she was looking at him. He wanted to reassure her, to convince her that he wasn't irreparably damaged.

It was hard to tell whether it worked or not. She didn't seem to know whether to laugh with him or burst into tears. "Let's go get some breakfast. Food will help," she finally said.

Naveed's stomach was so tight that he doubted he'd be able to get anything down. But he let Andi help him up and shuffled into the living room between her and Koffka.

Jake immediately went in for a hug, which Andi chided him for, whispering, "Dad! You can't just walk up and hug him like that! You have to ask first."

Inside Naveed's head, Nate said in a mocking baby voice, *Aww, isn't dat sweet? Andi thinks you're a poor wittle snowflake who can't handle a normal hug without freaking out.*

To prove them both wrong, Naveed said, "It's fine," and endured the hug even though his heart was speeding up and nausea was grabbing his throat. Jake finally pulled away, muttering condolences before retreating to the kitchen to finish breakfast.

Koffka, sensing the oncoming panic, had planted himself at Naveed's feet. *I know, boy*, he thought as he rubbed the dog's ears and tried to take deep breaths. His throat and lungs still felt constricted. He wasn't sure he'd ever be able to breathe normally again.

Andi led him to the table. The news was playing on the big-screen TV behind them, but the sound was muted.

"Jake," Naveed said. "Could you turn up the volume?" Andi shot him a questioning look, but he didn't care. If they talked about his mother on the news, he wanted to know what they were saying about her.

"You sure?" Jake brought over two plates of pancakes and fruit salad. Naveed nodded, and was grateful when their attention turned to the TV. His head felt so heavy that he literally had to hold it up with one hand. The pancakes would take too much effort to cut and to chew, so he ate a few mushy bananas from the fruit salad while the commercials ran. When the newscast returned, they talked about the weather before transitioning to their next story.

There she was, her photo at the top of the screen with the subtitle, *Tragedy at Mount Rainier.* "Officials confirmed that they have identified the body recovered during the search for a missing hiker at Mount Rainier yesterday. The hiker was Mahnaz Mirzapour, the former Nutrexo scientist who was slated to testify against Tara Snyder in the upcoming criminal trial. Due to the circumstances of her death, an investigation is being conducted to determine the cause, but police state that they have found no evidence of foul play. At this time, it appears her death may have been accidental, though suicide has not been ruled out. Opening statements in *The People v. Tara Snyder* begin on Monday, and it remains to be seen what impact this new development will have on the trial."

The words barely even made sense, because Naveed was paying more attention to the fruit he'd just eaten. It had tasted like nothing at first, but after this last bite a familiar scent filled his whole mouth before he realized what it was, before he saw the bottle of syrup that Jake had smothered their pancakes in, the kind with the imitation maple flavor that smelled just like—

Somehow he made it to the bathroom in time. He puked up the fruit, along with an impressive quantity of liquid, he had no idea where that had come from, and the room grew fuzzy around the edges, it was dark in here, he'd closed the door and hadn't turned on the light, dark and so small, the floor barely big enough for him and Koffka, who was trying valiantly to lick his wrist and keep him at Jake's house, but it was futile because that maple smell was stuck in his nose, the smell of the weedkiller that Tara Snyder had tested on him, which had wrecked his nerves and his lungs and quite possibly his brain too.

He gripped at Koffka's fur but it was fading beneath his fingers; he shouldn't have touched the dog because now Koffka was dead, too, his flesh rotting off his bones before Naveed's eyes, and he was left staring at an empty skull, and he was paralyzed on the floor, smelling the coppery blood, the urine, the vomit, the maple syrup.

Everything shriveled up inside him. That feeling he'd had last night, of the universe trying to crowd into his body—now it felt like everything was shrinking into a tiny dense mass, taking with it everything he'd ever hoped for.

The promise is empty, Nate said, and for once that voice was talking sense. Naveed could see that now. There was no *getting better.* There was no *time heals all wounds.* There was no *you'll feel better in the morning.* Not even *this, too, shall pass.* Lies, all of them lies. These things he'd once believed in—or hoped to believe in—were as flimsy as the advertisements cooked up by marketing executives and PR consultants. There was no justice, no retribution for the harm done to his family. There wasn't even a family—how could there be, without his mother in it?

"They don't know what they're talking about," Andi said. Her voice sounded watery and distant. One of her tears fell onto his cheek—he was lying on his side, his head in her lap, in Jake's bathroom. Koffka was beside him, warm and alive. Naveed wiped off her tear so she wouldn't touch his face.

"Your mom loved you *so much.*" Andi's voice was closer now, but quiet, wobbly with emotion. "She would never do that to you—she would never leave you like that. *Never.*"

Naveed remembered: they had just been watching the news. Andi must be upset because they'd suggested his mother committed suicide.

She doesn't get it, Nate said. *She doesn't have a clue what's really going on.*

Naveed opened his mouth to say, *Please help me, Andi, I need help, I'm in way over my head and I don't know if I can make it through this.*

But instead of saying anything, he found himself gagging, heaving nothingness out of his empty stomach. *Pathetic,* Nate scolded. *You think she can help you? She'll just turn you over to the enemy. They'll commit you, lock you up again, strap you down, force the meds down your throat or inject them straight into your veins until you become a useless zombie.*

Naveed didn't want to believe Nate. He'd trained for this, he'd worked so hard to keep Nate in check, he'd been doing so good lately, but....

Everything Nate was saying made sense. It was pointless to ask for help. The only place that could possibly lead was to a locked hospital room, where he would scream all night for someone to untie him while nurses rushed by outside the doors, pretending not to hear.

When Naveed looked up at Andi again, she felt very far away. It was like something between them had been cleaved, and their realities were no longer lining up. He had crossed some threshold, a doorway that she couldn't pass through. He had entered a place she could never understand.

That's right, Nate said. *That's what I've been trying to tell you all this time. She can't help you. None of them can. They just want to contain you. So you have to do whatever you can to stop them from locking you up. There's too much work to be done. We're the only ones who can do this, you know.*

We're going to find out who did this to Maman.

And then we're going to kill them.

Cyrus

SATURDAY, MAY 21

CYRUS WAS MAKING COFFEE IN THE KITCHEN WHEN SOMEONE tapped on the back door. He turned around and saw a ghost.

A startled sound flew out of his mouth. The terrifying face in the window was staring at him with deadened eyes while screechy violins played inside Cyrus's head, but the jump-scare moment passed quickly. As soon as he recognized who it actually was, he was just embarrassed.

He opened the door. Naveed breezed past Cyrus with barely a glance and bolted for the bathroom, slamming the door behind him.

Andi and Koffka followed him inside. They'd wanted to avoid any reporters hanging around in front, so she'd warned Cyrus they were coming the back way, which only made him all the more flustered by his overreaction.

"Oh, Cy." Andi embraced him in a fierce hug. "All of this is just completely, horribly, unbelievably awful. Are you doing okay? Where's everyone else?"

"Still asleep." Cyrus purposely didn't answer her first question. "Khaleh Yasmin gave us all some herbal tea last night that knocked us out. Sonbol-eh tib… I can't remember the English for it, but it's powerful stuff. She just left to get some groceries. And my aunt Leila is driving up from Oregon. Baba warned me that the cops will be coming by, there's an investigation I guess, but for now, it's just us." There was so much he needed to talk to Andi about, most of it having to do with the intel he'd gathered last night, but he was way too distracted by the retching sounds coming from the bathroom. "Is he… um… okay?"

Koffka was pawing at the bathroom door, probably wondering the same thing. "I'll go check on him." Andi opened the door and disappeared inside for a minute.

When she came back, she answered Cyrus's question. "He's kind of a mess. For obvious reasons. But I think my dad made it worse. It wasn't really his fault, I guess, he couldn't have possibly known, but—he made us pancakes and smothered them in maple syrup, the fake kind, you know, that smells just like—"

Cyrus knew exactly what she was getting at. "Like the weedkiller Dr. Snyder was testing at SILO. Shit."

"But it gets worse. He had the news on while we ate. The news! Why not a harmless home-remodel show or something? Or he could have turned it off when we came in, but no, he had to leave it on, and of course they ran a story about—about your mom and—"

She stopped there. "What did they say?" Cyrus prompted. He had so far resisted the urge to check social media and had been ignoring most of his texts, except for Andi's and the sympathetic condolences from the Quirqi team. Dev had told him he'd make an announcement that *D&C* would be going on hiatus, which was a relief to Cyrus. He couldn't even imagine trying to be funny right now.

Andi wasn't looking at him. She was staring in the general direction of the glass carafe where his pour-over coffee had just finished brewing. He tossed the filter and grounds into the compost bucket on the counter, divided the coffee into two mugs, then rummaged in the fridge for cream. He also pulled out a bag of sugar, which they were keeping in the fridge after the latest ant-break, since Andi liked hers sweet.

She dribbled in some cream and spooned a generous helping of sugar into her cup. "They said the police are investigating, but apparently there was no evidence of foul play. So it was probably an accident. But they also thought... they said... it might have been... suicide." Her voice dropped almost to a whisper by the last word.

"Well, it obviously wasn't *that*." The thought was ludicrous and Cyrus wasn't going to waste any brain space even considering the possibility. "It was an accident. The rocks were really slick from the rain, and she slipped. End of story."

"You don't think something else might have happened, though?" Andi asked. "Not that she jumped, not that, but... you don't think someone might have done this?"

Before Cyrus could answer, the bathroom door opened and Naveed stumbled out, Koffka at his side. Andi abandoned her coffee. "Here, I'll get your shoes, then let's head upstairs," she said, leading him to the couch.

Naveed slumped against the cushions while Andi wrestled with his work boots, which were caked in dried mud. He'd left a trail of dirt behind him. Cyrus thought of Maman then, imagined her sweeping up the mess, chiding his brother in Persian for not taking off his shoes at the door, and he was hit with an intense sensation. It felt like that time he'd been poisoned by Alastor Yarrow and his heart had briefly thudded to a stop. The tightness inside his chest was so painful that he had to pull up a chair at the dining room table so he could sit down and breathe for a minute. But the tightness didn't go away. It wouldn't go away, because this loss would be hitting him over and over, constantly, forever.

When he looked up, Andi was helping Naveed upstairs, Koffka keeping pace beside them. Good thing Cyrus had cleared out the bottom bunk. He stood slowly, grabbed his coffee and gulped a few sips that he barely tasted, then flopped down on the couch. The living room was dark. Baba had told him to keep the shades drawn.

Cyrus found himself thinking about what Andi had said before they'd been interrupted. *You don't think someone else might have done this?*

What if that was true, and it hadn't just been a horrible accident? What if someone had done this to his mother?

He didn't really want to think about it. He didn't want to think about anything.

He was still lying there when Andi reappeared, texting as she walked down the stairs. He scooted his legs in to give her room to sit near him, but she perched on a nearby armchair while her thumbs flew across her phone.

"Who're you texting?" he asked after a minute.

"Frida says she'll bring Naveed's things over later this afternoon," Andi said. "His meds, some clothes, stuff like that. They're giving him the week off. That'll be better. He should stay here for a while so we can keep an eye on him. I don't want him to be all alone out there. Not right now."

"Okay," Cyrus said hollowly. "That's good."

She didn't look up from her phone. "He had a bunch of promo stuff scheduled for the film today, too. He's supposed to be at Redwing for brunch in an hour, so I need to let Vanesa know he won't be able to make it in case she hasn't heard the news. Obviously he won't be going to the premiere either. I wish he could be there, I wish he could see it, but...." She trailed off. "Hey Cy... I feel kind of bad about this, but I still want to go tonight. Do you think that would be... you know, insensitive?"

"Oh—no, not at all. You should go if you want to."

"What about you?"

"Nah. You can count our family out. It would probably be weird for us to show up to something like that today. Plus, I'm just not up for a depressing documentary tonight."

There was a period of silence as Andi typed out a long text, then stood up to get her coffee before settling back into the armchair.

"I'm so glad you're here, A," Cyrus said. "You've always been good in a crisis."

She smiled wanly. "Only when it's not *my* crisis. I mean, this kind of is mine too, but... it makes me feel better to *do* stuff, you know? Still... I could really use a run later. Want to come with me, maybe?"

"Uh, have you ever *seen* me run?" Cyrus pictured himself trying to keep up with Andi on a jog, and actually laughed out loud.

Andi sipped her coffee. "I probably won't go anyway," she said. "It would be nice to clear my head a little, but I don't want to leave Naveed alone for too long. Oh—that reminds me, I told him I'd bring him some water." She sprang back up.

"Wait." Cyrus really needed to talk to her before everyone else descended, before she was pulled back into Naveed's vortex. "What you said earlier... about it not being an accident...."

Andi filled a glass with water, but to Cyrus's relief she didn't disappear upstairs with it. She set it on the coffee table and sat next to him on the couch, tucking her feet beneath her. "I don't know," she said softly, warming her hands on her mug. "I just don't know. I can't get Richard Caring's face out of my head. The way he looked at your mom during his trial—it was obvious how much he hated her. Not that he could do anything about it personally, but he's got plenty of connections. What if he sent someone? Like that guy who was following Naveed around last winter?"

"Maybe." Cyrus's assistant hacker (aka Todd) had been keeping an eye out for Tim Schmidt, but the trail had gone completely cold. Still, it didn't seem likely that Richard Caring was behind this. "I feel like Richard would be more careful—he wouldn't be stupid enough to plot a murder from behind bars and expect to get away with it."

"I know. But... there's something else. That photo I sent, you know, the one with my grandpa standing next to Alastor? I found out that Ah-gong used to sell green tea extract to Metafolia"—Cyrus raised his eyebrows, and she gave him a look that said, *I know, right?*—"so I figured that explained it.

But before I knew any of that, I accidentally sent the pic to your mom instead of you. And her response was kind of weird. She told me I should let it go. And that I shouldn't get you or Naveed involved."

A massive head-rush flooded Cyrus's brain. Good thing he was lying down. "My mom said that?"

"Yes. I have no idea why. Do you know? Did she say anything to you about it?"

Cyrus couldn't think about the last conversation he and Maman had without feeling a deep pang for how rushed he'd been, how impatient, not knowing it would be the last time he'd ever see her. Had she said anything about the photo? No, she'd asked about Andi, but only to make sure he could cook dinner when she came over Sunday, a detail that unexpectedly made tears spring to his eyes. He blinked them back. "No. Wait, you didn't send the pic to Naveed, did you?"

"Of course not. And I definitely won't show him now. We need to be extra careful not to trigger him—I don't want him to get any worse."

"Yeah." Cyrus sat up and took a sip of his coffee, then settled back into the couch cushions. "But there's something I wanted to tell you about, too. We had a meeting with a possible investor yesterday. At Blanchet Capital."

She winced. "Really? You're thinking of working with *them*? You know your mom's been campaigning against them for months, right? Akilah was just talking about it at dinner last night, how deeply they're involved in the for-profit prison industry and—"

Cyrus cut her off. "Just hear me out. The people we met with kept talking about this guy who has to sign off on everything. So I did a little sleuthing after our meeting." He didn't mention that this had happened after he'd found out about Maman, because he knew that might sound uncaring, but he'd needed to escape somehow. "His name is Raymond Whitaker. He's this super rich investor guy who has significant stake in a bunch of different companies from all over the spectrum. Tech, finance, PR firms—you name it. He's even served on the board of a few companies. Two of them stuck out to me. Genbiotix. And Nutrexo."

Andi stared at him over her mug, apparently speechless.

"Obviously, he's not on the Nutrexo board anymore," Cyrus went on. "Since the company doesn't exist—"

"Raymond Whitaker. That name sounds so familiar," Andi interrupted. "I've heard it before—where was it?" She pounded her forehead with her curled up fist. "Stupid short-term memory loss! Where have I heard it? This is going to drive me crazy."

"Hey, it's fine, I'm sure it'll come to you. Please don't go crazy." He smiled to show it was a joke, but she still looked upset. "Anyway, the strangest thing about all of this is... I think he was in that photo you sent."

"Seriously? Here... let's see...." She pulled up the pic on her phone while he did a quick image search for Raymond Whitaker. They put their photos side by side, staring back and forth at the men on their screens.

"That does look like him," Andi said. "I thought I'd seen him before. Maybe it was when I was researching Blanchet Capital during the whole Blazin Bitz thing I was working on last winter... but no, I don't think that was it." She set down her empty mug. "I wish I could just ask Ah-gong, but they're kind of, like, insinuating that Ah-ma had a stroke because she was so upset I was questioning them about this."

"Your grandma had a stroke? Is she okay?"

"She'll be fine. But, oh yeah, that was the same day I found out that Ah-gong sold his tea company. To Hannigan Foods—which, by the way, is owned by Blanchet."

"Holy shit," said Cyrus. "Well, that's an interesting development."

"Right? So now I get to pay for college with money from an industry I'm trying to fight against."

"There's no such thing as clean money," Cyrus said. "Doesn't matter where it comes from. It matters what you do with it."

She didn't say anything. Both of them stared at their phones for a minute, putting all of this together.

"Okay, so let me recap here," said Cyrus. "Your grandpa was in a partnership with Alastor Yarrow, selling green tea extract to Metafolia.

Raymond Whitaker was aware of it, too—he seems to be mostly good for throwing money around, so maybe he financed the operation."

"But who's the other guy? The blond one?"

"I have no idea."

"And why didn't your mom want me getting you involved? Do you think she knew something we don't, something that might have led to…?"

The unsaid words churned inside Cyrus's head. "No," he found himself saying. "No. In fact, maybe… maybe she was right."

Andi furrowed her eyebrows. "What do you mean?"

"I mean, we should let it go." As soon as the words left his mouth, Cyrus felt the release of tension that happened whenever he made a decision he knew was right. "What does it matter if Raymond Whitaker helped finance the start of Metafolia? Maman probably didn't want you to send that picture because Alastor tried to fucking kill us both and she didn't want to 'trigger' us or whatever. That's all. So just forget about it."

Andi swung her legs to the floor. "Why did you tell me, then? Why did you tell me that Raymond Whitaker—a guy who's connected to all these companies we're fighting against—was in that picture, if you just want me to forget it?"

It was a fair question, but Cyrus didn't know what to say. "Because you asked me who those guys were, and I figured it out—well, partially anyway—and I thought you should know. But it doesn't mean anything, so it doesn't do any good to obsess over it."

"Do you know what I think?" She caught his eye and didn't look away. "I think you don't *want* to know. I think you guys want to sign a deal with Blanchet, and you want to do it with a clean conscience. But turning a blind eye doesn't make it okay. It just lets people like Richard Caring and Raymond Whitaker keep doing whatever the hell they want, as long as it makes money for their companies and their friends. If you ignore what they're doing, the problems keep getting repeated."

Cyrus had to look away from her intense stare. Just moments ago, he'd been thinking how great it was to talk with her again, but now he felt awful. "I'm sorry, A," he said. "Maybe you're right. But if they offer us a deal, we'll probably take it. It might keep my family from losing one more thing—this house—because right now, we don't have the luxury of taking the high road. We're barely surviving here, and I'm going to do whatever I can to help."

Andi opened her mouth as if to say something else, but seemed to think better of it and closed it again. She picked up the glass of water on the coffee table so quickly that a thin river sloshed onto the rug. "I should bring this upstairs."

After she left, Cyrus closed his eyes again, mulling all of this over, feeling torn. He really didn't want to investigate Raymond Whitaker any further. If that made him a bad person, so be it.

A few minutes later, Andi texted, Hey could you come up here for a minute?

Cyrus hurried upstairs, worried he was careening headlong into yet another crisis. But when he stepped into his bedroom, all was quiet. Andi motioned for him to sit next to her on the bottom bunk. Then Naveed turned to face him, holding a phone tightly in his hand. He still looked like hell. Very ghost-like.

"What's going on?" Cyrus asked uneasily.

"I need your help," Naveed whispered. "This is her phone. I found it in the woods. I think she left it for me—for us. But it's dead, and I don't know the passcode anyway. I need you to open it up."

Cyrus looked down at it, the phone she'd so often left in weird places, balanced on top of an empty glass or hidden in sofa crevices or even, once, inside the chicken coop. He could almost hear her yelling from downstairs. *Kourosh-jaan, I can't find my phone, can you call it?*

"No. I can't," he told Naveed. "She had me tighten her security controls—I set it up so she has an eight-digit passcode, and it's encrypted, and you only get three tries before all the data's destroyed. I told her not to give the code to anyone. Not even Baba."

"There's got to be some way to get around that," said Naveed. "You have to open it."

"Even if I could—which I can't, because it's impossible—I wouldn't do it," said Cyrus. "That's her private stuff in there, Naveed. It doesn't do any good—"

"You have to get in," Naveed said again. "And you have to do it right now. Nothing is more important. The cops aren't going to help us. We have to find the answer."

"The answer to what?"

Naveed watched him with his ghost-eyes. "We're going to find out who killed her."

Andi

SATURDAY, MAY 21

ANDI HATED PARKING GARAGES. THE POORLY LIT CONCRETE mazes always set her on edge. She unfastened her seat belt, but didn't make a move to get out of Brooke's car.

"This was a bad idea," she said. "Let's just go back home."

"Nope. Not a chance," Brooke said. "It's the world premiere of the first film you ever scored! You have to be there."

"Are you sure it won't be weird? I feel bad, like we shouldn't be out having fun…."

"It's not about having fun. It's about showing up," Brooke said. "And yeah, I feel bad too. But Mahnaz wouldn't want us to miss this."

Andi's eyes prickled with tears. Tonight was going to be hard. "Thanks for being my date, Brooke."

"Of course! Anytime." Brooke balanced her phone on the dashboard, using selfie mode as a mirror while she applied a coat of bright-red lip gloss. "Naveed's probably a wreck, huh?"

Andi thought about the way she used to describe Naveed's moods for Mahnaz, and wanted to say, *He's sleet. He's freezing rain.* Was there even an emoji for that? It didn't matter anyway: Mahnaz was gone. It stabbed her in the heart every single time she remembered that. "Yeah. It's pretty bad. Cyrus said he'd keep an eye on him, though."

Brooke pressed her lips together. "My mom told me he totally went off on her, after they found... after they found the body. He told her it was her fault. That she shouldn't have let this happen."

Andi winced. "Ouch."

"I know. He can be so brutal—I hope you never see that side of him. Of course my mom feels horrible about the whole thing, and hearing him say that out loud... I'm sure he was upset, looking for someone to blame, and she was the unlucky one he took it out on. But still."

"Wow. That's terrible. I'm so sorry." Andi was angry on Brooke's behalf, but also she could hardly blame Naveed for his reaction. If she'd been in his situation, she probably would've lost it too.

Still, Brooke's words lodged uncomfortably in her mind. *Looking for someone to blame.* The explanation that it was an accident, though it seemed the most likely option, wasn't very satisfying. Maybe Naveed needed to believe she'd been murdered so that he could pin the blame on someone else. So that he didn't have to let in the possibility that she killed herself.

Andi sincerely hoped that hacking into her phone was as impossible as Cyrus said it was, mostly because she didn't want Naveed reading her text string with Mahnaz. All the same, Andi couldn't let go of the thought that Mahnaz had known something about that photo... and if they could just get into her phone....

But—now wasn't the time to be dwelling on this. She had somewhere to be.

Brooke zipped her phone inside her purse. "Shall we?"

Andi took a final glance at her own phone to make sure her waterproof mascara wasn't smudged, then stepped outside. She smoothed the black dress she'd bought that afternoon. The sundress she'd originally planned to wear felt way too cheery.

Brooke, who had dyed her hair a deep amber color earlier that morning, was dressed all in black too—a dark chiffon blouse, black skirt over black leggings, black combat boots. A CFJ button was pinned to her blouse. She'd brought an extra one, which Andi had fastened to the top of her dress.

She and Brooke walked through the dusk to the SIFF Cinema at Seattle Center. The Space Needle towered over them as they passed the metal dome of the giant fountain. Ecstatic shrieks from splashing children followed them as they rounded the corner to the premiere.

Andi hadn't expected much fanfare, so she was surprised to see the long line of ticketholders and the crowd of reporters gathered outside, including a few cameras from local TV networks.

"Wow." Brooke offered Andi her arm. "Okay. Here we come, two dour old ladies in mourning."

Andi linked elbows with her, knowing that photos would be posted all over social media along with speculation and commentary, but not caring. As they approached the doors of the theater, she noticed Vanesa standing next to Fernando, Marisol, and Ramón.

Vanesa caught Andi in a big hug. "Naveed's sorry he couldn't be here," Andi said into her ear. "And that he missed all the promo today."

"It's understandable," Vanesa said. "We were so sorry to hear about his mom."

Andi waved at Ramón and Marisol, who looked just as shell-shocked as she felt. She wondered what it would be like to see the film from their perspective. It followed them through a difficult time in their lives, and it wasn't like things had gotten much better for them. At dinner the night before, Vanesa had mentioned that they hadn't yet been able to find work this season. Ramón's reputation of standing up for worker's rights had so far made it impossible to get hired.

"Andi!" someone called. She turned around, only to be blinded by the bright burst of a camera flash. Is this what it felt like to be a movie star?

Because she'd much rather be lying around in her pajamas next to Naveed than dealing with this right now.

Once the afterglow had faded from her eyes, she saw that the person who had addressed her was a reporter. He stuck a microphone in her face, and she tried hard not to look directly at the giant KING5 News camera behind him. "Congratulations, Andi. So impressive—composing the music for a film at the age of seventeen! It must be such a proud day for you."

Proud? That wasn't how she'd describe this day at all. It had been emotionally wrenching, and it wasn't about to get any better.

"Well, it's bittersweet," she said. *Don't cry, don't cry, don't cry.* "It's an amazing movie, and I was honored to be a part of it. But it's hard to celebrate, because I know Mahnaz would have—" Andi swallowed hard. "She would have loved it too. I wish she could've seen it."

"Were you and Mahnaz Mirzapour close?" the reporter asked.

Andi didn't want to go into detail, so she fell back on an old cliché that, nevertheless, was true. "She was like a mother to me—she always treated me like I was her own daughter. So, yes. I really miss her."

Brooke must have been able to tell Andi was about to lose it, because she interjected, "This fight—the fight for food justice, for fair treatment of farmworkers—was her passion, too. That's why we're here tonight. Because even though this is a huge loss for the movement, we're going to keep on working towards a better world. Now, excuse us, please." She pulled Andi away.

"Thanks for rescuing me," Andi said. "I always clam up on camera. But you were awesome."

"Just trying to earn my keep as your hot date," Brooke replied with a smile.

Vanesa waved them over. "The doors just opened," she said. "We have reserved seats, a row in the middle, you'll see it. Oh, and Andi—we're doing a Q&A afterward, and would love for you to join us. Up to you, though."

"Wanna go in now?" Brooke asked. "Hide out from the reporters?"

Andi was about to say yes, but then she spotted her father approaching with a barely suppressed grin on his face. He, too, was wearing all black. He hugged her, and Andi heard the reporters calling to him, probably hoping to get a rock-star-father and composer-daughter interview. She was trying to drag him inside when she heard a voice in the crowd that she recognized. It was a familiar baritone, but she couldn't place where she'd heard it before.

"Wait," she said, looking back over her shoulder. But she didn't recognize any of their faces, and it was impossible to tell whose voice it was. "Never mind. Let's go in." Her dad turned around and waved, to a renewed surge of flashes, then followed her inside.

Moments after Andi settled into the seat between her dad and Brooke, someone tapped her on the shoulder.

"Sorry to bother you." The baritone-voiced man smiled. He had prominent black eyebrows and warm brown eyes. "Don't worry—I'm not here for an interview. I just wanted to thank you."

"Thank… me?" Andi didn't recognize anything about this man but his voice. Her dad and Brooke were also looking at him quizzically.

He stuck out his hand. "Jamal Montgomery. Editor at *Real Change*, and as of recently, a contributor to the *South Seattle Emerald* and *Seattle Times*, thanks to a certain article I published last June."

"Jamal!" Andi exclaimed. Of course—he was the reporter who had written the Nutrexo exposé last summer. Their interviews had been done over the phone, so she'd never met him in person. "So nice to meet you. Officially, I mean."

Andi shook his hand and introduced him to the others, and the three of them chatted until the lights dimmed. "No pressure at all, but if you ever want to do any follow-up interviews, you know where to find me," he said as he straightened up. Andi thanked him, even though she doubted she'd take him up on that.

She turned her attention to the front of the theater, where someone from SIFF was addressing the audience. Andi barely understood what they were saying. Her heart was pounding in her ears. Was it normal to be so nervous for something like this? It wasn't like she was playing live or anything, but she still felt as anxious as if she were about to serenade all these people.

After the previews played, the opening credits began—and with them, the theme that Andi had composed. She found herself holding her breath.

As the opening went on, she felt a subtle change around her. The audience stopped shifting in their seats, rummaging around for popcorn. They were transfixed, watching the image of the road while the music played. Then came Ramón's voice, reciting a Cesar Chavez quote in Spanish. Naveed's voice filled the theater next, reading the English translation. "It's ironic," he said, "that those who till the soil, cultivate and harvest the fruits, vegetables, and other foods that fill your tables with abundance have nothing left for themselves."

Brooke sniffled beside her. She leaned her head into Andi's shoulder. "Didn't even last a minute," she whispered, gesturing at the tissue in her other hand. "Andi—you are freaking amazing."

Andi hazarded a glance at her dad, who didn't even notice. He, too, was engrossed. Her song had already swept him away.

Her nerves left her then. She settled in to watch the film, imagining for a moment that Mahnaz was in the chair next to her, as absorbed as everyone else, silently cheering on Naveed through all his struggles and triumphs. The fact she wasn't here felt like the biggest knife-twist of all. She would have been so proud.

Roya

SUNDAY, MAY 22

ROYA LAY ON HER BELLY UNDERNEATH HER BED, PASHMAK AT her side, re-reading the letter she'd gotten from Kass last month. The one with her aunt's phone number. If Roya could just figure out a way to call her without anyone in her family finding out....

The bedroom door creaked open. Roya army-crawled out from under the bed. "Hey, what are you—oh, Koffka, it's you!"

Pashmak stayed beneath the bed, green eyes glowing in the darkness. She still preferred to keep her distance from Koffka. Roya reached out to pet the dog, glad that he'd come to see her. She'd stayed in her room most of the previous day, not wanting to be near all the crying people in her house, keeping her distance from them as if their emotions were catching. The longer she stayed away from their very real sadness, the longer she could pretend it wasn't true.

It was impossible not to notice that something major had changed, though. Obviously, Maman's death—if it really was real—was a big change, but that wasn't the only thing. The air inside the house still carried a sense of unease. Just breathing it in made Roya feel like she'd been in an ugly fight, one that had stirred up all sorts of messy feelings. The strange thing was, this sensation went away whenever she was outside, but opening the windows to let fresh air in didn't help. It seemed to be a shift within the house itself. It was subtle and hard to explain. Roya didn't even bother mentioning it to anyone else.

Koffka curled against her, whimpering. Roya wrapped her arms around him. The uneasy feeling shrank a little now that his strong calm body was next to hers.

"I'm glad you're here. I missed you," she told him. "Can you help me up? I have to go to the bathroom." Good thing he'd come in just then. It really hurt to put weight on her leg this morning.

Koffka stiffened up so that she could use him as a support, then walked beside Roya as she slowly made her way to the bathroom. When she passed her brothers' room, she saw Naveed lying on the bottom bunk, his back to her. He had been home for a whole day, but hadn't even bothered to come into her room to hug her or comfort her or even say hello.

She paused outside his door, daring him inside her mind. *Turn around and face me. Say something. Anything.*

He didn't. So she kept going. She wasn't going to speak to him, she decided, until he said something to her first.

Once she finished up in the bathroom, she thought about going downstairs. But all those stairs… and everyone would just be sad down there, all of them looking at her with pity in their eyes….

She was hungry, though, and she couldn't hide from them forever. She gestured toward her brothers' room. "You can go back," she said to Koffka. "I'm okay now. I have the railing."

But Koffka, sweet dog that he was, helped her all the way down the stairs. There were lots of people talking in the kitchen. When she rounded the corner, she saw Cyrus and Baba and the lawyer lady who was involved in the big trial starting tomorrow—but Roya's eyes went straight to the woman standing next to the back door.

"Auntie!" Roya exclaimed, and every head in the kitchen turned to face her.

"Roya!" Auntie Leila gathered her up in a warm hug. Roya couldn't help thinking about the last time she'd seen her auntie, back on Lopez Island. Back when she'd first met Kass.

When Roya pulled away, she noticed that Koffka was climbing back up the stairs, returning to Naveed. But there was no time to be sad he'd left, because Auntie Leila was saying, "Good morning, sleepyhead."

"When did you get here?" Roya asked.

"Last night," Auntie Leila said. "Are you hungry? I was just going to make some pasta—want some?"

"Sure," said Roya.

The lawyer lady looked over at Roya, then said a few quiet words to Baba before leaving through the back door.

"What was she doing here?" Roya asked once the door had closed.

Baba didn't answer. He looked lost, like he had no idea where he was. Roya scooted into the chair next to him. He put his arm around her robotically.

Cyrus looked up from his phone. "She thinks she can convince the judge to postpone the trial. To give us some time to get things in order. Plus, she has to figure out a new strategy, since she was counting a lot on Maman's testimony."

"Kourosh," Auntie Leila said warningly.

"What? Roya's part of this family, too. She deserves to know."

Roya thought Cyrus deserved a big hug for that.

"I have an idea, Roya," Auntie Leila said. "Why don't we go up to your room together? I'll help you pick out some clothes."

"Pick out clothes? Why?" Roya asked. "It's not like we're going any-where today. I can just stay in my pajamas."

They all stared at her as if she'd just said something weird, then exchanged glances. "What?" she asked at the same time Auntie Leila said, "You didn't tell her?"

"Tell me what?"

"The burial's today," Auntie Leila said. Baba and Cyrus both looked down, as if ashamed to meet her eyes. "Your dad and your brothers are leaving soon, and we'll meet them there. It's going to be a quiet ceremony. We'll have a memorial service next weekend."

"Oh." Roya's uneasiness grew. "Okay. I'll go get ready. You don't need to come with me, I know what I'll wear. But, Auntie, could I play some games on your phone while you make lunch?"

Cyrus side-eyed her, as if saying, *what, my games aren't good enough for you?* If Roya had actually planned on playing games, she definitely would've preferred to take his phone. But Cyrus was too nosy. He'd be able to figure out exactly what she'd done.

To Roya's relief, Auntie Leila unlocked her phone. "Sure, but just for a few minutes, okay?"

Roya nodded. "I'm going up to my room. Just tell me when my time's up." With that, she made her way up the stairs, barely holding back a squeal of glee. She was going to hear Kass's voice again!

Roya paused at her brothers' room to look in on Naveed. He still had his back to her, but he was coughing, so she knew he was awake. Koffka raised his head and whimpered as if asking, *do you need anything?* She just shook her head and moved along without saying a word.

When she got to her room, she closed the door and immediately dialed Ilyana's number. The phone rang three times before a woman picked up. "Hello?"

"Hi. May I please speak with Kasandra?" Roya was pleased with herself for sounding so grown up.

"Who is calling?" The woman had a Russian accent so thick it took Roya a moment to figure out what she was asking.

"This is her friend, Roya," she said.

"Oh! A friend. Please wait."

A second later came the voice Roya had been waiting to hear. "Hello?"

"Kass! I'm so glad you're there! I have so much to tell you, can you talk for a minute?"

"Yes," said Kass. "I'm happy you called. Ilyana doesn't usually pick up the phone unless she knows who's calling, but I had a feeling it was you. How's your leg doing?"

"Oh, it's all right. Healing up. But Kass…" Roya couldn't quite get the words out. She took a deep breath. "Kass, something really bad happened. My mom died."

Kass gasped. "Oh no," she said. "Really? How?"

"She went hiking. My dad said she slipped and fell off a cliff, I guess, but…" Tears stung Roya's eyes. "I think maybe this was my fault. She had these demons inside her. Like shayatin, if you know what those are? They made her angry. Mean. She seemed like a different person. And I did this banishing spell and I thought it didn't work but what if I did it all wrong and instead of banishing the demons I banished Maman? I used her hair, Kass, I made a poppet with her hair."

Roya was sobbing hard now, unable to hold back. Saying all of this out loud physically hurt, giving voice to the thoughts that had been swirling through her head for days, gathering more and more strength. What if it had been like the ants, where she'd been trying to do something good but ended up luring innocent creatures to their deaths?

"Oh, Roya," Kass said sadly. "I'm so sorry. Tell me about the spell you did. What else did you use for the poppet?"

Through her tears, Roya told her about all three parts of her banishing spell: the poppet, the song, the prayers at the mosque. After asking a few more questions, Kass said, "I don't think this is your fault, Roya. Your spellwork was good. The rituals you did were clearly trying to banish the demons, not your mom."

Roya wiped her nose with her shirt. Guilt still gnawed at her, but a little less so now that she'd consulted with an expert. "Okay, that's good. But is there anything I can do to, like, reverse it? To bring her back?"

"No," Kass said. "It can't be done. But don't worry, her spirit is still with you. It always will be."

Roya's throat felt very tight. That wasn't what she wanted. She wanted to squeeze into bed with Maman snuggling beside her. She wanted Maman to massage her knee with her cool, smooth hands. She wanted to smell her lavender-scented hair and her rose-oil perfume and even her morning cardamom-tea breath.

How could all those things be gone forever?

"If I could just talk to her again..." Roya mused. "That's something you can help with, right?"

"Actually... no. Ilyana caught me doing a ritual once and it really scared her so she made me promise I wouldn't do it again. If she caught me, she might send me away, and I *really* don't want to end up in another foster family. But... since I can't help... this just popped into my head, so maybe it means something. Nan had this friend, an old acolyte who became a shaman. She owned a crystal shop close to Seattle, but I have no idea if it's still there. I can't remember the name... something to do with the moon? Anyway, she was very skilled at moving between the spirit world and ours. Maybe I can track her down."

"I guess that could work." Roya didn't really want help from anyone but Kass, but she'd take whatever she could get.

"Wait—is there going to be a funeral?" Kass asked. "Maybe I could come, and we can figure out a plan then?"

"Yes! The memorial's next weekend, I think. I'll call you as soon as I know when." Roya hoped there would be a lot of people there, so Kass could blend into the crowd without her family finding out. Baba and her brothers would probably be too distracted to even notice.

"Perfect," Kass said. "Can I call you at this number?"

"No. This is my auntie's phone—she doesn't know I'm talking to you. And I'd better go, actually."

"Okay. Let me know about the memorial. I want to come."

"Thanks, Kass. I love you so much."

"I love you, too. We'll talk again soon."

Roya hung up. She felt all cleaned out, like she'd just scrubbed away a bunch of grime that had been sticking to her insides. It was going to be okay. She knew that now. Together, she and Kass were going to fix this.

IT WAS MOCKINGLY SUNNY by the time Roya and Auntie Leila arrived at the cemetery. During the long drive, Roya had covered her head with the same blue scarf she'd worn on the day Maman died. Something about it felt comforting, as if it had soaked up a bunch of protective energy that day in the mosque. *It's like casting a circle around my head,* she thought as she removed her shoes, then stepped inside the small building where everyone was gathering.

There was an open casket in the front of the room. A body was inside, covered completely in a white shroud. It seemed so impossible that Maman was in there. During the long drive, Auntie Leila told Roya that Khaleh Yasmin had done the ritual washing of her body earlier in the morning, had arranged Maman's hair into the traditional three braids, had wrapped her up in white linen. Roya knew these things in her mind, but it was still hard to connect that faceless shroud to the person who had kissed her cheeks and nagged her about finishing homework and pretended not to notice when Roya added potato chips to the shopping cart.

When she turned around, Roya saw that still more people had arrived, among them Andi and Brooke, both wearing scarves draped over their heads. She waved at them, then Auntie Leila helped her get settled on a prayer rug.

A few minutes later, the imam appeared and led the prayer service. There was a lot of wailing, and everyone wept openly. Well, not everyone, Roya noticed. Naveed wasn't crying. He was kneeling between Baba and Cyrus, both of whom had tears streaming down their cheeks. Naveed's head was bent, but his eyes were dry. He still hadn't said a single word to her.

After the brief service, Roya's dad and brothers and some of the other men from the mosque carried the casket outside, chanting and singing in low, sad voices. Roya, Auntie Leila, and Khaleh Yasmin followed the procession out to the grave, where the imam said a few more words. Then her dad and brothers gathered around the casket.

Khaleh Yasmin looked at Roya. "Would you like to say goodbye?"

Roya stared at the ground. Next to her right foot was a cluster of tiny white mushrooms, glowing in the bright sunshine. *No,* she thought. *No, I don't want to say goodbye! I don't want her to leave!*

But she nodded and stepped up to the casket. "You can touch her if you'd like. It's all right," Khaleh Yasmin said.

Tentatively, Roya reached in. She would have liked to hold Maman's hand one last time, but since the body was all wrapped up, she couldn't. It must be hard to breathe through all that fabric, Roya thought—and that's when it really started to sink in, the reality of all this: Maman was not breathing now. And she never would again.

Roya touched Maman's cheek. Through the cloth, she could tell how rigid the muscles were, how cold and lifeless the body was. And as she ran her hand across the contours of the shrouded face, she knew. They weren't lying. The body before her was all that was left of Maman.

She pulled away, into the waiting arms of Baba, who told her he loved her and kept repeating that he was sorry. She wished he'd stop saying that. None of this was his fault.

Baba and her brothers lifted the shrouded body out of the casket and lowered it into the ground. Watching them, Roya had a thought that made her heart hurt: now, she was the only girl in her family. Well, she supposed, Pashmak and the chickens were girls too, but that didn't feel reassuring at all right now.

Baba lowered himself inside to prop Maman up on small mounds of earth so that she was lying on her right side. Then he got out and sprinkled three handfuls of dirt on her. Roya's brothers did the same, and she noticed that Naveed had taken the silver star charm off his keychain, he was tucking it into his first handful of dirt, he was pouring it out into the grave. There it landed, shining for another second before it was covered up with dirt forever.

"No!" Roya yelled. How could he just toss it in there like that, as if it meant nothing? She lunged forward to jump inside and find it, but Auntie Leila and Khaleh Yasmin held her back. "No, no, no!" Roya kept repeating.

"It's okay," Auntie Leila lied.

Khaleh Yasmin caressed Roya's tear-streaked face with her hands. "Roya-jaan, are you ready to leave? We can go if you need to."

Roya wiped her face with the end of her scarf and pulled away. "No. Not yet." She turned back to the grave. Maman's shroud was now nearly obscured by dirt. There was no way she was getting that star charm back, but she couldn't let Maman go without helping to send her off. With a scathing glare at Naveed that he didn't seem to notice, Roya stepped forward, careful not to crush the tiny mushrooms at her feet.

She scooped a handful of earth in her hands, remembering all those times when Maman had been out working in the garden and Roya had been there digging beside her, relishing the squishy mud between her fingertips, and Maman had taught her about all the hidden things that happened underground, the conversations between the roots and the dirt and the mushrooms, whose tendrils reached everywhere, an invisible network beneath the surface....

One of Roya's tears fell into the handful of dirt, making a tiny drop of mud. She scattered it over the clean white shroud, watching the fine dust glitter in the sunlight as, handful by handful, Maman slowly disappeared into the earth.

Naveed

MONDAY, MAY 23

THREE DAYS. NO SLEEP.

Two-thirty A.M. on Monday. The sonbol-eh tib tea hadn't helped a bit, even though Naveed had brewed it so strong it was almost undrinkable. Should've been enough natural sedative to send an elephant into a deep slumber, but the dose wasn't strong enough for him, apparently.

It was the Serovia. Had to be. Someone had picked up his prescription at the pharmacy, and it was easier to just take the pills and suffer the consequences than go through the trouble of figuring out how to contact his psychiatrist, making an urgent appointment, explaining all the backstory, and transitioning onto some other drug that might not even be better anyway.

There were times when he thought about dumping them all down the toilet, quitting cold turkey. There were times when he thought about taking the whole bottle at once. Both of those were just fantasies, though. He was too tired to follow through on either option.

Anyway, he could deal with the lack of sleep, with the resurgence of the nerve pain that prickled inside his hands and feet. What bothered him the most right now was something much more pressing. Every day, it hurt more to breathe.

At first, he'd chalked up the chest pain to grief, but it never relented, it was there all the time, intensifying whenever he tried to take a deep breath. His inhaler didn't help anymore, either. The problem seemed to be deeper inside: his lungs felt like they were slowly turning to stone, barely room left inside them for air.

Naveed sat up in bed, the only way he could be remotely comfortable, and reached for his phone. It was time to ask Dr. Google what was going on.

The search results were far from reassuring. There were lots of possibilities, but one made a lot more sense than the others. Naveed read the symptoms, ticking mental boxes. *Shortness of breath. Persistent cough. Chest pain that gets worse when you breathe deep or cough. Feeling tired or weak. Weight loss and loss of appetite.*

"Lung cancer," Naveed muttered out loud.

God, Naveed, Nate said inside his mind. *You're such a fucking mess.*

It's because of the weedkiller at SILO, Naveed thought. *That stuff causes cancer, I was afraid this would happen, but I thought I'd have more time….*

Koffka looked up at him, as if asking, *Need your inhaler?* Naveed shook his head. What he needed was fresh air.

He got out of bed, not even bothering to be quiet. Cyrus was as heavy a sleeper as ever. Koffka followed him out the room and down the stairs.

Naveed grabbed a blanket from the couch and started making his way to the back porch so that he could sit outside for a few minutes, but stopped when he heard a noise.

Somebody was in the office typing on the laptop.

Maman, Naveed thought longingly. In his sleep-starved daze, it didn't feel so impossible.

Naveed and Koffka crept towards the office, a closet-like space off the dining room. The typing had stopped. He paused by the closed door and kept listening. The zipper of the laptop bag opening and closing. The squeak of a filing cabinet drawer. Then, another burst of typing. He didn't want to interrupt when she was writing, so he waited until it stopped before knocking softly and opening the door.

The room was empty. The laptop was closed.

But then he smelled it: the sharp scent of Maman's rose oil perfume. It hung in the air, the way it did when she had just left a room.

She had been here.

It felt like she was trying to tell him something. Just like with the phone, how she'd left it for him to find.

There was something in here. Some clue about who had done this to her.

Naveed had spent a lot of time dwelling on this. He'd been so frustrated with Cyrus for not even trying to help him figure out Maman's passcode. Nate, though, had convinced him not to mention it again. *Shouldn't have shown them her phone in the first place,* Nate said. *It was a mistake to think they'd help you find her killer. Just pretend you've given up.*

That hadn't been hard. He'd mixed truth and lies together to make it more believable, telling Andi it wasn't that he thought someone had killed his mother, not really, he just wanted it to be somebody else's fault, and he wanted Cyrus to open the phone so he could look through her camera roll and see the photos she'd taken at the mountain, he needed to know if she'd been happy in her last days, but really it was enough just to have the phone, to be able to touch the last thing she had touched. Andi had nodded tearfully, believing him, no doubt relaying it all to Cyrus the next time they talked about him behind his back.

None of them knew anything. And he intended to keep it that way.

Now, in the office, Naveed tried to wake up the laptop. But it had been powered down, so he had to turn it on again and wait for it to warm up. Instead of watching it spin its wheels, he opened the filing cabinet and started rifling through the folders. There had to be a clue in this room somewhere.

At first his search was haphazard. But then a thought occurred to him: what if she'd written down the passcode somewhere in here? Just in case she forgot it, since Cyrus had set up such stringent security controls? It seemed possible—she was always complaining about how she could never remember the password for Naveed's online health records. She refused to save it in her browser, since she wanted to keep his medical information as protected as possible. She'd finally written it down on a scrap of paper, which Cyrus had conceded was secure enough, as long as she hid it well.

That had to be it. The passcode must be written down somewhere too, but where would she have left it?

He started going through the files, scanning each page for a hand-written eight-digit number. It was tedious work, but at least it made him forget—temporarily, anyway—about his heavy lungs.

He leafed through a fat folder of past-due bills. Some of them were from Englewood. As far as he could tell, his parents still owed tens of thousands of dollars for his stay there the previous winter.

How could that be? Maman had assured him the stay was covered by his insurance. But if that was true, there was no way they'd still be in this much debt.

So... she had lied to him? Making him think it was covered so he wouldn't feel guilty that they were wasting so much money on him?

"You should have told me, Maman," he whispered to the empty room. "The fact that you lied about it—that just makes it worse."

He tried to ignore the squeezing pain in his chest and shoved the folder back into place. Practically the entire drawer was devoted to Naveed's medical records, with hanging folders labeled things like, "MRK," "Labs," "MICU Stay," "Peripheral Neuropathy," "PTSD." Each was stuffed with a hodgepodge of after-visit summaries, test results, scientific articles, pages of scrawled notes in Maman's handwriting.

Oh God. If this really was cancer, how was Naveed supposed to navigate all this medical stuff on his own?

How was he going to do this without her?

You don't get it, do you, Nate said. *We're not doing anything about the cancer—in fact, it only makes our path clearer.*

We're going to find out who murdered her. We're going to kill them. And then we're going to die on our own terms. Cancer treatments would just make you sicker, and you're going to die anyway. Wouldn't you rather be the one who decides when and how it ends?

Naveed sank into the desk chair. Koffka whimpered, reminding him, *Don't listen to Nate,* but it was all too much, problems mushrooming one on top of another, swelling like the tumors in his lungs. Even though he didn't want to listen to Nate, he had no choice. He was way too tired to fight anymore.

Cyrus

MONDAY, MAY 23

CYRUS BUZZED THE INTERCOM AT PHILIP'S DOWNTOWN CONDO. It felt strange to be coming here without the rest of the Quirqi team, but he'd received an intriguing text that Philip had sent only to him: There's something I need to talk to you about in person. Can you meet today? There was no way he could wait until the others finished their Monday classes to find out what was going on.

Luckily, his schedule was wide open, since court had adjourned early. The judge had granted a continuance out of "respect for the family" and concern that their testimony could be affected by Maman's sudden death, so opening statements were postponed until the following Tuesday. This was a huge relief to Cyrus, though it seemed to come as an annoyance to the jurors.

He'd asked Andi if she wanted to get coffee, but she said she had a headache and wanted to go home. He couldn't blame her. Seeing Tara Snyder in the courtroom, all smug-looking in a fitted blazer with her hair slicked back in that stupid bun, had gotten his temples pulsing, too.

He'd received the text from Philip as he walked through the front door with his zombie dad. Auntie Leila and Roya were taking Naveed to therapy and going to the park, but Khaleh Yasmin said she'd make sure Baba got some lunch. Even though he hadn't set a time with Philip yet, Cyrus said he had plans and hopped back in the car. Something about being inside his house just felt excruciating lately. Every time he stepped through the door, he couldn't wait to leave.

Now, the doorman let him in and escorted him down a short hall off the main lobby to the private office spaces. They were supposedly open to any of the building's residents, but Philip rented one of them 24/7 so he could use it whenever he wanted. He owned several condos in this building, one of which he used as his home-away-from-home since his main house was out on Bainbridge Island.

Cyrus's palms were sweating as he tapped on the door. It felt so weird being here without the rest of the Quirqi team.

"Come in," Philip called.

Cyrus opened the door as a small drone buzzed by. Philip was sitting in the desk chair with his FPV goggles on. The sleek white headset allowed him to see through the viewpoint of his "thinking drone" as it soared between houseplants and under chairs. He steered it over to a polished wooden platform labeled THINKING DRONE THRONE on top of a filing cabinet and brought it to a graceful landing.

Usually, Cyrus would sit at the table by the office window, but today Philip gestured for him to take the chair opposite his desk, which made Cyrus feel like he'd been called into the principal's office or something. "So. What's going on?" he asked.

"I talked with Kieran this morning," Philip said as he took off his goggles. "He and his team were really enthusiastic about Quirqi and sent your proposal to Raymond Whitaker for approval. But he declined because he had some... concerns."

Cyrus was surprised by the disappointment he felt, especially considering his mixed feelings after that tense conversation with Andi.

"What kind of concerns?" he asked.

"Well—I'll just come right out and say it. He thinks you're a liability. He would only consider funding Quirqi if you aren't involved."

It took a minute for Cyrus to digest this. "What. The hell. He thinks I'm a *liability*? I'm the one who came up with *Bugpocalypse*, you can't just cut me out—"

"Believe me, I don't want that either! The thing is—and I really hate saying this—it may be the best move. I've been pitching Quirqi to my other contacts, but the market's so saturated. Companies like this are having a really hard time getting funded right now. It's not like this is the end of the road, either, you're very talented and this is just the beginning for you. Besides, you have enough on your plate right now anyway. You don't need to add the pressures of leading a startup."

Cyrus felt like he'd been punched. No, worse than that: bloodied, stomped upon, pummeled. Raymond Whitaker's rejection of him, specifically, felt like a personal attack. Quirqi was *his*. Well, okay, it was Dev's too, and Shea's and Todd's. The four of them shared a vision. They knew how to make this thing great.

"Why me?" He looked at Philip, trying to keep his voice steady. "What makes me a liability, according to Raymond Whitaker?"

Philip shifted in his seat. "I don't know. I'm just relaying what Kieran told me."

"But if you had to guess?"

"I can't speculate. I've told you all I know."

"Okay, then let *me* speculate. He knows who my mom is—who she was. She's gone on the record as being critical of Blanchet Capital. But I'm not my mom, and anyway isn't that, like, discrimination? Doesn't he have to give me a chance, legally?"

"Unfortunately, that's not how this works," Philip said. "Look. I know it sucks, but all I'm asking is that you consider it."

Cyrus fumed. He opened his mouth, wanting to spout off, but Philip's phone buzzed before he could say anything. "Oh, I'd better take this,"

Philip said. "Just think about it—I'll tell the others, and we can meet to discuss it later in the week."

He answered his phone. Reluctantly, Cyrus walked out and closed the door behind him, the world in a blur as crossed the lobby under the watchful gaze of the doorman.

I'm not going to let go of Quirqi, he told himself as he made his way back to his car. *No. The rest of them won't stand for this, either. We'll find someone else to fund this if we have to.*

They couldn't just walk away from Philip, though. Right now, Cyrus was tempted to cut him out. See how *he* liked that. But, without him, they'd be lost. Philip knew how this business worked, which had saved them a whole lot of bumbling and prevented several potentially catastrophic decisions. They had trusted him to be acting in their best interests, but after this conversation, Cyrus wasn't sure if that was true anymore. Where did Philip want to steer the company? He'd been clear from the beginning that he appreciated their mission, but had drilled into them that it would never become a viable business if they didn't put their investors first. Which meant: it needed to be able to bring in the money.

Maybe Cyrus had been naive, thinking he could have it both ways. That he could make enough money to support the business and his family without compromising his values. Maybe there was no happy medium after all.

It was a depressing thought.

He had just turned the key in the ignition when Dev texted. Hey, glad to hear the trial was postponed, but wondering if u heard about this? (Warning, it's disturbing, but since it's blowing up I thought u should know)

Cyrus swallowed. Social media was his usual happy place, but he'd been trying to avoid it lately. Everybody had been talking about his mom. Speculating as to the real cause of her death and how this would affect the trial. Debating about her contributions to the food movement. Linking to articles about the warning signs of suicide and the importance of self-care for activists. All of which was bad enough—but even worse were the trolls jubilantly celebrating her death. Cyrus could usually tune out internet hate, but it was really too much for him right now.

Figuring that this would be more of the same, he unrolled the windows, cut the engine, and steeled himself before clicking on the link. But it wasn't about his mom—not exactly. The article was entitled, "Tara Snyder Is Not Who You Think She Is."

Just clickbait, he told himself. And then he began to read.

Tara Snyder Is Not Who You Think She Is

Editor's Note: This story went to press before the news broke about Mahnaz Mirzapour's death. No changes have been made in order to protect the integrity of the original piece.

By the time I arrive at the jail for visiting hours, I'm sincerely considering bolting back to my car. Though I'm usually the first one to jump on any assignment, no matter how bizarre or dangerous, this one has been weighing on me for weeks.

When I check in and tell the officer who I'm here to see, he raises an eyebrow. "She doesn't get many visitors," he said. "Kind of surprises me, to be honest. She's not like the others."

I ask what he means by that. "She's friendly," he says. "Never violent. Respectful. Damn smart, too."

This description doesn't exactly fit with the mental picture I have of Tara Snyder, the former Nutrexo scientist who will soon stand trial for allegedly abducting four children last summer. The Tara in my head is one of those empty-eyed serial-killer types, just like she appears in her mug shots, pale and frazzled and obviously psychopathic. But, as I've reminded myself more than once while preparing for this assignment, she never actually killed anyone. I repeat this in my head as the officer escorts me down the hall and I step inside the room where Tara is waiting.

Tara Snyder sits with her hands folded on the table. Her fingernails look well-manicured, even though she's been here for many months awaiting trial. Her hair is pulled back into a neat bun, and when she smiles at me, her blue eyes crinkle slightly at the edges.

I introduce myself and take a seat opposite her. A guard stands nearby, ready to intervene, but I can tell right away that this won't be necessary. Tara Snyder is eager to tell her story—in fact, she barely waits for me to start recording before it begins spilling out of her.

. . .

Tara Snyder was born in the suburbs north of Seattle. Her childhood, as might be expected considering her future fate, was a difficult one. Her father died when she was two, and her mother suffered for many years with undiagnosed early-onset dementia, which was extremely confusing and embarrassing for young Tara. To make matters worse, her older brother was emotionally and physically abusive. Tara's problems only compounded as she reached her teenage years. Her mother's illness worsened; her brother's drug abuse led to multiple arrests for a series of escalating crimes; Tara was sexually assaulted.

But Tara didn't let her dysfunctional home life interfere with her studies. She was a gifted child, understanding science so intuitively that her high school biology teacher began tutoring her in advanced concepts. He also helped her apply to colleges that would recognize her brilliance.

Though she was accepted into MIT, she was not awarded a scholarship so it remained financially out of reach. She ended up at UC Davis instead. In their department of genetics, she found her calling. She worked hard to prove herself in the male-dominated field, and was soon rewarded with a full-ride fellowship to continue as a PhD student, thanks to a grant from the Women in Science program—which had recently been started by none other than Richard Caring, then CEO of Nutrexo.

After graduation, Tara landed a job in Nutrexo's labs east of Seattle. By this time, her mother was living in a skilled nursing facility and her brother had fallen out of her life. Tara made Nutrexo her new home, her new family, impressing colleagues with her extraordinary ability to manipulate genes in complex organisms. While others were stuck on plants and rats, Tara began moving on to larger animals. She eventually created the first EcoCow, which was designed to improve the environment by increasing milk output and decreasing greenhouse gas emissions from cattle.

But Tara's rise brought with it some unexpected challenges. In an intensely competitive workplace, the success of her project was seen as a threat to several other research groups—including one headed by a woman named Mahnaz Mirzapour.

One morning, Tara arrived to find that her EcoCow—the first one of its kind, representative of years of incredibly difficult work—had become seriously ill overnight. The cow had been thriving up until this point, and was pregnant with a calf, just weeks away from delivery. Though Tara tried everything she could to save them, neither survived.

Tara was gutted by this loss, especially when she discovered that the animals' tissues contained toxic amounts of a veterinary drug she had never administered to them. She suspected that Mahnaz Mirzapour, who had long been vocal about her moral opposition to Tara's work, had been responsible. Mahnaz left the company in disgrace shortly afterward; though the terms of her departure were covered by an NDA, widespread speculation indicates that she was fired. (She did not respond to repeated requests for comments.)

Despite these setbacks, Tara did not give up. She only worked harder, pushing herself to deliver results under increasing pressure from the company's CEO, Richard Caring. He believed so wholeheartedly in her project, in Tara's ability to lift the company's flagging sales, that he bestowed upon her all the resources that SILO, the company's new state-of-the-art research facility, had to offer. He invested heavily in the EcoCows and told her that Nutrexo was counting on her. That she was to use any means necessary to make the project a success.

But, as we all know, the project was *not* a success. It was a complete and total disaster.

. . .

Tara Snyder relays most of this to me in an emotionless tone. "I've had a lot of time to think," she says with a wistful smile.

I prompt her to go on, but this is where the story ends. "My lawyer won't allow me to talk about SILO," she explains.

Fair enough, but I can't help asking, "How do you feel, now, about what happened there? Do you regret anything?"

Tara pauses. "I…" she begins, lowering her gaze to her hands, which are folded one on top of the other on the table. "I can't answer that question," she finally says, but the answer is written in her furrowed brow: an admission of guilt, but, also, regret.

A loud buzz startles me: my time is up. As the guard escorts me out the door, I look back at Tara sitting there, silent, repentant, the overhead fluorescent light shining on her blond hair.

• • •

Later, as I listen to our interview again, I try to make sense of it all, try to reconcile the woman I met with the image I'd had in my mind. If we are to believe the allegations against Tara Snyder, she's a cold-blooded, unquestionably evil criminal. But what if we see her with a bit more compassion, as a troubled genius who found herself under pressure so intense that she eventually cracked? As a person who has come to see the harm that she caused?

It's interesting to contrast the trajectory of her life with that of Mahnaz Mirzapour, who has by all accounts become more radical since the events of the past summer. She spent several weeks in Iran earlier in the year; she has been actively campaigning with anti-capitalist and Black liberation groups. Despite the public excoriation she faced during the Nutrexo scandal, she appears to be digging herself deeper into extremism.

I notice a change in the sound of Tara's voice when she speaks about both Mahnaz Mirzapour and Richard Caring. It tightens; she's trying not to show emotion, but her deep hatred is audible. It's easy to understand why she would be angry at Mahnaz, given their history, but why would she feel this way about Richard Caring?

It hits me, then: he heaped the pressure on, he sent her away to a facility so isolated that work became her entire life—and when Nutrexo's fortunes turned, he made her into the scapegoat.

When one considers all the press regarding the Nutrexo scandal—the intense focus on Tara Snyder, and the lack of similar scrutiny on the person heading the company—it becomes clear how the narrative played out in an all-too-familiar way. An ambitious woman was trying to make it in a man's world, playing by a man's ruthless rules, using any means necessary to get the job done—and when she failed, she was demonized for it. Richard Caring walks away with a short prison sentence, because "CEOs will be CEOs," and Tara Snyder becomes the monster, the banshee, the psychopath. She becomes a cautionary tale for all women who dare to want something more for themselves. *Be careful what you wish for, girls. Better stay in your place unless you want trouble.*

Though the outcome of the trial remains to be seen, it's virtually guaranteed that Tara Snyder will be given a harsher sentence than Richard Caring. But, if he has been given a second chance, why shouldn't she?

Annelise Stevens is a recent Yale graduate and contributing writer for *Medium*. Her articles have also appeared in *Vox, Gawker,* and the *New Yorker.*

Andi

TUESDAY, MAY 24

ANDI, ONCE AGAIN, HAD A BARB PROBLEM. THE HEADACHE JUST wouldn't go away. It had been pulsing nonstop ever since she'd read that article about Tara Snyder.

The article itself had been bad enough—but the response to it had been just as disturbing, with many people coming to Tara's defense and castigating Mahnaz. The only bright spot, from Andi's point of view, was the post that Akilah had written on a popular intersectional feminist blog.

> Nice job with the white lady feminism, defending your white sisters while throwing your brown ones under the bus. Regardless of whether Tara Snyder's allegations about Mahnaz are true (and this should not be a given), it's important to remember that Snyder is not a harmless woman who made a tragic mistake. Stevens manages to gloss over the fact that three of the four individuals Snyder abducted were Mahnaz's children, that she conducted horrific "experiments" on them during their imprisonment, that she engineered a car-bombing to mask their disappearance (playing on racist stereotypes in order to place the blame on Mahnaz and her husband Saman).

This doesn't even get into the fact that her SILO research protocol was designed to prey on marginalized populations by targeting recruitment at South End unemployment centers, or that her end goal was to introduce a product that would have had its most devastating consequences in these very communities. Yes, Richard Caring most definitely deserves a stricter punishment than what he got for his complicity in these crimes, but that doesn't mean Tara Snyder is innocent of them. She *is* "damn smart." Her crimes were premeditated; she knew what she was doing. She needs to be held accountable.

This, of course, had ignited a flame war, and things were getting so ugly that Andi had deleted all her social media apps so she wouldn't be tempted to check them. After a long conversation with Cyrus, they'd decided he would debrief Naveed about the article, since they didn't want him to stumble upon it without warning, but would keep a close eye on him to make sure he didn't get drawn into the drama.

Despite the raging headache Barb was inflicting, and Andi's frustration with the world in general, she had reached out to Jamal to set up an interview. Akilah's post had inspired her. Plus, there had been something about seeing Tara Snyder in court the day before, about reading that article—which did contain some details about her past that Andi knew to be true—and these things, coupled with seeing the film on Saturday night, knowing of the profound suffering of so many at the bottom of the food system ladder, had made her *angry*.

She wanted to do something to fight back.

Now, she sat at the kitchen island at her dad's apartment watching him "clean," which translated to shoving a bunch of clutter into his bedroom and closing the door. Jamal would be here any minute.

Even weirder, Naveed was on his way over too. Andi had mentioned the interview offhandedly, figuring he wouldn't be interested, but Naveed had surprised her by asking if he could join her for it. He'd been so lifeless lately that she was relieved to see him taking an interest in anything, and had told him that she'd love for him to be there.

The more she thought about it afterward, though, the more she wondered if it had been a spectacularly bad idea to invite him. Not much she could do about it now, though.

The buzzer sounded just as Andi's dad swept the last bits of fossilized fried rice off the table. "I'll go grab them," he said.

While she waited for them to come up, Andi massaged her forehead. *Please go away, Barb*, she thought. She could not wait until this was over.

A few minutes later, her dad returned with several others. A stocky middle-aged white woman with a camera hanging from her neck, Jamal, and Naveed. Koffka, of course, kept pace beside him, his toenails clicking on the wood floors.

It gave Andi a strange jolt to see Naveed up and about. His nerve pain had recently flared up again, and he stayed in bed most of the time because it was so painful to move around. Right now, though, he seemed... normal? He was wearing actual non-pajama clothes, a black button-down over a plain black t-shirt, black jeans, black sneakers. His eyes had dark circles under them, but he'd actually trimmed his beard and tamed his curly hair, which had been a matted mess the last time she saw it.

She had to restrain herself from kissing him. Especially when he caught her eye and smiled, actually *smiled*. He crossed the room and hugged her.

"Hey. It's good to see you," she whispered in his ear. "You okay? Feeling better?"

"Relatively speaking," he whispered back. Then he pulled away and headed for the now-clean dining room table. Andi sat next to him, but had to get up again when Jamal came over to shake her hand and introduce her to the photographer, whose name was Denise.

"Thanks so much for agreeing to be interviewed," Jamal said as he set a voice recorder in the middle of the table. "I'm working on a piece for the *Times* about the food movement, and was hoping we could get a few photos as well."

"Of course," her father said. "Have a seat. Would you like anything to drink? Coffee?"

Both Jamal and Denise accepted the coffee offer. Andi, though, set to work brewing a pot of tea to share with Naveed. Coffee would make her way too jittery.

Once they started talking, though, Andi felt more at ease. She remembered why she'd liked Jamal, who asked thoughtful questions and made her feel like her answers were the most interesting thing in the world, even while they were just debriefing about the movie, talking about her dad's upcoming Mile Seven tour and the album he was set to release in mid-June, about Andi's plans for college in the fall and Naveed's work at Zetik Farm.

Naveed, too, was friendly and charming. Which, truth be told, creeped Andi out a little. The person sitting next to her was acting just like the boy she had started crushing on over a year ago... but, she now knew, this was not the real him, not anymore. This was a mask he put on. Not that there was anything wrong with that, she had her own "everything is fine" mask that she wore often... it was just such an extreme difference compared to the rarely-talking, hardly-moving person he'd been for the last few days. Maybe that was why she found it so disturbing.

Jamal got Naveed to talk about the documentary for a while, then they paused for the photo shoot. The photographer had been taking snapshots as they talked, but her dad suggested going up to the roof deck to take advantage of its sweeping city views. Andi didn't enjoy the process much. She always felt awkward posing for professional shots, and was glad when they wrapped it up and headed back downstairs.

Her dad ordered Carribean-style sandwiches from a nearby restaurant as Andi refreshed her cup of tea. Naveed had barely touched his. Jamal turned the tape recorder back on and said, "So. Andi, Naveed. I was curious if you read the article on Tara Snyder that recently came out."

"Yeah, it crossed my radar," Naveed said grimly. Koffka whimpered, and he pet the dog's head.

"Really irresponsible. They shouldn't have published it," Andi added. Barb was begging for attention again. It was very distracting.

"The person who wrote that article spent an hour with a master manipulator and didn't interview anyone else who might have a different perspective—yet she has the nerve to suggest that she knows the 'real' Tara Snyder," Naveed said. "It's absolute bullshit. Tara was obviously trying to make herself look like some sort of victim."

"I mean, yeah, that's partially true, but—" Andi stopped. For a second, she'd forgotten herself. Forgotten that they weren't having a private conversation, that they were sitting at the table with a reporter, that everything she was saying, including a piece of information that she had never before shared with Naveed but had almost blurted out, was on the record.

"But what?" Naveed's eyes flashed fire.

"But nothing. Never mind."

Jamal had to sense that there was something juicy she'd almost let slip, but to his credit, he didn't push. Naveed looked like he didn't want to let it go either, but he stayed quiet while Andi went on, "You should read the post Akilah wrote, Jamal—I'll send it to you. She had some really good points, especially about how unfair it is to suggest that Tara Snyder deserves compassion but Mahnaz doesn't, when Mahnaz *never* stopped trying to make the world better. Even when it cost her."

To her surprise, Naveed picked up the thread. "True. Tara Snyder made sure my mom paid the price. And that nearly destroyed us. But we're still here. We're still fighting, still trying to fix some of the problems that Tara created at SILO. Like, for example, I've been involved with this fundraising campaign for farmworkers who have been infected with MRK...."

He went on about this for a while, and Andi was grateful that the conversation had turned to a less touchy topic. She stayed quiet until Jamal started listing other ways that they'd had an impact. "Getting Nutrexo shut down, for one," he said. "Now that's a pretty remarkable victory."

"Was it, though?" Andi found herself saying. Naveed was stroking Koffka's head, apparently deep in thought, and Jamal didn't interject, so she went on. "On the surface, it looks like a success. But they just spun off all their brands into separate companies that got bought up by other corporations—that's why Blazin Bitz are still around. It's not like anything was really fixed. The problems just got redistributed."

"That's because these are systemic issues." Naveed said. "It's much bigger than just one company. It's capitalism as a whole, it's the institutional racism embedded in American society. But what would you expect from a country built on stolen land, using stolen labor? I guess the usual way to spin these things is that the system is broken—that in some golden age companies were actually looking out for the best interest of their employees or whatever—but that's bullshit. The system is working exactly the way it was designed to. It was created to rely on exploitation of the workers at the bottom of the chain to enrich the resources of those at the top."

Andi winced. All she could think was, *the trolls are going to jump all over him.* After what happened with Jed, she knew that trolls weren't just bullies lurking in the shadows who never followed through on their threats. They were real people who could inflict real damage. She opened her mouth to interrupt him, but he was on a roll.

"And companies are legally required to grow every quarter so they please their stakeholders," Naveed went on. "We've all bought into the idea that things can grow and grow forever without any downsides. But that's not true. I mean, look at biology. Every living thing grows for a while until it finds a sustainable size. But if growth continues, unregulated? You know what that is? That's a tumor. It's *cancer.*"

Oh God, they're going to burn him alive, Andi thought. "But you can't really exist outside the system," she interjected. "We're all living within it. And I think that's what Mahnaz was trying to do with CFJ—"

As if he didn't hear her, Naveed plowed on. "I mean, here's an example of how screwed up things are. Pharmaceutical companies, like Genbiotix for example, make drugs, right? And they have to keep growing. Actually fixing problems, actually curing diseases—that's against their best interest. They'd be perfectly happy if everyone took daily medication. So what does it look like for the people who depend on those meds? Not only do they have their health problems to worry about, but they have to deal with their copays fluctuating, or finding that a medication they relied on suddenly isn't available because the company decided it wasn't bringing in enough money. And that doesn't even start with the other stuff going on in the 'health' industry. The cost of procedures and medical devices and insurance and everything! It's seriously fucked up!"

Jamal looked enthralled, like Naveed was handing him a pile of diamonds. All Andi could think was that she needed to stop his rant. Now.

"So you can see what we're up against," Andi cut in. "We all have a stake in this. Not just those at the bottom, but people at the top, too. Even CEO's have to make hard choices to keep up with the relentless pace. I bet they don't even realize how their decisions are going to impact people a lot of the time. It's not like they're out there cackling evilly, trying to ruin people's lives." Naveed was looking at her like she'd just committed treason, but she went on. "They're telling themselves that what they do is necessary for the 'greater good.' And their wealth insulates them from seeing the problems they're creating. That's why films like *Blood Apples* are so important. They shine a light on the things we'd rather not face. They force us to look, and think about what we can do to make things better."

The doorbell buzzed then. "Sandwiches are here," Andi's dad said. "I'll go grab them. Should we break for lunch?"

Jamal paused the recorder, and Naveed excused himself to the bathroom. Andi stood outside the door like she was just waiting for her turn, but when he emerged, she said, "We need to talk."

He nodded and followed her back to her room. Once the door was shut, he said, "Okay, so what were you going to say about Tara Snyder? What the hell was that about?"

Andi closed her eyes. Her head hurt so bad. She wished she didn't have to say any of this out loud. But she'd waited long enough. It was time to come clean. She sat down on the bed. "I have to tell you... that article. Some of the things Tara said were kind of... true."

"What do you mean?" Naveed was still standing against the door, facing her. Koffka stepped between them, like he was trying to prevent a fistfight.

"Not the stuff about your mom, I'm sure that wasn't true, but about Tara's past... her mom, her brother... she told me about all of that when we were at SILO. And she wasn't lying, I know she wasn't, she was kind of drunk and... unfiltered... when she told me. And I think part of the reason that she did... what she did... to you... was because you reminded her of her brother, who did horrifying things to her, and of course that doesn't make any of it okay, I'm just... I thought you should know."

Naveed sat down abruptly on the floor, but didn't say anything.

"I'm really sorry." She wanted to reach for his hand, but doubted he wanted to be touched right now.

"So that's it, then?" he said. "You're on Tara's side? That's why you were trying to undermine me out there?"

"*No.* I'm not on Tara's side. And, what? I wasn't undermining you—"

"Oh, really? Because it sounded like you were trying to defend Tara Snyder. Casting doubt in people's minds like that—that's how monsters walk free, Andi."

Andi was so confused. She hadn't said anything to defend Tara in front of Jamal, had she? "I just want you to be careful of what you say. You don't need people jumping on you right now."

"I know what I'm doing. So just get off my back, all right?"

Now Andi was exasperated *and* confused. This whole argument made no sense. Though she felt like yelling at him, letting things escalate, she paused for a deep breath. Then she told him the truth. "I'm just looking out for you. Because I love you. And I don't want you to get hurt."

Naveed crumpled then. Literally. His hostility seemed to melt away and he lowered his head to his knees, like it was too heavy to hold up anymore. "Too late for that," he said.

Andi slid off the bed and sat cross-legged across from him, Koffka still forming a furry dividing line between them. Andi bit her tongue and kept breathing deeply, trying to calm down, as they sat in silence for a minute.

"I'm sorry," Naveed finally said. "I shouldn't have gone off on you—that wasn't fair. I know you're on my side. All of this, it's just too much right now, talking to a reporter, dredging up all that shit, and I'm exhausted and my feet are killing me but I can't let on because I have to put on a good face for Jamal, you know?"

Andi exhaled in relief. "Oh, I know. Barb's trying to eat my brain as we speak."

"God, we're a mess." He peeked at her with almost-smiling eyes, then straightened out his legs and extended his arms. Koffka moved aside, as if opening the gates.

Andi took the invitation. She settled into Naveed's lap, leaning against his chest as he embraced her in a hug. "I love you so much, Andi," he said. "I know I'm not exactly fun to be around right now. It means a lot to know you're always looking out for me."

"Of course. I love you too, Naveed. And... you know... that you're going to be okay, right? That you'll get through this, even though everything hurts so much right now?"

She hadn't meant to go there, but the question had been nagging at her for days, and it felt good to voice it out loud.

He rested his head on top of hers. "Yes. You don't have to worry about me, Andi. I know. 'The only way out is through' and all that."

"Promise you'll tell me if you start feeling like you can't handle it, though?"

"I will." He ran his fingers through Koffka's thick fur. "We still have our pact, right? No surprises. No secrets. I promise."

Naveed

SATURDAY, MAY 28

THE MOON WAS STILL MOCKING NAVEED. IT HAD BEEN SEVEN days now since Maman died. Over a week without sleep. The nerve pain was always worse at night, but he'd grown so used to its constant presence that it was just background noise now. He kept the curtains open so he could stare out the window at the darkness. Koffka snoozed beside him, chest expanding and contracting against his back.

Every night, the fucking moon showed up in the window frame just before dawn. It was waning now, and looked like a sideways smile. He imagined it sticking a tongue out at him. *Ha ha, she's gone but I'm still here!*

Naveed thought about that book he used to like, *Keepers of the Moon.* He thought about those fictional Russians and their attempt to escape a totalitarian government by leaving earth entirely.

Escape. Naveed wanted that more than anything else in the world. Nate wanted it, too.

Maybe they weren't so different.

His mother's last night on earth had been just over one week ago. Had she slept that night? Had she looked up at the moon? Had she, too, been wishing for escape?

"Maman-jaan. Delam baraat tang shodeh," he whispered. It felt truer than ever, the tightness of his heart a never-ending ache in his chest. His eyelids were heavy as boulders. What was the point of wishing for an escape that would never be within your reach?

He closed his eyes and felt the gentle swoop inside his head that was the sensation of falling asleep. Usually, as soon as he felt it, he would jerk back to wakefulness, but tonight, there was no resistance. Tonight, he got carried under.

The sweet nothingness of deep sleep was elusive, though. He opened his eyes, and the room looked different, he couldn't even describe how, it was just *off*, just not quite right, and he tried to move but he was completely paralyzed.

That was when he realized his mother was sitting beside him.

She was looking right at him. She sat on the edge of the bed, like maybe she'd just brought him some chai nabaat or a bowl of cut fruit. She was perched there in her blue silk robe with her head tilted, her curly hair tied back in a ponytail.

Maman! He tried to say it, he tried to yell it, but his mouth didn't move. He couldn't make any sound come out. He felt frantic, because this was his only chance, and he was fucking it up. *Maman, you're here!*, he wanted to say. *Tell me what happened. I need to know! I need to know who killed you!*

She put her palm on his shoulder, and he could *feel* it, he could feel the weight of it, and he hoped that maybe it would unfreeze him but it didn't, he still couldn't move. He couldn't move, he couldn't breathe—

He sat up, gasping. Sweat pouring out of him. Koffka waited for him to take a hit from his inhaler, which he did, but the heaviness in his lungs remained. He sat there coughing for a minute, coughing with his eyes closed, because he didn't want the vision to vanish. He could still feel her hand on his shoulder.

It expanded inside him again, the enormity of this loss, and the perilousness of his situation, and the knowledge that he would never be free.

"It's okay," Cyrus said in a soothing voice. "Just a bad dream."

Confused, Naveed opened his eyes. Light was streaming through the windows now. Cyrus was sitting on the edge of the bed, the same way his mother had in the dream, or vision, or whatever it was, perching there in her blue silk robe—

The robe.

"Want to talk about it?" Cyrus was asking.

He shook his head. *No.*

"Okay. Well, just to warn you, we have to leave in an hour. Baba has a suit you can borrow. Try not to take too long to get ready, all right? We're helping Khaleh Yasmin get set up, so we need to get out of here on time."

"Where are we going?" Naveed asked.

A flicker of concern passed across Cyrus's face. "The memorial, remember? It's this afternoon."

"Oh. Of course," Naveed said. "Forgot that was today."

As soon as Cyrus left to take a shower, Naveed stepped through the creaky hallway, hesitating at the closed door of his parents' bedroom.

He knocked, and Baba opened up the door. His hair looked flat and greasy, his long beard wild and untrimmed.

"Kourosh said I could borrow a suit," Naveed told him.

"Areh, areh," Baba said distractedly. "In the closet. Help yourself."

As he walked through the dim room, Naveed tried not to look at all the little things that reminded him of Maman. Her glass perfume bottle on the dresser. Her collection of essential oils and homemade salves and balms.

Naveed was just about to open the closet door when Baba said, "I can't believe she's gone."

He kept his hand on the knob, but didn't turn it. "Me neither. I'm sorry, Baba."

"I never understood," Baba said. "All those times when she was depressed, I never got why she couldn't just look around at all the amazing things she'd created and be proud of all she'd done. Why all the love we tried to give her just bounced off and shattered at her feet. But now... now I get it. Now I see what it's like, and I hope... I hope she knew, before she...."

Baba began sobbing. Naveed embraced him reflexively, and his father returned the hug. "I hope you can feel it," Baba choked out. "I hope you know how much I love you."

"I do," Naveed said. "I know. I love you, too, Baba."

"I'm trying to tell myself that she's at peace now, but..." Baba sputtered. "But I'm just so angry at her for leaving us."

"That's normal. It's okay," Naveed said reassuringly.

Baba pulled away and put both hands on Naveed's shoulders, staring intensely into his eyes. "It isn't okay. None of this is okay. But Naveed-jaan, I need you to take care of yourself. I need you to do all the things you need to do to stay healthy, to stay safe. Because I can't lose you, too. Do you understand?"

Naveed's chest tightened even more. *Oh, I understand,* Nate was saying inside. *You think she killed herself, but she didn't, and I'm going to find out who's responsible so that you can stop blaming yourself. This will be the gift I leave you with.*

"Promise me," Baba insisted.

"I promise," Naveed said. *I promise I'll find out who killed her,* Nate added.

Baba hugged him one more time, then waved toward the closet. "Help yourself to whatever you need," he said in a dead voice. "I'll see you downstairs."

Naveed turned on the light in the closet. Maman's clothes hung there still, as if waiting for her to come back.

The blue silk robe was right in front of him. Naveed held his breath as he slipped his hand into the right pocket.

Empty.

But then he tried the left one, which did have something in it: a wad of tissues… and a piece of folded paper.

Hands shaking, he opened it up. It was a poem, he saw, written in Persian. One of her favorites, "I Will Greet the Sun Once Again" by Forough Farrokhzad.

He didn't read the poem right away, because his attention was drawn to the string of numbers that bordered the page. He counted—there were eight digits, repeating, but he couldn't tell where the sequence began and ended.

It had to be the passcode for her phone. But he would only have three tries to get the sequence right.

"Help me, Maman." The words escaped his mouth in a whisper. He felt a sudden pressure weighing him down, as if her hand had left an indelible imprint on his shoulder, a heaviness that would remain with him for the rest of his days on this earth.

Roya

SATURDAY, MAY 28

ROYA WRESTLED OFF HER TOO-SMALL SHOES AND WIGGLED HER toes in the grass. Ahhh, much better. The memorial service was about to start, and she was sitting in the front row of white chairs that had been set up in Khaleh Yasmin's backyard, fidgeting in her uncomfortable dress. At least her feet could breathe now.

She adjusted her scarf. It had soaked up the smells of saffron and fried onions and dried limes from the gheimeh polo she'd been stirring in the kitchen. Slowly, hoping the scarf would shield her face so that no one would notice what she was doing, she peeked behind her. Still no sign of Kass.

Baba sat down next to her without saying a word. He rarely talked anymore, and spent most of his days staring into space. "I'm designing a city in the clouds," he told Roya once when she asked what he was doing. "No foundations, nothing to anchor the buildings. How would you engineer something like that? I don't know, azizam. I'm trying to figure it out."

Roya had found that oddly reassuring. At least he was doing something, keeping his mind busy. Making things. Even if they only existed in his head.

Khaleh Yasmin tapped the microphone. "Good afternoon, everyone. Khosh amadid."

Roya glanced at Baba, who was sitting with his palms on his knees. She set her hand on top of his and leaned into his shoulder while Khaleh Yasmin welcomed them all and led a few prayers. She hoped he could feel what she was trying to communicate without words. *I love you and this is all so horrible and I wish none of it was happening to us.*

After that, Baba stood and talked briefly, but he was so choked up that he didn't manage to say much. Naveed stepped up to the microphone next and read one of Maman's favorite poems from a folded piece of paper in his pocket, first in Persian, then in English. It made Roya cry because the poem mentioned a flock of crows, and that made her think of all sorts of sad and happy things, including the baby crow that had given her its feather the same day Maman died. Since she didn't have pockets today, she had strung her velvet pouch onto a piece of yarn so she could wear it like a necklace under her dress. She pressed one palm to it as her brother read, imagining that she could feel the feather vibrating inside, like it had its own heartbeat.

Cyrus stood up after Naveed left the stage and announced that he and his friends had made a video about Maman. They had set up a viewing room in the office so people could watch it after the ceremony. This surprised Roya. She hadn't known he'd been working on a project like that. Then again, she never really knew what he was up to. Nobody in her house really talked to each other anymore.

The floor was then opened to anyone else who might want to say a few words. One of Maman's friends, a lady named Akilah, went first and gave a tearful speech about Maman's work with the CFJ, but then there was a pause when no one stepped forward. Even though nobody had asked her to, Roya felt like she should say something. So she walked up to the microphone and adjusted it, pointing it downward toward her mouth.

"Maman liked birds," she said. "And they liked her, too. A crow even gave her a gift once. But it's gone now." Roya glanced at Naveed, who was staring intently at his hands. She almost started telling the story about how she, too, had gotten a gift from a crow, but now that she was up here, with all these faces staring at her, she decided she wanted to keep that to herself.

What else could she talk about, though? She couldn't say what she was thinking. *Maman hadn't cared about anything for a while. She floated around like a ghost, and she ignored me all the time, and she poisoned hundreds of ants for no good reason.* All of those things were true, but this wasn't the right place to say them.

Something horrible struck Roya then. In a way, Maman had already been dead for a long time. Her body had been floating through life, possessed by the shayatin, but it wasn't her, not really. Was that why the banishing hadn't worked? Roya had been too late? But then, what had happened to Maman's soul? Was it really just... gone? Forever?

No, that couldn't be. There were times, still, when Roya would come down the stairs certain she heard Maman talking in the kitchen or typing on her laptop, only to find no one there. She had figured it was just her imagination. But what if it wasn't?

It felt like something had gotten ahold of her throat. Everyone was staring at her, waiting for her to speak.

All the faces in the crowd looked sad, or expectant, or pitying—except for one. Kass had arrived, Roya saw now, and she was smiling, beaming out encouragement. *You can do this.* "I really miss her," Roya finally choked out.

Once she got back to her seat she covered her face with her hands, upset and confused and embarrassed about her lame speech. Khaleh Yasmin rubbed her back comfortingly.

After the ceremony wrapped up and people began helping themselves to the feast Khaleh Yasmin had laid out in the dining room, Roya searched for Kass. But she didn't see her outside, so she wandered into the house. She thought about watching the video Cyrus had made, but the room was too crowded. Besides, it would be too painful right now. So she grabbed a few sweets off the dessert tray—golden saffron halva and Turkish delight, her favorite kind, rose-flavored with pistachios—and headed back outside.

Finally, she spotted her friend by the back fence. Kass was standing next to a woman who Roya assumed was her aunt Ilyana. As soon as Kass saw her, she gave Roya a huge hug.

"You came." Roya was still in disbelief.

"Ilyana's not excited to be here," Kass whispered into her ear. "But I convinced her that your mom was like a mother to me too and that I needed to pay my respects." Louder, she said, "Roya, this is my aunt Ilyana."

"Nice to meet you." Roya felt like she should curtsy for some reason.

"I am very sorry for your loss," Ilyana said. "It is tragedy."

"Yes," Roya agreed. "Thank you for coming."

Ilyana gave her an awkward shoulder pat, then left for the buffet line. Roya led Kass to an empty row of chairs. Since Khaleh Yasmin's backyard was a flat expanse of grass with a few trees and flowering plants around the edges, there was nowhere good to hide. Hopefully no one would bother them over here.

Kass took one of the pieces of halva from Roya's napkin, and Roya popped the Turkish delight into her mouth. Her eyes filled unexpectedly with tears. The taste of rose filled up her nose and her mouth and suddenly she felt like Maman was standing right next to her. It was the exact smell of her perfume.

She spat it out onto the grass.

"Got a bad one?" Kass asked.

Roya just nodded and bit into a piece of halva to distract her taste buds. Still, the smell remained in her nose. It seemed like she should enjoy this, the sensation that Maman was near, but she didn't. It just made her... uneasy. In a very familiar way. It was the same feeling of unease that filled the air inside her house. Maybe that meant something....

"I really need to talk to you, Kass," Roya began. "I don't know how to explain it, but things just feel... wrong... in my house. I know everyone's sad, and maybe that's all it is, but... I kind of feel like Maman's haunting us? Like she isn't at rest? Or something. There's this... energy... where everything feels... unsettled? Does that make sense?"

"It does." Kass nibbled on her halva. "It could be that your mother's spirit is having a hard time moving on. That happens a lot when people leave something unfinished."

Roya was relieved that Kass had taken her seriously. Her theory made perfect sense. "Is there anything I can do about it? I mean, I don't want to make things worse, but if she's... stuck... I don't think anything will get better until she moves on."

"Actually... yes. There might be something you can do." Kass pressed a small bag of dried green leaves into Roya's hand.

"What's this?" Roya asked.

Kass grinned. "Peritassa. Our ceremonial tea."

"What? Really?" Roya stared at the precious leaves. "But... how? I thought all the plants were destroyed."

"They were. But Ilyana has this box that she keeps on her dresser, and one day I asked her about it and she said my father sent it to her before he died. It was full of peritassa seeds! He asked her to keep them safe, so she never planted them, and doesn't know what they are. I took a few of them when she wasn't looking. I wasn't sure if they would sprout, it's been so long. Most of them didn't. But I got one plant to survive, and I just harvested and dried some of the leaves. Do you still have our Book of Shadows?"

"Of course," Roya said. "I thought about giving it back to you today, but it would've been too hard to sneak in."

"That's okay," Kass said. "It's for the best. Having it around would be too tempting for me. Besides, this way you can get the instructions for how to prepare it properly. It's *extremely* important that you do everything right. If you don't, it can be really bad. One time, I snuck a few sips during a ceremony, and I saw terrible things because I wasn't invited. Horrifying monsters and demons and things that still haunt my nightmares. So you have to be careful."

"I will," Roya promised. "If I follow all the directions, do you think I'll be able to talk to her? Find out how to help her cross over, or whatever?"

"I think so. But you'll need to wait till the new moon. And fire's important for calling in the spirits, but if you don't have anyone with you, put it out as soon as you drink the first sip just to be safe. I should warn you, too, you might throw up. So keep a big bowl nearby."

It all sounded very intimidating to Roya, but she would do anything to see Maman again. To apologize. To say a proper goodbye, and help her move on.

Something else struck her. "What about the demons, though? What if the banishing didn't work, and they come with her? I don't want to talk to them. I want to talk to her. By herself."

"You'll have to be extra careful about protection." As Kass went on about how to cast an impenetrable circle, Roya's vision blurred with tears. She couldn't believe how generous Kass was to share this with her. It wasn't just the tea, it was the way Kass listened, and understood, and made Roya feel like she didn't have to do any of this alone.

"Roya." The deep voice made her jump. She turned around.

Naveed was staring down at them, thunderclouds in his eyes, which were focused on the bag of leaves. "What's this?" he demanded.

"Just some herbal tea. For healing," Kass said.

To Roya's horror, Naveed snatched it right out of her hand. "Why did you come here?" he hissed at Kass. "No one invited you."

"*She* invited me," said Kass. "Now give her back the tea."

There was something about Kass, thought Roya. She looked like a little kid, but she talked like a grown-up—one who made you want to obey.

Unfortunately, though, it didn't work on Naveed. He put the tea in the pocket of his suit and stalked away.

But Kass wasn't going to let him go so easy. She grabbed his arm.

"Are you sure you want to do that? It's the only way she can see her mother again, and you're going to take that away? She'll never forgive you."

Naveed tore his arm out of her grip. Roya wondered if he was mad that she'd touched him—his face was all scrunched up in disgust. While his eyes were on Kass, Roya reached into his pocket, trying to take the tea out before he noticed.

But he noticed. Of course. And this time his hand shot out at Roya's and wrestled the small bag away.

No. He couldn't take it from her. This was all she had left: the one and only thing she wanted in this world. To see Maman, to sit with her, to talk to her again. The real Maman, not the one with the shayatin inside. The tea would show her the way, and he didn't understand, he didn't understand *anything*.

Roya looked up at the face that she used to see with such admiration. She used to think that he would do anything for her.

She knew better now.

"I hate you." The words came out low and cold, like she was blowing an icy wind at him. He froze, looking stunned, but she didn't care. He deserved it. She grabbed again at the tea, but this time he caught her wrist and twisted her arm so hard it hurt.

"Get your hands off her!" Kass bellowed. Roya attempted to pull away from his grip. Naveed abruptly let go, which made Roya lose her balance and fall back into the row of chairs behind her. She tried to grab onto one, but it tipped over and she fell to the ground, coming down on her bad knee.

There was a lot of noise from the clattering chairs, and from the people rushing to her side asking what had happened, but when Roya looked up Naveed was gone. She thought she saw someone leaving through the back gate, but it was hard to be sure, because the pain was blinding her, and she was crying because it hurt, and because Kass had brought her an irreplaceable gift that her brother had ripped right out of her hands.

Cyrus

SATURDAY, MAY 28

THE TITLE SCREEN OF CYRUS'S TRIBUTE VIDEO HAD JUST FLASHED onto the wall in Khaleh Yasmin's office when someone started wailing outside. At first, Cyrus figured it was just one of the mourners, so he ignored it. He really should have come up with a better title, he thought as the words faded to black. *Mahnaz Mirzapour: A Celebration of Life* sounded so bland. She deserved something with more personality, but he'd been in a rush and it was the best he could do at the time.

As the wail went on, though, he realized that the person sounded like they were in pain, not so much mourning-for-a-loved-one pain as oww-help-me-I've-injured-something pain.

Also, he knew that voice. It was Roya.

Andi was standing next to him, teary-eyed and red-nosed. She had composed a short piano piece for the video, which had really taken it to another level—and, as they discovered at the first showing, inspired a lot of weeping.

Brooke, Dev, Todd and Shea were all there too, but they were focused on the video and didn't seem to notice Roya's cry. Andi caught his eye, though, and they had a silent conversation. *I should go to her, can you handle things in here?* he transmitted, and she angled her head towards the door. *Yes. Go.*

He hurried outside to find a crowd of people gathered around an inconsolable Roya. She was on the ground near several overturned chairs, clutching her right leg. Someone was kneeling next to her, touching her shoulder and asking if she was all right, but Roya jerked back. "Get away from me!" she screamed.

"What happened?" Cyrus asked, but Roya didn't seem to notice him.

"I'm not sure," said the Asian woman crouching near Roya. She was wearing a black dress and a long necklace of elaborately painted beads. He vaguely recognized her as one of Maman's CFJ friends. "She and Naveed were having an argument. He looked angry and... I think he pushed her, and she fell into the chairs."

Shit. Cyrus looked around for his brother, but didn't see Naveed anywhere. He thanked the woman and squeezed in next to Roya. "Hey, sis. You okay?"

She cried harder and threw her arms around his neck. "No. He hurt me."

Cyrus wanted to ask what had happened, but he didn't want to get into it in front of the crowd. "Where does it hurt?"

"My knee... my leg... really hurts, I don't think I can walk... can you... I don't want... to be out here...." She sobbed into his shirt.

Cyrus lifted her up. "She's all right. I'm going to take her inside," he said to no one in particular.

Khaleh Yasmin stepped outside just as he was approaching the door, and he explained he was going to take Roya upstairs to lie down. She nodded and said she'd bring up some ice for her knee.

Cyrus carried Roya up the stairs, and once they were safe in the guest bedroom behind a closed door, sitting side by side on the bed against an impressive variety of throw pillows, he said, "So. What happened?"

"He was mad," she said. "Naveed. He was really mad and he pushed me and I fell into the chairs."

Cyrus was rattled by this news. He never would've thought that his brother, despite all his issues, would lay a hand on their little sister. "Why was he so angry? Do you know?"

Roya started crying again. He let her sob it out. Eventually, she took a deep breath and said, "I told him that I hated him."

"What? Why?" Cyrus had no idea there was so much animosity brewing between them. Though, come to think of it, the two of them had seemed frosty during the car ride over.

"He's barely talked to me all week," Roya said. "He doesn't care about me."

"That's not true. He loves you. He's just been... you know. Sick."

"Well, I haven't been feeling good either. Not that he would know. He hasn't asked."

Honestly, Cyrus was furious at Naveed for not being more attentive to Roya when she obviously needed him, for hurting her in front of all these people and then just running away. He was tempted to join in and start bitching about Naveed's shortcomings, but that wouldn't really help the situation at this point. "I'm so sorry, sis."

She sniffed quietly for another minute before saying, "Thank you for being here, Kourosh."

Khaleh Yasmin came in then, carrying a tray that contained a bag of ice and two plates of gheimeh polo, complete with crispy tahdig. Cyrus dug right in, but frustratingly, even the perfect wedges of tahdig didn't taste as good as usual.

After he finished, he excused himself and headed back downstairs. He texted his brother as he walked. Where the hell are you? We need to talk.

He glanced into the living room at all the people gathered here to say their goodbyes to his mother. Baba stood at the back surrounded by a crowd of well-wishers and condolence-givers, looking bewildered and sad. Cyrus spotted Kelly sitting near Dev's mom, her eyes red-rimmed.

Brooke had told him that Naveed had completely shunned them when they'd arrived at the memorial—Kelly had tried talking to him but he'd just walked away like she didn't exist. Total dick move.

Back in the office, the video had started up again. Andi was still on projector duty. *Everything okay?* she mouthed. He didn't know how to answer that, but nobody new was dead, so he moved his hand in a "so-so" gesture and she nodded. She knew that everything was relative.

After a few more cycles of the video, most of the crowds cleared out, and Cyrus set it to repeat automatically on a loop. He gestured to Andi, Brooke, and the Quirqi team, all of whom were standing awkwardly against the back wall.

"Let's go outside," Brooke suggested. "Fresh air will be good."

"Yes. Please get me out of here. There's so much crying," Shea said.

They spilled into the backyard, which was almost empty now. Most people had finished paying their respects and were getting ready to leave.

"So is Roya okay?" Andi asked.

"She'll be fine." The others looked confused, so Cyrus filled them in. "I can't believe Naveed sometimes. Does anyone know where he went?"

"Yeah. He texted me." Andi read from her phone's screen. "'Going back to the farm. Need to be alone for a few days.'"

"Huh. Guess he left with Gretchen and Frida... but, seriously. He couldn't make sure Roya was okay first? Why does he always run away when shit gets hard?"

"It's what he does," Brooke said solemnly.

"I'm worried about him." Andi spoke in a quiet voice. "I'm always so worried about him."

She sounded so sad that Cyrus felt like putting his arm around her, but Brooke had already beaten him to it. "He'll be all right. He just needs to cool down. Here, maybe this will help." Brooke pulled a baggie out of the knit pocket of her sweater. "Weed brownie, anyone?"

"Brooke, you're hopeless," Cyrus said.

"Hey, you gotta do what you gotta do." Brooke removed one and passed the bag around.

Cyrus hesitated when it got to him. He kind of wanted to try one—if ever there was a time to tune out your sorrows, your mother's funeral had to be pretty high on the list—but he, Todd, Dev, and Shea had a conference call scheduled this evening with Philip. They were supposed to be discussing whether to take Raymond Whitaker's deal, which Cyrus had so far managed to avoid talking about with the rest of them. He'd told them he wanted to wait until after the memorial, since he was too busy dealing with the fallout from the Tara Snyder article and working on the tribute video, which was true, but he also wanted to put off the conversation as long as possible. What if they felt the same way Philip did? What if they secretly wanted to get rid of Cyrus?

He passed the bag along. No one else took a brownie either. When it came back to Brooke, she said, "You guys sure? Might help you feel a little better."

"How long does it last?" Cyrus said. "We have to do something important for work in a few hours."

"It's a pretty mild dose. You should be fine."

"Is it okay with you if I try one?" Cyrus asked the group at large, mostly Shea, who was the designated driver of the Quirqi Train. "It's been... a rough week."

Shea shrugged. "I'm not going to stop you. But can we please talk about the call *before* you get stoned?"

"You've got time. It won't take effect right away," said Brooke.

Reassured, Cyrus took a brownie. "Andi? Want to join me?"

"My dad's here," she said. "He'll kill me." She reached into the bag, took one out, and ate it with a rebellious grin.

Dev and Todd both ended up taking one, too, and the three of them raised their brownies in a toast before popping them into their respective mouths. Cyrus chewed thoughtfully. It was fudgy and rich, with a strong nutty aftertaste—a pretty good brownie, actually.

Even though it was vegan. And weed-laced.

Soon enough, they fractured into groups. Andi and Brooke branched off into their own conversation, while Cyrus and his Quirqi buddies clustered together.

"So, what's the plan?" Shea asked. "What are we going to tell Philip?"

Something struck Cyrus then. A stupid idea, possibly. Or maybe it was brilliant? "I want to meet with Raymond," he blurted.

Silence.

"Uh, what." Dev raised his eyebrows.

"Raymond's problem is with me specifically. According to Philip, anyway. But think about how impressed the others were when they met us face to face. When they played *Bugpocalypse*. They *got* it, they understood what we want to do. I'm charming, right? So if old man Whitaker just met me in person, maybe he'd forget about his stupid vendetta against my mom or whatever it is that makes him see me as a 'liability.'"

Cyrus was hoping that the mellowness would have kicked in by now, but he still felt normal. Which was a disappointment. He was ridiculously nervous about how they were going to respond.

Todd was the first to speak. "Bold move."

"I'm sure this goes without saying," Dev added. "But you know we're on your side, right Cy? I mean, yeah, it would be awesome if Blanchet funded us, but not if it means cutting you out of the company. That's not even on the table as far as we're concerned. So yeah, if you want to ask for a meeting with Raymond, go for it. Can't hurt."

"Agree. It's worth a try," said Shea. "Tell Philip what you just told us and see what he says. We'll back you up."

"Totally," Dev said. "I don't think Philip sees this the same way we do. He's mostly in this to make money, he's always been honest about that. And, yeah, we all want Quirqi to be successful, but it's got to be about more than the bottom line."

Todd giggled. "Bottom line," he said, drawing an invisible line across his butt.

Dev laughed too, and Cyrus joined in, because suddenly the phrase was hilarious, and he hadn't even realized just how unconsciously stressed he'd been since that meeting with Philip, so worried that the rest of them would abandon him. But they hadn't. They were sitting here in the grass with him, and they were laughing, and the sun was shining on his face.

The grass was growing beneath him, too. He could feel it pushing through the earth. And look at it, what perfection! It was so green, so soft, that he wanted to lay on it. So he did. Brooke and Andi settled down next to him. Andi was sniffling a little, and he remembered when she'd stood next to him at the burial and scattered dirt over Maman's body, and there it was again, the shock that hit him whenever he realized that Maman was never coming back, when he thought about her there in the ground, where it had seemed so lonely and so... final. But it didn't anymore. He understood now: she'd been buried so that she could feed the earth the way it had fed her. Dust to dust. A never-ending cycle. It was sad—but also, it was okay. An intense peace descended on him. She was gone, and he would miss her forever, but he was still alive. He was alive! And it was okay for him to go on, it was okay for him to be happy and work on Quirqi and help keep his family together.

He looked around at everyone's faces. At Dev, twirling a blade of grass between his fingertips and murmuring to Todd, who was gazing at Dev like he was a god or something. At Shea, lovely Shea, absorbed in her phone. At Andi and Brooke, lying side by side in the grass next to him.

"You guys are like the best friends ever, did you know that?" Cyrus could see it stretching out before him, a satisfying life containing all these people. He envisioned the six of them sitting around a futuristic hovering table sharing stories of their happy relationships and good health and fulfilling work. "We're going to change the world! All of us, I mean, we're amazing, aren't we? Someday we'll look back at this and realize it was just the beginning, because everything's going to work out. Everything's going to be okay!"

It felt so true, here in the soft grass under the glow of the sun. Cyrus closed his eyes and let the moment fill him up until he was brimming with it. This was what Maman wanted him to know, he felt certain. Even though things might be shitty right now, they always worked out in the end.

Naveed

SATURDAY, MAY 28

NAVEED WALKED DOWN THE MUDDY PATH TO HIS CABIN, RELIEVED to be alone. The voices and laughter of the others followed him into the dusk. Aviva was visiting again, and had been sitting on the porch eating from a bowl of strawberries balanced on her enormous belly when he and Gretchen and Frida had returned from the memorial service. The interns, indistinguishable white women in their twenties with names like Carly and Camille, had also arrived during his absence. Everyone had gathered for a leisurely Shabbat dinner on the covered deck, safe from the drizzle that had rolled in. He stayed long enough to meet them all and take a few bites of challah from the plate they gave him, but everything he put into his mouth turned to dirt on his tongue. He excused himself and they let him go, saying they understood, but they didn't really.

He closed the cabin door, locked it, flopped down on his bed. Koffka curled up beside him, but he scooted away. Even Koffka couldn't comfort him right now. Everything was falling apart. Dissolving. It was getting so hard to tell now which inner voice was Nate's, and which was his own. He wasn't sure who he even was anymore.

In one pocket of his suit jacket was his mother's phone, as well as the poem bordered by the numbers that, he was certain, made up her passcode. In the other was the tea from Kass. He felt bad that he'd hurt Roya while taking it away from her, but he'd been infuriated to see his sister cluelessly accepting a baggie of illegal drugs from her "friend." It was the right thing to do, he knew, even though the way he'd done it had gotten a little out of control. So what if everyone else thought of him as heartless and cruel? They wouldn't be wrong.

It was better that he was on his own now. He had the tea. He had the phone. Between these two things, he was going to figure this out.

Tonight, he would find out who had killed Maman.

He got up and hung his suit jacket over the chair that she'd sat in when she'd visited. This cabin had been one of the last places she'd seen before she died. She had sat with him right here, across the table, drinking tea from the mug that he still hadn't washed—it was piled among the dishes that he'd never gotten around to cleaning.

He fished it out of the rest. There was still a thin ring of tea left at the bottom, and he could see the sticky half-moon impression that her lip balm had left. He didn't want to ever clean it off. He wanted to keep it this way forever, the way he would always keep that last voicemail she'd sent him, even though it ripped his heart to shreds every time he listened to it.

He positioned the mug in front of the seat she'd sat in, turning the handle so that she could grab it with her right hand and take a sip. The bowl of walnuts and dried cherries was still sitting in the middle, so she could have something to snack on if she was hungry.

He sat across from her seat and set the phone on the table. "I hope you don't mind," he said out loud. "I'm sure you understand why I'm doing this. If you won't tell me, if you can't tell me... then I'll have to find out what happened on my own."

Koffka perked up his ears at the sound of Naveed's voice. He loved Koffka, really he did, but he also kind of wanted to be alone right now. Alone with Maman.

"What's the code?" he asked. "Which number does it start with? Kourosh told me I only have three chances."

He was hoping for some sort of sign, but his question was met with silence.

Naveed unfolded the poem. Each of the four corners had a different number in it. Which one would she have started the sequence with? It could be any of them. He started with the top left: even though the numbers were in Persian script, which typically was written from right to left, numbers were always written left to right, same as English. He typed the code into his mother's phone:

7 9 4 3 6 7 1 9

It didn't work.

Okay, moving on to the second corner, then. That one started with the three.

3 6 7 1 9 7 9 4

No. It didn't work, either. The phone displayed a terrifying message that he had one more try. If he failed, all the data would be locked and could only be retrieved with the recovery password.

"What should I do?" he asked. His chances of guessing—or finding—the recovery password were remote. And he'd probably have only three tries for that one, too.

He sat for a while, thinking. Looking between the phone and the poem and the baggie of leaves. The sun disappeared below the horizon. Koffka was curled up on the bed with his head on his paws, watching quietly.

The tea. He couldn't wait any longer. He had to try it. Maybe it would work, and he would find her there, and he could ask her what happened without having to open the phone, or he would come across some clue that would make the correct sequence of her passcode clear.

But he would have to do this alone. Koffka would know something was up, and he couldn't risk the dog running to get help.

He turned on his own phone, ignoring the stream of notifications and opening the browser. Once he confirmed it would be safe, he powered his phone down again and started some hot water in the electric kettle. He brewed a strong cup of sonbol-eh tib tea. Not for him. For Koffka.

While he waited for it to cool, he pulled on a sweater, found a head lamp, and cleaned out a jar that he could use as a makeshift thermos. To keep Koffka from wondering what he was up to, he started on the dishes, scrubbing at them halfheartedly.

Once the tea was lukewarm, he fixed Koffka his dinner. Koffka preferred his dry dog food soft, so Naveed usually added water. This time, he added the tea instead. Koffka sniffed it, then looked up at Naveed.

"It's okay, boy. Go on. You'll like it," he crooned encouragingly. Koffka took a few tentative nibbles, then scarfed down the rest of the bowl. He was probably hungry. It had been a long day.

Naveed kept working on the dishes until Koffka finally curled up in bed, eyes drooping. He lifted his head briefly, looking at Naveed with inquisitive eyes, as if asking, *What did you do to me?*

He lay down next to the dog. "It's okay. Time for sleep. Here, I'll join you."

Once Koffka's breathing had deepened, Naveed got up carefully, but the dog didn't even budge. He was usually a light sleeper. So it must be working.

Still, he couldn't risk drinking the tea here in the cabin. Naveed had no idea how long this would take, and if Koffka woke up, he might ruin everything. So he poured hot water into the jar with the tea leaves, screwed on the lid, then put on his work gloves, head lamp, and boots. He closed the door quietly behind him and headed into the woods, holding the hot jar in his gloved hands.

It didn't take long for him to realize what a bad idea it had been to venture into the woods at night. The sounds here. The rustling branches. The snapping twigs. The creatures moving, slithering, creeping. Even though his mind kept repeating *you're okay you're okay you're okay*, his body didn't want him to forget that *WOODS AT NIGHT ARE NOT SAFE* and was sending all the usual warning signals. But even the racing heartbeat, tightened stomach, and breathing-through-a-pillow airway constriction couldn't stop him now. This was too important.

He stuck to the small trail he'd cleared after he'd first moved into the cabin. He wasn't even sure if he was technically on Zetik's property anymore; the farm backed onto public lands that were so hilly and densely forested that no one had ever developed them. His trail led to a clearing, at the center of which was something that had intrigued him so much he still hiked out here sometimes just to sit and wonder.

It was a pit in the ground. A square hole, about ten feet by ten feet, ringed by a crumbling stone foundation. He had no idea why it was here. He'd described it to Gretchen and Frida, but they didn't know either. The pit itself was maybe five feet deep, but the foundation stretched an additional few feet above ground.

He sat on a tuft of moss, looking at it from a safe distance. The ground was damp. Everything was. He unscrewed the lid of his jar and sipped the tea. It tasted similar to any other medicinal herbal brew. Slightly grassy, slightly bitter.

He didn't stop drinking until it was gone. Then, he waited.

Naveed focused on his breath for a while, but that just made him more anxious. He stood up and stepped to the edge of the pit. It might have been six feet deep, actually. Like his mother's grave. Like those graves at Orcinia, Alastor's compound, he'd seen their remnants in the distance once, mounds of dirt and fluttering yellow caution tape. In Orcinia, this tea had apparently been so important that they'd built an entire retreat experience around it.

A glimmer of hope flickered inside him. Would he really see his mother again?

A twig snapped. He turned, expecting it to be her, but no one was there. The trees were starting to look different, though. When he softened his focus, they became towering, hooded figures swaying above him. He sat down again, shivering.

"Maman?" he asked nervously. "Are you here?"

Oh. There was a big lurch in his stomach. It felt very distant, though. His whole body did now. When he looked down at his hand, it gleamed brightly, like all his cells had turned into stars.

Her hands glowed with points of light, as if she held every star in the cosmos in her tiny fingertips. The last line of *Keepers of the Moon*. The thought of it blew his mind: it was like he was understanding it for the first time, understanding *everything*. It was all starting to make sense in a way he couldn't even put into words. If he just stayed with it a little longer, he would finally figure everything out, all the connections that had eluded him in his normal life.

But this burst of insight fizzled quickly, because his body was making itself known again. The discomfort in his stomach was growing, and in his chest too, the tightness that just wouldn't go away. He could visualize it now, like he was peering inside his lungs, a dense black tumor that looked like a clump of earth, sending out tendrils that pulsed and threaded their way into his blood, his bones, his brain, traveling to every part of him.

He looked down at his hand again. It wasn't glowing anymore, it was hard and blackened, fingers shrunken against the bone.

Naveed was alone. Maman wasn't here. No one was here, no one but him and his rapidly decaying body. He wasn't even in the forest anymore, everything around him was barren and desolate. Nothing but gray. Gray everywhere he looked. Walls on either side of him. The ground sloped downward, curving into a dizzying spiral that had no end.

That same sense of expansiveness that had grabbed him earlier, when he felt like he was going to understand everything, came back to him, but twisted and upside-down. This is forever, he understood. This is the way it's always going to be. Een neez bogzarad, this too shall pass—that was the biggest lie of them all, because no, it would never end. He was on his own and this spiral was endless and he was stuck inside a decaying body and *he would never get out.*

"Do you want to see?" came a sudden, booming voice.

It startled him. He looked over his shoulder, but he was still alone.

"I want to see my mother," he said nervously. "Is she here?"

"Do you want to see?" the voice repeated.

He understood that the answer needed to be yes or no. Still, he was afraid to say yes to such a vague question: there were lots of things he didn't want to see. Yet if he answered no, he might never find out what had happened to her. Who had killed her. Wasn't that who he *really* wanted to see?

"Yes," he said.

The lights came on then. Fluorescent lights, humming, and he knew where he was: these were the corridors at SILO. He wanted to run in the opposite direction, back up the spiral, but his body wasn't cooperating. His legs were withering now. He managed one step before falling onto the hard concrete. He tried army-crawling, but his arms, too, had shriveled, become hard and useless.

The light flickered. It went out for a second, then returned brighter than ever. There was a puddle on the floor in front of him now. Not water. Smelled like piss. Somewhere else, he was puking his guts out, but not here. Here, all he could do was stare into the puddle, which was so still he could see his reflection.

But the face staring back at him was not his own. It was the one he'd been looking for, the one he should have expected all along.

Tara Snyder. She stared back up at him, her eyes empty but infinite at the same time, the ground beneath him shuddering and shaking as her eyes grew larger and larger, until the whole vision was swallowed up into darkness.

At that moment, something inside him shifted. Naveed had wasted so much time, so much energy, trying to fight Nate. But Nate's fury, Nate's desire for vengeance, Nate's impulses toward violence and self-destruction—all of these things belonged to Naveed, too.

There was no separation between them anymore. Finally, they were united, and the way forward was clear.

Andi

SUNDAY, MAY 29

"SO. ARE YOU READY?" BROOKE ASKED.

Andi sat across from her at a coffee shop. Two copies of the Sunday *Seattle Times* sat next to the lattes they sipped from paper cups.

"No." Andi's voice got drowned out by the bellow of the espresso machine, so she had to repeat herself. "No, I'm really not. This is such a weird feeling. I'd almost rather not know what Jamal wrote. Ignorance is bliss, right?"

"Well, you can sit there enjoying your bliss for however long you want, but I'm going in." Brooke flipped through the paper until she came to the magazine.

"Holy shit." She held it up for Andi to see.

Naveed stared back at her. Well, not at her, exactly, he was focused on a point just beyond her, some distant horizon. The photograph, a close-up in black and white, was remarkable, like an iconic shot of a world leader or something. His curly hair was attractively tousled by the wind, and his eyes... they were mesmerizing. Like they contained entire worlds inside.

She kind of wanted to stare into them forever.

She finally managed to tear her eyes away long enough to read the title. *The New Revolutionaries: How Seattle Youth are Changing the Face of the Food Movement.*

Andi flipped through the pages of her own copy until she came to the cover story. She skimmed the backstory about SILO and Nutrexo until she got to the section recapping their interview at Andi's dad's apartment. She winced when she noticed her face in a small photograph on that page. Annoyingly, they'd chosen one where Naveed was looking straight at the camera, while she was gazing up at him, like she was his disciple or something, waiting for his advice on an important matter.

Andi's temples pulsed as she read. Jamal had included a few quotes from her, but nothing memorable. However, he'd printed pretty much Naveed's whole anti-capitalist rant, with a pull-quote in huge letters repeating, "The system is working exactly the way it was designed to." The article wrapped up by talking about the documentary, but Vanesa's filmmaking contributions were barely mentioned. The main focus was on Naveed's role in the film.

Brooke slammed the paper down on the table. "Wow. That was. Just. Wow. I can't believe he's implying that Naveed is, like, our leader or something. That's crazy! He can barely get out of bed, how's he going to lead a movement?" Brooke paused. "I'm sorry. That was unfair. But you know what I mean."

"Yeah. I do." Except for the interview with Jamal, and the therapy and probation appointments Andi made sure he kept, Naveed had spent nearly the whole week in his bedroom. The suggestion that he was spearheading a social movement seemed especially ludicrous at the moment.

Andi folded the magazine in half, hiding Naveed's face on the inside. She suddenly felt very exposed. Like everyone around them was listening to their conversation. "Come on. Let's go."

They stepped onto the sidewalk, newspapers tucked under their arms. "I'm glad we didn't read it online," Andi said as they walked.

"I don't want to know what the comments say."

"Oh, I'll be writing one of my own. I mean, it's so typical, right? Focus on the charismatic guy who has a lot to say, but don't even *mention* the people who do the actual work. Like you!"

"And CFJ," Andi said. "I kept trying to steer the conversation there, but... I guess I'm just not as interesting as Naveed."

Brooke shook her head indignantly. "You are, though! He just focused on Naveed because it was easy, because that way the story fits right into the myth that one guy in shining armor—it's always a guy, right?—rushes in to slay the corporate beast and then everyone lives happily ever after. But that's just a fairy tale. It doesn't work that way in real life."

They crossed the street to a small neighborhood park, where little kids bumbled around the playground under the watchful eyes of their parents or nannies or whoever. Andi and Brooke headed for the swings and sat down.

Andi took out her phone, knowing that she should text Naveed, even though she had no idea what to say. He'd run off from the memorial service after hurting his sister, and had made it clear that he wanted to be alone. Now there was this article to talk about, too. So much to unpack.

When she checked the screen, she saw she'd missed several texts. One was from Ah-ma, who was back at home now. They'd discharged her earlier in the week, though she had many months of outpatient stroke rehab ahead of her. The message was short, only two words, but it made Andi smile nevertheless. So proud.

Her mom and dad had texted too, both variations on that theme. Andi didn't really want to think about the article anymore, or the complicated emotions it had dredged up, so she scrolled on until she saw that she'd also gotten a text from Frida. It was a response to one Andi had sent earlier asking how Naveed was doing. She'd been worried since she hadn't heard from him. I'm afraid Naveed isn't well this morning, came down with a stomach flu. He's getting some rest now but I'll check in on him later to make sure he's doing all right. Congrats on the article though!

Andi sighed and showed it to Brooke. "What is going on with him?" she muttered.

"Always something, huh?" Brooke said.

"I should probably check up on him, right? Just to make sure he's okay. But... it's just..." Andi paused, thinking about spending her day stuck in a small cabin in the middle of nowhere, listening to him vomit. She should probably be used to hearing that sound after Ah-ma's many months of cancer treatment, but the thought of it made her own stomach twist. "I'm just really tired of being around sick people," she said softly.

"He'll be fine, don't worry. Frida's got it under control. And you need to take care of yourself, too. Caregiver burnout is real."

"I'm not a caregiver," Andi said reflexively. "It's just..."

Brooke looked at her, head cocked, eyebrows raised in challenge.

Despite herself, Andi laughed. "It's just that everyone expects me to take care of them."

"Exactly." Brooke jumped out of her swing. "I have an idea for a much better way to spend the day. Let's get out of here."

"Where are we going?" Andi asked as they walked back to Brooke's car.

"I'm taking you to Folklife!" Brooke said. "We're going to listen to music and watch the buskers and eat junk food and just fucking relax for a few hours."

With everything going on, Andi had totally forgotten it was Memorial Day weekend. "Yes!" she shrieked enthusiastically, surprising herself. "It's perfect. But—can we make a quick stop first?"

An hour later, they walked into the festival, transformed. Andi had picked up an electric-blue wig and vintage go-go style dress at a thrift store, and Brooke kept tossing her now-long blonde hair over her shoulder. They mingled with the crowds, eating ridiculous amounts of kettle corn and French fries and vegan gelato. They stopped occasionally to chat with people who were tabling for various nonprofits, and to watch every busker that caught their ear.

One of the musicians had set up an electric keyboard, and Brooke managed to cajole him into letting Andi play a song. Brooke then borrowed the ukulele of a random guy who was strumming on a picnic blanket under a tree, and they stumbled through a cover of "Somewhere Over the Rainbow." Their performance was lamentable, but neither of them cared, because they were having too much fun. They laughed as they took exaggerated bows for their audience of five. After Brooke had returned the uke, they sat down on the grass and listened to its owner strum joyous tunes.

"Brooke, you're the best." Andi leaned her head on her friend's shoulder.

"Hey, Andi—can I tell you something? But you have to promise not to laugh. I haven't told anyone this yet."

Andi ran her fingers through the soft grass. "Of course. I'm not much of a laugher anyway."

Brooke smiled. "I like that word. Laugher." She took a deep breath. "So… yeah. I'm thinking of applying to law school."

Andi blinked in disbelief. Brooke—she of ten thousand hair colors, she of sleeve tattoos and vegan weed brownies—was nothing like Andi's idea of a straitlaced law school student. But the more she thought about it, the more it made perfect sense. "Yes. You should!" She paused. "You just want to legalize cannabis everywhere, don't you?"

Brooke snort-laughed. "Ah, you caught me! But… it's more than that. I feel like I could really make a difference as a lawyer. I know it'll be a ton of hard work—"

"But you'll be amazing at it," Andi said.

"Maybe I'll apply to UCLA. Or even USC. Follow you down to SoCal."

"YES!" Andi said with such ferocity that the uke player actually stopped strumming for a second. "Yes! Come down to LA with me. We can be roomies."

They turned towards each other on the grass and talked excitedly for a while, dreaming out loud, imagining what their college lives would be like. Maybe, Andi allowed herself to think for a moment, what Cyrus had said at the memorial was right. Maybe they really would look back on these days, years from now, and realize that they were just the beginning of everything.

Roya

SUNDAY, MAY 29

ROYA WAS ABOUT TO DROP A PIECE OF BREAD INTO THE TOASTER when she heard a small explosion.

The bread flew out of her hand. She crouched on the floor, pressing her back against the cupboards. What *was* that? It had come from outside, but it sounded close. She checked the back door. It was unlocked.

Too afraid to move, she listened until she heard it again. *BANG.* And again. *BANG. BANG.* Now that it had fallen into a rhythm, she relaxed a little. She knew this sound.

She stood up and opened the curtain. Baba was swinging his axe wildly, chopping at the trunk of the elderberry bush against the back fence.

Roya's breath caught in her throat. The bush was just getting ready to flower, and soon after that the berries would grow, the ones Maman used to harvest and make into a syrup that helped them feel better when they were sick. And now Baba was trying to destroy it?

She opened the back door and ran through the backyard in her socks, not even caring that they were getting wet and muddy. "Baba!" she yelled, but he didn't seem to hear her.

He swung the axe with so much raw energy that it scared her. This person was so different from the Baba she'd grown used to, the one who sleepwalked from his bedroom to the armchair and back again, lost inside the impossible cities he was building in his mind.

She called to him again, but he still didn't turn. It was like he didn't even know she was there.

Desperate to get him to stop, Roya pulled on his shirt. "Baba! *Stop it!*"

He turned around, axe still in his hand, and she pulled back just in time to avoid it slicing the end of her nose.

"What are you doing here?" he yelled.

"You have to stop! It's about to bloom! The flowers, she loved the flowers, and the berries—"

"She's not here!" Baba still hadn't lowered the axe. "It doesn't matter, because she's not here. She's gone, and it doesn't matter, nothing—"

"Sam!" Auntie Leila was coming down the path. She was still wearing her sleeping clothes, an oversized Billie Eilish t-shirt and purple sweatpants. "Sam! What are you doing?"

Baba lowered the axe blade to the ground, but didn't answer.

"Roya, come inside with me." Auntie Leila sounded stern. If Roya hadn't known better, she would've guessed that she was in trouble.

Still, she followed obediently, leaving Baba there looking deflated. She glanced back a few times to make sure he didn't pick up the axe again. It remained on the ground.

"Are you all right?" Auntie Leila asked once they were inside the kitchen.

The bread Roya dropped had landed next to the sink. She poked at it. "I'm fine."

"What happened?"

The bread had soaked up some water that was pooling around a dirty bowl. Roya mushed her fingers into it. "He was trying to chop down the elderberry bush. It was one of her favorites. She liked the flowers, and they're about to bloom. I had to save it."

Auntie Leila frowned. "This has been very hard for him. It was so sudden, and—stop that. It's gross." She scooped up the soggy bread and tossed it into the compost bucket on the counter.

Baba walked through the back door then. "Roya-jaan. I'm so sorry," he said. "I was just... I needed to do... to do something...."

"So you decided to kill one of her favorite plants? What good was that supposed to do?"

"Sam," Auntie Leila cut in. "There's something I want to talk to you about. Roya, can you go collect a few eggs? I'll make breakfast."

"No, thanks. I was just going to have toast." Roya didn't want to leave. Baba thought everything would be fine if he just said he was sorry? It didn't work like that.

"Roya. Please go." Auntie Leila stared intensely at her.

"Fine," Roya grumbled. She went outside, but not to check for eggs. She crouched right beneath the kitchen window, which was old and thin. If she listened closely, she could just make out their quiet voices inside.

"What do you think you're doing? You scared her half to death. You've got to pull yourself together," Auntie Leila was saying.

"I know. I'm trying. I didn't know Roya would come out here, I'm just..." He sighed. "I got a voicemail. The life insurance claim was denied."

"Oh," Auntie Leila said. "Oh, Sam. I'm so sorry."

"The whole thing... it disgusts me. They're basically saying her life was worthless, because... because of how it ended, and... I shouldn't have bothered. Should've known this would happen."

"You had to try," Auntie Leila said gently. There was a long silence, some sniffling, then she went on, "Remember when our parents died? I was Naveed's age, just starting college, and to have them both go like that, one after the other... I felt so alone, I had no friends, I was crying all the time... and then you all came to visit me for a weekend and rented that house on the beach. Cyrus was adorable, such a happy baby, smiling and clapping and making us laugh. And Naveed would snuggle with me whenever I cried, bringing me the things he found in the sand and telling these wild stories about them, and it was all just so sweet. That visit… it saved me, Sam. It was like a little light I could carry with me whenever things got dark."

"That whole thing was Mahnaz's idea," Baba said. "She always knew what to do."

Another silence. "I've been thinking," Auntie Leila continued. "Maybe it would be easier if Roya came back to Oregon with me on Tuesday. She could spend the summer down there."

What? Roya couldn't leave now! Not with Maman's ghost roaming the house still, desperately crying out for help crossing over. Since Naveed had taken the tea away from her, Roya was brewing another batch of herbal cider in her closet—but she would need to talk to Maman *here*, where Roya could feel her restless spirit everywhere. Besides, as much as she loved her auntie, she was distracted by her work and often didn't know what to do with Roya.

No. She couldn't go. She *wouldn't* go.

But, she knew, Baba would never let that happen. He wouldn't want them to be apart.

"Really?" Baba said. "Are you sure you'd be up for that?"

She couldn't believe it. He sounded relieved—like Roya was a huge inconvenience that he'd just been waiting to get rid of.

"Of course. It would be no problem. I'm mostly writing grants this summer anyway, and she could come along if I need to do any field work. Once the trial's over, maybe the rest of you could join us."

"Oh, I don't know. I'm already missing so much work—"

Roya stood up and limped back inside. "No," she said. "No! I'm not going to Oregon! I want to stay here!"

Auntie Leila winced. "It'll be fun. I'm not far from the beach. And there's an ice cream shop right down the block—we can go whenever you want."

"I'm sorry, Roya. This will be better for everyone," Baba said woodenly.

Roya fumed. So it was true: he really didn't want her here. "What about school?"

"We can work something out. I'm sure they'll understand."

"And PT? What about that?"

"There are plenty of physical therapists in Coos Bay," Auntie Leila said.

"No. I don't want to go." Roya crossed her arms, even though arguing seemed useless at this point.

"It'll be for the best," Baba said. "I'm going to miss you, azizam, but we'll talk every day, okay? And you can tell me about your adventures, and you won't be missing out on anything." Baba lunged forward and hugged her. "This is for the best. It really is."

Roya wriggled out of his grasp. None of them were even *listening* to her. She might as well already be in Oregon, far away from all the things that mattered.

Naveed

SUNDAY, MAY 29

THE DOOR SHOOK. SOMEONE WAS KNOCKING ON IT. "NAVEED? Are you in there?"

He didn't bother rising from the cocoon of his bed. His throat was all shredded up and he felt profoundly depleted. He was a hollow shell with all the meat scraped out, only the brittle exterior remaining.

Stupidly, he hadn't locked the door behind him when he'd come in sometime before dawn. The only thing he'd cared about then was making it to the toilet without puking on the floor.

Gretchen peeked her head in. Her smile faltered when she saw him. "Oh, my—are you all right?"

"I can't work today," he rasped. "I've got the stomach flu or something, I don't want you to catch it."

"Oh, dear. I'm sorry to hear that—I wish you were feeling well so that you could enjoy this more."

She held up a magazine. An actual paper one. It took him way longer than it should have to realize that his face was on the front page. "It came out this morning. A lovely article. We're so honored to have you here with us, Naveed. Would you like me to leave it with you?"

"Nah, that's okay, I'll read it on my phone later. Need to go back to sleep for a little bit."

"All right. I'll have Frida stop by with some broth." She began closing the door, then paused. "Oh, and Naveed, I wanted to let you know... if you ever would like to reconsider working the market when you're feeling better, we'd love to have you help out with that again. Sales really dropped off this last week without you there."

"I'll think about it. Thanks." He turned his back, and she closed the door.

He lay there shivering for a while as the cold air she'd let in floated through the room. Koffka woke up and whined, so Naveed crawled to the door, still under the blankets, and opened it so Koffka could do his business. The dog moved stiffly, groggily. Naveed supposed he should feel bad about that, but he was filled with numb.

Frida came by at some point. She bustled around in nurse mode, taking his temperature and pulse, cleaning up the mixing bowl he'd been vomiting into for the past few hours, making him drink a can of coconut water while she heated broth on the hot plate. She ladled a mug for him and turned off the burner.

"Drink up. Need to get rehydrated," she said as she handed it to him.

He sipped. Tasted like mud.

"You know, Naveed, there was a time in my life when I became very ill." Frida's eyes were focused on the dirt she was wiping off the floor. "I was still Fritz then. We were still living in East Berlin. I'd been feeling like a stranger in my own body for a very long time, but I was terrified of losing Gretchen and Aviva if I told them the truth. Then my father died. He was a difficult man, very cold, very strict—but it wasn't until after his death that my brother and I discovered he was a Holocaust survivor. It was a secret he kept his entire life, and it ended up poisoning everything around him. Can you imagine what it would be, to live with that weight?"

She paused, but he didn't answer. He just wanted her to stop talking, to go away.

"I fell ill not long after that. It was very bad. I had to stop working, but no one could figure out what was wrong. I kept thinking about my father, and finally told Gretchen my own secret. It took some time for her and Aviva to adjust, but they understood and wanted to support me. It wasn't that I became well again immediately, but I finally began to recover. I wasn't able to get better until I had become my true self, until everything was out in the open. Because what we bury, it has a way of resurfacing in painful ways. Sometimes even across generations. So if there's anything you ever want to talk about, I'm here."

What the actual fuck was she getting at? He couldn't take this anymore. "Thanks, but right now I just want to sleep," he told her, then retched into the now-clean mixing bowl.

Thankfully, she took the hint. "All right. Get some rest." She washed her hands and opened the door. "Zei gezunt. I'll be back to check on you later."

He stayed in bed for a while after she left. Eventually, he got up, blanket still pulled tight around him, and turned his phone on. As he waited for it to wake up, he reheated the pan of broth. Then he sat down at the table, across from his mother's place, where her mug and her phone and her poem still sat, and picked up his own phone.

The notifications flooded in. Baba had texted earlier in the morning. I love you, son. That was all.

Cyrus's last texts were sent after Naveed had abruptly left the memorial, a stream of messages berating him for hurting their sister and running away afterward, insisting that he needed to come back and apologize to her in person. Well, at least he could trust Cyrus to be real with him.

If he only knew the hell that Naveed had saved Roya from. But he wasn't going to bother explaining that to Cyrus.

There was a short message from Andi, too. I'm worried about you, please tell me how you're doing #ns2

Great. She had invoked the pact. To keep up appearances, he needed to come up with an answer that sounded sincere. After typing and erasing for what felt like hours, he ended up with something he hoped would appease her. I feel like shit the memorial was so hard and I know I freaked out and I'm sorry. Been puking all night, probably something I ate, don't worry Frida's taking care of me thank you for checking in but right now I just need to rest

She responded quickly. So sorry you're sick :(but thanks for being honest with me. Feel better! I'll check in tomorrow

Another text appeared on his screen while he was reading her reply. This one was from Jamal. Naveed, I'd like to thank you again for taking the time to talk to me. The response to the article has been phenomenal so far. I won't give out your contact info without your permission, but I've forwarded you an email that I received from a literary agent colleague interested in getting in touch with you. Best, Jamal.

While he sipped more mud-broth, Naveed found the article online and let his phone read it to him, since he couldn't get the words on the screen to make sense. The text-to-speech voice mispronounced his name, of course, and its robotic cadence gave the story an extra layer of detachment, so that even though it was parroting back words he vaguely remembered saying, they felt very distant, like a speech a different person had made.

Once it ended, he still felt nothing. He supposed that Jamal had done a good job of presenting him exactly how he wanted to appear publicly, like a person who was passionate about something, a strong person ready to fight. And it was good that his words had not been diluted, that his anger and resentment at the food and pharmaceutical industries, at the system as a whole, had come across very clearly. The focus on the documentary was great, too. But it was weird how Andi was barely in there, when he knew the truth: she was a whole lot better at fighting than he was.

The article also placed a sudden, intense amount of pressure on him. After all, words were one thing, action another, and he didn't have any idea what he was actually going to *do* about any of the issues he'd raised.

He opened his email. The literary agent gushed about Naveed's work in an enthusiastic letter, obviously eager for him to get in contact. It made him feel like vomiting again.

He set down his phone and stared across the table at his mother's empty chair. "I don't know what to do," he told her.

Koffka lifted his head. Was it only Naveed's imagination, or was there a hint of resentment in the dog's eyes?

Naveed thought about what Gretchen had said earlier, about how she wanted him to consider working the market again. And then it hit him, so obvious that he wondered why he'd never seen it before.

He was only here because Gretchen and Frida wanted him to be the face of their company, their salesman. Because he was good for business. He had been their pawn, he had been playing the great capitalist game just like they were, just like everyone was.

"Does it even matter what I do?" he asked. "Does any of this matter?"

The silence gave him his answer. The answer was the emptiness, the lack of response, the very definition of nothing.

The answer was no.

He picked up the poem his mother had copied down. *I will greet the sun once again.* Spoken like someone who actually looked forward to starting a new day. He definitely couldn't relate.

Naveed looked at the sequence of numbers around the edge, and this time, one string of numbers stood out. 1979. Yes—that had to be the beginning. 1979, the year Maman's father had been executed. The year she and her mother had escaped Iran at the beginning of the Islamic Revolution and emigrated to Lebanon and eventually to the U.S.

He typed in the sequence that he was sure, now, was correct. 1 9 7 9 4 3 6 7.

The phone opened up.

The background of her home screen was a glowing red tulip. He felt like he was watching something bloom.

The first thing he did was disable the passcode, so he could come in whenever he wanted without having to bother typing that long string of numbers. Then he decided to start with her texts, to see whether she'd gotten any strange or threatening messages.

He didn't see anything like that, but one message caught his eye. Ok, thanks! Have a good trip! It was from Andi.

What? Why was she texting his mom?

He opened the string and scrolled all the way back up to the top. It had started in April, right after he moved out. Sounds like he loves it at Zetik! He showed me around his cabin, it's so cute, Andi had written. His mother responded, Glad to hear it. How was his mood?

Andi had texted back a sun emoji. His mother responded with a rose. That means thank you. I appreciate you doing this, Andi.

It went on and on. For months. A weather emoji from Andi that apparently corresponded to his mood on a given day, a flower emoji from his mother.

Is that why Andi had called him every day? So that she could check up on him and report back to his mother?

He was so disgusted, it was all he could do to keep scrolling. But at the bottom of the string was something even worse. Andi had texted a photograph of four men, two of whom Naveed recognized.

There was Alastor, in his clean-cut alter ego, looking different, but still recognizable, without his long gray beard.

And standing right next to him was Tim Schmidt.

He looked exactly the same as the day Naveed had first met him back at Englewood, when he'd been masquerading as a CDC scientist studying MRK. Sandy blond hair, floury skin, tweedy jacket.

Oh, Tim Schmidt has big plans. Big plans.

Naveed found himself shivering again. Seeing those two men together was bad enough, but even worse was Andi's message beneath them: Hey Cy, I need your help figuring out who these guys are.

And then: Oops! Never mind. Sent by mistake.

Followed by Maman's reply: Let this go, Andi-jaan. It doesn't mean anything.

And please leave my sons out of it.

Naveed set the phone down, pulling his blanket tighter. Where had Andi gotten this picture? And she'd gone behind his back, asking Cyrus for help instead of telling Naveed about it, not even stopping to consider that he might have useful information, too. Whatever happened to *no surprises, no secrets?*

She had broken the pact.

She had been keeping so much from him.

He understood, now. Maybe it was the after-effects of that purge. By getting rid of everything, all that excess baggage he carried around, all the emotions that clouded his judgement, he could finally see things for how they really were.

Andi had just been a spy for his mother. She had never loved him. Well, maybe, at one point, she had loved the *idea* of him, but that wasn't really *him.*

"How could you do this to me?" he said out loud, slamming his closed fist down on the table, causing the bowl of cherries and walnuts to knock into Maman's mug. He looked beyond it to her empty chair. "Both of you—but especially Andi. She betrayed me. She lied to me. How could she. How could she."

He had to keep repeating it for another few minutes before he could move on, before he could touch the phone again and close the text string. But he couldn't do that without seeing the photo again, reigniting the fury—and the fear. What did it mean? Had Tim Schmidt been working with Alastor and those other two men? Had they been plotting something long before Alastor's death? *Big plans.*...

Had Maman known what they were up to? *Let this go. It doesn't mean anything.* Had *she* not let go, though? Had she figured something out? Is that what had killed her?

He opened her browser, hoping that he might find something useful in her search history, but of course Cyrus had set it up so that her searches were not tracked. So he decided to try looking in her email. There were hundreds of unread messages: notifications of upcoming events, appeals for donations from various organizations, petitions she would never sign. It was all so overwhelming that he nearly closed it again, but he forced himself to keep scanning subject lines for potential clues.

Then he saw something: a message, still unread, that had been sent the day she died. The subject line was, "RE: Genbiotix Application # 31336."

Dear Ms. Mirzapour,

Thank you for coming in for an interview earlier this week. We regret to inform you that we have decided to hire a different candidate with more recent experience in the industry. You may want to consider applying for an entry-level position as a lab tech in order to become familiar with contemporary research methods. We do not currently have any such positions available, but wish you luck should you seek to find employment at another company.

Best,
Charisma Cooper
Genbiotix Pharmaceuticals

"What?" Naveed said. "*What?* Genbiotix?"

Koffka looked up at him, weary. *Here we go again.* But Naveed couldn't hold back; he was too shocked. "What the fuck, Maman? Why would you apply to work there?"

Silence.

"And what a load of bullshit. 'Ms. Mirzapour.' You have a PhD, they should be addressing you as 'Dr.'! And Charisma Fucking Cooper is telling you to get a job as a lab tech? Yeah, I remember her. Of course I do. She's the one who gave you her card when I was in the ICU last summer. Were you hoping she would help you get your foot in the door? But why, Maman, why? Were you planning something? You had Big Plans too? Trying to take them down from the inside? Yeah. That makes sense. But of course Charisma would have guessed that, wouldn't she? You're probably blacklisted from every company Nutrexo was ever associated with…."

He trailed off, feeling queasy again, because now he was thinking of that article about Tara Snyder, the pieces of it that were true, the horrible things Maman had done to sabotage Tara's research at Nutrexo, the events that had been set in motion all those years ago. He hovered over the saucepan, expecting something to come back up, but nothing did.

Next he checked her sent messages, but that only made him feel worse: most of the emails were addressed to various debt collection agencies, as well as the bank that serviced their home loan. He could barely focus by this point, but the words "foreclosure" and "bankruptcy" came up a lot.

"How could that be?" Naveed asked Maman's empty chair. "The Nutrexo settlement... should have covered... I don't understand...."

He was exhausted by now, but he couldn't stop. He moved on to the next folder, her unsent drafts. This one only had a few messages. The most recent was a few months old, dated March 30.

Akilah,

I heard the news. Another innocent young Black man slain by the hands of the state, with no justice in sight. I am so sorry—though no words can make heartache like this go away. Every time this happens, I think of you. Every time this happens, I wonder, how do you do it? How do you keep fighting, day after day, when these tragedies keep happening over and over?

I think I know the answer: because you have to. And I understand that, because I have the same compulsion, but lately I'm feeling stuck. I'm constantly on the defensive, just fighting, fighting, fighting all the time. There is beauty in the struggle, I've always believed that, but sometimes the struggle doesn't feel so much like swimming against the tide as it feels like drowning. Maybe it's just the depression talking, but I can't stop wondering, am I making any difference? Am I doing the wrong thing, continuing on this path?

Everything's falling apart. The settlement money never came through, we're living on credit card debt and home equity loans, digging ourselves deeper every day. Which just makes me feel guiltier for sticking it out in the CFJ, when I could actually be putting my PhD to use. Makes me sick to think about working for a biotech corp, but I'm afraid that might be the only path left for me now.

Even that might not be open to me anymore though. I think I'm on their watch lists now, maybe I'm just being paranoid but obviously I haven't gotten over being interrogated by Homeland Security after coming home from Iran, stuck in that hell for hours when all I wanted to do was hold my daughter who was in the hospital at the time. I was just bringing my son some traditional medicines but all they could think was *Terrorist! Biological weapons!* It dug up so many of the things I work hard to keep buried so I can make it through each day... and then there's the trial... you have no idea how much I'm dreading that, watching Tara smirk at me while I testify, the things she'll say about me, I know she's going to dredge up a whole bunch of other traumas from the past, and having to relive everything that happened last summer, I don't know if I can take it.

Thank god for Saman, though. Seriously. When things get bad like this, he always manages to convince me that everything will work out. I don't know if it will or not. But I do know that I owe it to him, and my children, to not give up. No matter how much I want to.

I'm so sorry, this letter went sideways, I didn't mean to dump all this on you, of course I won't do that, I'm never going to send this so I guess I should just stop

Naveed lowered his head into his hands. He couldn't even look at her empty spot across the table anymore, couldn't speak to her. That heaviness had settled into his chest, into his whole body, and he felt her hand pressing into his shoulder, holding him down. He couldn't cry. He couldn't feel anything but this unbearable weight.

He opened her photos next. The one that appeared first, the last photo she had ever taken, was a view he recognized. It was the ridge right above the ravine where she had fallen. It was sunrise, and the whole valley was bathed in golden light. He could picture her there on the mountain, hiking up to the ridge to greet the sun, just like in the poem she had carried in her blue silk robe. But what had happened next? There were three paths, all of them seeming equally possible now.

She had greeted the sun before being attacked from behind, her phone dropping to the ground, not even time to fight back before she was thrown over the edge.

She had greeted the sun before saying her final goodbye to the earth, setting her phone in the underbrush so that it might give answers, however messy, to those she left behind. She leapt from the ledge, soaring into the empty air like a bird, feeling the brief release, the freedom, before crashing down to the rocky ground below.

She had greeted the sun, giving thanks for surviving another bout of depression, but the rocks were slick from rain and she'd slipped, her phone had clattered into the brush, she had fallen, she had tried to find something to grab onto but she couldn't, her head cracked open on the rocks and she died there, at the bottom of the ravine, her face pressed up against the dirt, bathed in the golden light of dawn.

Somehow, the last possibility now seemed the most painful.

It got his stomach churning again, so he crawled back to bed. Koffka curled up next to him, but he couldn't even feel the dog's warmth. He didn't think he'd ever feel warm again.

His thoughts swirled into a spiral, orbiting around one central figure. Tara Snyder. No matter what had really happened up there on the mountain, Tara Snyder was the person responsible for his mother's suffering—and for his. For his entire family's. No matter how you followed the threads, it all came back to Tara Snyder.

And Naveed was the only one who could bring her to justice.

III.

Scythes

Andi

ON THE MORNING THE TRIAL WAS TO BEGIN, ANDI WAS PULLED out of an anxious half-sleep by her buzzing phone. She'd been keeping it on at night in case Naveed called, though she hadn't heard anything from him since the day of the memorial.

She looked at the screen and blinked in disbelief. She rubbed her eyes, thinking that maybe she'd misread the name, but she hadn't. It was impossible, but somehow it had happened all the same.

Mahnaz had just texted her.

She opened the string. There at the bottom were their last messages to each other, the ones she kept re-reading even though they shattered her heart every time, Mahnaz informing her of her camping trip, Andi telling her to enjoy it.

Now, though, two more messages had been added, each in their own small bubble.

I just have to know one thing

Did you ever really love me?

It took a second for her to understand, but once she did, her whole body filled with numb dread.

Naveed had somehow managed to get into his mother's phone.

And he had seen their entire conversation. Andi scrolled all the way back to the beginning, when they'd figured out their code, when his mother had thanked her for keeping an eye on him.

Oh, no. This was bad. Very, very bad.

Heart pounding, she wrote in reply, Naveed? Of course I love you! I've always loved you.

It sounded so generic, but it was true. Part of her wanted to yell at him, *Are you for real?! Why do you have to doubt this—haven't I done enough to show you? The whole conversation is just proof of how much we care about you!* But at the same time, she could imagine how it would feel to be on his side of it, looking at how she'd boiled down his complicated moods into a little icon on the screen, reporting back to his mother like some sort of double agent. Plus, there was that photo of Alastor and the other men, and the accidentally-sent text showing she'd tried to contact Cyrus behind Naveed's back.

She didn't know what else to say. I'm really sorry about this, she wrote, even though that wasn't quite accurate. While she did feel guilty for not being entirely honest with him, she had been glad to have this connection with Mahnaz, and happy to do her part in relieving someone else's worry. I was just trying to protect you, she added, then sent the message.

His reply felt like a kick in the gut.

You're lying

I can't believe I ever trusted you

She started typing frantically. I'm not lying! It's the absolute truth, everything I did is because I love you, and if I can't convince you of that

But before she could finish her thought, let alone send it, a stream of new messages came in.

You broke the pact

You've been keeping so many secrets from me

We're done

Goodbye Andi

Andi threw her phone forcefully onto her bed. Rage swelled up inside, threatening to consume her. Though there were plenty of things she wanted to say to him, she decided against texting him back. Sometimes silence hurt more than words anyway.

She wished she could call Brooke and vent, but it wasn't even five in the morning yet. So she was left to soak in her feelings of resentment alone. Seriously, how could he do this to her? Just call off their whole relationship by text, not even giving her the chance to explain? Especially today, when she had to face Tara Snyder in court again. But as Andi and her father and Cyrus and Sam were undergoing the trauma of seeing Tara again and the torment of being questioned in court in front of her, Naveed would be hiding out in his little cabin at the farm, sulking and convincing himself that nobody loved him.

Well, fine. Hadn't she tried her very hardest to show him otherwise? If he couldn't see it, wasn't the burden on him? She couldn't force him to see something he didn't want to see.

Knowing that she wouldn't be able to find sleep again, Andi got out of bed. It was too early for a run, but she felt like banging on the piano. She got her MIDI keyboard set up on the small desk in the room, plugged it into her laptop and headphones, then started channeling her rage into music. Early on, she happened on a riff she liked. And, even better, she knew exactly where it belonged. Way back in the fall, she'd started working on an epic sonata that told her story through music. She'd stalled out on it a while ago, knowing it was missing something, but not sure how to fix it.

Anger, she realized now. That's what it needed. Most of the song had come from places of fear and anguish, but it needed this too, this bright raging energy, to balance the more sorrowful emotions. The fiery sun beating down on churning water.

She poured herself into the music. As time flowed around her, she slowly came to a heart-wrenching realization: she was angry, yes, but also relieved. How much brain space did she spend worrying about Naveed every single day? Wondering what he was doing, dreaming about their next time together. And even when they were finally reunited after months apart, he hadn't wanted to touch her, hadn't wanted to kiss, had been pushing her away this whole time, and she, too, had been pulling apart from him, but she didn't want to leave because she was afraid for him, and she didn't know if she'd ever stop caring about him, but maybe this was never meant to be a romance, he hadn't wanted it to be in the first place, maybe he'd known something like this would happen and both of them would end up getting hurt, and he had no space in his life to keep getting hurt, but then neither did she, and why was it always up to him to call the shots, he was the one to give permission for it to begin and end, while she went along with whatever he said, like that version of herself in the photograph who spent her life gazing adoringly at someone who didn't—couldn't?—love her the way she wanted to be loved, building her life around something that turned out to be an illusion.

She didn't want to be that girl anymore.

A knock on the door startled her. "Peanut? I've got breakfast ready— want to join me?"

"Be there in a minute." Andi pulled off her headphones and looked at the clock. Hours had flown by. She saved her work and slipped on the blouse and slacks she'd ironed the night before, after her dad went out and bought an iron. As she put on her makeup in the bathroom, she kept feeling a strange buzzing sensation that might have been anxiety, might have been anticipation, might have been… excitement. The buzz of freedom, maybe.

She would have to talk these confused feelings over with Brooke later, but there was no time now. Only time to force down breakfast and head out the door.

Her dad was preoccupied on the drive over, not that she wanted to discuss this with him anyway. She wanted to think about her composition instead of those cruel texts that still barbed their way into her mind from time to time.

At least she wouldn't have to see Naveed today. And she'd have plenty of other things to distract her. As she walked through security and followed her dad to the courtroom, she focused on her music. She couldn't stop thinking about how to work this new movement into her composition, about how amazing it was going to be now that she'd finally figured out what was missing.

They surrendered their phones at the door to comply with the courtroom's "no tech" policy. Cyrus and Sam were already inside, sitting close to the front, but all the seats near them were taken, so Andi and her father found a spot in the back. She watched them talk to the prosecution attorney, their heads bent together in quiet conversation.

Andi returned to her composition as the room filled up. Nervous chatter surrounded her, but it couldn't touch her, not when she had her musical shield insulating her from everything that hurt.

Tara Snyder was escorted in. As she took her seat at the defense table, Andi's heartbeat raced, but she breathed through it. She just had to get through this day, and her composition would be waiting for her at home. Tara Snyder was not going to ruin her life. Instead, Andi was going to make something great out of the horrible experiences she'd suffered through. That would be the ultimate victory.

The double doors at the back closed. Everyone quieted down. Andi was looking around the courtroom, wondering if things were about to start, when the doors opened again.

Naveed stepped inside, shoulders straight, head held high. He was wearing the same suit he'd worn to his mother's funeral, all black, and his beard was much thicker than he usually kept it. He looked older somehow. Skinnier, too. Almost skeletal.

But what surprised Andi even more than his sudden appearance here, in the place where she'd least expected him, was the fact that he was alone. Koffka was not with him.

That didn't make sense, Andi thought, increasingly panicked. Koffka went *everywhere* with him. She hadn't seen the two of them apart since the day he'd adopted Koffka.

Andi was so shocked that she almost didn't notice Tara Snyder swiveling around to see what the commotion was all about. But she saw the amused expression on Tara's face as Naveed walked down the aisle. Naveed, for his part, didn't look at anyone. He took a seat at the front, right behind the prosecution's table, still straight-shouldered, not hunched over like usual.

"I thought he wasn't coming?" her dad asked quietly.

All Andi could do was shrug, because the judge had entered and everyone was instructed to stand.

The trial had begun. And Naveed was here. And she didn't know why. Andi watched the back of his head as if that could give her clues, but there were no insights to be found in that tangled mess.

Naveed

TUESDAY, MAY 31

NAVEED DIDN'T EXPECT TO BE SPENDING HIS LAST HOURS ALIVE with one of the interns, but he didn't have a choice. Gretchen needed the pickup, so Naveed had to tag along with Camille—that was this one's name—as she drove the van up to the market. She seemed delighted that he would be joining her, and said she was happy to drop him off at the courthouse on the way.

He wondered how she would feel about it later, once it was all over and she saw what had happened on the news. Once she realized she had carpooled with a terrorist—since, by the end of the day, that's what everyone would be calling him.

He didn't feel like talking, but she kept yammering at him and some old sense of politeness, of general human decency, took over and he decided to listen to her instead of going over the plan for the millionth time in his head.

"Where's your dog?" she wanted to know, of course. "What's her name again?"

"Koffka," Naveed said. "His name is Koffka. And he's not feeling well today." Because Naveed had drugged him again.

"Oh, I'm sorry to hear that." Camille paused, like she was working herself up to say something. In the quiet space, Naveed watched the countryside rushing by outside the windows. It was like looking at a painting, at someone else's rendering of a thing that didn't actually exist.

"Do you like having a service dog?" is what Camille finally came up with. He glanced over at her and she caught his eye, then turned away, chastened. Maybe he looked too intense. He should probably tone that down.

"Uh, yeah," he said. "He's helped me a lot." He stopped himself from thinking about all the ways Koffka had made his life better over the past few months, because going there would make this a whole lot harder. This was for the best, Naveed reminded himself. Koffka was tired of being stuck with him. He'd be so much happier waking up in a Naveed-less world where he could roam the farm and play with Astro all day. Gretchen and Frida would adopt him, and soon the dog would forget.

He was only an animal, after all.

"How do you do it?" Camille said suddenly. "At the market, I mean. People come to the stand looking for you, asking about you... but then they leave, like they don't want to buy anything from me."

Naveed realized that, even though he'd just looked at her, he couldn't picture her in his head. But he didn't want to glance at her again. Better to not give her a face. He stared at his hands. He curled his toes inside his shoes. Then he knew how to answer. "I give out samples," he said. "Thin slices, right from my knife, instead of cutting up a bunch of things and leaving them on a plate for people to take and walk away. The human touch, that's what's important. Because the fruit tastes better when you feel connected to the place it's from and the people who grew and picked it."

Camille was nodding enthusiastically. "Connection," she said. "And belonging. That's what it all comes down to, doesn't it?"

She kept talking, but Naveed was distracted by the sudden burst of uncertainty exploding inside him. His plan was already in motion, he couldn't back out now, but... was this *really* the right thing to do?

Of course it was. Tara Snyder was a force of darkness, sucking all happiness from his family. As long as she lived in this world, they would never be at peace. And he was the only one who could stop her. He would gladly martyr himself to make sure justice was truly served.

He was dying anyway. Might as well make it worthwhile.

Naveed zoned out while Camille droned on. As they drove, the view morphed from trees and fields to warehouses and shipping yards. Eventually, they neared downtown. He looked out the window at a tent city encampment under the freeway. A shopping cart was turned on its side, spilling out a collection of indistinguishable items that could have been either trash or treasure to their owner. Impossible for him to know.

"Oh my gosh, I went off on a tangent there," Camille said. "And I almost forgot to tell you, but just yesterday, some guy came up to the farm stand and asked for you. Said he was an old friend of yours. Tim something... I want to say... Smith?"

"Tim Schmidt?" Naveed asked. At any other time, he might have found this alarming, but now it was just mildly interesting.

"Yes! That was it. I asked if he wanted me to pass on a message or anything, but he just wanted you to know that he stopped by and said hello."

"Thanks for telling me." For a second, Naveed was tempted to ask more—what had she said to him? Had she mentioned that Naveed lived at Zetik?—but that didn't matter anymore. This was, thankfully, the end of the line for Naveed. Tim Schmidt was irrelevant.

Camille was pulling over now. Naveed realized with a start that they were here.

It was time.

"Do you need a ride back? I could come get you after I finish at the market. I was going to grab dinner in the city—want to join me?"

He shook his head. "No. I have other plans."

"Of course. That's fine." She waved it off.

He should just go. Why was he stalling? "Thanks for the ride. Um, good luck at the market today." He slammed the door closed before she could respond and turned his back on her, on the van, on Zetik Farm and Gretchen and Frida, on everything but the task in front of him.

He moved his foot carefully. Even though the obsidian knife was safely wrapped up in his shoe, he didn't want to risk slicing his skin. He was certain he'd be able to foil the metal detector, but it would be a shame to call attention to himself by leaving a trail of bloody footprints on the floor.

He still had a few lingering worries about whether the knife would be sharp enough, whether he'd be able to stay conscious at the sight of all her blood rushing out when he stabbed the blade right into her throat, so that she would know how it felt to be unable to breathe, so that he could watch her struggle for her last breaths before he went, too. He wasn't sure how that part would go, it seemed likely that one of the guards would shoot him, but he would go ahead and slice up his wrist veins once he'd taken care of her, maybe slash his own jugular, just to make sure the job was done right. He wasn't going to prison. He would rather die than go there.

The promise of death offered so much freedom from worry. He hadn't even brought his inhaler, or his phone. Today, he was completely untethered.

Now, he squared his shoulders and headed straight into the crowd of reporters clustered in front of the building. Cameras flashed. People kept darting in front of him with their microphones, invading his personal space, but he ignored them and kept on walking. It was funny how having such a clear, important mission could make it easier to brush off these small annoyances.

Once he made it successfully through security—they patted him down, of course, but didn't make him take off his shoes—he met up with the prosecution attorney, who said he could testify after lunch. He had called her the night before, having found her number on his mother's phone, and had told her he'd had a change of heart and wanted to testify. But, she explained now, he would need to be prepped, so could he meet with her during the lunch recess?

He said he could, and then he walked into that courtroom and sat about ten feet away from Tara Snyder. He didn't look at her, he was careful to sit up very straight, he kept feeling her attention straying his way, like she was casting an invisible net around him, throwing out tethers, but he made sure that they didn't drag him in, he focused very hard on not returning her stare, all of this was much harder than he'd thought it would be, and the hours stretched by slowly, and while Baba was up on the stand Naveed recited poetry in his head so that he wouldn't have to listen to a word he was saying, he kept his eyes on his father's shoes, which had a little streak of mud at the tip that Naveed wished he could wipe off, and he waited and waited for it all to be over.

Finally, lunch came, and Naveed hurried out with the attorney before anyone could talk to him. He tried to pay attention to what she was telling him, even though he knew it would all be over before he even got to the stand. After they talked, he went to the bathroom and, in the safety of the stall, removed the knife from his shoe and held it in his hand. He sat there for a long time, just feeling it, the rightness of this, the relief that it would soon be over.

He walked back to the courtroom, holding the handle carefully inside his jacket pocket; he had to be cautious not to cut himself, since his unfeeling fingers could so easily slice against the blade. He took a seat in the nearly-full courtroom just as it returned to order. Tara Snyder wasn't back yet, the guards would be escorting her in at any moment, and then they would call him to the witness stand and he would start down the aisle, but then he would lunge at her, and it would happen so fast that no one would be able to stop him, and he would live his last glorious moments taking everything away from her, as she had taken it from him.

Andi

TUESDAY, MAY 31

AS EXPECTED, THE FIRST MORNING OF THE TRIAL WAS PAINFUL. Emotionally, of course, but physically, too. Andi's headache had started pounding when opening statements began, and it hadn't let up since.

Sam had been called up to the stand as the first witness. He stumbled through his testimony, obviously nervous, at several points close to tears. One thing came through loud and clear, though: Tara's actions had taken an immense toll on his family. Hopefully that would help persuade the jury. Andi wanted her to be locked up for a long time.

Through it all, Naveed sat ramrod straight. Andi found herself constantly distracted by his presence, wondering why he'd showed up. Only one option made sense: he was going to testify. Which she should probably be glad about. He could make any argument compelling, so his testimony would only help their case. But she couldn't let go of how *wrong* this felt.

As soon as they broke for lunch, Naveed and the prosecution attorney left through one of the side doors together. So he was really going to do it. Why was she so worried about this?

Her dad left to grab some takeout for their lunch. She and Cyrus made their way through the interior gauntlet of reporters, then ducked into a stairwell and climbed to the fourth floor where it was quiet.

They sat on a bench against the wall. Andi rubbed her forehead.

"What a circus, huh?" Cyrus asked. "Did Naveed tell you he was planning to testify?"

Andi sighed. "No, I had no idea. I hadn't heard from him in days, then all of a sudden this morning… he broke up with me. By text."

"*What*?" The outrage in Cyrus's voice was clear. "Wow, harsh. He can be such a jackass sometimes. Honestly, A, that's no way to treat someone as awesome as you are. Especially after all you've done for him."

"Yeah, well… he texted from your mom's phone. I guess he hacked in somehow. She and I had this conversation going, where I was checking in with her every time Naveed and I talked, just to let her know how he was doing. He saw it, and… let's just say, he was not happy."

"Hold up. He got in? To her phone?"

"Yeah. This whole thing… I'm just worried. I don't get why Koffka's not here. It's really bothering me."

"Same. Here's my theory, though: Naveed didn't bring him because he doesn't want to show any signs of weakness in front of Tara."

"That's ridiculous. Having a service dog doesn't mean you're weak."

"I know. But I think it's important to him that he looks like a 'normal' person in public."

Andi supposed that made sense. She wished she could just ask Naveed, but that was obviously out of the question.

Her dad texted to ask where they were, and once he arrived with sub sandwiches and chips, they ate in silence. Andi could barely force down a quarter of her sandwich. Even Cyrus didn't have much of an appetite for once. After he ate, he excused himself to the bathroom and said he'd meet them back downstairs.

This time, Andi saved him a seat when she returned to the courtroom. But before Cyrus got back, Naveed came in alone, hands shoved into the pockets of his suit jacket, and took a seat at the end of one of the rows. He still didn't look at them. He kept his hands in his pockets even after he sat down, looking slouchier than before. A slight tremor shifted through the curls of his hair. He was so nervous he was shaking.

She couldn't blame him. Andi was anxious enough about taking the stand herself, and couldn't imagine how much worse it must be for him. Especially without Koffka there to calm him down.

But she forced herself to look away, to stop thinking about him, because that's what he always did, he always took over her thoughts, and he had closed himself off to her, and she needed to do the same to him.

When Cyrus arrived, he slid into his seat, then whispered, "Hey, A, so this is weird, but... I think I just spotted our mystery man."

It took Andi a second to process that sentence. "Wait. What are you talking about?"

"The guy from that photo you texted me, the one with your grandpa and Alastor and Raymond Whitaker. The fourth guy, with the blond hair. I saw him as I was going into the bathroom. His hair was longer, and he didn't have a goatee... but, yeah. I'm almost positive it was him."

Andi turned around, scanning the now-full courtroom, but she didn't see the man anywhere. "What's he doing here?"

"I don't know. Not here for the trial, apparently, but there's plenty of other stuff going on in this courthouse right now. He could be on jury duty for all we know. Maybe I'm wrong, maybe I was just seeing things. But I don't think so."

This wasn't helping Andi's anxiety any. Next to them, Sam was leaning back against his chair looking exhausted. Andi did the same. She closed her eyes. She breathed. She tried not to think about anything. The headache was like a knife cutting into her skull, localized right behind the scar on her forehead.

Time passed. The judge still hadn't appeared, and neither had Tara Snyder. It seemed like they should be starting by now. What was taking so long?

After what seemed like ages, the bailiff rushed out of the judge's quarters and closed the heavy courtroom doors.

"Attention, everyone," he said. "We've been placed on lockdown."

Up until now, the room had been filled with a low murmur of voices, but after this announcement it grew incredibly loud. The reporters in the media section were in uproar, asking what was going on.

The bailiff motioned for them all to be quiet. "I don't have any more information at this time, but we'll need to stay put until we're given the all-clear."

"Is there a shooter?" one of the reporters asked, and a wave of dizziness nearly bowled Andi over. Good thing she was sitting down.

"I don't have any more information," the bailiff said gruffly. "As soon as I do, I'll let you know." He disappeared back into the judge's quarters as the room exploded into chatter. Several people asked loudly if they could have their phones, probably wanting to see if the outside world had more information than the useless bailiff, but no one answered their requests.

Andi looked down, breathing hard again, only to find that Cyrus's hand was very close to her knee, an open invitation. *I'm here for you.* She took it, squeezing gratefully.

"You all right, Peanut?" her dad asked from her other side. She leaned her head against his shoulder instead of responding. No, she wasn't all right. She was terrified that someone was going to burst through the doors any second, maybe even the man from the photograph, his blond hair blazing, letting out a storm of gunfire, was that what this was all leading up to, her whole life pushing her to this one miserable moment....

Stop. That didn't make sense. If someone was shooting up the courthouse, they would have heard gunshots, right? And everyone had to go through security, had to walk through a metal detector, there was no way they'd be getting a gun through there. The only people with guns on this side were the police, so there was nothing to be afraid of... right?

People were milling about now, pacing, anxious. Cyrus nudged her in the elbow. "If someone had heard shots, they'd be on it right away.

This place is crawling with cops. Don't worry. It'll be okay."

Andi appreciated that his thoughts echoed her own, but still, nothing would be okay until she knew what was going on.

There was something very claustrophobic about being stuck in a room with a bunch of anxious people, everyone desperate for their phones. She couldn't help sneaking glances at Naveed, who had curled into himself, head in his hands. Sam went over to talk to him and made the mistake of touching his shoulder. Andi watched him recoil, heard his cold, angry words cutting through the chatter, traveling straight to her ears: "Don't touch me. Leave me alone."

Sam came back looking like he, too, was about to lose it. Andi's dad took Sam aside to a corner of the courtroom, where they huddled together talking quietly.

"Should I go over to Naveed?" Cyrus asked her.

"Seems like he wants space," Andi said. "Don't want him to freak out in front of all these people."

"Agreed," Cyrus said.

Twenty long minutes passed before the bailiff came back out. When he did, everyone stopped talking. He asked for their attention, even though that was unnecessary: he already had it.

"There's no immediate danger, and we'll return your phones shortly, but the lockdown hasn't been lifted yet. Please be patient. I'll let you know when we have more information." The announcement was met with groans, but the bailiff seemed oblivious to them. Instead of leaving, though, he headed down the aisle, straight towards Andi.

"Sam, Jake, Andi, Cyrus. Please follow me. He should come too," the bailiff said, gesturing toward Naveed. Stunned, they all stood up. Sam got Naveed, and they followed the bailiff silently into the judge's quarters.

The room was small, but they crowded inside. Andi held onto Cyrus's arm for support, since she felt like she was about to faint.

Once the door was shut, the bailiff said, "Okay. I just spoke with an officer. No one can leave this courthouse until a full search has been conducted, because... Tara Snyder is missing."

Wait. But. How? How could Tara be missing? Andi barely had time to let this sink in before Naveed slid to the floor, holding his chest. His breath was labored, eyes frantic. Sweat beaded on his forehead.

Sam rushed over and crouched beside him. "Do you have your inhaler?" he asked. Naveed shook his head.

The judge looked concerned. "Should I call a medic?"

"No!" Naveed said hoarsely. "No medic. It's just. Panic."

"He gets panic attacks sometimes," Cyrus explained. "He'll be all right in a few minutes, once it passes. Just give him some space."

The bailiff got a call on his radio. "I need to go let the police in," he said. "I'll send one of the officers back. They want to talk to you."

Sam was speaking softly to Naveed in Persian. Andi tried not to look at them, but she could smell Naveed's sweat, she couldn't stop hearing that awful gasping sound he kept making, and her headache was roaring back with a vengeance, ripping into her, and she was about to lose herself into the current of fear that was trying to sweep her under, when she suddenly wondered if she could work something like this into her composition, to give that same staccato, gasping, breathless quality. Some sort of woodwind instrument, maybe.

What a weird thing to think at a time like this. She pushed it out of her mind, because she *should* be afraid. Tara Snyder was missing. Which meant she must have escaped. And if they didn't find her....

A police officer entered then, a woman with a thick black braid reaching down her back. Once the door behind them was closed and the officer had been reassured that Naveed didn't need a medic, Sam asked her what was going on.

The officer looked at him, then at the judge. "One of Tara Snyder's guards abandoned his post outside the room where she was being held when he heard a disturbance in a nearby hallway. Turned out to be nothing—well, it was *something*, a wireless speaker broadcasting what sounded like two people having a loud argument. He called for another officer to investigate and returned to his post. But when the other guards didn't come out at the end of the lunch hour as expected, he went in to find her gone and both of them unconscious."

"Are the guards all right?" the judge asked. Andi wasn't even thinking about them, though. She was thinking about the terrifying implications of this.

"They were taken to Harborview. I don't know their condition," the police officer said. "But, obviously, our main focus is finding her now." She turned to Sam. "Given your… history with her, I'd like to speak with you all about a few things. Can you follow me up to my office?"

Sam hesitated. "I think my son needs a few more minutes. Can we talk here?"

The judge sighed. "Go ahead. I better address everyone, since we'll need to recess for the day. Probably going to end up as a mistrial."

She left, and the officer said, "We're concerned for your safety. There's a possibility that Snyder escaped because she's considering retaliation. We'll give you a police escort home, but all of you should consider staying somewhere else for a while."

"Yes. Okay. Sure," Sam said.

"Maybe we could stay with Khaleh Yasmin," Cyrus suggested.

"Too obvious," Sam said. "I don't want to put her in any danger. We'll figure something else out."

All eyes then turned to Naveed, who was breathing more normally now. "You should come with us," Sam said.

Naveed shook his head. "No. I'm going back to the farm. She won't find me there."

"Maybe not, but I would feel a lot better if you were with us," Sam said. "I need to know that you're safe."

"Baba." Naveed said firmly. "I promise I'll be careful. But I *need* to be there right now. Working on the farm… keeping busy there… it's the only way I'll be able to stay sane through this."

Sam seemed to be doing some complicated mental calculations. Now was Andi's chance, the moment when she could jump in and offer to let Naveed stay with her instead. But she kept her mouth shut. Naveed had broken things off with her, after all, and right now she just couldn't deal with him on top of everything else.

"All right," Sam finally said. The moment had passed, the decision was made, and even though Andi still felt overwhelmed and uneasy, she couldn't hold back a sigh of relief.

Cyrus

TUESDAY, MAY 31

AS CYRUS DROVE HOME TRAILED BY A POLICE CAR, HE MADE A mental list of things he would need to pack. His laptop, of course. All his chargers, he couldn't forget those. But how many changes of clothes would he need?

How long would it take them to find Tara Snyder?

How long until this nightmare was over?

To Cyrus's surprise, Auntie Leila's car was still parked out front when they pulled up at the house. She and Roya should've hit the road hours ago. Why were they still here?

He glanced at Baba, who was spacing out in the passenger seat. "You didn't text Auntie about Tara, did you?"

Baba shook his head. "No. Didn't want them to change their plans."

Cyrus could see Auntie Leila through a gap in the hedges, pacing through the grass and stopping periodically to crouch down, like she expected to find something waiting for her under a bush. Even though the officers had told them to wait until they'd scoped out the house and yard to make sure it was safe, Cyrus got out of the car.

Auntie Leila turned sharply as Cyrus entered the gate. "You're back? So soon?"

The officers, two nearly-identical clean-cut white guys, were right behind him. "Afternoon, ma'am," one of them said to her. Auntie Leila literally jumped.

"Long story," Cyrus said. "Everyone's okay, but... we'll explain inside." He didn't want to talk about the courthouse drama out here in the open.

"Everything secure inside, ma'am?" one of the officers asked. "Or should we have a look around the house first?"

"Secure?" Auntie Leila said. "Oh—it's fine, you can go in. Yes. Let's all go in."

"Leila? Is something wrong?" Baba asked as they walked through the front door. "Where's Roya? She should be here for this. She needs to know what happened."

Auntie Leila, who had been wearing a pair of Naveed's slides, kicked the shoes off by the door. She kept her eyes on her feet as she said, "I don't know. She was playing outside, but when it was time to leave for her appointment, I couldn't find her. It's like she just... vanished...."

The police officers exchanged a worried glance. Baba sat down hard on the sofa, like his legs had just given up. But Cyrus knew his sister well, and he figured Roya was probably around here somewhere, hiding from Auntie Leila to avoid her PT appointment or whatever. "When did you last see her?" Cyrus asked.

"I don't know. I was working and lost track of time... so I'm not sure how long she was gone... before I noticed...." Auntie Leila said in a very small voice.

"We'll have a look around," said one of the officers. "Most likely, it's just a misunderstanding, or she wandered off and will come back home any minute. But—we need to fill you in first. Can we sit?"

Everyone except Baba pulled up chairs at the dining room table, and as the officers explained what had happened at the courthouse, it slowly dawned on Cyrus why everyone was so freaked out.

There was a possibility that Tara Snyder had come here. That she'd seen Roya outside, chasing after chickens or digging holes in the yard, and she'd come up behind her, so quietly that Roya never even heard her before—

The thought was so gut-wrenching that Cyrus didn't want to follow it any further. Roya had to be here somewhere. She had to.

He tore upstairs to check all the hiding spots Auntie Leila might not have tried: every cupboard large enough to hide her, every closet, behind all the doors, even inside the bathtub. He kept hoping she would pop out to surprise him, ending her epic game of hide-and-seek. When he got to her bedroom, he was briefly excited to hear a noise under her bed, but it was just Pashmak batting a chestnut around.

Once he was sure she wasn't inside the house, he scoured the backyard. Reflexively, he looked up into the walnut tree. There was a time when she'd practically lived up there, sitting in the branches playing her flute for the birds. She wasn't there, of course; she hadn't climbed a tree in ages. She wasn't with the chickens, wasn't in the workshop or the garage, wasn't curled up hiding beneath any hedges.

Eventually, he ran out of ideas, and had to admit to himself that Auntie Leila was right. Roya wasn't here.

He returned inside, the familiar knot of dread in his gut twisting in on itself. The house seemed too warm. Stifling. He was tempted to crack open a window, but he doubted that would help.

"So she may have been gone for as long as an hour." The officers looked grim. They didn't have to say anything out loud for Cyrus to understand what they were thinking. That would have given Tara plenty of time to come to their house and take Roya.

But, he reminded himself, lots of people were working on this case right now. As soon as they knew Roya was gone, they'd put alerts up, they'd do everything in their power to find her before—

No. They were going to find her, and she was going to be all right. There was no other option.

"Did you see or hear anything suspicious?" they asked Auntie Leila, who was now in tears.

She shook her head no, but the question made Cyrus think of something. "Wait," he said. "I did. At the courthouse. This guy—he might have had something to do with this." He pulled up the picture on his phone. "The blond one. He was coming out of the bathroom as I was going in, and I have a hunch that he's involved somehow. I mean, look at the guys he's hanging out with... Alastor Yarrow, Raymond Whitaker...." Cyrus purposely didn't call attention to Andi's grandpa, especially since he didn't even know the guy's first name.

"Thanks. We'll keep that in mind," one of them said, jotting down a note that Cyrus strongly suspected said something totally unrelated to the case, like, *Don't forget to stop for doughnuts on the way home.*

He supposed it did sound far-fetched. But if they weren't going to investigate, he'd have to dive down that rabbit hole himself. Later.

The officers headed outside to have a look around the backyard and the alley behind their house. Once the door closed behind them, Cyrus was struck by how quiet it suddenly was. All week long, there had been a steady stream of visitors passing through: people who had worked with Maman through CFJ, random Persians bringing sholeh zard, not to mention the detectives investigating her death. The silence was unnerving.

Auntie Leila turned toward Baba, who had been staring into space on the couch this whole time. "Sam, I'm so sorry, but don't worry, I'm sure she'll be okay—she's tough, Roya—"

Baba stood up. "I'm going to pack," he said in a monotone. "Kourosh, you should too."

"Pack?" Auntie Leila asked.

"Uh, yeah," Cyrus said, since Baba was already walking up the stairs.

"They don't think we should stay at home while Tara's on the loose. So we need to go somewhere else for a while."

"Where? Should I come with you?"

"You should go home," Baba called behind him. His bedroom door slammed, shaking the walls.

Auntie Leila pinched the bridge of her nose. "Oh God, poor Sam. I can't believe this happened. I can't believe I *let* this happen. I shouldn't have taken my eyes off her for a second! I should've paid more attention," she blubbered.

"You didn't know about Tara. It wasn't your fault." Cyrus patted her shoulder, but she only cried harder. "Sorry, Auntie, but I'd better get packed. It's going to be okay, though. They'll find her. I'm sure they will."

Cyrus backed away and headed upstairs. He paused by the door to his parents' room, wondering if he should say something to Baba. But he heard the floor creaking, followed by the low rumble of Baba's voice. He was praying, probably.

An unexpected wave of grief hit Cyrus then, swelling through his body and completely overwhelming him. He staggered to his room and sank onto his chair, touching his forehead to the desk and saying his own version of a prayer. *Come on, God,* he thought desperately. *Can't you give us a win? Just this once?*

The dread-knots inside his stomach were twisting themselves into the most unappetizing pretzel in the world. He honestly wasn't sure how much more of this he could take.

Even though he knew it probably wouldn't help, he escaped into his phone. There were tons of notifications waiting for him, but he didn't read any of them. The first thing he did was send Andi an encrypted text telling her about Roya. Then he wrote a group message to the Quirqi team. As he was composing it, he realized that he didn't even know where he and Baba were going to stay, so he asked if they had any suggestions.

He threw random items of clothing into a duffel bag as he waited for their responses. Shea won the gold star for being the first to reply with an excellent suggestion: Maybe Philip would let you stay at his condo for a few days?

Great idea, thanks, he replied, then held his breath as he wrote to Philip. They hadn't talked since the conference call on Saturday, which had gone surprisingly well: they'd actually convinced Philip to push for a meeting with Raymond Whitaker.

To Cyrus's relief, Philip replied quickly. Of course, you can stay at one of the vacation rental condos—let me check on the details & I'll get back to you.

Okay, good. One dilemma had been solved. As he was scrolling back through his texts, Cyrus had a thought: maybe Andi could stay at the condo too? She hadn't texted him back yet, so he wrote again asking if she and Jake wanted to crash with them. Philip would probably be fine with it, and if it was just Cyrus and Baba trapped together for the foreseeable future, he might go insane.

That done, Cyrus packed up all the electronics he could, his own laptop and external hard drive backups, plus all the test phones, which would make good burners. He should probably bring the family laptop, too, he figured, so that Baba would have one to use if he needed to check work email. He headed downstairs, pausing again at his parents' room, but this time he didn't hear any sounds inside.

Once in the office downstairs, he packed up the family laptop, stowing it inside the dusty bag that had been shoved between the desk and the bookcase. Weirdly, he was kind of excited. Living in a downtown condo did sound kind of glamorous.

But it didn't take long for the guilt to wash in. How could he even think such a thing when his little sister was missing?

When he returned to the dining room, the police officers were back inside, talking with Auntie Leila at the dining room table. Cyrus had a fleeting vision of his mother, of that horrible night when the police had come to their house investigating the murder of Brennan Walsh. Even though Maman had been through previous traumatic interrogations, she had nevertheless welcomed them into her home and served them tea.

An upswelling of grief threatened to drag him under again, but Auntie Leila was talking to him. He turned his focus to her. "So, Kourosh, I've made up my mind. I'm staying here," she said.

"Wait. You're—what?"

"I'm staying here. Someone needs to take care of the cat and the chickens." Oh, right. Cyrus had almost forgotten about them. "The police will be staking the house out, and it's unlikely Tara would come here. Plus… in case Roya comes back, I want someone familiar to be home."

"Good idea." Cyrus swallowed back a sob that had almost escaped. "I think I know where Baba and I are going. A condo downtown. Should be pretty secure. There's a doorman and everything."

One of the officers nodded. "All right. We'll escort you when you're ready."

As Cyrus piled his bags by the door, he heard someone at the front gate. He peeked out the window, half-expecting to see Roya skipping down the front path, but it was just a fat squirrel jostling the latch as it squeezed through the gap into the yard.

Naveed

TUESDAY, MAY 31

NAVEED WALKED OUT OF THE COURTHOUSE, TRAILING THE TWO police officers. They moved so quickly he could barely keep up. He was trying desperately not to think about the knife in his pocket. If he just kept his hands visible, no sudden moves, they wouldn't suspect anything. He hoped.

One of the officers paused before opening the front doors. The crowd of reporters had swelled in size. "Come on. Don't say anything to them, just follow us to the squad car and we'll get you home."

Flashes of light. A wall of people, wall of sound. Naveed forced himself to enter, sandwiched between the officers, who cleared a path. Bodies pressed against him. Microphones in his face. Sweat pouring from his forehead. The knife in his pocket—no, don't think about that. This endless walk. He wasn't sure it would ever be over.

Somehow, he made it to the squad car and they opened the door for him. He got into the back seat. But as soon as they closed it behind him, he saw the bars on the windows and realized that he was trapped. Oh no oh no oh no. Did they know about the knife? They knew about the knife, they were taking him back to the station, they were going to interrogate him, to lock him up—

"So where are we headed? Some farm?" one of them asked.

Naveed could barely keep up. So—they weren't—

"It's in Orting," the other one said. "Hop on I-5 South and we'll go from there." He glanced back at Naveed. "What's the farm called again? Forgot the name."

"Zetik," Naveed choked out.

"Got it. I'll find the address." They started talking amongst themselves, ignoring Naveed. Which came as a small relief. He still worried something would go wrong and they'd figure out what he'd been planning, but as long as he kept his lips shut tight, hands visible, no sudden moves, he should be able to make it home. One breath after another. His chest hurt so bad. *Just get through this car ride*, he told himself. *Then you can rest.*

After what seemed an eternity, the car pulled up in front of Gretchen and Frida's house. It felt strange to see it again after being so certain that he'd left it behind forever. One of the officers opened the door, freeing him, and he managed to stand, but he felt shaky on his feet, wished Koffka were there.

Naveed just wanted to go back to his cabin, but the cops insisted they needed to go with him, and then Gretchen appeared out of nowhere and Frida was not far behind, Astro trotting up alongside her, so the officers started telling them about what had happened at the courthouse, that Tara Snyder had escaped and they didn't know where she'd gone.

"Unfortunately, there's been another development," one of the officers was saying. "We just got a call—Roya Mirzapour is missing. She disappeared from her backyard this afternoon."

Everyone turned to look at him. The sudden attention was so blinding that he couldn't even process the statement before Frida spoke. "Oh, my. Do they think… Tara…."

"That's the current theory," the officer said.

Gretchen and Frida looked horrified. Naveed's legs wobbled. He leaned against the car hood, finally understanding what they were saying: Tara Snyder had abducted Roya.

God, he was such a fucking idiot. Why hadn't he killed Tara when he had the chance? He didn't have to wait for his turn at the witness stand, he should've just jumped up there and sliced her open the second he'd arrived, and now it was too late, now she was hunting them all down, and she had already gotten Roya.

"We'll be staked out here," the officer said. "Here's my number. Call or text anytime." He handed Naveed a card, which he slipped into his pocket.

"Naveed, you're welcome to stay with us in the main house tonight," Gretchen said.

Everyone was looking at him again. It made him sweat. "No," he managed to say. "No. I need to be alone."

They looked like they wanted to protest, but he just turned away and began trudging toward his cabin. Leaving footprints in the mud.

The police officers hurried ahead of him and entered the cabin before he did, doing a quick search. He was about to follow them in when that intern ran up. He couldn't even remember her name. But he did remember what she'd said as she'd driven him to the courthouse. That Tim Schmidt had come looking for him at the market. Yet another thing Naveed would have to deal with now. Fuck.

"Naveed, wait!" the intern called to him.

He turned, annoyed. He was seriously crashing. Needed to lie down. "What do you want?"

She must have heard the sharpness in his voice, because her smile faded. "I, um, I brought you some food. I heard about what happened at the courthouse—I'm so, so sorry about that, by the way—and figured your plans might have changed, so I got you some takeout."

"Not hungry," he grunted. Each word required so much effort. So much breath.

"Take it anyway. I'm sure you will be later. I'm helping out with the evening chores, so I'll be here a little while longer. I know this card game, it's really fun, might help take your mind off of things, if you want I could bring my deck by later?"

"No," he said firmly. "Need to be alone."

Luckily, the police came out then. They told him they were going to have a look around outside, and he should give them a call if he needed anything. Relieved, he caught one last look at the disappointment on the intern's face before he pushed the door shut and locked it tight.

The curtains were closed. It was dark inside. The first thing he saw were Koffka's eyes, glowing in the dimness, as the dog watched from his bed. *You betrayed me again,* those eyes said.

Even so, Naveed found himself crossing the room, collapsing in bed, throwing his arms around his dog and burying his face in the coarse fur of Koffka's back. Koffka seemed to understand that it had been an exceptionally bad day. *Okay, fine. I'll take care of you, but don't you dare do that again.*

"I won't," said Naveed. "I'm sorry." Mostly, he was just sorry he'd come back. He wasn't supposed to be here right now. Once again, he had failed.

He closed his eyes. For a while, everything faded out.

When he came to, the light had changed. It was darker; the sun was setting. Koffka was pawing at the door, whining. Naveed sat up. Was Tim Schmidt here? Or Tara Snyder? No, he wasn't ready for that, not ready at all—

But, he realized as the initial surge of adrenaline faded, no one else was around. Maybe Koffka just needed to do his business. Of course he did—he'd been asleep all day.

Something was itching at Naveed's brain, though. Tim and Tara. Schmidt and Snyder. Tim Schmidt wasn't that man's real name, Naveed knew, but did it mean something that his alias had the same initials as Tara's name? Was Tim Schmidt working for her? Gathering information, following Naveed around, figuring out where he worked, where he lived....

It made so much sense. *Tim Schmidt has big plans.* Maybe he'd been plotting to break Tara out all this time. But what was their end game?

Naveed didn't have to think about this too long before he knew the answer. They had come for Roya, and they were coming for him next.

He got up and sat at the table. He held his heavy head up with both hands. Stared at his mother's place, at the bowl of dried cherries and raw walnuts that still waited for her, at her mug, her phone, her poem, all waiting expectantly, like she'd just stepped out for a minute and would soon return.

"Maman," he whispered. "Maman, I'm scared."

I know. But the important thing right now is finding your sister. This leaped into his mind as if his mother were really there, talking to him.

"What am I supposed to do? Just wait until they come for me? I'm not strong enough to fight back—and what if Roya's already—"

I believe in you, Naveed-jaan. I know you can do this.

Koffka was still pawing at the door. Naveed crossed the room and kneeled next to the dog, wrapping his arms around his neck. "I'm going to let you out, but you need to be careful. They're coming for us, and when they do, we both need to be ready."

He opened the door. Listened. Only the sounds of dusk at the farm greeted him, the crickets just beginning their nightly symphony, the swallows swooping across the recently-tilled fields—

Something came to him then. Naveed followed Koffka outside. They walked slowly together out to the shed, where Naveed opened the door and the setting sun fell upon the curved metal blade of the scythe, glinting at him from the gloom like an inverted grin.

Yes. Oh, yes. When they came for him, he would be ready.

Roya

TUESDAY, MAY 31

ROYA KNOCKED ON HER BROTHER'S DOOR, PRAYING THAT HE could help her. Cyrus was her last hope.

She shifted her weight onto her good leg. Ever since Maman died, it had been harder to hoist herself up from sitting positions, more painful to put weight on her foot. Maybe it was just because she hadn't found the energy to do her physical therapy stretches like she was supposed to, but it kind of felt like everything was moving backward.

Cyrus opened the door. His hair was messy, but not in a way that looked intentional. A cowlick on one side swooped up towards the ceiling. "Hey, sis. Everything okay?"

"Your hair looks funny," Roya said.

"Yeah. Just got up." He opened the door wider, smoothing his hair with his fingers. She came in and plopped into his desk chair. It spun a little, so she anchored her left foot on the floor.

"I've got to hop in the shower in a sec," Cyrus said. "We have to leave for the trial in"—he glanced at his phone—"half an hour. Akh,

Roya, it's going to be painful. Good thing Auntie's taking you out of this mess."

"So you want me to leave, too?" she asked.

Cyrus blinked. "I didn't mean it like that. I'm just glad you get to go somewhere else. It could get pretty ugly while the trial's going on."

"I don't care! I want to be here. With you. Please, Kourosh, don't let them send me away."

He was digging through his dresser drawers, not even looking at her. "I'm sorry, Roya. I wish it didn't have to be like this. But you'll love it on the coast with Auntie, and it'll be over soon, and once I'm done with school maybe we'll all come down and hang out on the beach together."

Cyrus pulled a pair of black socks out of the drawer, then looked at his phone again. After a few seconds, he started typing something. Roya should've known better than to hope he could get her out of this. "Will you at least take care of Pashi for me?" she asked softly.

"Of course."

She wasn't sure he'd heard, since he was still typing away. Further conversation would be useless. "Okay. Well. I'll let you get ready."

He held his hand out to help her up. She felt a small surge of gratefulness for that, even though he was still absorbed in whatever was happening inside his phone. She shuffled into the hallway and was about to head downstairs when she heard voices coming from her parents' room. She paused, leaning against the wall, listening.

"Have you gotten a chance to look at any of those job openings in Coos Bay that I sent you?" Auntie Leila was asking. "The cost of living is so much cheaper there. And I think it would be good for all of you to have a fresh start."

"I don't know," Baba said quietly. "This house was so important to her... the first place where she was finally able to put down roots...."

"But there's no way you can stay here, is there? Not unless the settlement magically comes through. Maybe it's a sign that it's time to move on. Set down new roots somewhere else."

No. That wasn't right. Auntie was reading the signs wrong, she had to be.

Baba sighed. "There's no way the settlement will work out. Every option we had... it's all a dead end, so I guess... we'll have to...."

He didn't finish the sentence. All Roya could hear now were his strange laughing-sobs.

So... it was really true? They had to leave this place *forever*?

Roya couldn't let that happen. Baba was right—Maman had put down roots here. She was in this house still, she was growing all through it, through the walls, the soil, the plants in the garden. How could they just leave her behind? She would be stuck here forever without anyone to help her move on, wailing inside the walls and filling the house with her despair for the rest of time.

All through the morning, as she said goodbye to Baba and Cyrus, as Auntie Leila made eggs and toast and told her to get packed, Roya thought and thought. Eventually, a plan began to take shape.

Before packing anything, she snuck into the office and did a quick search on the computer: *crystal shop seattle*. She scoured the names that popped up on the map, but only one jumped out at her: Moonstone Apothecary.

That had to be the one Kass had mentioned, the shop whose name had something to do with the moon, the shop run by the Orcinian acolyte who had become a shaman. If Roya could just get there and explain what was going on, she had no doubt that the shaman could help her. She'd summon Maman so that Roya could talk to her, and maybe Maman would know how to help keep the house, how to make sure they could all stay together. Once that was done, Roya could call Kass and go stay with her and Ilyana until her family decided they wanted her back.

What if they never come back for you? Maybe they'll like it better when you're gone. The thought flew into her head even though she didn't want to think it. She pulled her scarf tighter. Sometimes it felt like the shayatin were all around her, making her think horrible things like this. Keeping her head covered made her feel a little more protected, but they were tricky, those demons.

No, she thought to herself. Her family would miss her, of course they would. But they were all so distracted now. It was going to take something big for them to sit up and pay attention.

After sketching out a map and writing down the directions to Moonstone Apothecary, which was only about a mile away from the Light Rail station closest to the airport, Roya packed her suitcase, throwing in all the clothes she never liked to wear. Then she stuffed her backpack full of her good clothes, the Book of Shadows from Orcinia and her own smaller version, all the letters Kass had written her, and a few magical tools. The Hekate chalice was too bulky and breakable to bring along, but she zipped Kass's athame into the front pocket. She hung the velvet pouch with its crow feather and bay leaves around her neck and tucked it under her shirt, so it would be extra close.

On the dresser in her parents' bedroom, Roya found the beautiful glass bottle of rose oil perfume that Maman used to wear, knowing that the shaman might ask her for something of Maman's to help with the ritual. But she also wanted to carry that scent with her on this journey, because whenever she smelled it, she felt like Maman was right there beside her, invisible but close. She spritzed it on her wrists before wrapping the bottle carefully in a pink pashmina scarf she found hanging in the closet.

Roya had a little cash in her wallet, the Nowruz money she hadn't spent yet, but she also took a handful of quarters out of the jar of loose change that Baba kept on the dresser. Then she gave Pashmak an extra-good scritch on her back right where she liked it, at the base of her tail. Pashmak purred and purred. "I'll see you again soon," Roya whispered.

Auntie Leila's eyes were glued to her laptop when Roya crept downstairs. She stowed her backpack in a shadowy nook before saying, "I'm going to play outside for a little bit."

Auntie Leila turned. "All right. You'll be ready to go to PT soon? We'll be leaving straight from there."

"I'm all set. My suitcase is upstairs," Roya said. "Could you carry it down?"

"Sure. I'll get…." Auntie Leila didn't even finish her sentence. She had been pulled back into the world inside the screen. Once Roya was certain her auntie wasn't looking, she grabbed her backpack and headed out the front door.

It was too easy, she thought as she stepped out the front gate, being very careful to latch it quietly. She quickly replaced her blue headscarf with an old black beanie of Naveed's, knowing the scarf would make her too conspicuous, and walked down the street with her shoulders as straight as they could be given the weight of her backpack.

When she arrived at the train station, she bought a ticket, feeling very independent as she shoved quarter after quarter into the slot. It didn't take long for the train to arrive, and she stepped through the sliding doors behind a lady with a rolling bag. Roya stayed very close and sat down next to her, latching on as her pretend daughter. The lady was so caught up in her phone that she didn't seem to notice. Roya smiled to herself. She didn't even have to bother with distractions. All these screens did the job for her.

Once on the train, Roya pulled out a small notebook that she had brought, the one where she had transcribed *Katerina and the Little Strangers*. She wanted to look occupied, like she was completely at ease, so that people didn't catch a whiff of her nervousness and know that something wasn't quite right.

As they got closer to SeaTac station, she unfolded the directions she'd written down and went through the route again in her head.

Finally, the robotic train voice announced, "Now arriving at SeaTac/ Airport station. Doors to my left." Roya shouldered her backpack and followed her "mom" out onto to the station platform. Soon she had to veer off, though, because the lady was wheeling her bag along with everyone else toward the airport terminals, and that wasn't where Roya wanted to go.

Instead, she followed the signs to a sky bridge, and slowly descended a long stairwell to the sidewalk of a very busy street. At first, there were still people around her, walking to their hotels or the giant parking lots that were all over the place, but soon the crowd thinned out and she was alone. She kept walking. No one stopped her, but all the cars made her nervous, especially when they slowed near her, like they were going to roll down their windows and ask her to get in, which of course she wouldn't do. She always felt silly when she saw they were just stopping at stoplights.

After a while she started to wonder whether she'd made a wrong turn somewhere, because the names of the streets weren't the same as the ones on her map, and now she was passing a bunch of houses that looked like they'd been abandoned; they were all boarded up and covered in graffiti. As she walked, she kept hearing footsteps behind her, but every time she looked around she didn't see anyone.

Someone was watching her, though. She could feel it.

She tried to shake it off. Tried to get the map to make sense. Thought about turning back around to retrace her steps, but decided to go one more block to see what the next cross-street was called.

A mocking voice called out from behind her. "Hey, little girl. Where you going?"

Roya ignored this. She folded up the map again, concealing it inside her damp palm, and sped up. The faster she walked, though, the worse her limp became.

Her heart jumped in her chest like it was skipping rope. The footsteps behind her grew louder. She shifted her backpack onto one shoulder and fumbled inside the front pocket. This street was so quiet, these small houses with peeling paint and barren yards, no people anywhere, no one to save her, no one in the whole world to protect her except herself.

Roya tried to walk faster, but her leg was really aching now. She couldn't escape.

In one swift movement, the person who'd been following her grabbed her shoulder. She tried to jerk away, but his strong grip made her lose her balance, and once again she was falling, trying not to land on her bad knee but coming down on it anyway, and she was lost and alone, and she couldn't move, and a stranger was standing over her, smiling a terrible smile.

Andi

WEDNESDAY, JUNE 1

AN EPIC BATTLE WAS RAGING IN THE NEXT ROOM OVER. AT LEAST, that was how it sounded to Andi. Tinny groans and clanging swords punctuated the silence.

It was a fitting soundtrack for the grisly hellscape playing out inside her head this morning. As Andi had left the trial yesterday, Barb had leveled up, adding a dizzy vertigo on top of a murderous headache. Andi had literally fallen over on the way back to her dad's car. Of course, he had insisted on getting everything checked out, which led to a night in the ER while they did a bunch of tests but couldn't find anything wrong. They chalked it up to anxiety and sent her on her way with a fresh bottle of painkillers.

Two good things had come out of the horrible evening, though. Andi's mom had been ready to book her a plane ticket back to Berkeley as soon as she found out about Tara Snyder's escape, but the doctors agreed that Andi needed to take it easy. Travel, they told Andi's mom at her request, was out of the question right now. Also, her dad had grudgingly allowed them to stay with Cyrus at a condo downtown instead of crashing with one of his bandmates. So now here she was, sprawled out on an extraordinarily comfortable king bed, listening to the battle next door and realizing that Barb, thankfully, was in retreat. For now, anyway.

She sat up and reached for her phone on the bedside table. She hadn't only wanted to stay with Cyrus so she could have a friend nearby, though of course she was grateful for that, even if she wished he'd turn down the volume on whatever video game he was playing. They needed to be together so they could figure out what happened to Roya.

After composing a few reassuring messages to her mom, who had sent about a billion texts asking how she was feeling, Andi scanned her other unread texts. Nothing important. She didn't feel like getting dressed or even putting a bra on, so she wrapped a throw blanket around her shoulders before sending a text to Cyrus. Hey can you come in here for a minute?

He appeared a few moments later, smiling in the doorway, eating oatmeal out of a paper cup. "Hey, A! How are you feeling?"

"Fine." Surprisingly, she could still hear swishing swords. In fact, they were even louder now that the door was open. "Wait. Who's playing the video game? Oh—are your friends over?"

Cyrus blinked. "Uh, no, it's like 7:30 on a weekday, and besides we're not allowed to have visitors at our top-secret undisclosed location. Believe it or not, our dads are totally obsessed with *Renaissance Slayer VII*. Baba wanted to drive around looking for Roya last night, but the cops said we all need to stay put for now, so I suggested we play some video games. Even though I was recommending games that were a little more... intellectual... I guess they just wanted to kill some shit."

"Makes sense." She patted the bed next to her. "So—did I miss anything? Have they found Roya yet?"

"Can I have your phone?" Cyrus asked.

"Uh... okay." She handed it over.

Cyrus powered it down, then left her room. Through the open doorway, Andi saw him burying her phone, along with the one he pulled from his pocket, under a stack of throw pillows on the couch. Then he re-entered her room, closed the door, and sat cross-legged beside her on the enormous bed. "You can never be too careful." He scooped up another bite of oatmeal. "So. Let's talk Roya. No news yet. But the cops are operating under the assumption that... that Tara... yeah. I can't even say it out loud."

"That's okay. I know." Andi didn't want to go there, either, but if they were going to figure this out, it couldn't be avoided. "Here's what I'm thinking: she took Roya because she's trying to draw the rest of us out. Lure us into some sort of trap. So she can get her revenge or whatever."

"I mean, it makes sense, but how stupid does she think we are? Like we're just going to head out on our own, roaming around the city searching for Roya until we fall into her evil clutches."

"It's not the two of us I'm worried about." Andi pulled her throw blanket tighter around her shoulders.

Cyrus scraped the bottom of his oatmeal cup with his spoon. "Yeah. Naveed was giving off definite loose cannon vibes yesterday. He's been texting with Baba, says he's staying inside the cabin, but still. You never know with him."

"The good thing is—well, it's not *good*, but you know what I mean—he had that panic attack at the courthouse. Usually, when they're that bad, they'll knock him out for a day or two. So even if he wants to go looking for Roya, he won't physically be able to, at least not right away. Which buys us some time to figure out where she is. Then we can tell the police and let them handle things."

"All right. Let's do this." He stood up. "I'll be right back."

He reappeared a minute later with two laptops. Andi told him she'd brought her own, but he insisted she use one of his since they were already set up for secure browsing. After he logged her on, he left again and returned with his hands behind his back.

"So this is embarrassing," he said. "We need some snacks—it wouldn't be a proper hackfest without snacks—but all I found were these." He held out two small bags of Blazin Bitz. "This place is a vacation rental, so I guess they keep it stocked with all the necessities."

"No thanks." Just looking at the bags got Andi's blood pressure boiling. "I helped start that Bitz boycott a few months ago, remember? Plus, I haven't even had breakfast yet."

"Oh, right! Let me make you an oatmeal cup. And I'll go throw these in the garbage, where they belong." He left the room holding the bags at arm's length, as if they were filled with rotten fish heads or something.

Andi turned her attention to the screen. Where to even start? Her intuition was telling her to look at the photo again, but her phone was still hiding under the couch cushions, so she had to reconstruct it from memory. Four men, standing against that polished wood backdrop, glasses of champagne raised: Raymond Whitaker; the blond dude Cyrus said he'd seen at the courthouse; Alastor Yarrow; Ah-gong.

Alastor had started the herbal supplement company Metafolia. Ah-gong had provided the green tea extract ingredient. Raymond Whitaker had probably funded the operation, but Andi didn't know that for sure. She decided to start her search with him. It still bothered her that she'd heard his name somewhere but couldn't recall what the context was.

Cyrus brought in her oatmeal, and she ate it while they browsed. It tasted like sweet glue.

"Not sure if this helps any," Cyrus said after a time. "But the logo on the badge your grandpa was wearing in the photo is from an herbal and vitamin supplement expo."

"Makes sense. Ah-gong used to go to things like that all the time. So I guess that's where they met, and... started Metafolia or something?" For a second, Andi felt incredibly stupid. What if this whole thing was a wild goose chase, and Ah-ma's Mystery Box had just contained some boring vitamins?

But, if that were true, why had Ah-ma treated the whole thing like a forbidden mystery? And why had the blond man showed up at the trial?

No, this was all leading somewhere. It had to be.

Andi turned back to her Raymond Whitaker search, but everything she found focused on his role at Blanchet Capital. So she tried searching *raymond whitaker alastor yarrow*, but nothing came up for those two together. Then she tried *raymond whitaker nutrexo* and found an article talking about how he'd guided the imploding company into selling off its brands. Which wasn't surprising, since he was on the Nutrexo board and also ran the parent company of Hannigan Foods. He'd found a way to profit from Nutrexo's downfall, but there was nothing particularly scandalous about that.

It wasn't until she searched *raymond whitaker metafolia* that she finally hit gold. This led her to a *Wall Street Journal* article about the acquisition of Bountiful Earth Markets, which had happened shortly after Brennan Walsh's death. *The acquisition of the natural foods chain by Blanchet Capital has some critics questioning the judgment of the company's CEO, Raymond Whitaker. It comes on the heels of a risky venture that ultimately failed: Mr. Whitaker was a majority shareholder in the supplement company Metafolia, Inc., which was shut down by federal investigators just before its planned IPO.*

It felt like she'd just stumbled on the answer, but, annoyingly, she couldn't quite put her finger on why it mattered. "Hey Cy, listen to this." She read the snippet to him.

"Whoa. Blanchet owns Bountiful Earth now? Brennan would've hated that. Remember when we went to his place for dinner that one night, and he was grousing about not wanting to sell out to Wall Street or whatever?"

"The vultures," Andi said. "The vultures! Cy, that's it!"

Cyrus tilted his head. "That's what?"

"That's where I've heard his name before. I even met him once! Well, sort of. At the Walsh Foundation fundraiser right after Brennan died. I wanted to talk to Senator Bittner, and she was in the middle of a conversation with him, and when he left she offhandedly said something about vultures swooping in. That's what she meant, that Raymond, or Blanchet or whatever, had their eyes on Bountiful Earth. But—oh no." Andi had to close her eyes as a wave of dizziness swept over her.

"You okay?" Cyrus asked.

"Raymond and Alastor were standing together in that photo," Andi said. "Alastor killed Brennan, who didn't want to sell his company. What if...?"

Even though her eyes were still closed, she could feel Cyrus scoffing. "So, like, Raymond wanted Bountiful Earth so bad that he had his buddy Alastor kill off Brennan? And, not to get too self-centered here, but he tried to kill me, too. Why would Raymond want me dead?"

"I don't know," Andi said. The more she thought about it, the unlikelier it sounded, and the more overwhelming it all seemed. "I'm just saying. That photo's trying to tell us something, and I have a feeling the blond guy is the key to all of this. We need to figure out who he is."

"I'm with you there. I told the police about him yesterday, but they didn't seem to think anything of it. Have you asked your grandpa about him?"

"No. But he's really cagey about anything to do with Metafolia. He wouldn't tell me anyway."

"Even if my little sister's life depends on it?"

Andi opened her eyes. "Okay. You're right. I'll text him. But I still doubt he's going to give us anything useful."

"It's worth a try. Just make sure you use encrypted messaging." Cyrus rubbed the back of his neck. "Um, there's one other potential option, maybe. I actually have a meeting scheduled with Raymond Whitaker next Monday."

"You *what*?" Andi asked.

"I know, I know, you disapprove of me selling out, but—"

"It's not just that," Andi interrupted. "What if I'm right? That he was behind Brennan Walsh's death?"

"It's an interesting theory," said Cyrus slowly. "Honestly, though, I think Alastor was just psycho, and it made him mad when me and Brennan exposed Metafolia. It doesn't seem like something a powerful rich guy like Raymond would bother getting his hands dirty over. But—never mind, it's not like I can just go into our meeting and say, 'Hey, so I have this random pic of you, mind telling me who this blond dude is? I think he has something to do with my missing sister.' Plus, it's like five days from now. Too long. We need to figure this out now."

Andi rubbed her forehead. There was one other avenue that had popped into her mind, but it, too, felt like a long shot. "I think you need to talk to your brother."

"Why? I thought we didn't want to drag him into this."

"I know, but remember what I told you about how he got into your mom's phone? I think she knew something about that photo, and that's why she didn't want us investigating. But she might have gone looking into it herself."

"You think we can convince him to let us have it?"

"He may not care about me anymore, but he cares about Roya," Andi said. "And this might help us find her. Well, not *us* us, but if we can get the police a name, some compelling evidence for a link to Tara Snyder, they'll have a suspect to track down."

"The problem is… then we have to explain the whole thing to Naveed, rely on him to search the phone, and report back to us without going rogue and trying to find Roya by himself. Or, I guess we could ask the cops to take it from him, but I don't think he'd hand it over willingly, and they might even charge him for keeping evidence from them… I don't know. I'm just not sure it'll work."

"Then what are we supposed to do?" Without warning, tears prickled her eyes. This was all so incredibly frustrating.

"Don't worry. We'll figure it out." Cyrus closed his laptop. "You doing okay, A?"

Andi rested her head against the padded headboard. "I've been trying to rank them. The worst days of my life. Yesterday definitely makes the list."

"Oh, yeah? Did it beat out the old number one?"

"Hard to say. It's not easy, because do you go by the day when you felt the worst, or the one you can barely remember, but was full of objectively terrible things? Does that even make sense? I don't think I'm making sense." She laugh-sobbed, and he reached over to pat her knee. She grabbed onto his hand and held it.

"It makes perfect sense. We've all had horrible days—but you know, we've also always gotten through them. And there's always good stuff waiting on the other side," Cyrus said. "It'll be okay in the end. I'm sure of it."

Andi nodded, but she felt like burrowing back under the covers. Their amateur investigation had gone nowhere. Roya was still missing, and they had no idea how to find her, and the longer this went on, the more likely it seemed that everything could only end in disaster.

Naveed

TIME WAS BEHAVING STRANGELY. SOMETIMES THERE WAS AN eternity between seconds; sometimes hours raced by in a blur. Naveed's phone had numbers on it that corresponded to some objectively agreed-upon time, but such things were meaningless for him now. His phone was only useful as his tool of deception. How are you Naveed-jaan, Baba would text. I'm doing fine, don't worry about me, Naveed would reply.

He was growing tired of this meaningless performance. *What's taking you so long?* he kept asking Tara Snyder inside his mind. *I'm waiting for you. I know I'm next on your list. Come and find me, so we can finally end this.*

At some point on Thursday, Frida stopped by. "Aviva just went into labor!" she said. "So we need to head down to Olympia. It might be a few days. We've arranged for the interns to take care of the farm chores and feed Astro—but would you like to stay in the main house while we're gone?"

"No," Naveed said. "That's okay. I'll just stay here."

"You have everything you need? I'll bring some groceries from our fridge. The interns won't be around much. But the police are still here.

If you see anything suspicious, call them right away."

"I will."

Frida hesitated. "Are you sure you will be all right?"

Naveed closed his eyes. "Frida, I'm fine. Go be with your daughter."

She and Gretchen returned shortly afterward to fill up his small refrigerator with food that would inevitably rot. Every time he tried to eat, the mud in his mouth nearly choked him. So he'd stopped bothering with that pointless ritual.

He kept the window cracked so he could hear if anyone was approaching the cabin. Everything was eerily quiet. Occasionally, he saw the police officers patrolling outside. Sometimes they'd hang out on his porch or roam the fields, but mostly they remained by the road.

Eventually, his exhaustion gave way to restlessness. The four walls of the cabin seemed to be growing closer, pressing against him.

He couldn't stay here any longer. He hid Maman's phone under his mattress, sent a few final texts, put on a black hoodie, grabbed his supplies, and stepped outside.

The rain fell in sheets, drenching him instantly. After making sure no cops were around, he trekked up the hill into the woods, but not so far in that he lost sight of the cabin.

He talked to Koffka, softly, about what the dog would need to do when Tim Schmidt and Tara Snyder came. He wasn't sure Koffka was up to the task. All the feral violence had been trained out of him when they'd turned him into a nurturer, so it was up to Naveed to put it back.

He set a simple trap, putting some granola bar crumbs underneath a rock propped precariously on some sticks, then retreating to the shadows. A clueless squirrel crept by some time later, upsetting the sticks in his quest for the sweet oats and nuts, the rock slamming down on his body.

Naveed rubbed Koffka's back. "Go get him, boy," he said.

Koffka just looked at him quizzically.

"Get him. That's your dinner," said Naveed.

This time, Koffka listened. He was probably hungry. Naveed had no idea when he'd last fed him. The dog got up, almost reluctantly, but when he pawed over the rock and found the helpless squirrel wriggling there, his animal instincts took over and he bared his teeth, growling, before tearing into it. The squirrel let out a shrill, human-like shriek as it died.

Naveed lay back and rested for a while with his eyes closed, trying not to listen to the sounds of flesh being ripped from bone. His lungs felt so heavy, an eternal weight in his chest.

"Good boy," he said when Koffka returned later, wet blood still visible on his black lips. Naveed hoped the squirrel had been treat enough, because he didn't have anything to reward him, but from the look in Koffka's eyes, he thought it had. He had reminded the dog who he really was, deep down. A hunter, primed for attack.

Time passed. The sun dipped down to the horizon. Night fell. Naveed kept his eyes fixed on the cabin. Waiting for a flicker of the light, a passing shadow, a bend in the grass. Nothing. What if he'd been wrong? What if they weren't coming for him after all?

Didn't matter, he decided. He wasn't going back. One way or the other, tonight would be the end. If the dawn came and they still hadn't found him, he was going to make sure he never saw another sunrise.

The night grew thicker. He shivered in his wet hoodie, fighting to keep his eyes open. He was so tired. So. Very. Tired.

The next thing he knew, Astro was barking frantically in the distance. He sat up, instantly alert. There was a sharp bang—

And then—

Silence.

Koffka lifted his head off his paws. Naveed tightened his grip on the scythe and returned his eyes to the cabin. What seemed like ages later, someone began walking up to it, slowly, covering their tracks in the mud as they went. As they drew closer to the light, he could see silvery blonde hair pulled back in a tight bun.

Tara Snyder was here. As far as he could tell, she was alone.

Koffka was watching, too. "That's her," Naveed whispered. "Come on."

The two of them moved as quietly as they could through the brush. With each step, Naveed closed the gap between them, and even though he knew this could go very wrong at any moment, he anticipated their reunion with a sort of thrumming excitement.

She was at the front door of the cabin by the time he emerged from the woods, Koffka right behind him. She turned at the sound of his approach and raised the gun in her hand.

He stopped at the edge of the tree line. She was below him in the valley, and he was up in the forest, looking down on her from beneath his black hood, scythe propped beside him, the blade right next to his ear. He could hear it singing to him.

"Now!" he told Koffka, and the dog ran toward her, teeth bared. But something strange was happening: Tara had caught his eye, she had recognized him, and she was bending now, setting the gun on the ground, raising her hands to the sky in a gesture of surrender.

It didn't make any sense, but it was too late to stop what was already happening. Koffka grabbed on hard to her leg, dragging her to the ground.

She yelped in surprise, but not loudly, much quieter than the squirrel, actually, and Naveed ran down, careful to keep his footing on the muddy slope. He had no idea what she was playing at, giving up her gun like that, but he wasn't even going to try to figure it out until she was safely restrained. As soon as he reached her, he rammed the blunt wooden end of the scythe against her head.

She fell back. He rolled her over and fastened her hands behind her back with the rope he'd been carrying in his hoodie pocket, making sure to tie it extra tight around her wrists, cutting off circulation to her hands. Then he bound her ankles before gagging her with the black tie he'd worn to Maman's funeral.

All the while, he kept his ears open in case Tim Schmidt was somewhere nearby waiting to ambush him. But the only sounds were the chirping of crickets and the rustling of wind through leaves.

Once she was tied up, he collected her gun, shoving the barrel into his waistband, then stowed the scythe back in the woods. Still no sign of Tim Schmidt—if he were here, he probably would have shown himself by now. Tara must have come alone.

Koffka was sitting at attention, so Naveed gave him a quick pat and some praise before hooking the still-unconscious Tara under her arms and dragging her into the forest.

Their journey was long. It started raining again, but not much water leaked through the thick canopy of trees overhead. He hadn't thought about how physically difficult this would be, and soon his back and arms were aching, his chest on fire from all the exertion, every breath like a knife tip stabbing his lungs, but still he kept going.

He dragged her all the way to the pit, the one he'd visited the night he'd taken the tea, and heaved her up and over the crumbling stone foundation. She fell silently to the ground, landing hard on her right side, her head thumping against the compacted mud.

Naveed sat back against a tree, panting. He had accomplished exactly what he'd wanted to, which should have felt good, but seeing her body in there like that, muddied and limp, lying on her side, reminded him of his mother in her grave, and then he thought about Tara setting the gun down and raising her arms, surrendering unexpectedly. He'd attacked her anyway. Did that make him the hero or the villain in this story? He didn't even care. He couldn't feel anything anymore; what was wrong with him, holes in the dirt, holes in his soul, holes in his lungs, or stones maybe, rapidly growing tumors that made it hard to breathe, all of this and he still couldn't breathe. He hadn't fixed anything.

The gun was digging into his back. He took it out and set it on the ground. There it was: the answer, the out. So easy, over in one shot—no, two, since he'd have to take her out first.

He picked it up, imagining how cold the steel must be, not that he could feel it in his hands, so instead he touched the barrel to his hot forehead. It felt good, like a mother's touch: comforting, promising sleep, promising peace on the other side.

Koffka whimpered. Naveed put the gun down. He needed to bear this just a little longer.

He walked back to the edge of the woods. It was pouring out there, and his hoodie was soon soaked through again, but he grabbed his scythe and hiked back to the pit to find that Tara was now sitting up.

Her eyes gave away nothing, but her arm was hanging strangely, dislocated probably, and there was a slight furrow to her eyebrows. If he wasn't mistaken, tears were actually leaking down her muddy cheeks.

She was in pain. Which was good.

Still, he wasn't satisfied.

He sat against the tree again, cross-legged, his black hood still on, the scythe propped up next to him. He wanted her to know who he had become. *I am the butcher,* he thought. *The master of Death.*

She stared into his eyes. Her lips curled against the black silk tie. She was trying to speak to him. He didn't want to hear her words, because always her words were weapons, but he had his own questions that needed to be answered.

He searched the ground and located a short, hard stick. He took out his obsidian knife and started working on it, whittling the tip into a sharp, flat point.

She watched him. Her gaze didn't bother him at all anymore. A big gust of wind rolled through the trees, shaking their branches and sending a fresh batch of raindrops falling to the ground. They fell mostly on Naveed, since there was a clearing over the top of the hole, which meant the bottom of the pit was very muddy and Tara was just as soaked as he was by now.

When he was done, he stuck the sharp stick into his pocket and tied Koffka to a tree with his last length of rope. He needed the dog to stay here with him until the end.

Then, after grabbing the gun and the scythe, Naveed lowered himself down into the pit with her.

Andi

THURSDAY, JUNE 2

ANDI AWOKE ON THURSDAY MORNING FROM AN ANXIOUS DREAM. She'd showed up late to school only to find everyone taking an exam she'd failed to study for, and she tried to explain to the teacher about her headaches and the trial and everything else, but he just stared down at her and said that none of it mattered. The test was what mattered, and she had to take it, he didn't care if she was dying, it was that important of a test.

So she sat at an uncomfortably tiny desk, but the test was written in some foreign script she'd never seen before, maybe Persian, she thought, although it didn't look quite right, and one of the other students coughed, an awful rattling cough she knew all too well. Naveed was hunched over the desk next to her. She leaned closer and asked him for help translating. He just shook his head, wiping his mouth hurriedly like there was something he didn't want her to see, but she saw it anyway, the blood smeared around the edges of his mouth, the red stain on his sleeve. In a cold voice he said, "If you can't figure it out, that's not my problem."

Her eyes flew open then. It took her a few minutes to remember where she was, but that didn't bring much comfort. She was still stuck here in purgatory at Philip's condo. Roya was still missing. Naveed was still out at the farm ignoring everyone except Sam, who got texts from him occasionally. Ah-gong still wasn't responding to Andi's messages. Ah-ma hadn't been feeling well, so she hadn't been able to talk. In short, a whole lot of nothing had happened.

Andi glanced at the clock on the nightstand. It was almost noon, and now that she was more awake she felt antsy and restless. So she got up, showered, changed into a different pair of sweats, and made her way to the kitchen.

Cyrus sat at the dining room table behind his laptop. The dads were still in the study, slaying knights or whatever. Andi wished her dad would come out to check on her, but he seemed totally immersed in that alternate reality. It was infinitely better than if he'd escaped into the vodka and Oxy he was probably craving, but still. Watching him get sucked so completely into a video game failed to bring Andi much comfort.

When she sat down across from Cyrus, he looked up. "Hey, A. You hungry? I was about to make some lunch. Did you know there's a deep fryer in the kitchen? So what do you think: tempura for lunch, doughnuts for dessert?"

"Okay." She drummed her fingers on the table.

"I could use a little help chopping vegetables," he hinted.

"Oh, fine," said Andi. "Not like I have anything better to do."

It turned out to be the most pleasant hour she'd passed in a while. She put some music on, and they settled into a rhythm as they chopped, breaded, and fried a strange assortment of vegetables Philip had dropped off. But every so often, she would jolt back to reality and wonder, *what the hell are we doing? Roya's out there somewhere, probably being tortured by Tara Snyder, while we're hanging out at a luxury condo frying mushrooms?*

Cyrus called the dads in as Andi stuck a serving spoon into the too-wet rice. This place had every kitchen gadget but a rice cooker, so she'd made it on the stovetop while Cyrus handled the deep frying. Frankly, she was embarrassed to serve such mushy rice, but she brought it to the table anyway.

The dads wandered out of their gaming lair. "Just made it to the Red Queen's castle," Sam said. His bloodshot eyes had dark circles beneath them.

"She's going down," Andi's dad added.

"Okay, well, once you're done vanquishing her, I think it's time to take a little break from video games," Cyrus said as he helped himself to a tongful of fried vegetables.

Both dads looked down at the table, chastened. It was all very surreal.

A phone buzzed. Andi checked hers, hoping it was Ah-ma saying she was finally up for a chat, but it was Sam's. He stared at it a minute, reading a text on the screen.

"What does it say?" Cyrus asked.

Sam let out a sigh. "No news. It's just Naveed. He says his phone's dying and he lost his charger, so he might be out of contact for a little while."

"Maybe he can borrow one from somebody at the farm?" Andi didn't like to think about him being all alone out there without a working phone. But also, something felt off.

"Good idea," Sam said as he helped himself to a generous serving of tempura. Andi, though, couldn't stomach another bite.

After they'd helped to clean up—"No problem, just throw it all in the dishwasher!" Cyrus exclaimed, as if dishwashers were a brand-new invention—Andi went back to her room.

She flopped onto the bed. Naveed's text was really bothering her. He'd been stuck inside a tiny cabin for days and suddenly couldn't find his charger?

Andi had been trying valiantly to put him out of her mind, to stop worrying about him, but she couldn't ignore the nagging suspicion any longer. It felt like he was sending an ominous message: *I won't be responding to your texts anymore.* She might be wrong, that was possible, but all of this was reminding her way too much of the previous summer. The patterns were so similar. Naveed's irritability, his breakup with Brooke, his insistence on isolating himself—all leading up to the night of his overdose.

The thing was, it was so hard for her to tell what the line was between "not okay but getting through it" and "not okay and at imminent risk of suicide." He'd promised that he'd tell Andi if he didn't feel like he could handle it. At the time, she'd chosen to trust him. But so much had changed since then. The pact was over, his promises meant nothing, and what did she really know about what was going on inside his head?

Nothing. She knew nothing at all.

She'd probably been lulled into a false sense of security, figuring he would be okay because he had so many supports. Koffka—but his service dog hadn't been there when he'd showed up unexpectedly in court. Therapy—but he hadn't seen his therapist since he went back to the farm. His meds—but he'd gone on that rant about pharmaceutical companies during their interview with Jamal. What if he'd stopped taking them or something?

The fear was so big, it paralyzed her. She was lying there in terrible pain, from her ever-present headache and her never-ending heartbreak, and she felt like she couldn't move, she was stuck there with terrifying thoughts cycling through her mind. *Is this how it is?* she wondered. *Is this what it feels like to be Naveed?*

If so, she could understand how badly he might want to make it stop.

Which probably wasn't a healthy thought at all.

But there was one thing she could do about this. She texted Gretchen and Frida to ask them to check up on him. Then she took a painkiller, because why not? Only one, of course, just enough to take the edge off while she waited for a reply. Unfortunately, it didn't do anything to help with the agonizing thought-loop.

Her phone rang a few minutes later. When she saw who was calling, she managed to force Naveed from her thoughts, at least temporarily, because she'd waited a long time for this. She accepted the call. "Hello?"

"Hello, Andi."

"Ah-ma! How are you?"

"Fine, how are *you*?" Ah-ma asked. "I heard. I'm sorry. About. Everything."

She didn't even know the half of it. "Thanks. Ah-ma, I'm wondering if you can help me. But first, there's something you need to know. Remember, the day before you had the stroke, you got a package? Like you always did on Tuesdays."

Ah-ma didn't answer right away. Andi held her breath. Her mother had warned her that she needed to allow extra time for Ah-ma to process things.

"Yes," said Ah-ma finally.

"Well, I... I opened it. I saw the photograph inside."

"Oh." There was a definite note of disappointment in Ah-ma's voice.

Andi rushed on. "I'm sorry I lied about it. I was a little freaked out, because I saw Ah-gong standing right next to Alastor. But that's not what I'm calling about. I need to know—who's the blond guy in the photo? I think he has something to do with Tara Snyder, and if we can track him down, we might be able to find her. And my friends' little sister."

"I was afraid," Ah-ma paused. "You would ask."

"Why? What's going on, Ah-ma? Please tell me. I need to know."

"Yes. You do."

It seemed to take forever for Ah-ma to collect her thoughts. Eventually, she continued, "When the cancer was diagnosed. They said I wouldn't live. It had already spread. I was. We were. Desperate."

"Wait," Andi cut in. "That's not what Mom told me. She said you caught it early? That the prognosis was good from the beginning?"

"Listen," Ah-ma said, so Andi shut up. "It is hard. To talk. Cancer was very bad, but your ah-gong didn't want to lose me. He knew someone. Who had recovered. From cancer as bad as this. One of those men—you said his name?"

"Alastor?" Andi prompted.

"Yes. But we called him different name. Ah-gong met him at expo."

"And they decided to collaborate on Metafolia?"

"Metafolia was only the beginning," Ah-ma said. "The plant. Peritassa. They drink leaves like tea. But its seeds. Alastor found they could heal. He had tumor in lungs. From Agent Orange spray. In Vietnam. But peritassa seeds made it go away."

It all sounded very far-fetched to Andi. "And you believed this?"

"It's true. I am proof."

"But… how can you be sure…?"

Ah-ma didn't answer that. "Other men still working on this cure. Raymond gave Torsten funding."

"Torsten?"

"Blond man. Chemist. He need to isolate. Active compound. To make drug. Not easy. Plant not legal. Makes research hard."

"So… you were… testing it for him?"

"Ah-gong contacted Torsten. After cancer." Ah-ma abruptly switched to Mandarin. "I'm sorry. English is too hard right now. Is this okay?"

"Of course." Andi hoped she would be able to keep up, and wouldn't lose anything in her less-than-perfect translation.

Luckily for her, Ah-ma was still speaking slowly. "Torsten sends me samples. But it is hard. To get the dose right. At first it wasn't working. So I had to do chemo too. And sometimes it's too strong. It makes me feel very sick. But Torsten is working to make it better. And the doctors are surprised that I have recovered this much. The tumor is still shrinking. But the other cancer cells are gone."

Andi was so stunned, she had no idea what to say.

"Ah-gong thinks I shouldn't tell you this. If you tell the police. Torsten will go to jail. They'll shut down his research. I won't have the pills anymore. The cancer may start growing again."

"Oh," Andi said. "Oh, no."

"But it's okay," Ah-ma said. "It doesn't matter to me if I have one more day or a thousand. I got to see you grow up. That's all I wanted."

Tears were flowing fast from Andi's eyes now. "It matters to me. I don't want you to go, Ah-ma. I'd miss you too much."

"I don't want to leave you either, Andi. But at my age, all I'm doing is buying a little more time."

Andi wiped her nose on her sleeve. "Wait. What about Tara Snyder? Where does she fit in with all of this? Was she involved in the research too?"

"I don't know. No one ever mentioned her."

"So, where's Torsten? Do you have an address? A last name? Anything?"

"I don't know where he is. And I have to go. But, Andi, I trust you to do the right thing. Don't worry about me. About Ah-gong. It will be all right."

"Okay," Andi whispered. "I love you, Ah-ma."

"I love you, too."

After she hung up, Andi closed her eyes. She was exhausted. Overwhelmed. It was impossible to be relieved at finally knowing the name of the blond man, because now that she knew the consequences of turning him in, she wasn't sure what she should do.

Torsten. As with Raymond Whitaker, she felt certain she'd heard that name before. She kept replaying the conversation with Ah-ma, but try as she might, she couldn't find the memory she was searching for. *Remember,* she thought as sleep pulled her under. *Remember. Please.*

Cyrus

THURSDAY, JUNE 2

CYRUS HAD JUST TAKEN THE LAST DOUGHNUT OUT OF THE DEEP fryer when Andi screamed.

A million thoughts went through his mind at once: had someone broken in? Was she being attacked? But he had eyes on the locked front door, and this place was eleven floors up. No one could get in, right? Unless they climbed Spiderman-style along the walls... or hijacked a window-washer's platform or something....

No, that was ridiculous. Nevertheless, he grabbed a butcher knife from the magnetized rack and flung open her closed bedroom door, afraid of what he might see.

He crept inside, knife raised. Andi was tangled up in her sheets and appeared to be asleep, though she was muttering in an odd, creaky voice.

Cyrus exhaled and lowered the knife, glad that she hadn't woken up to see him charging into her room like a madman. She was just having a nightmare. That was all. He closed her door quietly and returned the knife to its spot on the rack.

Jake wasn't around—he had left for some important meeting with his band—but Cyrus briefly wondered if Baba would emerge from the room they were sharing to check on things. When he didn't, Cyrus peeked in to make sure his dad was still alive. All good—he was snoring loudly. Cyrus was glad Baba was finally getting some rest, now that the Red Queen had been vanquished.

Looked like he'd be eating doughnuts for dinner all by himself. Cyrus took down a few plates from the cupboard. Their clanking echoed through the eerily-quiet condo.

As he bit into his first doughnut, pausing for a moment to appreciate the ecstasy that was fried dough, he heard Andi calling his name.

Before heading to her room, he took a second to dip another doughnut into raspberry glaze for Andi. "Hey, A. Bad dream?" he asked once he got to her doorway, plate in hand.

When she looked up at him, he realized she'd been crying. "No. Yes. Sort of." She hid her head in her hands.

He closed the door behind him and set the plate on her nightstand before sitting next to her on the bed. "Want to talk about it?" he asked. By now, his post-nightmare bedside manner was well honed.

"I have a name," she said.

He didn't have a clue what that meant. "Uh, do you not like me calling you 'A'? I can call you Andi if you want."

"No. Not that." She sniffled and scooted closer to him. "The blond guy. I have a name."

"What? How did you find it?"

"Ah-ma finally called," Andi said. "She told me his name, and I knew I'd heard it before, but I couldn't figure out where. Then I fell asleep, I guess, and I remembered. I heard it at SILO, when I was in Tara Snyder's lab trying to get information from her, and she said that there was one other scientist there. Torsten. A chemist."

Now she had Cyrus's full attention. "Oh shit. The blond dude was a researcher at SILO? But I thought they all got thrown in prison?"

"Not everyone did. Just the people who were working directly with Tara and covering up what she'd done."

"Whoa. So he knew Tara before, and he helped her escape? Why? What's in it for him?"

Andi explained what she'd learned from Ah-ma. It was a lot. Cyrus tried his best to keep up.

"Holy shit," he said when she was finished. "So *that's* what this is about? Their evil plan is to... cure cancer?"

"Yeah." Andi leaned back against her pillows. "Cy, I don't know what to do. I mean, I want to tell the police, but also... I don't want Ah-ma to die."

"I don't want that, either. But Roya... oh God, do you think that's why Tara took her? To experiment on her or something? We have to tell them. This is our chance to save her. It's a good lead, it totally fits...."

"But we don't even have his full name. We don't know where his lab is or anything. And besides, if it's true, if they really do have some sort of miracle cure, then... it's not just about Ah-ma, think of all the other people out there who could be helped."

"If it's really that amazing, then it needs to be researched by *real* scientists," Cyrus said.

"Yeah, but it sounds like that's complicated, since the plant's illegal, you know, kind of like cannabis or something, Brooke's always talking about how it's hard to do good science on it because of the federal laws—"

"Look, A, all I'm saying is that we shouldn't leave this up to a couple of crazy people in a secret lab! People who don't think twice about kidnapping little girls and—"

"Stop." Andi massaged her forehead. "Okay. I get it. We have to tell them. Even if it means I'm handing my grandma a death sentence."

"It's not like that," Cyrus said. "You're doing the right thing, no question."

She turned her back on him. He could tell she was crying, so he rubbed her back until she shook him off.

"I'm so sorry, A," he said. "I'll leave you alone, but I, um, I brought you a doughnut, it's still warm, even... I mean, if you're hungry, which you're probably not right now, but.... yeah. I'll be right outside if you need me."

He found his phone at the table and finished the doughnut he'd abandoned, plus one more for good measure, while he browsed for information about Torsten. At least he had a mission now. Baba had said the detectives would come by sometime this afternoon, and if Cyrus could track down Torsten's lab before they arrived, Roya might still have a chance.

Cyrus had slowly been losing faith that they'd find her. At first, he'd been certain that everything would be fine. Even though he knew it hadn't been anything more than a weed-induced vision, the version of the future he'd glimpsed at Maman's memorial was so comforting that he'd been reaching for it often, like a magical talisman, like that star charm Roya had once sewn to her flute case. Back when all this started, holding onto that feeling had been enough to reassure him.

But it had been two whole days. The police had zero leads on where Roya or Tara had gone—the officers who'd been guarding Tara at the courthouse had apparently been poisoned and were still unconscious. This new development, the likelihood that Tara Snyder was experimenting on his little sister, quite frankly scared Cyrus shitless.

At least Andi had made some progress. They had a name now. Torsten. Not exactly common, which was good. It shouldn't be difficult to figure out where the guy's lab was. Right?

But after searching for like an hour and still finding nothing, he decided to call in his assistant hacker. Maybe Todd would have more luck.

Cyrus still had an itchy feeling that Maman had known something, so he spent some time thoroughly searching the family laptop. He didn't find anything, though that was partly his fault for setting up the browser so that the history wasn't saved. He was about to throw the power cord across the room in frustration when he had a thought.

Maybe the information he needed wasn't on the laptop.

Maybe it was on her phone. The phone that Naveed had found the day she died.

He stood by what he'd told Andi, though. They couldn't get that phone unless they went down to the farm and wrestled it out of his brother's hands. It was unlikely to contain any useful information, anyway, since he'd set it up with such stringent security controls.

Cyrus closed the laptop with a heavy sigh. No leads anywhere. Might as well just wait for the police to get here, tell them what was up, and hope they could figure out where to find this Torsten dude.

He drifted to the kitchen. Out of habit, he scrubbed his glaze-smeared plate, scouring it with a soapy sponge, before remembering that he could've just thrown it in the dishwasher. Oh well. Might as well finish the job. As he rinsed it off under a stream of hot water, something else came to him.

All this time, he'd been focused on electronic devices. But Maman was old school. She wrote notes to herself on scraps of paper all the time. Writing things by hand helped her remember better, she always said.

Obviously, since he wasn't at home, he couldn't search the filing cabinet or the stacks of paper on the office desk. But there was one thing he could check: the laptop bag. She'd been using it to carry the laptop to work recently, since the computer in her office had crashed.

He felt inside the front pockets and found a small notebook. It was mostly empty, except for a few barely decipherable notes in Maman's handwriting. Nothing important, though. Just mundane things she'd jotted down.

Check in w/Akilah re: GiveBig. Roya PT resched for Tues. Interview tmrw @ 1pm. Pick up canned pineapple.

Cyrus had to put a hand on his heart to guard against the painful tightness in his chest. That canned pineapple had been for him. It was still in their cupboard. He'd never gotten around to making the sweet-and-sour tofu he'd requested it for.

He continued turning pages, even though he wanted nothing more than to stop. This was pointless, and it hurt, and he was wrong, Maman hadn't known anything and—

Wait. Hold on, was that—

Yes. Tucked between pages in the back was a loose sheet of folded paper. He unfolded it and found a list.

Torsten Ostrom: Silo/consulting for Metafolia —> Genbiotix? —> founder of Pharmabox Inc

Raymond Whitaker: funding? Pharmabox board?

Alastor Yarrow: supplier of raw materials, Metafolia founder

Henry Lin: producer (gr tea extract for Metafolia), conn to Pharmabox = ??

So she *had* been investigating the photo. And it was just like Andi had said. This shit was all connected.

Several addresses were listed on the other side. The first few were labeled *former Nutrexo lab space*. Those addresses were crossed out. Then there was one labeled *Genbiotix?*, also crossed out. The last one was circled. It said, *Pharmabox Inc.*

Cyrus opened the laptop and looked up the Pharmabox website, but found only a slick-looking landing page that said the site was under development. When he searched the address Maman had written down, it turned out to be a big warehouse in Tukwila that looked creepy as hell on street view. Windowless. Shadowy. The perfect location for a secret lab.

How had Maman found this address? All of her tracks had been erased, so, he supposed, he might never know. *Thank you, Maman*, Cyrus thought. *You're a genius. This is everything we need to find Roya.*

He resolved to celebrate with sweet-and-sour tofu once he was back home and all this was over.

A loud knock startled him, but the video doorbell's screen showed two of the detectives who had been working the case. Cyrus opened the door and offered them each a doughnut. Detective Dotson took one, but his buff partner Detective Radley declined. The guy probably ate a zero-carb diet or something. Dotson's eyes lit up with bliss when he bit into the doughnut.

"Should I wake up my dad?" Cyrus figured Dotson wouldn't be

sitting there happily eating doughnuts if the police had horrible news, but he never knew with these people.

"Not necessary. We don't have any new leads," Radley said.

"Actually... Andi and I thought of something," Cyrus said. "There was another scientist at SILO—Torsten Ostrom. What happened to him after it was shut down?"

The detectives looked at each other. "There was no evidence he was involved in any wrongdoing at SILO," Radley said. "He, and several other staff members, weren't charged with anything when it closed. We've been able to reach a few of them for questioning to see if they know where Snyder might have gone, but we haven't been able to locate Torsten."

"Do you know what he looks like, though?" Cyrus asked.

"Yes," Dotson said before he polished off his last bite of doughnut.

Cyrus pulled up the picture on his phone and zoomed in on the blond guy's face. "Is this him?"

Radley squinted at the photo. "Could be," he admitted.

"Well, like I told your officers before, I saw him in the courthouse the day she escaped during the lunch recess," Cyrus said. "So can you think of a reason why a former Nutrexo scientist who worked with Tara Snyder would've been hanging out there? He wasn't there for her trial, or he would've been in the courtroom during the lockdown."

They were quiet for a minute. Cyrus went in for the kill. "Have you heard about the company he founded? Pharmabox, Inc.?"

"How did you know about that?"

Cyrus shrugged, not wanting to implicate Andi's family. "I've been digging."

"Did you find an address?" Dotson asked. "The business license only listed a P.O. Box."

"Yep. Right here." Cyrus turned the laptop around, careful to conceal Maman's notes beneath it.

Dotson was writing the address down. "Thank you," Radley said. "We've got it from here." They rushed out the door, leaving no evidence of their visit but a small plate littered with crumbs.

Even though his stomach was starting to feel leaden—the inevitable consequence of doughnut overindulgence—Cyrus turned on a baking show and got lost for a while in the drama of runny custards and soggy bottoms and ticking clocks.

Andi crept out of her room as a new episode started. "Did you hear the police when they came in?" Cyrus asked. "I found the address of Torsten's lab, and—"

"Yep. I heard." She did not sound happy, so he shut up. She puttered around in the kitchen for a bit before sitting next to him with a plate full of doughnuts.

He ate another as they watched, but by now he felt kind of sick. He couldn't restrain himself from checking his phone often. Andi was doing the same. Nothing from the police. Nothing on the news. How long would it take for them to raid the place? Had they decided against it? There were probably protocols to follow, he figured. Or maybe they wanted to wait until it got dark. Or something.

After the star baker was crowned, Cyrus glanced over at Andi. "The doughnuts are good, right? I really miss baking. Maybe we should make something together tonight? Or tomorrow, those were kind of a gut-buster, I guess, but—"

Andi interrupted. "Cy—I think Naveed's in trouble."

"When *isn't* he in trouble?" Cyrus half-joked.

"No, really. Something's wrong. The way he texted about being out of contact for a while—that was weird, right? And with all that's going on, Roya missing, Tara on the loose, I'm afraid that he... what if he couldn't handle it?"

Another episode started, its peppy theme music filling the living room. It really did not fit the vibe. Cyrus turned the volume down. "He'll be okay. If nothing else, he's got Koffka—"

"Does he, though? He didn't bring Koffka to court."

"What are you saying?"

"I don't know," she said miserably. "Just that I'm worried. I texted

Gretchen and Frida to see if they could check on him, but they haven't replied. That was hours ago."

As if on cue, her phone lit up. "It's Frida!" she exclaimed, but her face fell when she opened it. "Oh."

"What's wrong?"

Andi turned the screen toward him. Cyrus stared at the photo of a beaming Gretchen, who was holding a tiny pink newborn, its face all squinched up. "They're not at the farm. Their daughter just had her baby."

"They just left him there? By himself?"

"I guess so." A few more texts came in, and Andi paused to read them. "She says he promised to stay inside the cabin. The police are still staking it out, and Astro's on guard dog duty. Apparently Naveed's been in contact by text, but he messaged her a few hours ago to tell her his phone was dying and couldn't find the charger, same as he told your dad." She sighed deeply.

"We could ask the cops to check up on him," Cyrus suggested.

"Yeah, but you know how he feels about the police. If they confronted him when he was... you know. That would probably push him over the edge."

"Well, we don't really have any choice, do we?"

"Oh, hold on, I know who to ask." Andi's thumbs got busy with her phone.

Cyrus halfheartedly watched the bakers prepping their signature dishes. When Andi paused, he prompted, "So? Who is it?"

"I'm talking to someone at the Crisis Text Line. Don't worry, it's all anonymous. They're awesome, and—hold on." She typed some more, then frowned.

"What did they say?"

"They can send medics out to the farm to make sure he's okay. But that still feels risky to me."

Cyrus's stomach did a clumsy somersault. "True. That time last summer, it wasn't until after I called the medics...." He couldn't say the rest. His voice always failed him when he tried to talk about that night.

Andi exhaled slowly. "They can't give us advice on what to do, but I really don't think he should be alone right now. He needs to be with someone safe. Someone he trusts. Like us."

"But we can't...."

"Who else can, Cy?"

"You want to go to the farm. Seriously?"

"I don't know. I think so. Yes."

"Let me think." Cyrus turned the show off. The screen went black. "Okay. You're right, the cops and medics are almost guaranteed to set him off, so we can't rely on them. And I'm, like, 100% positive Tara's hiding out at Torsten's lab in Tukwila. That's the only thing that makes sense. Which means it should be safe for us to go to the farm. Especially since the police are staking it out. Not that our dads would agree, but... Baba's zonked, he probably won't be up for ages. And your dad said not to wait up. He might go out after he meets with the band."

A flash of anger passed across Andi's face. "Well, if he can go out, why can't we? And this is way more important than some band meeting."

By the time Andi had gotten dressed and they'd composed a vague note for their dads that included the number of Cyrus's burner, the only phone they were bringing, dusk was falling. Cyrus pulled out of the parking garage, hopeful that they'd missed rush hour and would get there quickly, but traffic through downtown was at a standstill. They chugged through the gridlock as darkness fell. The wind lashed sheets of rain against the windows.

Finally, they pulled up in front of Gretchen and Frida's small yellow house. There was a police car parked on the side of the road just before the driveway, but it looked empty.

Andi, who had been resting with her eyes closed, breathed out and ran her fingers through her hair. "It looks the same," she said. "I haven't been back here since... you know."

"Yeah, me neither," Cyrus said.

"Really? You haven't come to visit him?"

"Nah. Haven't had time. I think his cabin's in the back, though. There's a side road…"

Cyrus rolled slowly down the road, leaning forward to see through the windshield better. "It's so dark out here—oh shit," he swore as his car bottomed out. "Looks pretty rough ahead. Better walk from here, I guess."

He parked. They pulled their hoods up as they walked along the road, briefly veering into the squishy grass to avoid a huge mud-pit, all the way to the little cabin at the edge of the woods. The porch light was on, their only beacon in the darkness. He kept expecting to hear Astro barking or see a police officer patrolling, but everything was silent and still. Andi had her keychain-pepper-spray at the ready, so Cyrus followed her lead and opened the pocketknife he'd taken from his dad's jacket before they left.

Andi knocked on the door. No answer.

She jiggled the knob and knocked again. "Naveed, it's me. Please open the door. Please. We need to know you're okay."

Still nothing.

They circled the perimeter. Andi tried to peer into the curtained windows. "I can't see anything." Her voice shook in frustration. "Should we… what should we do?"

Cyrus stumbled on a patch of uneven ground. He turned on his phone flashlight and looked where he'd stepped. It was strange, there was a muddy track through the grass, which was flattened in the middle as if…

As if something had been dragged along the ground. Something heavy.

Like. For example. A body.

He traced the track with his flashlight. It was continuous, unbroken, about a foot wide. And it led straight up the slope into the woods.

That was when they heard a distant sound. A frantic bark echoing through the trees, finding its way to them.

"Koffka." Andi took off running up the slope toward the forest.

Good thing the cops were right out there on the road. Cyrus dialed 911 as he rushed behind her, following Andi into the dark woods.

Naveed

NAVEED STAYED IN THE CORNER OF THE PIT, KEEPING HIS distance from Tara Snyder. She watched as he took his weapons out of his pocket, lining them all up on the muddy ground in front of him, as if preparing for surgery. He glanced at her and saw the red stain above her knee where Koffka had clamped her leg in his jaws. It made him dizzy, so he looked up. The clouds above him whipped by, revealing splotches of dark sky and the waning moon, thin as a clipped fingernail now. *Glory of the moon*, he thought, returning his gaze to the ground. He added the gun to the end of the lineup.

Then he walked over to her, behind her, scythe in hand, boots squelching in the mud. He heaved her into a sitting position, then passed the curved metal blade over her head, slowly, pulling it closer to her neck as it descended. He'd sharpened the blade, and it curved so beautifully around her, sickle blade under a sickle moon. Forget guns. Once the interrogation was over, this was how he would kill her. A proper execution.

But he wasn't ready for that yet. "If you try to scream for help, the police are close by, they're going to find you and haul your ass back to prison. I'm only taking this off so you can answer my questions," he told her, keeping the blade against her neck, loosening the tie with his other hand and letting it fall away to the ground.

"You're wrong," she said. "They won't come, I took care of that."

Before he could even register what that meant, she continued, "I didn't come here to hurt you. I just want to talk. Why don't you put that thing down?"

He waited for the hatred to surge up, but it refused to come. He was back to numbness, even with her right in front of him. "No. I'm not letting you get away with what you did to my mother. You killed her. And now it's my turn to kill you."

"You're not going to blame *me* for that, are you?" Her words sent a fault line racing across the icy numb. "She did it to herself, Naveed. Life is hard for everyone, you know, but some of us get back up when we're pushed down. Some of us keep fighting and fighting even when it seems like all is lost. Others… well, others just give up."

Naveed felt like he was on fire suddenly, like maybe fire had been hidden beneath the ice all this time, and it had finally burned through. He had to restrain himself from slicing her head off right then and there.

"Look, I know you don't want to live either," she went on. "I saw what you were doing with my gun. It feels good, holding something that powerful, doesn't it? So let me help you. That's what this is about, right? You want to die, you want to stop this cycle you're stuck in, but you're too scared to do it yourself."

"What? No!" he yelled. "No. Stop this—just tell me. Where's Roya?"

That shut her up. He was still behind her, but even though he knew he wouldn't have gotten any clues from her face, he wished he could've seen her expression.

"Where is she?" he asked again.

Still, she said nothing. He removed the scythe from around her neck and walked over to his array of weapons. Now he could see her eyes, but they showed no fear. He took the small stick and returned behind her.

Her hands were pale and blood-starved. He held her index finger tight and jabbed the sharp stick deep underneath her fingernail. "Where is she? *What did you do to her?*"

She cried out, so he moved on to the next finger. "I won't stop until you tell me," he said.

"Please," she said through clenched teeth. "This isn't about Roya. Just give me a chance to explain."

"Go right ahead." He went in for another jab, but the drop of blood beading on the tip of her index finger stopped him. He had to look away while the world got fuzzy.

He was a terrible torturer.

Naveed stepped out from behind her and returned to his tools. Next was the obsidian blade, though he wasn't eager to use it.

"You don't care about dying," Tara said. "That's not what you're afraid of. You're afraid of being forgotten. You want to make your mark—you want your death to *mean* something. And I can make that happen, if you just help me with what I need."

"Help? With what?" He felt like he was losing control of the conversation, but he had to know.

"You and me," she said. "Strange that it had to be this way, but you and me are the only ones who can make this work. We can only do it together." She didn't seem to be feeling pain anymore. He had lost his upper hand, but still he listened. "I'm sure you know by now that many herbicides are potent carcinogens, and Compadre was no exception."

"What are you saying?" It was like she'd reached a hand inside his chest and was shredding his lungs into tiny pieces.

"It's only a matter of time before the cancer develops," she said. "And I know you don't care about saving yourself, but your sister was exposed, too. Cyrus, Andi, all of you. But I'm closing in on a cure. If you could help save them—and thousands, hundreds of thousands, of people with cancer, why wouldn't you do it? That's why I'm here, that's what got me out, there's a new path for both of us, a new life's work. We're so close, Naveed. And you can help. You're the last piece of the puzzle."

"You expect me to believe you have some sort of miraculous cancer cure, that I'm going to go back with you willingly, turn myself into your lab rat again? You. Are. Absolutely. Insane." Naveed decided to skip the obsidian blade in favor of the scythe. He needed to get back on top of this.

She snorted. "Like you're one to talk. Multiple psychiatric hospitalizations in the past year, trouble with the law, locked up in a mental institution for three months…. don't act like you're any saner than I am."

He tried not to show any emotion, but those words cut deep. They also, he realized, gave him an opening to ask something else he wanted to know. "So that was Tim Schmidt's whole deal?" Naveed asked. "You sent him to spy on me. At Englewood. The urgent care clinic. He kept asking me to release my medical records. I didn't give him permission. But you got them anyway, didn't you?"

"He knows how critical this project is," Tara said. "And he knows that you're an important part of it. I needed to monitor your labs, your records, and he knew how to get me access. If you come with me, I'll tell you all about the project and how you fit into it. It doesn't have to be like it was before. As long as you cooperate."

Naveed tightened his grip on the scythe. "No. Just tell me where the lab is."

"That isn't how it works," she said. "We go together or not at all."

"Then I choose not at all."

"Are you sure about that? You don't care about helping Roya? Or Cyrus, or Andi? You'd rather be stubborn and—"

"Don't you see where you are?" Naveed interrupted. "This is it, Tara. This is where you die."

He dropped the scythe on the ground and seized her throat with both hands. He pushed her backwards until he was on top of her, pressing her further into the mud, she couldn't scream, couldn't do anything because he was choking the air out of her, he was going to kill her, right here right now she was lying lying lying but but but—

Roya. What if the research project was real, and she had taken Roya and was experimenting on her in a secret lab somewhere? If he killed Tara, no one would ever know where Roya had gone.

So, at the last moment, when her lips had turned purple, he relented, and she made awful gasping noises while air rushed back into her lungs, awful because they meant she was alive; they meant he had spared her, which meant that she had won.

For now.

He slid off of her, but as he did he caught sight of her leg again, the one Koffka had attacked, the section of fabric that was soaked with her blood, and the sight of it brought him back to the barn at Englewood where he had found Roya, her leg crushed by the horses, the flames closing in, the thick smoke engulfing them—

The next thing he knew, he was face down in the mud. Why was he lying in the mud? Didn't even matter. He wanted to go back to sleep. Sleep, so elusive; he'd just had a taste and didn't want to let it go, but the skies had opened up in a downpour, fat raindrops hammering down on his head, and there was another sound, a strange one, like sawing, and Koffka barking in the distance.

He started to sit up, soaked to the bone, he had just been burning hot but he wasn't anymore, he was shivering with cold, and this all felt very familiar, so he wasn't surprised when he saw Tara there in the pit with him. But he *was* surprised when he realized what she was doing, that she'd managed to cut off her wrist bonds by scraping them against the scythe lying on the ground beside her—and just as he realized this, she lunged at him.

Her left hand dangled limply by her side—something was very wrong with her shoulder—but the force of her body knocked him back down, and she threw herself across him. Though she wasn't able to restrain him completely, with only one hand in use and her ankles still tied, she pressed the heel of her palm against the base of his throat and leaned on it with all her weight.

Naveed gasped, but no air came through. None at all: she would make sure he never took another breath. She didn't need blades or guns, no, her words and her hand were the only weapons she needed, and they had worked, that's what was so disgusting, he was going to die in a muddy pit, wriggling and wet like a fish, her hand forcing his neck against the ground.

He tried to get out, he tried, growing increasingly frantic; he didn't want to open his eyes because he didn't want her face to be the last thing he saw, but then all he could feel was her hand, her hand on his throat, Maman's hand down in the ravine, Maman's hand holding the glass mug in his cabin, her hand ripping apart the sprouts at Sizdah Bedar and scattering them into the river, those sprouts that meant rebirth, a fresh start, the green things growing from dirt and decay.

With a force that surprised him, Naveed managed to whack Tara in the bad shoulder with his right fist.

She cried out in pain and relented just enough for him to get a breath in, a small one, it felt like the passageway had narrowed, his windpipe collapsing, but it was a breath just the same, and it gave him the strength to tear her hand away, knocking her off balance and allowing him to overpower her, and the next thing he knew he was free. He still gasped for breath and felt like he was going to pass out any second, darkness trying to close in, but he wouldn't let it. He wouldn't let her take this from him. For so long she had been controlling every part of his life, even in her absence, and he wanted it back.

He punched her in the shoulder again and she went down, howling. He could barely hear it through the pouring rain. He rolled her over so she was lying on her stomach, then picked up the scythe and sat on top of her, restraining her hands with his knees, and he pulled her head up by her fucking bun, which had come unfastened and was now a muddy ponytail, and he hooked the scythe around her throat. He'd find another way to save Roya, if she could be saved, but he couldn't let Tara Snyder live any longer.

There was a strange sound, it was dry and rustly, like wind through reeds, like coughing, but not coughing, it was a happier sound, and it took a minute to realize that *he* was making the sound, he was laughing, he was about to separate Tara Snyder's head from her body and he was giddy about it, and just as he realized this he heard his name coming from above.

He looked up. Andi and Cyrus stood at the edge of the pit. He supposed he should be relieved to see them, but he wasn't, not at all. He was annoyed—no, *furious*—at being interrupted. As far as he could tell, they were horrified. Their identical expressions of shock distracted him just long enough for Tara Snyder to wriggle her right hand loose. He had no idea how it happened so fast, but the next thing he knew she was clawing at him, digging her sharp fingernails into the sensitive skin on the underside of his wrist, which made him reflexively relax his grip on the scythe, and then she was tackling his arm to the ground, taking advantage of his loss of balance by rolling out from under him, and though he kept his grip on her hair she had the scythe now, and the last thing he saw was Andi's face, the terror in her eyes, and he noticed her lips were moving, like she was saying something, maybe his name, though he couldn't hear anything anymore.

Then Tara Snyder slammed the wooden shaft hard against the side of his head and the world plunged into darkness.

Andi

THURSDAY, JUNE 2

OF ALL THE THINGS ANDI HAD SEEN, ALL SHE'D BEEN THROUGH, the sight awaiting her when she and Cyrus ran into that clearing was one of the worst.

She had prepared herself for finding Naveed's lifeless body. As horrible and traumatic as that would have been, she never would've predicted that she'd find him down in that pit under his black hood, wild-eyed and laughing maniacally—there was no other word for it—while holding an actual scythe up to Tara Snyder's throat. Andi instinctively jerked backwards, knowing with certainty what was about to happen: he was going to cut her head off.

But he caught Andi's eye then, and froze mid-laugh. He glared at her. There was no sign of regret in his expression, no embarrassment or shame. Only anger.

His hesitation lasted only seconds, but while he was distracted Tara had twisted out of his grip. Andi yelled to warn him. Too late. Tara wrestled him to the ground and shoved the scythe handle into his temple. He fell back limply into the mud.

Andi crouched, hoping the raised stone foundation would conceal her and Cyrus. Maybe Tara hadn't seen them or heard Andi cry out.

"Where are the police?" Cyrus muttered. "They're on the property somewhere—they should be here by now."

Andi peeked over the concrete edge. Tara was using the scythe to cut the ropes binding her ankles. Her left arm drooped at her side, but that didn't slow her down. She moved quickly once free, and the first thing she did was to cross the pit and pry something out of the mud. Andi's heart clenched when she realized what it was. A gun.

Tara returned to Naveed, whose body lay face down. She kept the gun trained on him as she stepped closer, and Andi knew what came next. There was no way he was getting out of this alive.

Then Tara pointed the gun at Andi and Cyrus.

"Thank you," she yelled through the driving rain. "Thank you for distracting him. I'm going to need a hand getting out of here, and you're either going to help me out and let me go, or you're going to die."

Andi and Cyrus looked at each other. What choice did they have? They had been so stupid to come back here, should have waited for the police, but how could they have possibly known?

Cyrus closed his pocketknife and returned it to his jacket. Andi did the same with her pepper spray. Neither weapon was useful from this distance. Neither would protect them from her gun.

Across the foundation from them, Koffka was snarling, straining at his rope. He seemed frantic to get to Naveed, who still hadn't moved.

Tara threw them the rope that had been used to bind her ankles. Andi caught it and tied it around a nearby tree. Before she threw the end down to Tara, though, she yelled, "If we help you, you have to let us go."

"Of course. Now throw the rope down."

Andi knew better than to believe Tara. At the same time, she knew Tara liked to think of herself as an honorable person, which of course was insane, but if Andi made her promise something, maybe she would keep her word.

Or not.

Andi lowered the rope. As soon as it landed in the pit, she took Cyrus's hand and pulled him around the foundation to Koffka.

Her secret weapon.

Right now, Koffka was nothing like his normal gentle self. He bared his sharp teeth, growling like an attack dog.

"Hold onto the rope while I untie him," Andi whispered to Cyrus. Cyrus nodded reluctantly and veered behind the two of them as Andi approached the dog.

"Koffka," she said in a quiet, calm voice. She glanced over her shoulder. Tara was climbing out slowly, since she only had one hand to work with. "Koffka, sit."

The dog whined, licking his lips, pulling at the rope again. Andi examined the knot. It was so tight she doubted she'd be able to untie it.

But—duh, she didn't need to. "I need the knife," she said to Cyrus.

He handed his pocketknife to her. While he held onto the rope restraining Koffka, she sawed at it, and when Tara Snyder emerged from the pit and raised the gun at them again, they were both holding tightly to Koffka's rope. As soon as the dog saw Tara, they had to pull hard to keep him from going after her.

For one tense moment, Andi thought her plan wouldn't work. Tara was going to shoot them, every single one of them, and it would all end here in this rainy forest.

But Koffka was moving back and forth, side to side, as he tried to escape from their grip. He wasn't an easy target. And if Tara shot either of them instead, Koffka would be on her in seconds.

Tara lowered the gun and backed out of the clearing, then disappeared into the woods behind her.

Koffka was still straining at the rope, barking frantically. Andi and Cyrus looked at each other. Then they let him go.

For a second Andi thought he would jump down into the pit to be with Naveed, but he didn't. He tore away into the forest, streaking through the dark woods in pursuit of Tara.

Andi hesitated. Down in the pit, Naveed was stirring. Should she really go check on him? What if he turned against her for letting Tara get away?

But she couldn't just abandon him, either. She knew she needed to be with him right now. She had to remember—and she had to help *him* try to remember—who he really was.

She lowered herself into the pit, slipping when she landed. Naveed lay nearby, shaking and sputtering, wiping at his face with his sleeve and straining to breathe through his mouth.

Andi's head was spinning by now, and it hurt of course, and she felt like time was sliding around again. She staggered toward him.

That was when she heard a gunshot in the forest, followed by the unmistakable howl of a dog.

Koffka, she thought. *Oh God. She got Koffka.*

But then another possibility occurred to her: Cyrus had disappeared, too. *He went to get help,* she told herself. *He's fine. He has to be fine.*

It struck her that jumping into the pit had been a very stupid move. Now she was trapped. If Tara came back, it would be so easy to pick off the two of them.

Andi was incredibly tired all of a sudden. She lowered herself down in the mud near Naveed. He recoiled from her.

"It's just me," Andi said, though he probably knew that. "She's gone."

Slowly, he rolled over so he was facing her. The rain was starting to let up a little. "Is she coming back?" he asked between gaspy breaths.

"I don't know." Andi had to close her eyes. Her head was hurting so bad now.

"Well, then what the fuck are you doing here?" he asked. "Go! Run!"

"No. I'm not leaving."

"Don't do this," he gasped. It was painful to listen to him trying to force air into his lungs. "Leave. I don't want you to die."

"Well, I don't want *you* to die, either," she countered. "I think she's gone. Let's just breathe together for a minute." She inhaled slowly.

His eyes were darting around, not focusing on hers. "I can't... breathe... Andi, I fucked up and I can't... do this anymore... can't live... with myself...."

"Is Nate back?" Andi asked. "Don't listen to him, Naveed. You've gotten through this before. I know you can do it again."

"No," Naveed said. "This time... it's not going to get better. It's just... it's not." To her surprise, he got up and crawled through the mud away from her.

Andi stood, but a wave of dizziness kept her anchored to the spot. By the time it had passed, he was crouched in the corner holding a knife. Black blade, ivory handle. He pushed his left sleeve up, exposing his forearm.

"Naveed. Listen to me," she said desperately. The knife blade hovered above his wrist. "So you've made some mistakes—we all have. But what really matters is what you do next. You have a choice. Please, don't do this. Don't leave us. Please."

Naveed opened his mouth, and Andi dared to hope she had changed his mind. But then, before she could even react, he plunged the blade into his arm.

So many things rose up in Andi then. Horror. Frustration. An unexpected fury. She crossed the distance between them and kicked his shoulder hard.

He howled in pain and dropped the knife, which fell to the ground. He, too, lost his balance and landed in the mud.

"Oh, did that hurt?" Andi yelled as she picked up the knife. "Good! Because that's only a fraction of how much you're hurting me right now!"

He curled up on his side, wheezing, holding his wrist.

Her heart jumped with worry—she'd been so focused on getting the knife out of his hand that she wasn't sure how deeply he'd cut himself, but she couldn't see any blood, so maybe it wasn't too bad. She sat beside him, hugging her knees to her chest, exhausted. "We need you here, Naveed. So stop thinking of all the bad stuff, and look at the good things

you've done, here on the farm... how many people you've helped...."
Her vision was getting swimmy, from tears in her eyes or her pounding
headache, she wasn't sure which, so she closed her eyes again, and rested
her head on her knees.

"You know what I've been thinking about," she murmured. "Last
February. Not the day—the day with Jed, but the weeks after that. I
remember canoeing on the lake, our picnics, the sun shining on us, but
even the days we'd just lie around listening to music together were perfect
too. Because I love you. You're, like, the person I always looked forward to
talking to, and being around, so when your mom asked if I could keep an
eye on you when you moved out, I wanted to help, because I care about
you, and I'm sorry if you hate being watched over like that, but you know
what? You can't do it alone. Nobody can." She paused to catch her breath.
"You're the strongest person I've ever met, Naveed. You can get through
this. You *have* to get through this. Because we need you."

She peeked at him. His eyes were still closed, but he looked unbearably
sad. Her gaze traveled down to his hand, which was still holding his wrist,
and a tidal wave of dizziness hit her when she saw it: his fingers were
covered in blood. It oozed out from between them, it ran down his arm,
pooling on the wet earth beneath them.

"I can't," he whispered. "I'm so sorry."

"No. You can get through this. You can." Andi looked frantically for
something, anything, she could use to stop the bleeding, but saw nothing,
so she pried his fingers off and clamped one hand firmly beneath the cut,
squeezing hard, hoping it would cut off the blood flow. She pressed her
other hand to the wound itself and raised his arm high, because weren't
those the things you were supposed to do? Apply pressure. Elevate. But
it didn't seem to be helping at all, it felt like her hands were beneath a
faucet of warm water that grew cold as soon as the air touched it, and
the liquid running down her fingers looked black, not red like blood
was supposed to look, it was coming from that deep inside him, it was
coming out that fast.

"Stop," she found herself whispering, as if that word could fly into the wound, stanching the flow, fixing everything. But words couldn't help. They hadn't helped. He was literally slipping away, and she couldn't save him this time, and she was hurt and afraid and horrified and angry all at once, because there was nothing more she could do, nothing but sit here with him until it was all over.

But a sudden sound made her tighten her grip: the rustling trees. The heavy footsteps, growing closer.

Someone was coming.

Roya

TUESDAY, MAY 31

ROYA LOOKED UP AT THE STRANGER TOWERING ABOVE, THE person who had been following her as she wandered these empty streets looking for Moonstone Apothecary. She couldn't see his face because he was backlit by the afternoon sun. Her knee was on fire and she wanted to cry, but she bit the tears back. At least she'd managed to get what she needed from her backpack before she fell.

"Aw, a poor little cripple out all by herself." The stranger's voice squeaked slightly at the end of the sentence. He wasn't a grown-up, Roya realized suddenly, he was probably younger than Cyrus even. He cleared his throat and added, in an extra-mocking tone, "Where's your mommy?"

"Actually," Roya paused for emphasis. "She's dead." She curled her fingers around the agate stone in her palm, then flung it at the boy.

He howled as it made contact right between his eyes. While he was distracted, Roya rifled through the front pocket of her backpack until she found the athame. She pointed it at him, imagining that the pain sending shock waves through her leg was being transformed; she was channeling it into a river of energy that flowed out through the tip of the knife.

Think about your intentions, Kass had said to her once as they stepped inside a circle of thirteen birch trees. Roya didn't want to hurt this boy, she just wanted him to leave her alone. *I want you to go away,* she thought, directing the flow of energy straight to his chest.

"Don't come any closer," she said. Her voice sounded different when it came out. Deeper. Older. "Unless you want me to cut out your eyes."

The boy was staring at her. She stared back, unblinking, fierce. He was the one who broke eye contact. "Crazy little bitch," he muttered. Then he turned around and walked away.

Despite the roaring ache in her knee, a rush of joy swept through Roya. She had done it! She had actually performed magic, and this time the results had been immediate and satisfying. To that boy, she'd looked like a helpless little girl. But she wasn't helpless at all. She was powerful.

All the same, she was still lost—and now she was also hurt. She knew she wouldn't be able to stand on her leg, let alone retrace her steps back to the train station. Not yet, anyway.

Maybe, she thought, she could find her way into one of these abandoned houses. That would at least get her out of the open, into a place where she could rest while she figured out what to do next.

She raised the athame again. *Show me the way,* she thought, moving it in a semi-circle as she scanned the houses around her.

It took a few minutes of careful looking, but finally something caught her eye: an open window at the base of a nearby building that she figured she could squeeze through.

The hard part was getting there. Roya tucked the knife back into its sheath, then returned it to her bag. She hoisted it onto her back before half-crawling, half-dragging her way to the gap. It was only once she got there that she realized her agate stone was still on the sidewalk, but there was nothing to be done about it now. She could go back to get it once she could walk again.

Roya inspected the window. It was impossible to tell what was inside. Everything was pitch black.

Anything would be better than staying out here, though. The boy might come back at any moment. And he might bring his friends.

She wriggled through feet first, but even though she stretched her good leg as far as it would go, she couldn't touch the ground. Bracing herself, she slid through, reaching her good leg downward, hoping that she'd be able to land on it without putting pressure on the bad one.

But the drop was too far, and she landed clumsily again, falling to her knees and reaching her hands out to absorb most of the impact.

"Owwww," she howled into the darkness as the pain in her knee exploded like a firework, bright and sudden, lighting up her entire body. Strangely, a sharp sensation shot through her hands, too. It was only after her eyes adjusted to the dim light that she understood why: the ground was littered with broken glass.

Once the initial shock had worn off, Roya scooted herself to a clear spot and took stock. The room was large and empty, as far as she could tell. Her left hand was all scraped up, and there was a big piece of glass stuck to her right. She took it out and saw a deep cut running across her palm. The sight of blood made her dizzy, but she made herself open her backpack and wrap it up tightly in one of her t-shirts. Then she tied the leather sheath around her waist. She felt a little safer now that the athame's handle was in easy reach. Once that was done, she let herself lie down, using her bag like a pillow, not that there was any way to be comfortable on this cold concrete floor.

For a while the pain swallowed her up. She drifted, trying not to think about the hunger gnawing in her belly, the thirst tearing at her throat. She would get up soon, she kept telling herself. She'd get up and climb back out and find someone who could help as soon as the ache faded.

But it didn't lessen as the day went on. Standing up was impossible, and even scooting around on the floor hurt so bad she almost passed out. The sliver of light from the window above grew dimmer and dimmer until darkness covered her entirely. Sometimes Roya heard scurrying sounds. Sometimes things that sounded like footsteps. Remembering the boy from earlier, Roya took the athame in her left hand since it hurt to move the fingers on her right, and traced a circle around and over her. *Protect me,* she thought, directing energy through the knife again. For some reason it exhausted her to do this. Maybe she'd let too much energy flow out of her. She would need to be more careful.

In the night, the seriousness of her situation started to sink in. She couldn't stand up. Couldn't get out of here. She had no food, no water. No one in her family had a clue where she was. Even Kass couldn't be counted on. She had sworn off witchcraft, so it wasn't like she'd be able to do any spells that would lead her to Roya. Plus, Roya had all her friend's magical tools anyway.

The tools. An idea struck her. She dug through her backpack, tossing clothes out until she found what she was looking for.

Her first wand.

She raised the flute to her lips and played quietly, hoping that the message would get through to someone who could understand. But it really hurt her cut hand whenever she moved her fingers to play different notes, and it made her even more thirsty and tired, plus she started to worry that it might get the attention of any boys lurking outside. After a few minutes, she stopped playing.

So much for that idea.

As she picked up her clothes and stuffed them back inside her bag, she found the pink scarf, still wrapped around Maman's rose oil perfume. That was the whole reason she was here in the first place: she'd been looking for the shaman, who could channel Maman so Roya could talk to her again.

But… what if she didn't need the shaman after all? Roya was powerful on her own: magic ran through her veins. She used to think that the wording of the spell was the most important part. Now, though, she knew that the feeling behind them was just as critical. The incantation, the ingredients, the intention, the action—the spell would only work when all of those pieces were put together.

Newly energized, Roya laid out all her magical objects before her. The candle, the crow feather, the trio of bay leaves, the flute. The Book of Shadows from Orcinia, since that one felt a lot more sacred than her little store-bought notebook. The bottle of perfume.

She removed the beanie she'd been wearing and replaced it with the pink scarf, wrapping it carefully around her hair. Maman had bought it while in Iran, but Roya had never actually seen her wear it. Still, it felt good to be surrounded in something her mother had once touched, and she could almost feel the ghost of Maman's fingertips brushing her hair out of her eyes. She spritzed the bottle of perfume until the fragrance of rose filled the air.

"Maman," Roya said out loud. "I need to talk to you. Please come."

She held her breath and unwrapped her hand, the one with the big deep cut. As soon as she stretched her fingers out, it opened up again. Roya touched the wound to her objects, anointing the candle, and the blade of the knife, and the flute. Her blood glistened in the dim moonlight.

Roya re-wrapped her hand and gazed at the crow feather. She played, softly, the finding song she'd written for Maman the day she died. The crow feather tried to float away on the little tufts of air escaping her flute, so she had to stop mid-song and anchor the feather safely under the Book of Shadows.

After playing through the song a few times, she set her flute down and took the knife in both hands, directing the energy to the perfume bottle, smelling roses every time she breathed. *Maman, please come. Please.*

Roya sat there for a very long time, focusing as hard as she could. *Maman, where are you? I just need to tell you that I'm sorry. I need to say goodbye. Is that why you're haunting us? Because I didn't say goodbye?*

Nothing happened. Maman didn't materialize in front of Roya, she didn't whisper reassuring words into her ear, she didn't float across Roya's skin, leaving a trail of goosebumps.

"No," Roya said, angry now, yelling. "No! Maman, you have to come! I need you! How could you just leave me?"

There was no answer.

No one was coming. What did that mean? Had the shayatin completely devoured Maman's soul, leaving no trace of her in the spirit realm or anywhere else? Or what if...

What if the shayatin had never been there at all?

What if Maman had just stopped loving Roya?

What if Maman had abandoned her in the same way Naveed had when he moved out, disappearing from her life suddenly without even a backward glance?

Roya set down the knife. She wished she'd been able to light the candle so she could blow it out, signaling that the ritual was over. As it was, she just lowered herself down, too tired to do anything but sink into a fitful sleep.

Cyrus

WHEN ANDI JUMPED INTO THE PIT, CYRUS RAN THE OTHER WAY. He couldn't help feeling slightly annoyed as he followed the muddy track out of the woods. Andi had to see if Naveed was okay, Cyrus got that, but she was the much better runner, and now it was up to him to find help. Even though the 911 dispatcher said they would contact the police, it seemed like the patrolling officers should have turned up by now, so Cyrus might have to search this massive property himself, and by the time he found them Tara would probably be long gone....

Right now, though, he just wanted to get out of these woods. He tore through the wet brush, glancing over his shoulder frequently in case Tara was creeping up behind him. All he saw were dark outlines of trees shaking in the wind.

When he finally emerged, he jogged towards Gretchen and Frida's house. The lights were on inside. He didn't remember them being on when he pulled up. Maybe they'd come back home, or the cops were checking it out?

As he ran closer, a police officer came out of nowhere. She pointed her gun right at Cyrus. "Stop! Hands up!"

Cyrus stopped. "You've got to help," he panted as he raised his hands. "Tara Snyder. She's out there. In the woods. Right now. Please. Help."

The officer lowered her gun and called over her shoulder to a few others who were clustered near the side of the house.

Sirens screamed in the distance. Red lights flashed against the walls. There were so many cops here. But he'd told the dispatcher, and now this officer, that everyone was in the woods, so why were they hanging out here instead of rushing to the forest to catch the escaped fugitive?

One of the officers broke off from the group, looking somber. "Follow me," the officer said gruffly, leading him toward the front yard.

They arrived as an ambulance screeched to a halt in the gravel driveway, but the officer led Cyrus to another police car that had just pulled up. "He says Tara Snyder's out in the woods," the officer said to the two others as they got out of the squad car. "Let's go."

"Wait. We need a medic too, actually. For my brother. She, um, attacked him...." Cyrus trailed off when he realized that there was another ambulance across the street, and someone strapped onto a gurney was being loaded inside. "Who's that?" he asked.

"Two on-duty officers were shot," one of the cops said.

"Oh shit, are they okay?" Cyrus asked, then added, "I forgot to tell you, she has a gun." Immediately he felt stupid for saying that last bit, because obviously.

"Where is she?" the other officer asked.

Cyrus led the two officers down the road toward Naveed's cabin. As they walked, two others ran up—the detectives Cyrus had talked to at the condo earlier, Dotson and Radley. He thought about making a doughnut comment, but decided against it. Definitely not the time.

Once they made it to the tree line, Cyrus pointed to the spot where he and Andi had entered the woods. "Tara's in there somewhere. Follow the trail to a clearing, that's where my brother is... and Andi, too... but I don't know where Tara went, my brother's dog chased her and I don't know... I don't know."

"Stay right here," Radley said. "Don't move until we send an all clear."

Cyrus didn't know what to do with himself. Of course he wasn't going to follow them, but it felt so weird to be standing at the edge of the woods doing nothing while all this activity was going on around him. Soon enough, though, a medic ran up, her headlamp bobbing toward him through the darkness.

"Your brother's hurt?" the medic asked, catching her breath as she set down her heavy bag of supplies. "Was he shot?"

"No, no... he was... fighting with her, she whacked him in the head and he passed out, he wasn't awake when I left...."

The medic nodded curtly. "Does he have any allergies? Any medical conditions I should be aware of?"

Cyrus actually laughed, even though it was totally inappropriate. As they waited for the go-ahead, he described a few of Naveed's many problems and quirks, warning her that he didn't like to be touched, that he sometimes freaked out around cops and medics so she might need to sedate him, all that stuff. She seemed grateful to know this ahead of time. He wondered what her job was like. She probably saw all sorts of crazy shit.

Their conversation was interrupted by an explosion of distant gunfire. Cyrus got so light-headed that he literally had to sit down right there in the mud. He touched his forehead to his knees, praying once again. *Oh God, don't let them hurt Andi and Naveed. Please keep them safe. Please.*

After some unknown stretch of time that felt endless to Cyrus but may only have been seconds, the medic's radio roared to life. "We need you in here. An officer's coming out to meet you."

When the officer appeared, Cyrus followed the medic. He couldn't just stand around anymore, and figured that if they were allowing her in, the situation must be contained. The officer didn't stop him.

"The dog led us to her," the officer said as they walked. "She was trying to get away, so we fired and—she's still hanging on. Come quick."

Cyrus didn't think these people had their priorities straight at all. What about Naveed? But then he realized that they still needed to question her. If she died, all her secrets would die with her.

Including the one that mattered most to Cyrus.

Eventually they came upon the other cops, one of whom was placing her gun into a plastic bag. The others parted to reveal Tara lying on the ground on top of a crushed fern. Cyrus felt sorry for the plant.

A sudden bright light illuminated the scene—someone had propped a floodlight against a tree trunk, and now Cyrus could see everything a little too well. There was blood everywhere. *Everywhere.* Cyrus had to look away.

Radley noticed him then. "Hey—thought I told you to stay put."

"Did they raid the lab?" Cyrus asked. "Did they find my sister?"

Radley stepped away from the group, and the two of them turned their back on the others. "We found the lab and arrested Torsten Ostrom, who confessed to helping her break out. But when the squad got there, Snyder was already gone. She had knocked Ostrom out and restrained him, and he didn't know where she was. He says he doesn't know anything about your sister, either, that he and Snyder went straight to the lab after they left the courthouse. We did a thorough search—took a while, they were experimenting on dogs, there must have been dozens, lots of empty cages—but didn't find her. Doesn't mean there's nothing *to* find, she might be somewhere else, and I hate to say it, but you might want to prepare yourself for—"

Cyrus stopped listening. He turned around and charged toward Tara Snyder, wanting to shake her by the shoulders until she answered the most important question of them all, but the officer blocked him. "Where's Roya?" he yelled. "WHERE IS SHE?"

Tara's eyes were closed. She didn't show any signs of having heard him. Her neck and chin were covered in blood. That was as far down as Cyrus dared to look.

"Nothing I can do," the medic was saying. "She's already lost too much—"

"She's not breathing," an officer crouching next to her said. The medic started CPR, and Cyrus turned away again, thinking about Roya. He refused to believe what Radley was hinting at. That his little sister was already dead.

Focus on the facts, he told himself. They had found the lab. Roya wasn't there. Torsten said she'd never been there. He could be lying, sure. But what if he wasn't? Was it possible Cyrus had missed something?

He thought back to the day she'd disappeared. How his first reaction was that she'd been hiding from Auntie Leila so she didn't have to go to PT. But there was another place she really, really didn't want to go, based on the last conversation he'd had with her: Oregon. He pictured Roya that morning before the trial, how she'd come into his room practically begging him not to send her away....

Cyrus felt like smacking his forehead. What if she hadn't been abducted at all?

What if she'd just... run away?

But where would she go? How could two days have passed without anyone recognizing her? Her face was plastered all over, there were Amber Alerts out and everything....

The medic sat up. "She's gone." Tara lay on that poor blood-drenched fern, unbreathing, motionless.

Gone.

Dead.

Tara Snyder was actually dead.

Something wet touched Cyrus's hand. He drew back in surprise, but looked down to see Koffka nuzzling against him.

Cyrus kneeled beside the dog. "You okay, boy?"

Koffka flicked his ears. There was a hole right through the tip of one of them, ringed by a thin rim of blood. "Dodged a bullet, huh?" Cyrus laughed as he said it, he was just so relieved, it was over now, or part of it anyway,

Koffka had hunted Tara Snyder down, had led the cops right to her, and she had bled to death here in this forest, alone and defeated.

For some reason it made Cyrus think of the stories from the Shahnameh that Maman used to tell him and Naveed when they were younger, the tales of the warrior Rostam and his fierce steed Rakhsh, who had once slain a lion that tried to attack Rostam while he was sleeping. Cyrus hugged Koffka, burying his face in the fur of his back as he laughed and laughed.

After a minute, the medic touched his shoulder. "You all right?" she asked. Cyrus had laughter-tears in his eyes, and they probably all thought he was completely insane, or in shock, which maybe he was, a little. But he could tell the officers were more relaxed, too, knowing that their long search was over, that Tara Snyder wouldn't be hurting anyone ever again.

"Show me where your brother is," the medic said. Cyrus told Koffka to come, and the dog led them back to the pit.

Andi was sitting inside, her back to Cyrus. "She's dead!" he proclaimed as they approached. "Tara Snyder's dead!"

Andi turned slowly. She didn't look remotely relieved. It didn't make any sense, but she was holding something that looked like a ghoulish Halloween prop, a zombie arm with grayish purple skin, its hand flopped into a lazy claw-like position. She was holding it high, like a trophy, but there was nothing triumphant about the gesture. "Please help," she said in a desperate voice.

The medic went in first, and Cyrus lowered her supply bag down into her arms. Then he followed. Koffka hesitated for a second, but soon jumped down to join them.

It wasn't until Cyrus got closer that the scene began to make sense. Naveed was lying on his side, his head on Andi's knee, and then Cyrus saw it, the blood all over Andi's hands, the blood on his brother's arm, the blood on the ground beside him, mixing with the rain and the mud.

"I tried," Andi was saying to the medic. "I tried to stop him… tried… but the bleeding… it won't stop…."

"You're doing great. Keep it elevated for me." The medic unzipped her bag.

"What happened?" Cyrus asked.

"He... cut himself... he... I'm so glad you're here," Andi said through chattering teeth. Koffka settled next to her, lowering his head closer to Naveed's, whimpering softly.

Cyrus sat next to Andi, letting her words sink in. It sounded so benign at first, like Naveed had cut himself on accident or something, but slowly he understood. It didn't make any sense, though. Tara Snyder had inexplicably, miraculously, let Naveed live—and here he was, finishing the job for her?

Seriously. What was wrong with that guy?

Cyrus bit his tongue and took a deep breath, determined not to lash out right now. He had done that once before, letting his exasperation show at the worst possible moment. He wasn't going to repeat the mistakes of the past.

The medic called for backup before applying a tourniquet and pressing a wad of gauze to Naveed's wrist. It was soaked within seconds. Naveed was just lying there, not even trying to fight back. Which seemed like a bad sign.

"Kourosh," Naveed whispered. Cyrus had to scoot closer to hear him. "I think she... took Roya... to a lab...."

"Is that what she told you?" If she'd confessed to Naveed that she'd taken Roya, maybe Cyrus's alternate theory wasn't true....

Tara Snyder had lied about a lot of things, though. He sincerely hoped this was one of them.

Naveed didn't answer. Now that he was bathed in the glow of the medic's headlamp, Cyrus could see his brother was having serious trouble breathing. His neck tendons popped out sharply as he tried to force air into his lungs. There was a huge bruise above his collarbone. Damn. Had Tara tried to strangle him or something? This was way worse than Cyrus had thought. He should've insisted that the medic come here first.

To fill the unsettling silence, Cyrus told them, "The cops found the lab. Roya wasn't there. I think maybe something else happened. Roya really didn't want to go to Oregon, and they were supposed to leave while we were at the trial—I think she might've just run away."

Naveed closed his eyes. Cyrus nudged him in the shoulder. "Hey—stay with me here. Do you have any idea where she might have gone?"

"No," Naveed muttered, eyes still closed. "She. Hates me."

"That's not true," Cyrus said. "She felt terrible about what she said to you at the memorial, you know. She was just taking stuff out on you. Nothing personal."

Naveed's eyes flew open. "Kass," he said.

"What?" Cyrus asked.

"Kass... friend... was at... the... mem... the mem....."

Cyrus thought Roya and Kass had long been out of touch since they weren't allowed to talk to each other. He had no idea she had come to the memorial. "You think Roya went to see Kass? But doesn't she live in Tacoma or something? How would Roya get down there?"

"Does anyone know her address?" Andi asked. "Do your parents—does your dad have it somewhere?"

"I doubt it." It hurt just to think about Baba right now. Who was going to call him and explain all this? Cyrus hoped like hell that he wouldn't have to.

"Did they ever talk on the phone?" Andi asked. "Maybe we could figure out her number?"

Out of habit, Cyrus pulled the burner phone out of his pocket, the default response when he needed to look something up. For whatever reason, this jogged his memory, and he remembered something odd that had happened the day after Maman died: Roya had asked Auntie Leila to borrow her phone to play some games for a while. Cyrus had way better games than Auntie Leila did—why hadn't Roya asked to borrow *his* phone? He had felt slightly insulted. Even though he probably wouldn't have given her his phone anyway.

"Yeah. Maybe... hold on." Cyrus mentally thanked his past self for adding Auntie Leila to the burner phone's contacts. It was super late by now, but to his relief she picked up on the second ring.

"Hey, Auntie," he said. "It's Cyrus."

"Kourosh! Is everything all right?"

"Uh, it's okay-ish, I think," he said, not wanting to get into it now. "But I need you to do something for me. Look back through the recent calls on your phone, and there should be one that was placed the day after my mom died, it was while Roya had your phone, and it would be a number that's not in your address book, and I need you to find that and send it to me, like, right now. It's really important."

"Oh—sure," she said.

Cyrus thanked her and hung up as a stern voice said, "Hold this."

The medic indicated the zombie arm, which was now stitched up and bandaged. "I need to make an incision in his trachea and insert a breathing tube."

"You need to... what?"

"Just keep this elevated." The medic sounded impatient. "Hold on tight. Make sure he doesn't move."

Cyrus swallowed hard. Naveed had cheated death so many times that, in a weird way, he seemed almost invincible. But the gravity of the moment hit Cyrus then. These could be the last moments he spent with his brother.

He tucked the phone into his coat pocket and took over, stretching the arm up as far as he could while the medic positioned Naveed on his back. Cyrus, not exactly eager to watch this part, scooted behind Andi. His hand came down on something hard, and he jerked back in surprise. The scythe handle was half-buried in the mud behind him. He shoved it out of the way, both the object itself and the memory of Naveed standing in the pit with the blade around Tara Snyder's neck. Now was not the time to process that disturbing image.

He settled in, encircling Andi from behind, holding Naveed's shoulder down with his now-muddy hand. She leaned her head gently against him.

Koffka nuzzled Andi's knee, and she stroked the dog's wet fur.

"I hope Roya's all right," Andi said. "I can't believe... after all this... we're still alive." She glanced at Naveed, whose labored breaths confirmed that this was true. At least, in this moment, it was true.

"We're still alive," Cyrus repeated. "And it's going to be okay. We don't have to worry about Tara Snyder ever again. And we're going to find Roya—so you'd better stick around for that, Naveed. She'll want you to be here when she gets back."

Cyrus looked down, hoping for some sign that Naveed had heard, but he was staring blankly up at the sky. He followed his brother's gaze up to the break in the clouds above their heads, at the rich texture of the stars, at the thin crescent moon that shone down on them all.

Roya

THURSDAY, JUNE 2

ROYA SUCKED ON A CHERRY LOLLIPOP SHE'D FOUND BURIED IN the depths of her backpack. Her teacher had given it to her a while ago for turning in her homework on time. Roya wondered if today was a school day. She honestly had no idea. It was daytime now, but she didn't see the point in trying to get anywhere. All of this had been for nothing.

She hadn't been able to conjure Maman or transmit a distress signal to Kasandra or Khaleh Yasmin, the two people she felt would be the most receptive. She'd managed to explore the room she was in, but it was an empty space aside from a single door, which was stuck shut. She had tried throwing her body against it, and when that hadn't worked, she'd tried magicking it open. That had failed too.

Of course it had. She wasn't good at this the way Kass was. It had been stupid and childish to think she could use magic to get herself out of this mess.

Was magic even real? Roya was beginning to doubt it. She'd probably just imagined that she'd had some sort of power because she'd wanted to believe it, when in truth she was just a dumb little nine-year-old who had no control over anything.

The cherry lollipop was sweet, and helped her feel a little less thirsty, but with that artificial cherry flavor filling her mouth she thought unexpectedly of SILO, a place she tried hard to never bring to mind. She remembered that day she'd crawled through a broken window and escaped into a cherry orchard. And now here she was again, trapped in a space she might never be able to leave.

Roya gazed at the open window longingly—and even though she'd been looking at the same view for days, she noticed something different this time. Two brown mushrooms had sprung up overnight. Their caps were still attached to their stems and they looked moist and brand new, but one was almost twice as tall as the other. *A mom and a baby*, Roya thought, and a deep sadness weighed her down like a heavy blanket, because now she was thinking about the burial, the mushrooms at her feet, Maman in her white shroud lying at the bottom of a deep hole, the silver star charm disappearing beneath the dirt, the magic that had been lost that day.

And now, Maman's body was rotting, all sorts of things were eating away at her skin and her eyes and her hair, and the ants were probably rebuilding their tunnels to point away from her, the one who had killed hundreds of their friends, but also the one who had taught Roya about so many things while they sat in the spring sun plunging their fingers into the mud, giving plants new homes, making little piles of cottonwood fluff and bendy sticks for birds to use in their nests. Maman had given life and taken it away, and was Roya going to be just like her, wasting away in a hole in the ground until there was nothing left? Was this really the end? She would never get to see Kass or Baba or Cyrus or Khaleh Yasmin or Pashmak or Koffka or Naveed ever again?

Roya realized that she was wailing now, the same anguished cries that the women from the mosque had made at the memorial service. The sound suddenly made sense, the only way to get the pain out, or lessen it a little. It hurt so much. Like it was crushing all her bones.

She hugged herself. She wished she'd never left home.

The lollipop was almost gone. Roya scraped the last sugary crystals from the soggy stick with her teeth. Now she felt even hungrier—and thirstier—than she had before. Still sucking on the empty stick, she curled up on the floor.

She needed to get out of here. But how? The window was too high. The door was too stuck. No one knew where she was. Well, the mushrooms knew, she supposed. Not that they would be any help.

Mushrooms. Ants. Underground. Eaten away. Eating. Cherries. Orchards. Farms and crows. Trees and sky. Cats and chickens. Home.

She drifted to sleep and found herself being carried beneath the earth by a massive stream of ants. Down they went, down and down, and it was dark but there were beautiful glowing threads all around her, like she was a tiny creature inside a thick, cozy sweater. When she looked down, she realized that the stream carrying her wasn't made of ants after all: she was floating along on strands of her mother's long black hair. No matter how she moved, it remained steady beneath her. There was so much comfort in this simple fact, knowing that no matter what, it would be there holding her up, keeping her safe.

Roya sighed, burrowing deeper into that pleasant feeling. The glowing threads were changing now, gathering into a thick spiral like a piece of yarn, multiple threads spinning together until she finally understood what they were.

A mushroom! she thought with delight, she was watching it from below, a baby mushroom about to push through the surface, but just before it emerged into the light, something startled her awake.

It was a familiar noise that she couldn't even place yet, because she was still filled with the feeling from the dream, the safety and peace of being bundled in a comfy sweater, embraced by someone she had loved more than anything.

Tears sprung into her eyes; goosebumps bloomed on her arms. She looked down to see that she was clutching the crow feather to her chest.

She came, Roya thought in amazement. It was like the mushrooms in the window had heard Roya's cries and reached through their underground threads all the way to those other mushrooms growing beside Maman's grave. They'd relayed her message to Roya, but it didn't come in words, because that wasn't the way mushrooms talked. It came instead as a feeling, like Maman was holding her again, like she was whispering into Roya's ear, *Don't worry, Roya-jaan, I will be with you always.*

The noise came again, and this time Roya recognized it: a dog was barking nearby. And its bark sounded kind of familiar....

Could it be? "Koffka? Is that you? I'm over here, please help!" she yelled as loud as she could. But her voice was weak from not being used. It came out croaky and not nearly as loud as she wanted.

That was okay. She had other ways of being heard. Roya set the crow feather gently onto the floor, then picked up her flute. She played some screechy notes—on purpose, to get their attention—before settling into an actual song.

She'd only been playing for a minute or two when she heard a voice nearby. At the sound, her breath left her, and the song stopped abruptly. What if she'd been wrong? What if the boy was back, and he'd brought a vicious dog with him this time?

"Roya! Where are you?" Cyrus yelled.

Cyrus. It was Cyrus! "I'm down here! But I can't get out. Kourosh, is that really you?"

"Yep! It's me." His face appeared in the small window. "Whoa—what are you doing down there? Are you okay?"

Roya didn't even know how to answer the first question, so she ignored it for now. "I hurt my knee when I fell. I can't walk on it. And I'm hungry. So so *so* hungry. Did you bring any food? Or water?"

"I'm sure we can find some. There's no way I can get through that little window, though—hold on, I'll be right back. Hang in there."

Roya sat up stiffly and began packing her magical tools away. Of course, she was glad she wasn't going to die down here after all, but she was also… disappointed somehow? Her feelings were all mixed up for some reason. Before she could figure out what that was about, she heard another voice at the window.

"ROYA!" Kass roared.

"KASS? You're here too?" Just like that, her disappointment vanished, and was replaced by a soft glow in her heart.

"Hang on. I'm coming in," Kass said.

"Be careful! There's broken glass on the floor."

Kass slid through the window easily. She was much taller than Roya now, but still skinny. Clutching Roya in a tight hug, she asked, "Is anyone else here?"

"No. I just came in because I hurt my knee and needed a place to rest until it felt better, but I ended up hurting it worse when I fell in. How did you know where I was?"

"Cyrus called me—they've been talking about you on the news, and I was so afraid you were in danger, so I was doing everything I could to try and protect you. I know I said I was done with witchcraft, but this was too important, and there were plenty of things I could do without Ilyana noticing. But anyway, Cyrus called and told me that you might have run away from home, so I thought about where you might go and remembered how we talked about the acolyte who had that crystal shop, and I thought since Naveed had taken the tea away from you, maybe you'd want to see your mom some other way, and I convinced Ilyana to drive me up here so we could help look, and we were searching all over, and finally Koffka picked up your scent and—here." Kass held out her hand. In her palm was the agate from Lopez.

Roya rested her head on her friend's shoulder, grateful. Then, remembering something, she pulled away. "I'll trade you." She took the stone and handed Kass the Book of Shadows. It was time, finally, to return it to its rightful owner.

Kass gasped and hugged the book to her chest. "Thank you for keeping it safe. You had it with you this whole time? Did it help?"

"Definitely." It was hard to believe that, just a short while ago, Roya had doubted there was any magic in the world. But there was no denying it now. Her prayers had been answered: Kass and Cyrus and Koffka had managed to find her. That was an unquestionable miracle.

"Oh, wait! One more thing." Roya untied the sheath from her waist. "Your athame. I used it a few times, so you might need to cleanse it or something before you use it again? I don't know. Anyway, it belongs with you."

Kass unsheathed her ritual knife with gentle reverence. Its silver blade caught the faint light coming through the window, as if greeting its long-lost partner. It reminded Roya of that time she had watched Naveed and Koffka joyfully reunite at Englewood. Two parts of a whole, back together at last.

The glow in Roya's heart grew brighter than the sun. It was so dazzling she almost couldn't stand it. "I love you, Kass."

Kass sheathed her knife and hugged Roya again. "I love you, too."

A huge bang startled them. Across the room, the door flew open, and a police officer burst through. Roya gripped Kass tighter. She never knew if things were going to get better or worse when the police showed up.

But Koffka came through the door next, followed by Cyrus. The beam of his phone flashlight bounced as he jogged over. Koffka licked at her fingers and face, and she hugged him and Cyrus, both at the same time. The police officer asked if she was okay, and she said she was but she couldn't stand up because her knee was hurt, so after a minute he left through the door, talking on his radio.

"Is anyone else here? Where's Naveed? And Baba?" Roya asked.

"You'll see them soon," Cyrus said. "But first, tell me. How the hell did you end up down here?"

So Roya had to explain exactly what she had done, and by the time she finished telling him, several police officers had arrived and asked her to start over at the beginning. They scolded her for running away and said they'd been looking all over for her. Which actually felt kind of nice.

People had noticed she was gone. And they wanted her to come back.

When the medics came, the police stopped their lecture and let them look her over.

"Can I go home now?" Roya asked as they braced her knee.

"Sorry," said one of the medics. "We've got to take you in, get some fluids in you."

Roya really hated hospitals and didn't want to go, but she was too tired to argue. "Can I have something to eat? I'm so hungry."

The medics gave her a small bottle of water and a few packets of crackers, which didn't help much. To Roya's surprise, one of the police officers handed her a sandwich from his lunch bag. She thanked him and tore into it. It tasted like tuna, which she usually didn't like, but right now it was the perfect thing. She devoured it so fast that Cyrus said she'd probably just broken someone's speed-eating record.

Kass hugged her goodbye and said that Ilyana wanted to go home, but told Roya to call in the morning. Roya promised she would. Even though she knew he'd overheard their conversation, Cyrus didn't seem to care. Maybe that meant their friendship didn't have to be a secret anymore.

"So you'll never believe what happened while you were gone," Cyrus said as they loaded her onto a gurney. She was grateful he was there holding her hand as they poked her with needles and cleaned up her cuts. The story he told was extremely distracting, too. She listened in disbelief as he told her about how Dr. Snyder had escaped from the police and hunted down Naveed at the farm, but the police found her in the woods, and they shot her when she was trying to get away. They had killed her. She was dead. Roya made him repeat that a few times, just to make sure she'd heard right.

Then Cyrus explained how they were all convinced that Dr. Snyder had taken her. Roya found that a little insulting—there was no way she'd let that happen ever again!—but it also made the truth more embarrassing. Everyone had been thinking of her as a tragic victim, but in fact this whole situation was entirely her fault.

"Do you think Baba's going to be mad at me when he finds out what really happened?" Roya asked.

"No way. He's just relieved you're safe, and that nothing terrible happened to you. I mean, this... it's not great, but... it could've been worse."

"Wait, what about everybody else? You said Andi went with you to the farm. Is she okay?"

"Andi's fine. She's with Naveed at the hospital. He, um." Cyrus paused, and Roya got that heavy-blanket feeling again. "He hurt himself pretty bad."

"What do you mean? Hurt how?" Roya asked.

Cyrus crushed a discarded sterile wrapper into a tiny, dense ball. "He... cut himself. Really deep."

Roya was afraid to ask, but she made her mouth say the words. "On purpose?"

"Yeah."

"Oh." Roya watched Cyrus as he rolled the wrapper-ball between his palms. "So, like last year. He wanted to die."

Cyrus just nodded slowly.

"How could he?" Roya whispered. "How could he do that to us?"

"I don't know, Roya. I think everything's been really hard for him these past few weeks, and he just couldn't take it anymore."

"It's been hard for all of us," Roya muttered.

Cyrus dropped the wrapper-ball into his pocket and placed his hand on top of hers. "It has."

"But he'll be okay?"

"I think so. I hope so. But it might be a while until he comes back. They'll probably keep him in the hospital until they're sure he's, you know. Not gonna hurt himself again."

"Okay." Roya looked at Koffka, who sat at Cyrus's side, keeping a respectful distance to give the medics room to work. "But what about Koffka? Can he stay with us while Naveed gets better?"

Cyrus glanced down at the dog. "Oh—yeah, probably."

"Good. But, Kourosh… what's happening with our house? I heard Auntie and Baba talking the day I left. How Baba can't afford our house anymore. She wanted us all to move to Oregon."

Cyrus's eyes widened. "Whoa—I mean, I knew things with the house were bad, but…" He made a face. "I don't want to move."

"Me neither! I love our house, and it kind of feels like Maman is still there, if that makes sense? And I don't want to leave her."

"But we'll take her with us wherever we go." Cyrus's glasses were fogging up. He took them off and wiped them on his shirt. "We won't forget her. Ever."

"Never," Roya agreed. She was thinking about the dark stream of Maman's hair threading underground, always there beneath her feet, no matter where she went. "Thank you for finding me, Kourosh."

"Sure thing, sis. Now don't ever do that again," he said.

Roya grinned and snuggled into his soft shoulder. She felt like she was home already, maybe because Cyrus *was* home, and so was the rest of her family, and it didn't matter so much where their house was, because she knew now that Maman would be with them everywhere, always.

Cyrus

MONDAY, JUNE 6

IT WAS KIND OF AMAZING, CYRUS THOUGHT, HOW QUICKLY things could change.

Only days ago, he had been in full-on crisis mode. And now here he was, sliding his arms into a button-down shirt once again, this time to go meet with a new potential investor.

Life was so weird.

When Shea texted that the Quirqi Train was out front, Cyrus hustled down the stairs. He couldn't leave without giving Roya a goodbye hug, though. She was on the couch, her right leg stretched out straight in front of her. She had to wear a knee brace for another few weeks, but she seemed to be in good spirits, especially since Koffka never left her side.

Auntie Leila sat across the coffee table from her. She rolled the die for one of Roya's favorite games, Harvest Time. "Oh no, another white!" She groaned. "Yikes. We might not get everything harvested before winter comes."

"I'll be back in a few hours. Wish me luck," Cyrus said as he slid on his shoes.

"Good luck, Kourosh!" Roya smiled at him.

"It'll go great. I know it will," said Auntie Leila. "Your dad just called, by the way—the transfer got approved, so they're headed to Harborview. I'm not sure they'll allow Naveed to have visitors yet, but if they do, can you come with us later?"

"Of course." Cyrus was happy to hear this, because it meant Naveed was stable enough to be transported. The small hospital where they'd taken him the day Tara Snyder died ("T-Day," as Cyrus called it inside his head) was an hour away and didn't have much when it came to psychiatric facilities. They'd also gotten the disconcerting news that Naveed's lung scans had come back with several abnormalities, but Cyrus had faith that the Harborview doctors, who had a much better grasp of his brother's complicated medical history, would get things figured out.

He glanced at the window, where a small slice of Shea's car was visible through the overgrown hedges. "Gotta go, see you later!" he said as he left through the front door.

Todd and Dev let out whoops of excitement as Cyrus slid into the passenger seat. "Ahh, he's back!" Dev gave him a sloppy bro-pat on the shoulder while Todd trumpeted an imaginary horn. "He who faced down the legendary supervillain Tara Snyder and lived to tell the tale!"

"Glad you're okay," Shea said as she pulled into the street, flashing him a grin.

Cyrus grinned back. He wanted to tell them how happy he was to be here with them, too, but a lump in his throat prevented him from saying it. He did manage to get out a simple "Thanks, guys," without sounding too emotional about it.

They started talking about their plans for the upcoming meeting, but it soon devolved into a discussion about where they should grab lunch afterward. Todd had been researching nearby restaurants, and he had opinions. They were debating whether to go for ramen or barbecue when a text came through from Andi. Hey Cy good luck at your meeting today. I'm rooting for you!

Cyrus hadn't seen Andi since T-Day, when he'd left with the cops to find Roya while Andi stayed with Naveed. They had figured they'd reunite at the hospital, but Andi's dad had apparently been livid when he heard what had happened. He had whisked her away to the airport and sent her off on the first flight to Oakland. They both thought that was pretty harsh, so they'd spouted off about it in a long text conversation. Cyrus sort of wished that his own father had been angry too, but he'd pretty much spent the whole weekend weeping. Cyrus had nearly asked a nurse to hook Baba up to the IV to replace all the fluids he must be losing through tears alone.

But Cyrus knew why Andi approved of this new potential funding option, which was pretty much the exact opposite of Blanchet Capital. It had been amazing the way the stars had aligned. Shea had started a conversation on T-Day about considering other fundraising models, like crowdfunding, which she thought would work well for Quirqi since they already had a large platform. The next day, while Cyrus was hanging out at the hospital, he'd gotten a text from Kelly asking if he could give her a call. It turned out she'd mentioned Quirqi to one of CFJ's major donors, a woman named Kamiko Watanabe, and Kamiko had been very interested in meeting with them.

So they had set up today's appointment, despite the fact that their meeting with Raymond Whitaker was still scheduled for the afternoon. Cyrus didn't exactly want to go through with that, but he needed to meet with Raymond face to face. He had some questions that had nothing to do with their startup.

"You good with ramen, Cy?" Dev asked, pulling him back to reality.

"Definitely," Cyrus said.

For the rest of the drive, they talked about Quirqi and their plans for the summer—normal stuff that had nothing to do with psycho scientists or medical drama or depressed fathers or police investigations.

Cyrus was so relieved not to be thinking about those things that he almost cried.

Eventually, they pulled up in front of Kamiko's house, a midcentury rambler in an upscale neighborhood by the lake. The front garden was beautiful, with carefully tended bonsai-style trees, flame-leafed Japanese maples, and a winding stone path to the front door.

"I feel like we're going to a spa or something," Shea whispered.

"Me, too." Cyrus silenced his phone. He remembered how he'd felt while walking into the meeting at Blanchet Capital in the former Nutrexo tower, the stress and dread that had almost overwhelmed him. This time, even though so many things hinged on this meeting, he couldn't bring himself to feel anything but calm.

The moment Kamiko opened the door and greeted him with a warm smile, he recognized her as the woman with the beaded necklace at the memorial, the one who had seen Naveed and Roya's argument. Apparently, he had also met her several other times at the CFJ fundraising events Maman used to drag him to. Kamiko reminded him of this as she led them into her dining room, which had huge picture windows looking out into a backyard that was even more impressive than the front. There was a koi pond and everything.

Philip was already at the table, sipping green tea out of a small cup. Even though he'd been reluctant to set up the meeting in the first place, he looked completely at ease.

Kamiko poured cups of tea for the rest of them as they gathered around the table. Cyrus wasn't quite sure what the protocol was here. It felt very informal, and he quickly dispensed with the idea of doing any sort of structured demo. As it turned out, Kamiko had done her homework. She'd already downloaded *Bugpocalypse 3K* and had looked over their business plan.

"I'll be honest," she said in such a way that Cyrus immediately set down his cup, bracing himself for rejection. "I didn't love *Bugpocalypse*. Sure, I liked it, it's a perfectly fine game. Could just be that I'm the wrong demographic." She smiled and threw back her gray-tinged black hair. "But it felt kind of... tossed off? Like it was a rush job."

Cyrus's cheeks burned. They *had* put it together quickly, and some things were sloppier than they should be. But she wasn't supposed to notice that.

"It looks like so many games already out there," she went on. Cyrus looked down at his tea. Here was the part where she said, *This isn't for me, but good luck.*

"Same with your show." She waved a hand at Cyrus and Dev. "It's very charming, but it also feels like it could be tighter."

Cyrus wanted to speak up in their defense, but he could tell she was building to something, so he stayed quiet. Dev was following his lead.

"It feels like it could be so much *more*," she continued. "And I appreciate that you need more resources to bring it to its full potential. That's why I'm interested in working with you. I admire your mission. Spreading happiness through pro-social, accessible games and content—yes. The world needs that. But to really make yourselves stand out, I don't think you need to go wider, as you proposed in your business plan. You need to go *deeper*. That's why the episode of *D&C* that stuck out most to me was the one with—what was his name? Your brother's character."

"Navotron?" Cyrus asked.

"Yes!" She smiled fondly, as if remembering an old friend. "If you keep your sense of humor while occasionally touching on serious topics in a creative way, the way you did in that episode, I think you could have something great. Life is hard, but that doesn't mean you can't find joy even in the darkness. It's a tough balancing act—but I don't have any doubt that you can do it. So, if that matches your vision at all, I'd be glad to help by funding your salaries and incidental expenses, in exchange for a seat on the board."

Cyrus glanced at the others. They all looked as stunned and amazed as he felt. *It's perfect,* he thought. This was exactly what they needed: someone who would push their business, and their art, to be the best it could be. And, frankly, she was right. After the year he'd had, he was finding it harder to relate to the snarky humor he'd once been drawn to. It just wasn't satisfying in the way it once was… because, he realized, it was missing something. Depth. He craved that now, in a way he never had before.

Kamiko refilled her cup from the cast-iron teapot on the table. "I want to be clear up front that I see this as a good investment, because I believe you have the drive and passion to grow Quirqi into a successful business. I've inherited a lot of blood money, and I'd much rather back you than a soulless company that might offer me a little more return on my investment."

There was a brief silence, then Cyrus said. "Wow. Thank you. That all sounds… amazing."

Of course, there were a lot of details that Philip wanted to discuss, but to Cyrus's surprise he seemed jazzed about her proposal too.

After talking for nearly two hours, they said their goodbyes. "I can't believe it. We found our angel," Shea said dreamily as they walked back to their cars.

"Well, she's not proposing to fully fund the project," Philip reminded them. "There's still the capital equipment, office space…."

"But we could crowdfund for those things. We shouldn't pass up the chance to work with someone who really *gets* it," said Dev.

"She's not coming from the tech world, though, so she doesn't know how it works," Philip said. "This isn't the easy path. If we took the deal with Blanchet, everything would be taken care of, and we'd have the heft of a big company to help with promotion. They'd be able to help with an IPO, too, if we decide to go that route in the future."

Cyrus looked around at the others. What was it that Maman always used to say? *There is beauty in the struggle.* "Nah. I'm good. If there's one thing I learned from my mom, it's that the right path is usually the harder one."

"Looks like the majority wants to go with Kamiko," Dev said. "Maybe we should just cancel that meeting at Blanchet."

"No," Cyrus said quickly. "Philip went through the trouble of setting it up—I don't want to back out. But I don't think we all need to be there."

After some discussion, they decided that Cyrus and Philip would go to the meeting and meet up with the others for ramen and drone racing at the condo afterward. They'd let Raymond know that they had another offer on the table, which Philip thought might give them some bargaining leverage—apparently, he wasn't quite ready to give up on a more traditional funding plan. Cyrus, though, had other reasons he wanted to see Raymond Whitaker.

As Cyrus followed Philip to his car, he noticed a bunch of new texts from someone he didn't expect: Naveed.

Hey Kourosh I'm on my way back to Seattle

Never commuted by ambulance before haha it's weird very bumpy

Bet they'll take my phone away when I get to Harborview but good news Baba said Dr. Imari's the attending right now so maybe it won't be so bad

Anyway was just thinking I might want to bring Navotron back can you check w Dev if I could do another d&c episode maybe this time make it even more epic

Cyrus almost laughed at the mention of Navotron. The stars just kept on aligning. But then he read the remaining texts and found himself blinking back tears.

We can talk later gotta go now but also wanted to say I'm sorry

I fucked up in a lot of ways but thanks for being there when I needed

You have no idea how much it means knowing there are people who won't give up on me

Love you brother

The texts had been sent while he was in the meeting with Kamiko, so Naveed was probably already settling into the psych unit by now. Cyrus sent a short response as Philip drove downtown, even though he had no idea when his brother would see it. Sorry I missed this was in a mtg. I have some great news too, will fill u in when I visit, and YES we DEFINITELY want Navotron to come back. Guess I've learned a thing or two about crisis counseling haha but srsly I'm so glad we found u in time and that u made it thru. Love u too

The whole ride over, Cyrus's brain felt like an overloaded circuit board. There were so many thought loops and possibilities and connections firing all at once, countless ways that his brother could help with this new direction that Quirqi would be taking. He was so preoccupied that he barely paid attention as they got in the elevator and ascended to Raymond's floor. But before he knew it, Kieran was there, ushering them into an empty conference room.

"Let me do the talking," Philip said. Cyrus only nodded, because Raymond Whitaker had just appeared in the doorway. Kieran closed it behind him and sat down.

Philip launched into a heartwarming speech about why Cyrus was not a liability but an integral part of the company, and that Blanchet should reconsider funding the team as originally proposed. Raymond, though, barely seemed to be listening.

After Philip wound down, Raymond said, "I'm glad you've found another investor, because we've decided to fund a different company. Just signed off on it, otherwise I would have spared you the trouble of coming down here. Best of luck," he added and stood up.

So that was it. They were being dismissed.

Before he could chicken out, Cyrus stepped toward Raymond. Kieran and Philip were talking amongst themselves and didn't seem to notice. "Excuse me, sir—"

"Ah, Cyrus. There's something I wanted to talk to you about," Raymond said.

Well, that was unexpected. Cyrus's palms were sweating so enthusiastically that they were practically dripping on the carpet. Good thing Raymond was making no sign of initiating a handshake.

Raymond lowered his voice. "I was questioned by the police regarding Pharmabox, which turned out to be a bad investment on my part, and I was told that you have a photograph of me and several men with whom

I don't wish to be associated."

It was pretty irresponsible of the cops to tell Raymond where the photograph had come from, Cyrus thought, but Raymond was probably tight with the chief of police, like Richard Caring had been. Or he had other ways of finding out.

But, he quickly realized, Raymond had just handed him exactly what he needed. Bargaining leverage. "I'll delete it," Cyrus said. "I'll make sure the original picture is destroyed, that it never gets posted anywhere. But—on an unrelated note, I was actually going to ask you for a favor."

He forced himself to hold Raymond's stare, even though he was quaking in his proverbial boots.

"What do you need?" Raymond asked grudgingly.

"So, you might know that my family came to... a settlement... with Nutrexo," Cyrus said, hoping he was using the terminology right and didn't sound like a complete idiot. "But the thing is, the company never paid us before they shut down. My dad's been getting the run-around for months, and we haven't been able to pay off the medical debt the settlement was intended for. I know you sat on the Nutrexo board. You have connections. Is there any way you can unfreeze those assets?"

He managed to stop himself before adding an unprofessional, "Or whatever." Raymond Whitaker stared down at him. Cyrus felt like a slacker kid in the back row of class, forced to answer a question even though he had no idea what the teacher was talking about.

To his surprise, Raymond said, "I'll see what I can do." He extended his hand.

Great. There *was* a handshake involved. Cyrus hastily wiped his palm on his slacks and shook Raymond's hand.

As he walked out of the conference room, a serene lightness came into his heart. He had done all he could. Maybe things would work out with the settlement money, but even if they didn't, he would be able to help support Baba financially now that he'd be bringing in his own salary.

Even better, he would never again have to set foot in this building.

Once again, he re-envisioned the future he'd glimpsed that day at his mother's memorial. This time, it wasn't just a pie-in-the-sky ideal. This time, he knew for sure that everything was going to work out. Quirqi had their angel, and he was about to go celebrate with some fantastic ramen, and he would spend the entire summer with his best friends as they built their virtual community from the ground up.

Mon, June 6, 10:19 AM

Hey Andi

They're transferring me to Harborview

Back to psych unit fun times
so before I go off grid
for a while I wanted to say...

You have every right to be angry
w me. And if you never want to
talk to me again I understand

But

I'm so sorry

For everything

I know that prob feels
hollow but it's all I've got

I love you Andi

And I'm not saying that bc I'm like
demanding that you feel the same way

I'm saying it bc it's true

and will always be true

no matter what

Ok gotta go now, see
you on the other side

Oh so sorry just saw these

Probably too late but
thank you for saying that

Heal up and text me
when you get home 🩶

June 15

Dear Nate,

Dr. Imari asked me to write a letter to you, so here I am, mostly because I'm trying to be a Good Patient so they'll let me leave this horrible place. Also I need a distraction. I really don't want to do this though. All of this is YOUR FAULT, here we are locked up thanks to you, and I messed everything up with everyone I care about and my arm hurts so. much. because of what you made me do. Still recovering from surgery, botched the whole wrist-cutting thing and sliced through some tendons in my left arm, so stupid. So stupid.

Been thinking about that night a lot. Reliving it, trying to make sense of it. There I was lying in the mud, barely able to breathe, blood rushing out. I thought that was what I wanted (or you thought? I don't even know anymore). I thought that would be the moment when I'd finally find peace. But Andi was sitting with me, and all I felt was regret for how badly I'd treated her. Also I was disgusted by what I'd almost done to Tara. I think I said it out loud. I think I apologized for making so many mistakes. I have this memory of her staring down at me, her wavery voice saying, "Yeah. Well, you can start making it up to me by not dying."

I didn't even consider that not-dying was an option by that point. Like, I had already dug my grave. My windpipe was swelling shut, it felt like I was getting oxygen one molecule at a time and I knew it would close up soon and that would be it. Andi was hovering above me though, and Koffka too, then Cyrus came in at some point and put his hand on my shoulder, which made me think about Maman from my dream, resting her hand on my shoulder, sitting beside me in her blue silk robe, and then the moon came out through a break in the clouds and I remembered how it used to make me think of escape, but that wasn't right at all.

Gravity. That's what it meant. The moon was like an anchor, keeping me grounded here on the earth to all the things I no longer wanted to leave.

Literally the weirdest shit comes to you when you're dying, I guess.

Then it happened. My throat closed up. That was it. My last breath. I tried so hard but nothing else got through. Death had come for me at last. But I didn't want to die anymore.

As I thought that, suddenly I was flooded, the air finally got in (because they cut a hole in my throat, which is horrifying but damn it felt amazing at the time)—and THAT was when I felt the relief I'd been hoping to find. THAT was peace. Just breathing. Just being able to breathe.

True, it's not the first time something like this has happened to me, but it felt different somehow? Like I lost something important during one of these other brushes with death, and this time I finally found it again. Because Andi and Cyrus and Koffka were there, watching over me, helping me through. I know this sounds super cheesy but I remember thinking of that line from Maman's favorite poem. "The threshold filled

with love." That was really the only way to explain where I was, what I
felt. There was nothing but love all around, flowing into and out of me,
holding me.

I can feel you rolling your eyes, Nate. Trust me, I know it sounds
dumb. But... it felt good, and Dr. Imari keeps telling me I need to hold on
to anything that feels good, especially when things are as shitty as they
are right now.

I mean, they could be worse? At least I actually like Dr. Imari, and
she doesn't put me in restraints, and I've been sleeping so much better
now that they switched me to a new antidepressant, plus yeah it feels
good to be on oxygen, I didn't realize how O2-starved my brain must
have been all this time. Still it's pretty terrible, they're doing a lung
biopsy today, I'm so afraid of what they're going to find and I guess
talking to you is better than dwelling on that.

And the other thing, too. You know. The anniversary. Today, it's been
one year since Tara Snyder drugged us and trapped us at SILO. I've been
watching the clock, counting milestones. A year since my family packed
up our old minivan and left for the protest. A year since we arrived at
Nutrexo Headquarters. A year since I bought that issue of Real Change
while Cyrus and Andi disappeared into the building. A year since I saw
Tara Snyder for the first time. A year since...

Better stop there.

Nate, can you explain something to me? I do not fucking understand

Tara Snyder. Did she seriously hunt me down at Zetik because she expected me to come back to her secret lab (which apparently was real btw)? Or did she want to kill me? Or did she want me to kill her? Or was there some other reason? I just don't get it.

Sometimes I think she just liked playing her sick little games with me.

Sometimes I think I liked it too.

Messed up, I know. But hear me out. Didn't it feel good to have a justified, clear outer target to pour our rage and hatred into? Now that she's just... gone... and we don't have that anymore, what am I supposed to do with all of that instead?

Oh my God, Nate.

Shit.

You're right.

She's not gone.

She's you.

I thought your voice was my voice, but now that I think about it, the things you say, the way you talk to me... it's the same way SHE talked to me.

So what does that mean? Need to ask Dr. Imari about this. They're coming to get me for the biopsy soon anyway. Back later.

June 16

I'm back. Biopsy was hell but at least it's over. And now we wait for the results...

So I talked to Dr. Imari. And I realized something, that even though we got out of SILO I never really escaped. I've been imprisoned all this time. By Tara Snyder, by the memory of her, by the things she stirred up that you parroted back to me whenever I fell back down into the shame spiral. You'd sneer at me and my weakness, and it was her sneer, which I thought was mine, and this is where it gets confusing, because I start wondering how much of me is really me? And how much of me is her? And how much of her was even her. If that makes sense.

Dr. Imari pointed out that it might be an oversimplification to think of you as Tara. Because obviously she's not the only person I get those messages from (like: that being the disabled, mentally ill son of Iranian immigrants makes me inherently worthless and also potentially dangerous, at least as defined by American society). Tara soaked up similar messages in her own way, and she felt worthless too, deep down. Also trapped. Maybe that's why she came to Zetik that night. Tim Schmidt (or whatever his real name was) broke her out, but she knew the truth. She would never really be free. She'd just traded one prison for another. And she wanted some kind of closure with me, even if she didn't know for sure what that would look like.

It feels so weird to think of her that way. Like a person who wanted some of the same things I do.

Also it's a little horrifying, isn't it? That we soak up all these harmful messages from the world around us without even realizing it, and unless we work hard to challenge them, they can so easily turn us monstrous. We're all teetering on ridges above deep ravines and it doesn't take much to push us over the edge.

So what does all of this mean for you and me? "What you resist persists," says Dr. Imari. If I keep fighting you, we'll be stuck in our miserable inner prison forever. Once the biopsy comes back we'll know how bad the cancer is, and if we don't have long to live, I really don't want to spend the rest of our days like this.

At the same time, I know that buying into the shit you're spouting hurts me and everyone around me. And that's not okay either. So what do we do?

Dr. Imari sees you as a part of me that's working incredibly hard to protect me, and okay, I'll give you that. You never let your guard down. You're always trying to keep others from taking advantage of me. It's just, the way you go about it really isn't doing either of us any good. And it's not your fault. This is all you know—all we know. But maybe we could just... try something else for a while? See how it goes? And if it works out, maybe you'll be able to learn how to trust me, so that you can rest, and we can finally be free?

Worth a try. You with me?

-n.

Wed, June 22, 8:51 PM

Hey Andi

Wanted to let you know
I'm finally back home

Hey Naveed

So glad to hear that!!!

Can you call me
so we can talk?

I'd rather text if that's ok.

I'm a total mess right now

Okay so I don't even
know where to start

How are you feeling?

Tired but okay

Feels like I just had a
20-day-long panic attack
but not too bad considering

Did my brother fill you in
about the lung drama?

Haha The Lung Drama

Sounds like a bad TV show

Yes he filled me in a little,
but I want to hear it from you

Ok so they did a bunch of
tests and it turns out I have
pulmonary fibrosis

Like, scarred lungs

It's not curable but now I'm on some new meds to keep it from getting worse, and they gave me a portable oxygen tank to use when I need it

I really hate it but I was convinced it was cancer so I guess this is better?

Though honestly I don't know. Prognosis uncertain at this point. Could end up needing a lung transplant someday ugh

I'm so sorry Naveed

I really wish you could catch a break

Yeah. Me too.

I'm glad you texted. Been thinking about you a lot.

Especially this past week, with The Anniversary

Same!

Every day it's a fresh hell of remembering "oh this is where I was a year ago"

Yes! I've been doing that too. Not just day to day but like moment to moment. Today was especially bad.

Always fun reliving some of the worst days of your life lol

UGHHH YESSSS ITS SOOOO BADDDDD

You been getting thru it okay?

Barb bothering you at all?

Haha remember Barb

Of course, oh god Barb
has been driving me crazy

But yeah, I'm okay.
Thank you for asking

I love you so much Andi

I'm sorry, that was probably
out of line but I can't stop
thinking of how horrible I've
been to you and I want to
explain but I don't want it
to come off like a bunch
of excuses. Still I feel like
I owe you an explanation

Explain away

I'm listening

Thank you

So

There were so many things going
wrong when my mom died

Like, I was sure I was dying of cancer.

My meds got switched up and I
was having serious side effects,
I couldn't sleep at all for weeks.

And the worst thing was

I started to believe Nate

Even as he dragged me down
to some really terrifying places

I was convinced that if I asked
for help I'd get locked up and
strapped down in the psych ward

Trapped there driving my family
deeper into medical debt

Maybe it doesn't make sense why
that felt like a fate worse than death

But it did

So I tried as hard as I could to hide it all

Didn't matter who I lied to,
ignored, cut out of my life

That really hurts Naveed, because all of
that is awful and we could have faced it
together if you just told me!

And yeah I owe you an apology too
because I wasn't entirely honest with
you either and I'm so sorry about that.

But everything I did was because I love
you and wanted to protect you

And then you went and
ripped my heart out

I really thought you were going
to die!! And I felt like it was all my
fault for not doing enough, for not
saying the right thing.

I never would've forgiven myself,
it would have ruined me forever,
and your dad & Roya & Cyrus

I hope you know by now that you can
tell me what's going on and I'll do
whatever I can to help. I WANT you to
tell me! It doesn't do ANYONE any good
if you just keep it all in until it explodes

So, just... remember that.
If you're ever there again.

I will. I promise.

Sorry I didn't mean to go off on you, I've just been so angry and frustrated, and I'm sad that you felt like you had to go through all of that alone

Honestly tho, I'm not saying this to dump on you

I just want to be open

Because I still care about you, of course I do

But I def don't want to make you feel worse

You okay?

I mean, it hurts of course but

Thank you for being real with me Andi

I don't want to get that low ever again

So I'm working on it

But it's good just to talk with you again

I really missed you

I missed you too

Call you in the morning maybe?

Not sure.

Have to go back to the courthouse tomorrow. My probation officer is pissed with me

I've got a bunch of other stuff going on this week, have to start pulmonary rehab and PT, there's follow-up appointments and therapy and a bunch of other crap, not to mention my dad and Roya are still super mad

Honestly, in some ways it's easier being in the hospital than coming home

That sounds exhausting

If you can't call that's ok

I'm here if you ever want to talk tho

Thank you Andi

I'm so tired guess I should go but I want you to know that you are an incredible human and I'm ridiculously lucky to have you in my life

Talk soon

Yes plz call whenever you can, my life is sooooo boringgggggggg

Anyway I bet it feels good to be back in your own bed

Sleep well

You too

Don't let the Barb bugs bite

Lolololol

Good night 🩶

Naveed

NAVEED KNOCKED ON THE DOOR. HE WIPED HIS SWEATY forehead with his long-sleeved shirt. Koffka regarded him with his big dark eyes. "It's okay, boy," Naveed said softly. "Just nervous."

Behind them, Baba was helping Roya up the steps. The two of them had been mostly silent during the long car ride. Naveed had dragged them down here, and he hoped more than anything that it would be worth it.

Frida opened the door and greeted him with a shining smile. "Welcome! Come in." She shook Baba's hand and waved at Roya, who waved back awkwardly.

"May I?" she said to Naveed, extending her arms. He nodded and embraced her, grateful that she pulled away quickly to rub Koffka behind the ears. The dog whimpered as she did so. "Missing Astro, are you?" she crooned to him. "We miss him too. But you should meet the new dogs—they are very shy, though."

Naveed settled his right hand on Koffka's head. After Astro was killed by Tara Snyder, Gretchen and Frida had adopted two dogs that were rescued from the Pharmabox labs. Naveed didn't like thinking about what they had been through.

"There's one!" Roya gestured behind the sofa, where a yellow lab was curled up. "Can I pet him?"

"Approach slowly," Frida said. "Let him come to you, if he wants."

Naturally, less than a minute later the dog's head was in Roya's lap, and she was singing a soft little song to him as she stroked his head.

"She is good with animals," Frida said. "Come, would you like some lunch? I was just setting it up outside."

Naveed mentally kicked himself—he'd forgotten to tell them it was Ramadan. Baba and Roya were both observing it this year, and though Naveed had never found much solace in religion, he was joining them in his own way. Instead of asking for God's forgiveness, Naveed was trying to show all the people he'd hurt that he was worth forgiving. Which was hard to do since he was still struggling to forgive himself.

"I'm sorry, when we talked earlier I forgot to tell you," Naveed said. "They're fasting for Ramadan. Can't have anything to eat or drink until after sundown."

"Oh, I see! That's all right, we can clear it away—"

"Don't worry about it. You should go ahead and eat," Baba said.

Naveed was glad for the permission, because he was starving, but still felt a little weird as he loaded up his plate with Frida's amazing rosemary potatoes. Baba stared out at the orchard. Roya decided to stay inside with her new dog friend. Gretchen, who had been weeding the vegetable garden, clomped up the back steps to join them.

Once everyone was settled, Frida said, "Thank you for coming down to visit. I know we've said it before—but we are very sorry, because we feel that we let you down. We're glad that you are interested in a second chance here, Naveed. And we would be happy to have you back."

Baba cleared his throat. *Here we go*, Naveed thought. He squirmed in his chair, suddenly very conscious of the brace on his left wrist.

"As you know, I have some concerns." Baba sounded so gruff. It had been like this ever since Naveed came home: Baba was stern, strict, humorless. "For one thing, he can't handle the physical demands of farm work. His arm is still healing. And the fibrosis in his lungs—he just can't work at the same level as he used to."

Naveed hated it when people talked about him like he wasn't there. "But the air's so much cleaner down here, Baba," he interrupted. "They did say it might help to be away from the city—"

"And he's still adjusting to his new meds. He needs to be closely monitored. Plus, he has lots of follow-up appointments in Seattle. We've also signed him up for an outpatient counseling program that meets every weekend for three months. So it doesn't make sense for him to live down here."

Gretchen was nodding. "I understand your concerns. Perhaps, Naveed, you could just work at the market? That way you could stay in Seattle—"

"No." Naveed was fully aware of how desperate he sounded. "No. I want to be down here. I can still do farm work, the doctors said it would be okay, I just have to ease back into it gradually, use my oxygen if I need to."

"We've talked about this. I don't think I can trust you to take care of yourself," Baba said coldly.

"Baba, you can. I'm doing fine now. It's not like it was. I'm not going to make the same mistakes—"

"I. Can't. Trust. You." Baba gave him that look again, the one he'd been shooting Naveed often. It was a painful expression, hard to look at. Nate always interpreted it as, *I hate you, and you disgust me, and I'm ashamed to call you my son.* But Nate never got the last word anymore, and Naveed's spin on it was different. *I love you, and you betrayed me, and these are the consequences.*

Once again, Naveed had a lot of rebuilding to do.

Gretchen interjected, "If you're not up for physical labor, Naveed, there is another option. Frida and I saw *Blood Apples*. It got us thinking about Zetik and… we realized we could do better. We hire many seasonal pickers this time of year. But we do not speak Spanish, and can't communicate with them well. Perhaps you could help with that. Help us understand the needs and concerns of our workers. Suggest changes."

"We want to start transitioning out of being full-time farmers, so that we can spend more time with our new granddaughter," Frida added. "We could use help planning for the future. You'd still be welcome to stay in the cabin when you're here, even if it's just for a few days a week."

Naveed paused mid-chew, consciously willing his jaw not to drop. He swallowed quickly and said, "Yes! I'd love that!"

Of course, Baba wasn't nearly as enthusiastic. "I still think Naveed isn't able to handle living independently yet."

"I can do it, Baba. I'm not helpless. I know how to manage it all, I'll take my meds religiously, I've got Koffka…"

"That's what you said last time. And look how that turned out."

Naveed slumped in his chair, defeated. He and Baba had been looping through these same conversational circles for weeks now.

Frida jumped to his rescue. "I agree that the way we handled things last time was not ideal. We would need to work more closely with Naveed to make sure he keeps up on his treatments. But I'm sure we could find a plan that you both are satisfied with."

Baba shook his head. "That's very kind, but his medical needs are complicated. It's a lot to ask."

Frida stood firm. "It isn't. Really. I was a nurse for thirty years. Taking care of people is second nature. And this farm, it is a special place, very healing. I'm sorry it didn't work out last time. But we hope you'll give us another chance to help him. To help you."

Baba was watching the swallows out in the distance. They wheeled through the June gloom, playfully dipping and diving from the fields to the trees and back again. Naveed took his silence as a potential good sign.

"Think about it," Frida said. "You don't have to decide right this minute."

Gretchen asked if Baba wanted a tour of the farm and orchards, and to Naveed's relief he said he did. Roya, who had probably been eavesdropping that whole time, opened the screen door right on cue and said she wanted to join them. Naveed stayed behind and offered to help Frida with the dishes after he'd shoveled down two helpings of every dish on the table, but she waved him off. "I'll take you up on that some other time. After you move back," she said with a wink.

"Frida." Naveed didn't even know what to say. "I can't thank you enough. For giving me another chance."

"The pleasure is mine. Oh, and if you want to head back to the cabin, feel free. We cleaned up a little, but all your stuff is still there."

Naveed nodded. "Think I'll do that. Thanks."

As he walked back to his cabin, he found himself thinking about the changes he might suggest for how their farm was operated. Of course, the first step would be to talk with the workers to see what they wanted to change. And he should contact Ramón... maybe, if he was still having a hard time finding work, Gretchen and Frida could hire him... and maybe they could totally change the structure of the workday... have a communal lunch in the middle of the day so everyone could rest... maybe Marisol could bring her kids along and help with that, since she still had health problems and couldn't do farm work anymore. Someday, maybe they could even convert Zetik to a worker-owned cooperative.

There were so many possibilities.

Plus, if they could show that their model worked, show the positive benefits to everyone involved, maybe the effects would ripple out, leading to broader changes in the food system.

It wasn't going to be easy, he knew that. But he was excited to try. And for him, being excited about anything was worth celebrating.

Naveed reached the cabin at the same time Gretchen and Baba walked up. "Oh! Naveed! Come see." Gretchen led him around the side. The mushroom logs he'd half-buried the day Maman had visited were now covered with ruffled stacks of turkey tails.

"We've been watering them for you," Gretchen said. "These just popped up the other day."

"They're… wow. They're beautiful." Naveed was surprised at how emotional he felt. He'd planted these mushrooms because he'd heard that they could fend off cancer, and even though he knew it was irrational, it felt like they were sending him a message. *Everything's going to work out.*

"I'll let Naveed give you the tour of his place," Gretchen said to Baba. "Roya's feeding the chickens. I'll go keep an eye on her." She smiled at them before walking away up the dusty road.

Naveed held the door open for Baba. "After you," he said.

Baba stood awkwardly just inside the doorway. Naveed gestured for him to sit in the same chair Maman had sat in during her visit. He didn't mention it, hoping that Baba would somehow know, on some level below words and below thought.

"So what do you think? The orchard's beautiful, isn't it?"

Baba grunted noncommittally.

"I know you don't want me to do this, but I really feel like it's the best option. Oh, plus, Frida didn't mention it today, but when we talked earlier she said they could still give me a stipend, and I'm pretty sure it would cover the monthly cost of my meds and oxygen. Plus, I've been in contact with this literary agent that Jamal referred me to, and she thinks she can get me an advance if I put a proposal together for a memoir, so that might help take care of some of the inpatient bills—"

"Naveed-jaan," Baba interrupted. "You don't have to worry about any of that. We're going to be okay—the settlement money finally came through. All you need to do is focus on getting better."

Those words cleaved something inside him—but in a good way. It felt like being cut free from the invisible sack of boulders he'd been dragging around all month. "Then please let me do this," Naveed said. "Please. Let me prove that you can trust me. Let me live here for half of the week, and I'll come home every weekend, and if it isn't going well, we can re-evaluate. Just give me a chance. Please."

Baba was silent for a minute. Then, finally, he sighed. "All right. We can try it."

Naveed wanted to shriek with joy, but he restrained himself. "Thank you, Baba. I won't let you down. Oh—and I have something for you."

Naveed crossed the room and took Maman's phone from its hiding place under his mattress. He traced the starburst crack with his thumb one last time, then held the phone out to his father. "I found it... that day... at the mountain. It's unlocked. I think she would've wanted you to have it."

Baba's eyes filled with tears. "Her phone?"

Naveed nodded. "She loved you so much, Baba."

Baba kept his eyes on the phone. Naveed knew he was trying hard not to lose it.

"I'm sorry for being the worst son in history," Naveed went on. "Thanks for not giving up on me."

"I'll never give up on you." Baba said through choked sobs. "So don't give up on yourself. Promise me?"

"I promise," Naveed said. And this time, he meant it.

"I LOVE IT HERE," Roya exclaimed as she spread a patchwork quilt over the golden stubble of the fallow field. To Naveed's surprise, Baba had accepted when Gretchen invited them to stay for dinner after sundown. Once the feast had been devoured, Baba insisted on helping them clean up, so Naveed and Roya went for a moonlit walk.

It had been cloudy all day, but the sky had cleared as the sun set. Naveed lowered himself down next to Roya, who was already on her back, looking up at the sky. Koffka sat next to him, still at attention. Naveed had a feeling that the dog had not forgotten what had happened in those woods. Obviously, Naveed hadn't either, but he still felt unexpectedly relaxed. It was as if this land could soak up pain and grief just as easily as it could absorb water.

Naveed turned his head towards a glowing orb illuminating the clouds from behind. Soon enough, the moon peeked through. It had been forty days now since Maman had died, and still the moon was shining. Always the same, always changing. Its gravity a steady, unyielding force. An invisible anchor.

Roya spoke. "Do you think... maybe sometime, like later in the summer, Kass could come here for a visit? And Ilyana, we could all camp out or something. They would love it."

"I don't know," Naveed said. "I don't want any trouble—"

"She wasn't the one who burned down the barn. *I* did that, remember?"

"I'm talking about what she gave you at the memorial. Do you know what that tea really was? It was a drug. The same stuff that almost killed Kourosh."

"It wouldn't have killed me." He could practically hear Roya rolling her eyes. "It was a very small dose."

"Maybe not, but—" He hesitated, not really wanting to admit this, but deciding to do it anyway. "I took it, Roya. I brewed the tea. And the things I saw... the way it made me feel afterwards... I'm just glad you didn't have to go through that."

"It's because you were uninvited," said Roya. "Kass told me all about it. You're supposed to take a lot of preparations for it to work right. You can't just jump in there without knowing what to do, because then it will only show you horrors."

That was an interesting way to look at it, Naveed thought. But he still wasn't about to apologize.

They were both quiet for a while, lost in their own thoughts. Naveed took off his wrist brace and flexed his fingers, moving through a sequence of physical therapy stretches. They got a little easier every time. Woodcarving would probably be off the table for a while yet, though.

Out of the blue, Roya asked, "How come you never invited me here before?"

"I didn't know you wanted to come," Naveed said. "When I first moved out here, you had your cast on still... you had to do all that PT when it came off... plus I was so busy all the time."

"You left me." The depth of pain in her voice caught him off guard. "I really needed you then, and I needed Koffka, he helped so much too, but one day you were like, 'oh by the way, I got a job at a farm, I'm moving out, see you later' and left me all alone."

Those words landed like a gut punch. "You weren't alone, Roya. You had Kourosh, and Baba, and Maman…"

"No. Kourosh and Baba were never home, or if they were, they were busy with stuff. And Maman… you didn't see it, did you. I think maybe I was the only one who saw it."

"Saw what?"

"The demons," said Roya. "She had these demons inside her. You know, like shayatin. It got really bad after you left."

"Oh, Roya." Naveed turned towards her, propping himself up on his elbow. "What did—what did the shayatin make her do?"

"She just didn't like me anymore." Roya was still staring up at the moon, but tears flowed from her eyes, running straight down the sides of her face and falling onto the quilt in small drips. "She was annoyed at me all the time. And grumpy. I think she hated taking me to all the appointments."

"Hey. Come here." He sat up and opened his arms. She snuggled closer. Sometimes she acted so mature that he forgot her age, but she was only nine. Still small enough to crawl into his lap. "You know what, Roya?" he whispered into the dark. "Something like that happened to her when I was your age. I called it the shadow. It wasn't anything to do with you, though, I promise. She had depression—a disease, a horrible one. It makes you hurt inside, so bad that sometimes you can't help taking it out on other people. But she still loved you. So much."

Roya was quiet for a minute. "Is it going to happen to me too?"

Naveed didn't know how to answer that. He wanted to soothe her fears, but he also wanted to be honest about this. "I don't know. It might. But, lucky you—you've got me, and I know what it's like." Without meaning to, he glanced down at his uncovered wrist, at the scar that shone pink in the bright moonlight. *I've been through hell*, that scar said, all of his scars said. *And I survived.* "You can talk to me about anything, anytime, and I promise I'll listen."

"Sometimes I feel like they're already there," she whispered. "The demons, the shayatin. Sometimes I just get so *mad,* and they make me want to hurt someone, even though I know it's wrong." She paused, then added, "I was really mean to you. I'm sorry."

"It's okay," Naveed said. "Believe me, I get it. And I'm sorry too. That you felt so alone. Let's never let that happen again. From now on, we stick together. Deal?"

"Deal." Roya sat up and dug around in the front pocket of her hoodie. "Here. I want to show you something."

"What's this?" he asked when she handed it to him. It was a small box about the size of a deck of cards, the edges sanded smooth. Baba's work, he could tell immediately.

"It's my phone," Roya said. "A special one. See, when I was stuck in that basement, I realized that the mushrooms in the window could talk to the ones by Maman's grave, and she always said it was underneath us everywhere we went, the mycelium"—she pronounced it carefully, syllable by syllable—"so I had Baba make me a spirit telephone, and now I can talk to her whenever I want." She opened the box. "I found some mushrooms growing in the woodchips, so I put some of the wood inside my phone and I charge it up by keeping it damp, and soon the mycelium will be in this wood too, and... anyway. Do you want to talk to her?"

"Um." There was a sudden pressure in Naveed's chest. He wished he had the backpack he carried his oxygen around in, but he'd left it inside the house.

"Don't be afraid," Roya said. "But, you should know, she might not talk back in words. The mushrooms have to translate, and they speak in other ways. Like, in pictures that pop into your head, and goosebumps and strange dreams. Basically, you have to pay attention to how it makes you *feel* to talk to her. That's the important thing."

Naveed took the phone. He held it up to his ear. "Maman," he whispered, and the pressure in his chest grew stronger. He felt like he was going to burst. Couldn't say another word. He remembered the question he'd so badly wanted to ask her: *Who killed you?*

He sat there waiting to feel something. To see or hear something. To get some guidance. Even though that was ridiculous. Wasn't it?

Did you jump on purpose, Maman?

Or were you tempting fate, balancing there on the ridge, seeing what would happen?

All he felt was that pressure building in his chest. Should he ask Roya to run back to the house and get his oxygen? No, she couldn't run... but... it hurt, oh God it hurt....

Roya touched his chest and he flinched. But she didn't take her hands away. She held them right under his pecs, or where his pecs would have been if he actually had any muscle, one hand on each side of his ribcage. "Yes," she said. "You can let it out now."

For whatever reason, those words broke him open. He could feel it, the pressure in his chest like a dense mass, traveling up through his mouth, exploding out of him in a loud wail. He wept. He wept and he wailed, and Koffka looked worried but Roya was telling him it was okay, telling Naveed to let it out, let it out.

"But Baba—might hear—" Naveed's voice shook out of him, disjointed and high-pitched.

"I'll just tell him we were howling at the moon. C'mon, Koffka, you too!" She launched into a loud howl that merged nicely with Naveed's wail, and he cried and laughed and rocked back and forth, and even though Nate was in there castigating him for carrying on like this, it felt so damn good that he couldn't stop.

Eventually he wound down, even though he felt like he still had a whole sea of tears inside. It had helped so much to release some of the pressure.

"How did that feel?" Roya asked once he'd stopped sniffling. He had set the spirit phone down at some point, and she was tucking it gently back into her pocket now.

"Amazing." He was flooded with a rush of appreciation for his weird and wonderful little sister, even though he'd learned nothing. No clear answers had appeared to him. And yet, for the first time in forty days, he no longer felt that gnawing sense of agitation when he thought about Maman's death. He felt... cleaned out and...

At peace.

Which, he supposed, if he went by Roya's logic, might be an answer in itself.

He may never know how she had died. But maybe that wasn't the important thing, anyway. Maybe all she wanted him to know was that she was at peace. That now, she could rest.

And so could he.

"I miss her." Roya stroked Koffka's back. "But sometimes, I get this kind of nice feeling, like she's everywhere, like she's all tangled up with the mycelium in the dirt underneath us, in the trees, in the air..."

"And the mountain. And the moon." *She's everywhere and yet nowhere,* that was how Naveed felt. It still hurt so much, but it was, now, a bearable pain.

They settled onto their backs again. Roya snuggled her head into his shoulder, reaching one arm across his chest to rest on Koffka's head. They lay there together, watching the moon until the stars began twinkling to life, only visible once the darkness set in.

Andi

FRIDAY, JULY 22

THE GOLDEN SALMON TILES ON THE AIRPORT FLOORS HAD ALWAYS reminded Andi of stepping stones. She leapt from one to another, like she'd done when she was younger, balancing her weekend bag on one shoulder, laughing at herself when she missed one and almost slammed into a humorless business traveler. She was eighteen now, and she'd been through a lot, and she didn't care what Mr. Random Businessman thought of her.

Naveed was waiting on the other side of security, smiling his dazzling smile. Koffka greeted Andi with a gentle hand-lick. She and Naveed both had that awkward moment when they weren't sure whether to hug, but after a second he opened his arms and she dove into him. It felt so good to be near him again, to be held by him, and of course that dredged up tons of complicated emotions, weakening her resolve for what she knew she needed to do. It was time to have the difficult conversation they'd both been avoiding.

"Happy belated birthday!" he said when they pulled apart. "Believe it or not, Kourosh is actually baking an eighteen-layer cake as we speak."

"Wow," said Andi. "That sounds… tall."

Naveed laughed. She loved that sound. "They're thin layers. But still."

They walked through the crowded airport. She was tempted to hold his hand, but she didn't reach for him, and he didn't reach for her.

"So, how was the flight?" he asked.

It was a little sad, Andi thought, that they were starting off with such neutral small talk. But it made sense. They hadn't talked much over the past few weeks. "Great, actually. Cy sprung for business class tickets. Pretty luxurious."

"Only the best for the birthday girl," Naveed said.

"Thanks for flying me out here. It's good to be back." Andi said reflexively, though she wasn't sure if that was true or not. The invisible baggage crowding the space between her and Naveed could fill an entire cargo plane. "So, by the way, Brooke and I have plans to see a show tonight, then I'm going to crash at her place."

"Oh. Okay." He sounded slightly hurt, but quickly recovered. "You can stay with us tomorrow if you want. Kourosh was planning to spend the night at Dev's anyway. So we'll have an extra bed."

"Maybe. We'll see." Andi almost wished her dad was still in town so she didn't have to figure out her own sleeping arrangements, but he was currently on tour and had sublet his apartment to a friend. When he'd called on her birthday from Philadelphia, he hadn't sounded high at all—which was in itself a perfect gift, since she constantly worried about him falling into his old habits—but their conversation, too, had been strained and generic. She hadn't seen him in person since the night Tara Snyder had died, and that hadn't exactly gone well.

He'd been angrier than she'd ever seen him, yelling at her for how stupid she'd been to go down to the farm without telling anyone, how he was trying so hard to keep her safe and she just kept putting herself in harm's way, how *that family* was nothing but trouble, meaning the

Mirzapours, not even seeming to care that this was all happening in a hospital waiting room and Sam was right around the corner getting updated on Naveed's condition. When he insisted that Andi would be leaving on the first plane out of Seattle in the morning, she screamed that she wasn't going to abandon Naveed and stormed off to the bathroom. But in the end, after a few tense hours in which they both cooled off and she processed her angst with a Crisis Text Line counselor and word came back that Naveed would be okay, she had given in. By the time the sun rose, she was at the airport saying goodbye to the city.

Now, they walked through the parking garage until they arrived at the farm pickup truck Naveed had borrowed. They each climbed in their separate doors, Koffka forming a buffer between them. Naveed turned the key in the ignition. "So, where exactly are we going?"

"Get back to I-5 and take the Mercer exit," she said. "I'll tell you where to go from there."

He made his way to the spiral ramp to exit the garage, which kept going down and down for so long that Andi had to close her eyes to avoid getting dizzy. Eventually, they emerged into the bright sunshine.

"So," Andi said. "How's it going at work?"

"Great, actually. We had our first farm lunch the other day. Marisol and the interns cooked us this big feast while Ramón and I talked to the other workers, and we're coming up with some great ideas for restructuring things. It's hard, but I like it."

"You've been feeling okay, then?"

"Yeah, mostly. You wouldn't believe how much time all this health care stuff eats up, though. Maman always used to… but it's okay, it's time for me to figure it out on my own." He glanced over his shoulder as they merged onto the freeway. "Oh, I was going to tell you—this is kind of interesting. One of my doctors mentioned that they've been seeing the same type of fibrosis I have in a lot of patients who had severe MRK. They're still trying to figure out why it's happening, but now that the epidemic is petering out, they'll probably start to see it popping up in the survivors. At least they know it's a common complication and can start treating it before it progresses too far. Not that the treatment will be accessible to all the people who need it, though. I've been brainstorming with Vanesa about that. She's thinking about doing a follow-up short film to help raise awareness."

"That sounds like a good idea." Andi wasn't yet ready to dive into the conversation she was dreading, so she asked, "How's the book coming?"

"Oh. The book." He shot her a sheepish glance. "I've been meaning to say, Andi—I still feel guilty about that. You deserved a lot more attention in that interview we did with Jamal, but I just swooped in and stole all the glory from you. I'm really sorry."

It felt good to hear him say that. "It's okay. Honestly, I wouldn't even want a book deal. Way too stressful."

"Yes! It's *so* stressful. The whole thing's so daunting... but I think it'll be good to write about everything that happened, you know? I'll be in control of the narrative for once. Maybe I'll finally be able to make sense of it all."

"I bet that'll help a lot," Andi said. "Can I read it when it's done?"

"Sure, if you want. But it'll be a while. Won't be getting to it until I finish my counseling program and things slow down at the farm. Plus, Kourosh is talking about hiring me as a consultant for some suicide prevention content they're developing at Quirqi, and I want to bring in Max—remember him, from Englewood?—to help with that. I might try taking a night class at community college in the fall, too. See how it goes, maybe even reapply to the UW eventually."

"Really? Wow, good for you." Andi was amazed at how fast he'd turned around. The last time she'd seen him, he'd been half-dead at the bottom of a muddy pit. Though, she supposed, almost two months had passed since then. She just hadn't gotten the play-by-play of his recovery since they barely texted anymore.

He shrugged. "It kind of sounds like too much when I say it out loud.

We'll see how it goes in reality. What about you, though? What have you been up to lately?"

"Oh, the usual. Practicing piano. Running. Sleeping. Going to therapy every now and then. And jiu-jitsu. Nothing exciting."

"How's your grandma?"

Andi fiddled with the zipper on the backpack between her feet. "Not great. She's still recovering from her stroke. And the cancer's getting worse. She wants to stop treating it, but my mom and Ah-gong want her to keep going. It's this whole big thing." It was a gigantic thing, actually, a conflict that had consumed them over the past few weeks. Ah-gong had treated Andi with coldness ever since her return from Seattle, and it only got worse after the results of Ah-ma's latest scan came back. Ah-ma, on the other hand, seemed completely at peace with her decision. "This wasn't your fault, Andi," she said often. "I'll convince him of that eventually. He just needs time."

For a while, Andi had followed the news to see what would become of Torsten's research. It turned out that he had been working on the project ever since the SILO days, when he'd technically been a Genbiotix employee. Though Genbiotix insisted it had never sanctioned his research, they were now trying to take over R&D of the active compound. Apparently, Torsten had made a lot of progress on artificially synthesizing it so that they could bypass growing the illegal plant. The problem was that the compound didn't seem to be as effective when it was taken in isolation, which was why he'd wanted Tara to help bioengineer a more complex mixture of compounds mimicking those in the original seed. Andi had been disappointed by this news. Even if Genbiotix did pick up where Torsten had left off, it would be years and years before the drug hit the market. In other words: far too late to help Ah-ma.

Koffka nuzzled Andi's hand, as if reading her mind. She gave his ears a grateful scratch with one hand, discreetly wiping her eyes with the other.

"Oh, Andi, I'm so sorry," Naveed said. "That's horrible." He moved his hand on top of hers, and she interlaced her fingers in his. They lapsed into silence, but she liked that he didn't try to change the subject or offer advice or anything. They just sat with the sadness for a while, and it was a little easier to handle, because they were feeling it together. The tall buildings of downtown grew closer. Andi made a conscious effort not to look at the old Nutrexo tower.

Once they exited the freeway, she directed him to a parking lot off Dexter. He pulled into a space and cut the ignition. "Do you want me to wait out here?"

"No, I want you to come in with me. In a minute, though." Okay, it was time. Andi scooted closer, and Koffka moved aside so she could rest her head on Naveed's shoulder. She brought her hand up to his chest, feeling his heart tapping beneath her fingertips, the rise and fall of his ribcage as he drew breath after breath. She remembered that morning when she had woken up beside him and thought she was in heaven, until she came back to reality and remembered why he was there, and that small moment somehow encapsulated their entire tumultuous relationship. It had been filled with beauty and sadness and horror, with hope and confusion and love.

"Naveed..." she paused. "Naveed, I love you so much. But... we're kind of going our separate ways, aren't we?"

The air whooshed out of his lungs. When he spoke, his voice wobbled. "Yeah. I guess we are."

"Part of me wants to hold on," Andi admitted. "Because I love you, and I love this, being here with you, and I don't want you to feel like you're so broken that you don't deserve love, because that's not true at all, but long-distance relationships are hard, and I know school's going to be really tough for me, and I don't want to mess up my shot at this."

His arms encircled her. "You won't mess up. But I understand. I love you, too, and you've helped me so much, but I need to figure out how to stand on my own two feet, I guess. Honestly, I'm not in a place yet where I can be in a romantic relationship with anyone. I want you to enjoy college. I don't want you to spend all your time stuck in your dorm room talking to me when you should be out meeting new people. But I *do* want to come visit you sometime. After I finish my probation, once the harvest season's over. Maybe by then I'll have my shit together. I was thinking of taking a writing retreat down on the coast, actually."

"Yes! I would love that." She pulled away from him, and it was hard, but necessary.

He cleared his throat. "So. Now we're here, which is... where exactly?" He indicated the nondescript building in front of them.

"It's a recording studio. My dad's friend owns it. I finished a piece I've been working on for a long time, since last fall, actually, and this was my dad's birthday present to me. Getting it professionally recorded."

"Really? That's awesome. And I get to watch?"

"Yep." She was a little nervous about playing in front of him, but at the same time, she knew he needed to be there. She wanted to feel his attention flowing toward her as her fingers flew across the keys, she wanted to channel it into every note, and she wanted him to hear it the first time it was ever played as it should be, in a quiet room on a grand piano, and even though it was kind of her goodbye to him she hoped it would also show him how much he had given her, how his belief in her as a musician had carried her not only to this moment, but would keep her afloat far beyond.

"Wow. I'm honored," he said with such gravity that she had to laugh to lighten the mood.

"Don't get too excited," she said. Then she got out of the car and they stepped into the studio together.

The sound engineer, Brian, greeted her and she entered the soundproof room to get warmed up. On the other side of the glass, Naveed settled onto the couch with Koffka, looking so eager to hear what she was about to play that she had to quickly return her gaze to the piano. *Focus. Just focus, and you won't screw up.*

"Okay, ready when you are." Brian's voice came through her headphones after she'd played a few warm-up pieces. She nodded at him, took a deep breath, relaxed her fingers on the keys. And then she began to play.

As it always did, the room melted away; it was only her and the music now. She poured everything she had into the melody, and just as she'd hoped, Naveed's presence fed her, bumping up the tension, making her performance better. This song was her story, her way of transforming her experiences into a narrative, not a linear retelling, but something that evoked the emotional truth of it. Layers and layers built upon each other right up to the precipitous climax, before spiraling down into a quiet movement where everything fell away and was slowly pieced back together. She had once wondered how it would end, and had toyed with the idea of it going on and on, looping back on itself with endless variations, but everything had to end sometime, nothing was permanent, and she had decided on something more subtle: ending the song on the same note with which it began. The amazing thing was that, even with her perfect pitch, the last note didn't *sound* the same as the first, as if the journey of the song had changed her so much that she was hearing everything in an entirely new way.

When she was finished, she lowered her hands, afraid to turn around. When she did, she couldn't see Naveed, but Brian was giving her a thumbs-up, so she took off her headphones and stepped out of the room. Then she saw him curled up on the couch, sobbing into Koffka's chest. Brian was pretending not to notice.

"That was great—I think we got it! Unless you want to run through it again. Up to you," Brian said. "Here—give me a second and we'll play it back."

Naveed looked up as she shut the door. His eyes were all red. A beautiful mess. He wiped them hurriedly as she joined him on the couch. "Andi. Wow," he said. "I'm sorry, it's not that I didn't like it, because I did, I *loved* it, it's just... damn. I don't think I can listen to any music ever again after hearing that perfection." He looked at her with curiosity, as if seeing her for the first time. "Do you have any idea how powerful you are?"

"Just another one of my amazing talents. The power to make grown men weep," Andi joked, because although she couldn't bring herself to say so out loud, the answer was yes. It was something she sensed deep in her bones, a power that had been with her always, but that she was only just beginning to know.

WHEN ANDI AND NAVEED arrived at the Mirzapours' house, they made their way to the back patio, where Brooke, Cyrus, and Roya were waiting. Vast amounts of hugging ensued. Even Sam, whose grief now seemed permanently etched into the wrinkles around his eyes, embraced Andi and gave her cheek-kisses, the way Mahnaz used to do. Everyone talked excitedly for a while, and they ate the crazy-decadent eighteen-layer cake that Cyrus had put together, and it was warm and shady and perfect, perfect, perfect.

After they ate, Brooke said to Andi, "Hey, so I'm planning a road trip down to California in a few weeks. You think I might be able to crash with you?"

"Oh my God, yes!" Andi was sure her mom and grandparents wouldn't mind. "Yes! Stay as long as you want! We've got plenty of room."

"Yay! We can explore the city together... see the sights, eat all the things, hit the museums. I can't wait!"

Andi couldn't either. A visit from Brooke would be just the distraction she needed from family drama.

"You know what?" Cyrus said. "I was just thinking, have we ever gotten a picture of all of us together?"

"I don't think so," Andi had to admit.

"Let's do it!" said Brooke. "Maybe out in the garden? I'll be the photographer."

They trooped out to the back. "The light's good over here," Brooke suggested, gesturing to a corner of the yard where the sun wasn't too bright, near the overgrown, fruit-laden elderberry bush.

"Perfect!" Roya struck a pose. Andi, Cyrus and Naveed all crowded in behind her, Andi in the middle, flanked by two boys she had once dated but still dearly loved, Koffka sitting at attention near Naveed.

Brooke was just backing up to take the picture when a crow cawed above them and fluttered down near Roya's feet.

"You've got to be fucking kidding me," said Cyrus.

All four of them burst out laughing, startling the crow, who immediately flew off, but none of them could stop, they all just laughed and laughed, and Brooke asked them what was so funny, but how could they possibly explain?

As they took more pictures in various combinations to immortalize the afternoon, Andi realized she had no idea when she would be back in Seattle again. Her dad was talking about settling down in California after the tour, and she might not have much reason to come up here anymore. It made her sad, but also excited, to think about all the changes ahead.

Once they had finished, Brooke said, "Hey guys, I'll be right back." A few minutes later Naveed excused himself too, so Andi sat in the grass and talked to Cyrus about Quirqi until his tech-speak made her eyes glaze over.

When Naveed and Brooke returned, they were carrying a large, heavy-looking package wrapped in dark blue paper.

"What's this?" Andi asked.

"Your present! Open it up!" Roya sat eagerly next to Andi while she pulled the paper off.

When she saw what it was, she drew in her breath. "Oh, you guys. Oh, wow."

It was a work of art: a photo collage fitting inside a hexagonal frame, crisscrossed by strips of wood that formed a beautiful geometric pattern, with a photograph inside each space. There was a selfie she and Naveed had taken when they'd gone canoeing, Koffka peeking in at the back; there was that photo Andi had taken of Naveed giving Roya a piggy-back ride at Seward Park when she still had her cast on; there was Cyrus posed behind the absurdly tall cake they'd just eaten, smiling proudly; there was a selfie Brooke had taken the night they went to see Invisible Noise; there was Naveed at his cabin, lying next to Koffka, both of them looking at the camera with identical puppy-dog eyes; there was even Mahnaz, a picture of her smiling in the garden with dirt-streaked hands, holding up a bunch of carrots and beets. And at the center, in the middle of a many-pointed star, the photograph they had just taken—Brooke must have disappeared to print it, she realized—Andi, Naveed and Cyrus all with genuinely delighted smiles, Roya's face upturned in wonder at the fleeing crow, only visible as a streak of black tail feathers.

Andi had to fight to keep the tears out of her eyes. "It's beautiful. I just... I love it. It's perfect."

"Naveed made the frame," said Roya. "But me and Kourosh helped choose the pictures!"

"Don't want you to forget us down in SoCal," Naveed said with a smile.

"Oh, I could never. I could never," Andi managed to say before the lump in her throat choked her up. She could visualize it already, this gorgeous collage propped on the desk in her dorm room, and knew that just glancing at it would make her feel less lonely. She loved how it captured all the time they'd shared, all they'd been through together. And she loved that even the reminders of unpleasant things, like Naveed's struggles and Roya's leg injury and Mahnaz's sudden tragic death, weren't scrubbed out to avoid painful memories, because those memories were a part of her too, a part of all of them: a part of life in all of its endings, in all of its beginnings.

IF YOU'RE STRUGGLING...

It doesn't mean that you're broken or defective. You deserve support. None of us can do this alone.

Crisis Text Line
> United States and Canada: Text HOME (or AYUDA for Spanish) to 741741
> UK: Text SHOUT to 85258
> Ireland: Text HOME to 50808

Suicide Prevention Lifeline
> United States: Call or text 988, or visit suicidepreventionlifeline.org.

International Helplines
> Visit findahelpline.com to search for helplines in your country.

Other Resources
> Many additional resources (including BIPOC and LGBTQIA+ focused resources) are available at alannapeterson.com/resources/mental-health.

ACKNOWLEDGMENTS

It has now been ten years since the initial glimmer of inspiration that led to *When We Vanished*, and from there to the rest of the quartet. The close of this book marks a significant end for me, so here I am on the threshold, looking back and giving thanks to everyone who has guided these stories into existence.

This time, at the risk of sounding weird/crazy/dorky, I want to begin by thanking my characters. Through them, I have learned so much. Special shout out to Mahnaz and Tara for helping me explore my darkest corners—and, of course, to Andi, Cyrus, Roya, and Naveed for your extraordinary courage and resilience. I will miss spending my days with you all.

Gratitude galore goes to: Janice Kao, for seeing the real story inside a bloated early draft and guiding me towards what it was trying to be (also, for sharing your lǔ ròu fàn memories); Pontia Fallahi, for your gracious Persian culture and language support; Pam O'Shaughnessy and Melanie Peterson for your insightful feedback; Joe Fahr for your techspertise; Simone Adler for helping me name Zetik Farm; and Jacob Covey, who made it possible to offer these books in physical form, and whose cover designs are perfection on every level.

Many thanks to the artists who have inspired me through their music, images, and words, especially Forough Farrokhzad, Sholeh Wolpe, and Kaveh Akbar, whose poems had a major influence on this book. I must also thank the writers whose work Naveed cribbed from while ranting about food system injustices: Eric Holt-Giménez, Douglas Rushkoff, and Marion Nestle.

Thank you to my friends, family, parents and ancestors. To Amber Lenore, who journeyed with me through the underworld and back. To my beloved Brett, Cora and Desmond, for never giving up on me.

These acknowledgments have generally centered on humans, but they aren't the only ones nourishing and inspiring me! All of my pets past and present have been a source of much joy and comfort, most recently my cat Chouquette. Any typos in this book are due to her habit of walking across the keyboard while I'm working on pivotal scenes. (Just kidding, Chouqi! Mistakes of any kind in this book are my own.)

Thank you to the Source from whence these stories came. To the mycelium beneath our feet. To unknowable mysteries. To crows and orcas and dogs and ants. To bread and apples and pomegranates and mushrooms. To yarrow, birch, mint and rose. To Tahoma. To Delta, Reno, Berkeley, and Seattle. To the moon and the sun and the stars. To wind, water, fire and earth. To this entire maddening and beautiful and incredible world.

And of course, to you, dear reader. Thank you for sticking around to the end.

ALANNA PETERSON is the award-winning author of the *Call of the Crow Quartet*, a series of young adult eco-thrillers. She delights in tromping through the mud, singing while roller skating, finding patterns in data, spacing out while washing dishes, and writing stories that are ambitious, entertaining, and strange.

CPSIA information can be obtained
at www.ICGtesting.com
Printed in the USA
LVHW031547280722
724575LV00001B/158

9 781952 149078